Caught in the Baltic Tide

Young Love Set Against the Sweep of Occupying Forces in Latvia

Russell John Connor

lots of love

Russell

Published in May 2022 by emp3books Ltd
6 Silvester Way, Church Crookham, Fleet, GU52 0TD

©Russell Connor 2022

ISBN: **9781910734469**

The right of Russell John Connor to be identified as the author of this work has been asserted in accordance with sections 77 and 78 of the Copyright Designs and Patents Act 1988.

About the Author

Russell John Connor was born in Altrincham, Cheshire. After his family moved south, he was educated at Charters School, Sunningdale and University College London. On gaining a diploma from the London School of Economics in Personnel Management, Russell entered the business world and worked for a range of companies as a manager and consultant.

Russell's work took him to Riga, Latvia in 1994 and this led to a continued interest in and connection with the country.

Riga Prison, Latvia, July 1940

As the khaki canvas curtain at the back of the Soviet lorry swayed open, Rupert glimpsed the sanatorium, bone white in the weak, early morning sun. It was his last look. Cold, crawling fear worked its way up his body from his toes. With it, he felt he was rising in his seat, his body trying to climb out of itself, his mind whirling.

The lorry bounced on the rutted road and the jolting shook Rupert's thoughts as if they were lemonade in a bottle. Half-formed, they rose, fizzed and burst before he could draw a conclusion or make a plan. As they travelled through Riga, the only thing he could recognise were the cobblestones as they made the lorry shudder, straining the almost non-existent suspension.

He enforced calm, steadying his mind and a single, desperate thought coalesced- *Irene. Did they find her hiding? Did she escape?* A shifting of feet and he became aware of the hard gaze of the guards opposite him, their rifles resting against their thighs, their eyes cold. The truck was filled with the thick, oppressive musk of damp, stale clothing and the sour tang of their breath. Rupert fixed his eyes on the floor.

When at long last the lorry passed through huge iron gates and stopped, Rupert didn't know where he was at all; certainly, he wasn't in any part of Riga he recognised. He looked up at a greenish-brown building, its windows boarded or heavily barred. A high brick wall with sentry towers that looked like stunted lighthouses enclosed it. He had never seen something that looked so inhumane.

The guards pulled Rupert from the truck and bundled him into a wide, grey, empty room with low ceilings and a thick, tarry mixture on the floor. The smell of disinfectant caught him at the

1

back of the throat.

'Stay there, do not move.' The soldiers left.

His head swam, his thoughts stumbling over one another, bouncing off the dark, stained walls. Yet with some odd, still certainty, he understood that he had to prepare himself for some sort of humiliation.

A side door opened and a smell of wet cloth and boiled cabbage wafted in. One of the soldiers had returned. He eyed Rupert with cold indifference.

'Undress'.

The single word made Rupert flinch, but he obeyed, taking off his jacket and shirt. The soldier's lip curled and he shook his head.

'Everything off.'

Rupert stood shivering in his underpants, as the soldier went through his things, tore out shoelaces, stripped the lining from his jacket, then threw everything into a corner. Rupert took a crumb of comfort from the fact he had taken Irene's letter out of his pocket that morning— she could not be implicated.

'Open your mouth,'

Drawing his round, sweaty face close, the soldier yanked Rupert's jaw open and jabbed a dirty finger inside, running it behind his lips and teeth. Rupert suppressed the urge to gag.

Then he was ordered out. Moving in an icy daze, a series of corridors seemed to flicker by around him, each one barer and colder than the last. At the end of one corridor, he was pushed into a room where an un-shaded, weak light bulb shed dim light

2

over a single chair. There his head was roughly shaved. His clothes were tossed in and he was ordered to dress. His insides squirmed and his mind pulsed and clattered precluding any rational thought.

Inside a dark stockroom he was handed a padded mattress, a rough, dark green blanket, two grey bed sheets, a pillow with a grey case, one aluminium bowl, a mug and a spoon. All he was aware of was the weight of the items and their dusty smell, the imminent descent of his unbelted trousers and a prickling sensation emanating from his roughly shorn scalp.

Without any assistance with the precarious pile, and hitching up his trousers with his elbows, he was escorted up two staircases caged with metal netting and onto a wide, echoing landing. The concrete beneath his feet was spattered with dark stains. Horizontal slits in the boarded windows let in a minimal amount of light, their upward angle preventing any view of the ground. His escort ran a heavy bunch of keys along the iron railings and the metallic sound reverberated eerily around the huge, black vaulted roof.

The corridor stretched onwards and Rupert walked in the guard's wake, trying to distinguish odours in the mingled stench of stale fat, urine and fear.

At the end of the corridor, a heavy cell door was unlocked and, as it opened, there was rush of hot, stale air. Without any orders, or word from the guard, Rupert trudged in and placed his issued items on the iron bedstead, fitted with rough wooden slats. He scanned the room: a wooden chair, a small desk, three bars of a cast iron radiator and, in the corner, a bucket. He also noted something new as it slithered from his chest to his gut— a feeling of utter isolation. This, he thought, as he glanced at the grey walls, could only grow in intensity.

The cell wasn't unduly small and had a large, high, barred

window at the far end, but, in the heat of the day, it felt suffocating. The door slammed shut, its reverberations following the guard down the corridor. Rupert rolled out the thin, dirty mattress and stuffed the prickly, yellowed pillow, sharp feathers poking through, into the grey case. In the heat, he longed to lie down but the shallow depression in the pillow made him hesitate. He stared at it, wondering how many countless heads had made its hollow permanent as they lay, awaiting their fate. Where were they now? He shuddered. At length he succumbed, lowering his head into the dip with a cold sense of finality. The rough linen closed around his ears and he allowed himself a shaky laugh. 'It fits my head as if made to measure.', he said aloud to the muffled silence.

His mind turned to Irēne. Had she been able to escape back to Riga? He replayed what she had said to him the previous day, 'We have made the decision. Now we need to live with it without looking back or with regret. What is done is done and we can only look forward.' *Perhaps*, he thought. *But if we'd set off to Germany there would have been at least a few weeks before life turned harsh. We would still have our freedom.*

Rupert had lost track of time when he heard footsteps. The door ground open and a guard entered, seized him by the upper arm and walked him along the corridor in silence. They halted outside a wide space without a door. The guard jerked his head, gesturing Rupert inside. The powerful smell of stale urine advertised the toilets.

Along one wall was a row of metal sinks and along another, lurking in the gloom, was a row of diabolically black, gaping holes. Although he had never squatted to defecate before, Rupert understood he needed to do this, or risk being caught short at night. He was handed pieces of newspaper cut into four two-inch squares. Under the uninterested gaze of the guard, he managed to go to the toilet and then washed his hands at the sink in a trickle of icy water, grateful that there was no mirror, which would doubtless have too miserable to look into. He cupped his hands and bent to wash his face but there was a sharp movement and the guard spat into the corner and waved him out with a terse 'Time.'

The noxious smell of fear that Rupert had noticed in the corridor settled in the stillness of the night, crept stealthily under the door and pooled under his bed. Then it rose, twisting up the iron legs. He breathed it in and it became him. He lay with his eyes wide, his fingers knotted in the filthy sheet, his breath catching in staggered gasps and watched as first unspeakable shadows, then the weak sunrise slid across the mildewed ceiling.

Shortly after dawn he was jerked from his sleepless torpor by a braying klaxon and, shortly afterwards, the spy hole in the cell door shot up with a loud clank. The key turned in the lock and, with a rough shout from the guard, he was escorted to the toilet where, once more, he was rushed through the proceedings with indecent haste. *Perhaps,* he thought, *if I wash one ear today and another tomorrow, by the end of a fortnight I'll have completed a full wash, just in time to start again.* Breakfast was thrust through the hatch in his cell some time later, but Rupert wasn't hungry. He eyed the watery porridge and tin cup of *kvass* without any appetite. The yeasty smell of the *kvass* masked something more malodorous. It stayed untouched until it was collected by a guard who took Rupert with him, directing him down the stairs and into a courtyard sectioned into separate areas, cages that kept prisoners apart. They reminded Rupert of market day cattle pens. There and alone, he was ordered to walk in a circle around an enclosure and he did so for about twenty minutes. It was of some relief to be in the fresh air, even if the view was obscured by netting with only the jagged, black watchtowers looming above. All too soon he was back lying on the bed in the stuffy cell. Sleep overcame him and when he awoke, he was surprised to find, by the position of the sun, it was the afternoon. He closed his eyes but there was no relief from merciless awareness. He tried to remain passive and let the plankton of thought float through his mind, but it did nothing to stave off the sense of dread. It continued to be afternoon and did not cease to be afternoon for what seemed to be an eternity.

The evening meal consisted of soup, a dessert and black tea. Rupert used his issued spoon to taste the soup and after a few slurps surmised that it consisted of bull's heart or liver, oats, sour cabbage and plenty of water. He pushed it away. The dessert was stewed apples and he kept these in his mouth for a while trying to savour the pure acidity in place of cruel thought.

The next night's sleep was disturbed but he felt less fearful, only dreadfully lonely. The prison was unnaturally quiet and he longed to hear Irēne's voice. Then, as time passed, he longed to hear any human voice.

The morning brought no change to routine, nor would it, Rupert guessed, for the rest of his stay. In the pressing gloom of his prison cell he was like a deep-sea diver who knows that the cable connecting him to the outside world has broken. Submerged in a vast ocean of silence he looked out of his brass and glass helmet over a scene of nothingness. There was nothing to see other than the lifeless chair, table and piss pot. There was nothing to hear other than the inhuman banging of doors and the occasional animal grunt.

The evening meal arrived with barely any warmth. Before taking a sip of the soup, he smelt it and noted that it was not as obnoxious as it had been on his first night. He recalled how the stench of the prison when he first arrived had been almost unbearable. The next day he noted the foulness of his own body odour. Now, he lifted his arm and breathed the sour musk of his own armpits with some interest. He understood that he was now part of the scent of the prison.

Apart from his gaolers, who said little or nothing, the lack of a face or human voice meant that his senses gained the minimum of nourishment from the silent objects he had for company. He was in a void and found that as he paced around his small world, so his aimless thoughts circled too.

He thought about his early life at home on the Wythenshawe Estate, of going up to Cambridge and then of living in Manchester and, being an employee of Metropolitan Vickers. He recalled in great detail proudly signing the contract for his overseas assignment and joked to himself that he must have missed the section on spending time in a Soviet prison. He thought of his mother and of how her life might have changed since the declaration of war. Mostly though, his thoughts returned to Irēne; how he had met her and fallen in love. He feared what might be happening to her and the undercurrent of dread flowed beneath his constantly wandering thoughts.

The thoughts merged into his dreams and after a night of tossing and turning, chasing the illusive oblivion of deep sleep, he awoke drained and bleary eyed.

He was aware of the huge expanse of time. He understood that his biggest challenge would now be to keep himself sane. He knew the solitude, the emptiness and torturous silence would blight his rationality unless he found some structure and was able to marshal his ill-disciplined mind. Without food providing any proper sustenance, he realised that he had to take charge of his own nourishment and that meant thinking about the people whom he loved even if the sense of loss burned into him, searing even through sleep.

After the visit to the exercise yard, he took to wandering forward and backwards in tight steps either side of his bed. The memory came back to him of a caged tiger he had once seen at Bellevue Zoo. Having been used to seeing the deer, pheasants and other wildlife on the Estate roam free, he had felt sick at the sight of such a sad, misplaced creature. Rupert remembered how the tiger had paced around every inch of the barred cage and turned his eyes to his own restless feet.

He managed to fit exactly seven paces into a length of the cell and turn in such a way that he hardly broke his stride. After a while, he developed an automatic rhythm to this walking pattern. He found that it enabled him to direct his thoughts to an area of his own choosing as he took his exercise.

Seven exact paces with a turn acted as a meditative device and he knew this was the key. In this manner, time would pass and sanity be maintained.

Out loud, he said 'Thank you.' In his prison cell he was conscious that his voice sounded disembodied, like it was rising from the depths of a dark well. The thanks were directed to Irène. He knew that his most life-affirming event was meeting her. Now, with time on his hands, he planned to recall in painstaking, absorbing detail the path he took to falling in love with her. *Was it at first sight?* He asked himself. No, he was not impulsive enough for that to be the case. He knew he had been attracted to her from the first meeting but understood that love had only ignited when he began to hear about her history and how her upbringing had been so different to his own.

Riga, 23rd August 1939

Rupert wasn't used to feelings of regret, but he couldn't help mouthing the words, 'If only,' and repeating them. Sitting at the desk in his apartment opposite the big, double-paned window looking out onto *Elizabetes Iela*, he picked up the diaries he had kept since his arrival in Riga and looked through them to find the exact date on which he had first met Irēne.

> **28th November 1938.** *Attended a briefing on the planned construction of the dam. All potential suppliers there including Siemens. Translator spoke excellent English and German. Very pretty too. Irēne – Pronounced Eareeney – slightly rolled R. Had a few words. Works for the Ministry of Interior Affairs.*

Rupert flicked through his entries.

> **15th December 1938.** *Delivered the official notice to the ministry of our intention to bid for the turbine and switchgear contract. Had to wait and was given coffee by Irēne. Shorter than me but not small. Dark hair, which flicks up to her cheeks. Slight crescent moon in her left eye. I was stupidly tongue-tied. She must have thought I was very distant.*

Picking up and opening the 1939 diary, he read.

> **6th January 1939.** *Metropolitan Vickers Export Company fully registered. Met Irēne briefly again at the Ministry. Very friendly. Lovely smile. So nice to have a few words in English but difficult to talk much in the office.*

> **21st January 1939.** *Saw Irēne walking through Vermanis park arm in arm with a very handsome*

chap. Damn.

After reading this entry, he quickly turned the following pages as he knew that Irēne didn't feature again until August, 1939. The intervening diary pages were full of the work at the port and then, when the weather suddenly turned warm in late April, the daily entries were about mapping the route from the port to the site of the proposed dam and detailing any necessary enabling works. There were also many entries about chess games, locations of matches and names of winners. Mostly, there was a simple marking of 'won'. Then, he found and read his last entry, written the evening before:

> **22nd August 1939.** *Delivered the confirmation that work on the contract is suspended until further notice. Met Irēne again. Proved to myself that I am a complete fool.*

He thought back to the previous day. He had fallen into conversation with Irēne as she escorted him from the Minister's office.

As they reached the wide stairs leading down to the reception area Irēne asked, 'What will you do when back in England?'

'I'm not sure. No one has said anything to me, but Metro Vicks is a huge company and makes more than turbines and switchgear. There'll be something for me. In any case, I have to finish a report on the dam project before I can move on.' He decided not to point out that if there were to be a war, he might be required to join up or, at least, be redeployed for the war effort.

At that point they could have shaken hands and departed, their destinies forever unconnected but Irēne asked, 'They say the girls in Riga are very beautiful. Will that be in your report?' Rupert gave a small cough.

'I can honestly say that some are.'

'What of girlfriends or even a wife; do you have someone special waiting for you in England?' Rupert's eyes widened and he felt heat rising to his face.

'No. Sorry. There isn't anybody waiting on my return.'

'There is no need to be sorry, only I am disappointed. In that case, I thought you might have invited me to go somewhere with you in your time in Riga.' Rupert was taken aback. He wasn't used to women being so direct with him and it took him a few seconds to collect his thoughts.

'But... but Irēne, what about your boyfriend?'

'What boyfriend?' Irēne looked at him and narrowed her eyebrows to form a polite frown. Rupert could feel himself blushing in earnest now.

'I'm sorry but I thought... I thought I saw you walking through Vermanis Park arm in arm with a rather dashing looking man. I presumed...'

'You did presume.' The corners of Irēne's mouth twitched into a small smile. 'I think you must have seen me with Pēteris - my father.'

It would have been easy and natural for Rupert to turn and leave in embarrassment, but he was seized with the need to salvage something – he wasn't quite sure what. He started talking as if just outlining his diary arrangements. 'I'm leaving for England in four days and the day after tomorrow I'm off to Saulkrasti to go on a fishing expedition with Stanley, my boss and Andris Ozols, the owner of the cement works.' Giving himself time to think, he asked, 'Have you heard of Andris's father, Guntis Ozols? He has a senior position in the Government.'

11

'Everyone in Latvia has heard of him.' Irēne said.

'If I can get the tickets,' He was now sure of the right question to ask, 'would you be so kind as to come to the opera with me tomorrow night?'

'That would be lovely. I look forward to seeing you in a bow tie.' Rupert didn't possess a bow tie and enquired as to what he should ask for when shopping for one. He left with a smile knowing he was now looking for a *taurinš*, which, Irēne informed him, could also be a butterfly.

Now, sitting at the large secretaire in his apartment, Rupert, acknowledging the regret of wasted opportunity, mouthed, once more, 'If only,' and gazed out of the window. As he studied the elaborate art nouveau façade of the apartment block opposite, with its two long-nosed faces adding a magnificent flourish to the architect's confection, he felt an impending sense of loss for a city that he had come to love.

A flood of images and their associations passed through his mind from the ice yachting he saw in January on the frozen White Lake to standing in the Riga Post Office in winter, overpowered by the smell of sweaty sheep that came from the thick coats many people wore, cured in such a way that the natural oil remained.

He stood up and scanned the street below where lorries and cars jostled with the horse drawn carts and cabs. This mixture of the old and new was one of the things that fascinated him about Riga. He wondered whether, unlike in Manchester, the horses would ever be replaced, as they were so efficient pulling the sleighs in the winter. Through the open window, he could smell the faint odour of fried potatoes rising from the streets. The local petrol was mixed with the potato spirit used in making vodka but, as this smell also emanated from every kitchen, he wasn't sure he could blame the pervading scent on the traffic fumes.

Looking around his big apartment, rented for him in a stylish block, with its high ceilings, intricate coving and the tiled Dutch stove rising from the floor to ceiling, his gaze fell on some of the presents he was taking back to England to give to his mother, aunty and uncle; socks, gloves, linen towels and tablecloths, all woven with intricate designs. He had bought them at a Christmas market in the Dome Square where the magical-looking booths were lit by gaslights and candles to show off their spicy cakes, painted wooden toys and handmade garments.

A pair of amber cufflinks lay on the secretaire. Rupert looked forward to giving them to his patron, Lord Simon, and telling him he had bought them in the Moscow District. He thought Lord Simon would be amused when he told him this was where serfs used to come to hide and by law, if they were not recaptured by their master within two years, they won their freedom. Having completed the inventory, he decided that, if there were sufficient room in his bags, he'd buy some Rigas Balsams for his colleagues at the factory. In its earthen bottle and with its initially repellent, bitter taste, it would prove quite a talking point.

The evening ahead beckoned and he began to wonder what it was about Irēne he was so vehemently attracted to. He knew it was more than their facility to speak common languages. He thought of her face. It wasn't that she had big eyes, or full lips but rather that all her features seemed to suit her and worked so well together they turned into real beauty. Above all though, he was struck by her bearing and gaze. She had a confidence about her and when she looked at him there was a flash of something, a spark that sprang between them, a glittering in her eyes.

He picked up the tickets for the evening performance of Eugene Onegin. He had bought them at the last minute and now the two slips of embossed, cream paper carried more than their value - one last chance to see Irēne. Rupert slid them into his jacket pocket, tucking them into the dove-grey silk lining. Then, he

13

checked his bow tie in the mirror and left for the National Opera.

Having plenty of time to spare before the rendezvous, he bought, en route, some flowers for Irēne at the newly opened Army Economic Store. This had become his favourite shop in Riga and, on a free day, he enjoyed wandering around looking at the exotic merchandise and taking in the features that made it such a characterful building: the broad, theatrical-looking staircase that swept up from the ground floor, the ceiling lights encased in burnished bronze and edged with intricate floral motifs, the chrome fish tanks full of live fish and the array of beer taps dispensing a huge range of local ales. He delighted in riding Latvia's first escalator and watching the awed faces of those youths who had managed to evade the doorman when they saw people being levitated perpendicularly up a staircase without moving a muscle.

That evening, the high number of shoppers, large queues for food and the emptiness of some of the shelves surprised Rupert. Typically the shops were well stocked and, although always busy, never overly crowded. There was a hint of tension in the air and the faces Rupert saw looked pinched and ill at ease. He wondered whether the populace, with so much talk of war, anticipated hard times ahead.

After purchasing a large bunch of pink roses from the florist, Rupert was handed them, heads downward, unwrapped with the thorns removed. This was one of the first things he had noticed about the local customs; people carried bunches of flowers heads down and they were never wrapped in the gaudy paper he was used to seeing in England. He had enjoyed identifying these small differences between the British and Latvian traditions and immediately wondered whether, on returning home, he'd soon get used to doors that open into a room rather than out? Would he get used to drinking tea in the morning rather than coffee, would he get used to Manchester's constant drizzle in winter and summer? He knew he was being frivolous and that the largest question remained, would he ever again, after the light, air and beauty of Riga, get used to working in the dark, musty confines of a factory?

Walking from the store towards the National Opera, his thoughts drifted to friends, family and work colleagues waiting for him at home, *How can I summarise my experience or pick out the highlights?* His mind was drawn to the Latvian Song Festival in the Esplanade Park, which he had attended earlier in the summer. He tried to capture a clear mental image, one he might describe to his sceptical colleagues, but his memory could produce only an exhilarating kaleidoscope of linen cloaks, shirts and headgear embroidered with ethnic patterns and the strange, ethereal sound of thousands of harmonised voices that made his hair stand on end.

Looking up to the rooftops, he saw, against a cerulean sky, a statue of two men holding the world aloft. Their figures were hunched and contemplative, burdened by their load but Rupert could not bring himself to feel their gravity tonight, his footsteps were light and his conscience free.

He arrived at the theatre and looked across the park towards the recently built *Our Land, Our Freedom* monument. The figure of a woman carried aloft three stars symbolising Latvia's regions; Kurzeme, Vidzeme and Latgale. The sun glinted off the stars and the golden ribs on the cupola of the Russian Orthodox Church just visible over the crenellated rooftops of the university. The park was busy with people, homeward bound or alive with their evening activities.

In the pink light of the early evening sun, a profusion of pretty parasols shielded elegant ladies whilst young couples meandered along the paths and old ladies sat by the fountain, deep in conversation. Flocks of sparrows chirruped and danced in the dusty soil of the flowerbeds in front of the theatre. Rupert liked the planting scheme used for the summer flowers. It was less formal than the Manchester Corporation's way of arranging its beds and reminded him, in a way, of the cottage garden at home, natural and full of variety.

The call of home was strong, but Rupert knew he would miss Riga and the many aspects of its character; beautiful architecture, wide boulevards, parks, sculpture, the reserved but friendly people and the food. *Ah the food, a life without cold beetroot soup and soured cream in the summer and sweet pickled mushrooms and sauerkraut in the winter would be sad indeed... and what about potatoes? I will miss the many varieties of delicious potatoes each with a girl's name; Andretta, Vivita, Laura, Irēnīte – little Irēne.*

An image of Irēne's mouth, the corners turned softly up in a smile rose in his mind. He wondered if he would be lucky enough to kiss her that night.

Prison Requests

Rupert started on his seven strides and turn routine. In his mind he was waiting for Irēne by the opera house, the tickets in his breast pocket, his *taurinš* crisp at his throat, the scent of flowers in the air. Sharp footsteps in the corridor broke his reverie and the spy hole was raised. The door was unlocked and in strode the same officer who had interrogated Rupert at the sanatorium, Lieutenant Dmitri Kuznetsov, State Security. Rupert looked into his face. It was the face of man paid to facilitate cruelty, his mouth thin, his eyes too bright in the gloom. He took off his cap and made a show of wiping off the desk before he perched on its edge, smiling over at Rupert beside the bed. The smile, though it showed rather small, pointed teeth, did not reach his eyes. 'I hope everything is up to your satisfaction?' he asked.

Rupert matched the lieutenant's banter. He would play the man's game; after all, what was there to be gained by resistance now? He inclined his head. 'If you have ever stayed in a Cambridge college, you would know this is luxury.'

'Now, is there anything you need?' The sincerity of the lieutenant's tone surprised Rupert. Once again, he decided it prudent to return the favour.

'I would appreciate something to read and the use of a toothbrush, razor and writing pad and pen.'

'And what about your Minox? Don't you need your spying camera too?' Rupert had become so used to carrying around his miniature camera he instinctively patted his empty pocket.

The lieutenant smirked. 'We have an extensive and well stocked library full of Russian books, which are no good to you,' he leaned forward and voice was silky with threat, 'unless you were lying to me about not reading Russian.' Rupert waited for a similar rebuttal to his other requests, but it did not come.

'Toothbrush and writing pad I can get, but razor and metal pen are prohibited, however, you will be able to shower and shave every ten days and I will make sure you have pencil to go with your pad.' The lieutenant said, sitting back. Rupert felt like he had won the football pools.

The lieutenant did not seem to be in a hurry to leave and, given his conciliatory tone, Rupert risked asking, 'Do British authorities know of my imprisonment?'

'Is this famous British humour? Do you think Churchill is losing sleep thinking of you over here? No, he is, at this moment, learning German. The British army is routed, Luftwaffe is blowing what is sadly called Royal Air Force from sky and London is ablaze. You can be thankful you are not on receiving end of German bombardment. But, you can rest assured Comrade Stalin knows of your presence. Given you English have been so troublesome, I don't know why he thinks so highly of your nation, but he is happy to be your host and maybe, one day, you will be of use to him.'

'What about Legation, do they know I am here?' Rupert asked and the lieutenant gave a forced laugh.

'Didn't you get postcard? Your Ambassador, Orde has left to sun himself in Chile. As for rest of those at Embassy aiding Jewish cause, they have until next week to leave or they will have no diplomatic protection thereafter. Keep your cell tidy, you might be having visitors.' The lieutenant got up, and said, 'By the way, Vilis Lācis sends his regards.' With that he banged on the door and was let out of the cell. The mention of Vilis Lācis jolted Rupert. What had this man, who he had only met briefly at the sanatorium, got to do with his incarceration?

Alone in his cell, Rupert dwelt on what the lieutenant had told him about the war. He decided the talk of London being ablaze was simply propaganda or at least a tactic in some cruel sport to weaken him mentally. He put it from his mind. England would not fall and the power of British diplomacy would win his freedom. That is what he must believe.

The requested items did not arrive the next day and Rupert attributed this to the lieutenant reminding him exactly who held the cards. This was not, after all, a hotel. He resolved to entertain himself, between his seven-step pacing, by trying to catch the flies that buzzed around and swatting the occasional mosquito that seemed to drill into his ear.

After a few tedious days, to his huge delight the toothbrush, book and pencil arrived with the evening meal.

He used the toothbrush at once. Even though there was no toothpaste, and he had to use the *kvass* to wet his teeth, brushing the bristle over the rough enamel felt like one of the world's finest luxuries.

After that, he rested the pad on the desk and thought, *I must not squander this lifesaving resource.* It was like it had printed on it, 'Only to be used in case of emergency', and he knew that time had not yet arrived. However, he sat at the table and, holding the pencil, made tiny little marks on the back cover to indicate the days he had been in prison.

Rupert awoke the next day and felt the prickliness of the rough blanket against his unshaven chin. *Such hope,* he thought, gazing around his drab, grey-green world. *How did it come to this?* The clean, unused notepad and pencil on the desk seemed to stand apart, an untapped source of solace. Rupert rose to begin his pacing, content to return to the streets of Riga that filled his mind, back to the summer and to a night at the opera.

A Night at the Opera

Scanning the paths in front of the National Opera, Rupert was trying to predict from which direction Irēne would arrive when someone tapped his shoulder. *'Labvakar* Rupert'

'Labvakar Irēne, you surprised me... and how lovely you look.' This was the first time he had met Irēne outside of a business context and was used to seeing her in a rather plain jacket over a cream or white shirt. It was a warm evening and Irēne wore a floral dress with short sleeves and her arms were covered with a loosely knitted, lacy shawl. She was the essence of a summer evening. He thought, *How lovely, how natural.* She took a step back and looked him up and down as if inspecting a soldier on parade.

'Very handsome! I see you bought a bow tie.'

'Yes, from a butterfly farm.' They both smiled and he presented the roses. 'These are for you but now I'm wondering what we can do with them in the theatre.'

'Oh, such a lovely pink colour.' Irēne took hold of the bunch. 'How did you know it is my favourite and, not to worry, we can leave them in the cloakroom.'

The café downstairs was already quite full with smartly dressed couples enjoying a pre-performance aperitif. Joining the small queue at the bar, Rupert enquired, 'Champagne?'

'What a lovely suggestion,' replied Irēne, 'it would not be the opera without a glass, would it?' Moving away from the bar, they clinked their champagne flutes and looked into each other's eyes, which Rupert had soon learnt was the local custom before taking the first sip.

'*Priekā.*' Rupert said.

'Bottoms up, if I am not mistaken.' Irēne replied and as she laughed, Rupert noticed the small whitening in the blue-grey iris of her left eye. *If the eye is the window on the soul*, he wondered, *what does this crescent moon reveal about Irēne?* She interrupted further speculation by commenting on his tanned face and added, 'People will think you have been to the south of France and not to the frozen north.'

'If I tell them I've been to Latvia, they may well think it's a republic in Africa anyway, not many English people have even heard of the country.'

A couple vacated a table and, once Rupert and Irēne had taken their place, he picked up the conversation. 'I'm amazed I could get tickets - especially as this is a premier.'

'Riga is quite empty. Normally the opera would be booked up months in advance with visiting Swedes, Finns and Germans. All this talk of war is making everyone nervous and no one is travelling – unless going home of course.'

'Going home.... It is very strange but my first thoughts are to my room in Elizabetes. I really feel like it is home there. By the way, I like the way you pronounce my name. With a slightly rolled R it sounds very continental.'

'That is nice to know,' Irēne smiled, 'and thank you for pronouncing mine so well. Foreigners often forget the stress is always on the first syllable in Latvian. I like the name Rupert; are there many Ruperts in England?'

'Yes, it's quite common but we all have to live under the shadow of a very famous Rupert Bear. He's a cartoon character who appears in one of our newspapers. If you see me wearing yellow-check trousers and a yellow scarf you'll know I'm trying to

21

look like my namesake.'

'Oh, very smart. I hope Rupert's a friendly bear.'

'All Ruperts are friendly.' He said and smiled to reiterate the point.

'I am very happy to hear that.' Rupert liked the way Irēne's smile seemed to almost extend to her prominent cheekbones. Looking at his pocket watch, he was pleased to see that there were still twenty minutes before the commencement of the opera. Plenty of time to watch the way her eyes sparkled with laughter as she spoke.

They talked of opera, and Rupert was enchanted by Irēne's capacity to recount the sweeping stories and recite her favourite lines. She asked Rupert whether he had seen Eugene Onegin before and when he said he hadn't she deftly summarised the story.

'Now you will not be all at sea, as I think the English say.' she said. *Oh,* thought Rupert, *But I think I may already be so.* They both drained the last drops of champagne.

'I suppose you will have many stories to tell when you are back in England.' Irēne said, dabbing her lips with a folded paper napkin.

'Oh certainly,' Rupert responded, 'I'm not joking when I say no one in England has heard of Latvia. When I go back, I'll tell them Riga's the most beautiful city in the world. They'll think I've been living in some sort of fantasy. Standing in front of the theatre I was just comparing it to Manchester. I can't tell you how different it is to my hometown.'

'Well, everyone has heard of Manchester but I do not have any idea what it is like.'

Irēne's assertion immediately made Rupert think of the fog and sulphurous air that often shrouded the city for days on end in the winter months. 'You would find Manchester interesting, maybe even shocking. It's so different to Riga.' He looked at Irēne and wondered what she'd think if suddenly transported to Manchester's Piccadilly Gardens. *Certainly her lovely cream coloured shawl wouldn't be the same after an evening out,* he mused and then said, 'It's a huge industrial city. With the exception of open countryside creating a breathing space to the south, it is encircled by factory chimneys spouting smoke, soot and goodness knows what else. This all leaves behind a black deposit on the masonry and, as for washing, it instantly dirties any newly cleaned linen.'

'You must be looking forward to going home.' She raised her eyebrows and he smiled.

'We do have some very grand buildings but you have so many new, clean and coloured buildings and the plasterwork. Well, there's nothing like it in Manchester. Manchester is very masculine. It's built on free enterprise and sweat. Riga is very feminine. Built on... well all things nice. The art nouveau architecture makes everywhere seem bright and happy... the dawn of a new age.'

'A new age. If only. It is very interesting what you say. In Latvian mythology there are many pagan goddesses. There is much feminine energy in Riga.'

'Let's drink to pagan goddesses.' He raised his empty glass, 'Oh dear, such a poor toast... By the way, I like your accent. Behind the German accent, you have, to my ear, the faintest traces of an American one.'

'How can you tell?' Irēne looked surprised and he mimicked it.

'Ameerican. You have a long sounding e.'

23

The buzzer called them to their seats and, as they went up the steps and into the dress circle, Irēne slipped her arm through Rupert's. The only other woman whom he had linked arms with was his mother. This felt completely different. The slight sensation of his arm touching Irēne's right breast intoxicated him. At that moment, he couldn't remember ever being as happy.

Although Rupert had never been to an opera before, he had seen pictures of Covent Garden and whilst it had looked impressive, he had felt it looked austere and cold. Now, sitting in the dress circle on the sumptuous velvet seats looking at the gold leaf around the balcony, the grand buttresses of the stage and the elegant ladies in their long dresses and jewels, he was transported to a different world; of empires and high art, love and tragedy, death and destiny.

At the interval, they joined the rush to the bar in the vestibule on the first floor. Whilst waiting to be served, Rupert caught the eye of the British Military Attaché standing further back in the queue and he nodded in recognition. Rupert remembered his last meeting with the attaché at a Christmas party at Schwarz's restaurant and how he had been given a lecture on the poor state of the Latvian army. He recalled the clipped tone of the attaché's Sandhurst accent as he listed the failings from the poor physique of the average soldier to the lack of armament and power to make decisions.

When the attaché eventually stopped detailing the limitation of the Latvian military he started pontificating on the threat of the IRA and Rupert had become bored to the point that he vowed to keep away from the British contingent. In thinking back to that, he was rather proud of his achievement in immersing himself in the local culture rather than seeking refuge in the expatriate community, who to him, seemed to be trying hard to be terribly British.

With glasses of champagne in hand, Rupert managed to evade the attaché by stepping out with Irēne onto the balcony overlooking the park with its full flower beds, the reds and yellows of the blooms seemingly on fire in the evening light. He returned to their previous conversation. 'So, if I'm right, how come you speak with a slight American accent?'

'Well, I guess I could sound American.' Irēne gave a faint shrug of her shoulders. 'I learnt English in Berlin from a lady called Alexandra Fischer whose mother was American. Alexandra did not really teach me though. She just constantly spoke to me in the language and I picked it up without any struggle. If I sound American it must have been passed from Fischer's mother.'

'What does Alexandra Fischer do?'

'She was the private secretary for a theatre director. He used to produce the work of Bertolt Brecht. Have you heard of Brecht by any chance?'

Rupert threw his head back in surprise. 'Heard of him? I studied his work at Cambridge as part of a modern German course.'

'No! Really? Brecht used to call the boiler suit he always wore a Manchester workers' suit. Is this what people in Manchester wear?'

'Well, plenty of people do wear boiler suits at work. I will have to let them know it has become the height of fashion in intellectual circles.' Rupert sniffed in amusement. 'But, somehow I don't think the fashion will catch on there. A friend of mine at university, Count Orlonsky told me of a funny story he'd heard about Brecht when he visited England; the doorman at the Savoy mistook him for a worker when he was due for lunch and barred his entry.'

'I doubt whether Brecht saw the joke in that. You have some well connected friends, a Count you say?'

'Ah, we called him the Count because he apparently had a distinguished Russian ancestry, but he never told me what that was.' The buzzer for the next act sounded. 'It's amazing both of us know Brecht in some way. It just shows how the fabric of life is tightly woven. Strands in our lives are overlaid. How wonderful.'

'How poetic.' He looked at her, not quite sure whether she was being ironic.

At the next interval Rupert bought two more glasses of champagne and Irēne asked, 'Are you trying to make me drunk?' He wasn't sure how to respond and Irēne had started to say she was only teasing when a tall, prematurely balding, man in his mid-thirties carrying a camera around his neck interrupted them.

'Walter, good evening.' Rupert warmly welcomed the visitor. 'I didn't know you liked the opera. Can I introduce Irēne Kalnins? She works at the Ministry of Interior Affairs.' He experienced a warm feeling, one he took to be pride, when indicating that Irēne was his companion for the evening and he turned to her. 'Irēne, this is Walter Zapp.'

'I am sure I recognise the name. Are you the inventor of the Minox camera?' Irēne asked. By way of answer, Walter took out of his jacket pocket a metal object, about the size of two small fountain pens arranged side by side and showed this off in the palm of his hand.

'This takes pictures as well as being a thing of beauty.' Rupert exclaimed, having already been shown the camera. 'Walter is an artist and a genius.'

26

'I am not sure about being a genius,' said Walter, 'but it does take good photographs, although we are still working on adding a flashlight. To supplement my income, I am the official photographer at the premieres and have to take pictures of important people in the audience and of the singers at the curtain call. Here, let me take your picture.' Without waiting for an answer, he scooped up his Leica camera, took a few paces back, and pressed the shutter release. Everyone looked towards them when the bulb flashed and popped.

'Very important people.' Irēne commented.

After allowing Walter to change the flashbulb, Rupert faced Irēne and continued. 'As part of the report on the dam, I had to evaluate its impact on the local population and wildlife. That meant walking along the banks of the River Daugava with Walter and taking lots of photographs. Walter is a great photographer as well as inventor and he has taken the most beautiful pictures of the Daugava valley including the spectacular gorge at Staburags. Of course the dam, when it's eventually built, will change the valley forever. The current dam has just raised the water level by three and a half metres, but the new one will increase it to thirty-five metres... but, at least, Walter has captured a record of what was there.'

'I am for beauty rather than progress. In one way it is good the project has stopped.' Irēne said.

Rupert raised his glass, looked into Irēne's eyes and said, 'I am for beauty too.' The bell for the end of the interval sounded and, after bidding Walter farewell and on the way back to their seats, he explained, 'I was put in touch with Walter because he speaks English. His father is a British subject, but I don't know what he does. Anyhow, Walter thinks, one day, every woman will have a Minox in their handbag and every man one in their briefcase.'

'I like his ambition; certainly every spy in the land will

want one.'

'I think you might be right.'

It was still warm when they came out of the opera and, having collected the roses, they walked towards Laima clock, where horse drawn cabs were to be found. They talked about the opera and Irēne asked, 'When you get back to England will your life return to nothing more than a full diary of balls, concerts and parties as Eugene Onegin's was?'

'It can be so tiresome.' Rupert replied and put his head to one side in mock exhaustion.

'And would you give me a lecture if I was to send you a letter professing my love, as did Tatyana?'
'Yes, just like Onegin.' He mimicked the stern voice of the character he had just heard on stage, 'I'd coldly advise more emotional control in the future lest another man take advantage of your innocence.'

'Are you so like Onegin?'

'I hope I'm not like Onegin at all.' He thought it best not to be seen as facetious and returned to his normal tone. 'When he sees Tatyana later in his life, he realises he has made a mistake because she is beautiful. I already know you are beautiful.'

'Are all Englishmen such flatterers?' Irēne jabbed him gently in the ribs. They walked on towards the cab, quiet for a while.

Rupert broke the silence. 'I'm sorry I am going away tomorrow. Andris Ozols, has invited my boss and me to spend the day fishing with him in his boat out on Riga Bay. I've become friends with Andris over the course of the project and it seemed like a good way of spending our last day in Latvia. Also, I have got a feeling he will want one final opportunity for revenge.'

'Revenge!'

'Yes, revenge for all the times I've beaten him... at chess. It is nice he has offered.' He decided not to explain why he was sorry to be going, as he was afraid that admitting he'd rather see Irēne might sound rather too sentimental.

As they walked on, arm in arm in the limpid evening air Rupert focused on the impending separation and wanted desperately to kiss Irēne goodnight. Then, he thought of his leaving for good in three days. *How silly to leave with an aching heart,* a sensible voice sounded in his head. When they reached the cab rank there was no opportunity for a long goodbye. A row of carriages stood awaiting passengers and the horses' hooves shifted and danced on the cobbled boulevard. On their approach, a cabbie had already jumped down and was holding the door of the open topped carriage.

Rupert became rather formal and took Irēne's gloved hand and kissed it. The cabbie helped her up into the carriage and Rupert passed the roses to her. Rupert and Irēne looked at each other without saying anything. Then, feeling he hadn't seized the moment, he said, 'I have one last night in Riga, the day after tomorrow, can I take you out again? Maybe dancing if you know a place where they let men in who have two left feet.' The horse had already started, but he clearly heard a reply, caught on the rosy air, 'I would like that very much.'

Rupert turned for home, his heart light and his gait buoyant. The days ahead seemed newly inviting. Fishing with good company, a night out with a beautiful woman, a cruise over the Baltic Sea, a train ride and home to sleepy Wythenshawe. What could be more idyllic?

A Trip to The Seaside

In the borderland between sleep and wakefulness where time and space cease to constrain, Rupert's bow wave of consciousness left the summerhouse nestling by the coast where he lay and hovered over the Baltic before pushing on past Germany and Holland and, rising over the Channel and English coastline, deposited him, with a swoosh, into his mother's kitchen. There was no big welcome home; it was as if he had never been away. He sat by the fire burning in the stove even though it was August and his mother asked whether he wanted another cup of tea.

As he bubbled up from the depths of a deep slumber he understood that he was still dreaming and tried to bring his thoughts back nearer home. He recollected the night at the opera and how he had taken Irēne in his arms and kissed her. Her lips were full and her waist was surprisingly slim; so slim, in this half awake state, his arms seemed to go around her twice. He breathed deeply and enjoyed the erotic sensation.

The sharp point of consciousness finally pierced the carapace of sleep and he realised, with regret, he had let Irēne disappear into the night leaving only an impression of his lips on her laced-gloved hand. He pictured her standing at the steps in her pretty dress, a few locks of hair curling forward accentuating her high cheekbones. *How very feminine but strong too,* he thought and then, recalling how she pronounced his name with the rolled R, *I like the sound of her voice, and such proper English; quite remarkable.*

Stretching luxuriantly in his bed in a large airy bedroom, covered only by a crisp linen sheet and thin, down filled quilt, Rupert had the sense of space and freedom that had epitomised his time in Latvia. In England he, realised with a smile, he had been tucked in under sheets and blankets all of his life. In

Latvia, he had enjoyed throwing off some of the constraints imposed by society's expectations. Although he knew he hadn't pushed hard at any boundaries, and had tried to behave in a way his mother would be proud of, he nevertheless felt liberated and more empowered than at any other time in his life.

Having washed and shaved he swept back his sun-lightened hair, much longer than he had ever worn it before, and looked at his arms, where the hair was a sun-bleached blonde. He was pleased with the effect.

His pocket watch showed eight o'clock and he knew there was no need to rush. Andris might soon be up but his boss had been set to enjoy a rare night away from his wife. Rupert had left him eyeing an unfinished bottle of Andris' favourite scotch with calculating intent.

Whilst rekindling the fire in the kitchen's wood burning stove and brewing a coffee, Rupert pondered upon how his habits had changed, 'For a start, back in England, everyone will think I've become French if I ask for coffee at breakfast.' Coffee in hand, he made his way to the balcony and from there he looked through the pine trees to the smooth Baltic Sea beyond, the colour of smoked glass. Just below the balcony was a terrace with an area for outdoor cooking. The discarded utensils used for grilling the fish the previous day were now the only evidence of three men enjoying preparing and eating their catch, as if none of them had any other care in the world. Rupert had complimented Andris at the time on his culinary skills; the fish had been astonishing, melt-in-the-mouth and somehow fresher and more vital than anything Rupert could recall eating, even from the cottage gardens at home.

Yesterday's newspaper stared up at Rupert from where it lay on the sun lounger. On the front cover was a photograph of a beaming Stalin standing beside the German foreign minister, Joachim von Ribbentrop, in the large reception hall of the Great

Kremlin Palace. Behind them, a portrait of Lenin looked down from the wall. In the foreground, Vyacheslav Molotov, the Soviet commissar for foreign affairs, sat at a desk signing The Treaty of Non Aggression between the German Reich and the Union of Soviet Socialist Republics.

Rupert took hold of the newspaper and was picking his way through the Latvian when Andris emerged onto the balcony, a mug of coffee in his large hand. He was much shorter than Rupert but powerfully built. Working in his father's cement works in his earlier years had been as good for his physical development as it had his business acumen. Although he was only five years senior to Rupert, Andris had the presence and character of a much older man, with his steady, iron-grey gaze and purposeful silences.

After the customary morning greetings, Rupert pointed to the picture in the newspaper and, speaking in German, commented, 'Although my Latvian isn't that good, I can see this is some sort of neutrality pact.'

'Yes,' said Andris, looking away from the newspaper and out over the bay, his mouth a grim line. 'It says it guarantees that both nations would remain neutral if either were attacked by other countries. Also they would remain neutral if either of them were the aggressive party – which is the more likely option.'

'Maybe a neutrality pact might be good news for Latvia and the Baltic States; neither Germany nor Russia would want to annoy each other by invading countries close to their own borders.' Rupert wasn't convinced by his own optimism.

'You don't want to believe Hitler and Stalin are suddenly best friends.' Andris responded in an authoritative voice. 'Remember, Hitler denounced Stalin's regime as a band of international criminals. He even wrote in *Mein Kampf* of his wish to destroy the Soviet Union. On the other side, Soviet propaganda is active; even promoting, I would say, confrontation with the Nazi menace. No, this is to cover up something else. I expect the very worst. A whirlwind is building. It is a good job you are going. Don't take this the wrong way, only, I think you will be safer in Britain.'

Rupert was thinking about how to steer the conversation away from politics when Andris ventured, 'I think we might not be seeing Stanley for a while this morning. So we have a little time. As this is our last opportunity for chess, how about a game?' He was already on his way to fetch the chess set before Rupert had time to agree.

Andris unfolded the board on top of a small table on the balcony and they both drew up chairs. Andris looked at Rupert and said. 'You've gained quite a reputation in Riga for your chess. Now it is time for you to go, how about handing over some of your secrets? I really could do with beating my old rival, Ivars - the smug bastard.'

'I'd be afraid for his health if you started to beat him. His reddened face when I win, makes it look like he is going to burst a blood vessel.' Rupert made the first move and added, 'I'm not sure I can pass on any skills, but I'll have a think about it.'

'Happy to receive any tips.' Andris remarked making his first move, to which Rupert made a swift response.

As the game progressed, Rupert gave some thought to his chess strategy and said, 'There is a difference between theoretical strength and actual strength. A well-positioned pawn, played with skill, possesses more strength than the bishop moved in a way that lacks strategy.'

'That I understand.' Andris' voice had a hint of irritation.

'I'm sorry, I didn't mean to sound like I was teaching a

33

cat how to climb a tree.'

'I am not offended, but you play in a different way. My strategy never quite works with you and I don't understand why.'

'I don't really know either, perhaps it comes down to being able to handle unfamiliar and unexpected things, outcomes I cannot know, with blind confidence.' Andris raised a bushy eyebrow, already growing unruly, wiry hairs.

'Very abstract!'

The sun hadn't come fully onto the balcony before the game came to a characteristic end with Rupert declaring, 'Checkmate'.

'If your mother wasn't looking forward so much to your return,' Andris flung up his large hands in mock exasperation, 'I could easily take you into the bay and drop you overboard.' They laughed and Rupert promised to write if he found the key to his winning game.

Draining the cold coffee from his mug Andris asked, 'Anyway, have you enjoyed yourself?'

'If you mean the fishing, I certainly did and if you mean my time in Latvia, then definitely. This job here has been the best I've done. I didn't really know much about dams and electricity generation before I came, but I do now. The work has been fascinating.'

'In what way?'

'I hadn't realised how vital transportation could be to a contract. Where bridges were too low or roads not wide enough to easily transport the equipment, I needed to factor these constraints into the contract. What does the postponement of the project mean for your cement works?'

'There are some minor consolations for not building the dam. We own the dolomite quarries that would get flooded by the dammed river. So we can continue to work these for a while longer.'

Rupert recalled a similar conversation at the opera. 'I am for beauty too,', he had assured Irēne. Rupert realised he had tacitly agreed that postponing the project was a good thing. He wondered whether he'd ever make a good dam-builder. His mind handed him an image of Irēne stood before him, her face upturned awaiting his kiss. Andris interrupted the development of this scene with an interjection, 'It has been good to work with you. I see why everyone I know has a good word to say about the British.'

'I appreciate that.'

'Yes, I hope to work with you again. In the meantime, please keep sending Welsh coal and Scotch whiskey; if not, dried peat and local vodka will be a very poor substitute.'

Andris cleared away the chess set then leant forward, lowering his voice. 'I read some time ago that employees of Metropolitan Vickers were charged with wrecking and using their cover as businessmen to spy on the USSR. Of course it must have been a trumped up charge. It didn't seem right to ask you about it when we were working on the project, but did you know any of the men?'

Rupert knew what Andris was referring to. A few years before he had joined the firm, five engineers from the company were arrested in Russia. One of the men signed a detailed confession detailing the spying operation and two of the men were given short prison sentences in Russia. Rupert answered, 'Oh I'm sure the whole thing was fabricated and, no, they left before I joined.'

Andris opened his mouth to continue, but stopped short at the appearance of Stanley on the balcony, who gave a considerable yawn and greeted them with surprising chirp and vigour. 'Good morning to you both on this beautiful Baltic blue day', he said, his hoarse voice indicating that a late night of solitary drinking had taken its toll. Andris replied in faltering English that he indeed was well and, after a brief conversation about the weather, added, 'Stanley, with this *schönes Wetter*, I stay on here and Christa join me later. You take *vagon* and my wife drive it back when later she come here.'

As soon as Stanley had finished his coffee they were ready to depart. After a great deal of handshaking and promises to keep in touch, Rupert and Stanley set off in Andris' BMW 328 roadster, its long, sleek bonnet suggestive of the power underneath.

The road wound away from the water and through first trees, then open fields. They had not been travelling long before Stanley began to talk about the project. 'I think we can go back home proud of what we did lad. If it weren't for all this political posturing I'm sure contracts could be signed int' mornin'. The specifications for turbines are clear and we could begin shippin'em out to the dam in less than eighteen months. It's a bloody shame.' Stanley's return to his broad Manchester dialect told Rupert he was settling into the idea of returning home.
Stanley turned the car onto the main road and accelerated towards Riga. The wind noise increased substantially and Rupert raised his voice. 'Do you think that war is now imminent?'

'Honestly, it looks right likely. The ambassador wouldn't be pressuring us to leave if this were just sabre rattlin'.'

'Yes, I suppose you're right.' Rupert had purposefully not engaged with talk of war on his assignment and, even on the verge of going home, preferred not to think of it.

'We've been so focused on project, all this mess in Europe

seems a long way away but Germans and Italians have become right restless. Remember, the Germans aren't too far up coast at Klaipeda, or Memel as they now call it. That's all of a four-hour tank ride away. No, I think the best thing is t' get all our contracts safely out of here and if and when all this talk of war dies down, or more likely after the war is finished, we come back and finish t' job.'

Driver and passenger stopped talking for a short while as the road curved and the glimmer of the sea was visible through an arc of silver birch trees, their leaves sparkling in the sun like a shower of gold coins. As the road straightened Stanley increased the speed and shouted, 'What will you be telling people when you get home?'

'Oh it is difficult to say... the food, the proper winter, the warm summer.' He didn't really want to think about going home. It suddenly felt a long way away and he wondered whether he would ever see Irēne again once he was back in England. 'By the way, tonight I'm taking Irēne Kalnins out; you know, the girl from the Ministry. Do you know of any good dancing places?'

'I will ask the missus if she knows of anywhere. If it were beer and sausage, I might be able to help. But, remember we have t' be packed and ready t' go at ten o'clock tomorrow. The boat isn't going to wait for you if you have t' get out of a warm bed and are late getting home... Remember what the ambassador said!' With that, Stanley lent over and gently nudged Rupert on the arm.

Rupert and Stanley had been guests of the British Ambassador, Charles Orde at the Legation in Riga. After lunch, and when the ambassador's wife had left the men at the table, the ambassador had addressed Rupert directly. He remembered exactly the lecture given in a hectoring tone. 'On this project you represent Metropolitan Vickers and Britain. Proper behaviour is to be expected at all times and there is to be no fraternising with local girls. If you want to learn the local language, a sleeping dictionary is not the answer.' At first, the reference to a dictionary hadn't made sense, but the ambassador's words stuck in his head for some time afterwards, especially the warning, 'Don't forget, many of the women have TB'. He suspected at the time this was just scaremongering; now he had a deep sense of lost opportunity.

Trying to dismiss ideas of loss from his mind, Rupert asked, 'Will you be pleased to get back to England?'

'Too right lad. Won't you?'

'Well, yes.' Rupert sounded far from convinced.

'I'm looking forward to a proper pint, talkin' with people who understand me and seein' United. T' wife can't wait either. It is very lonely and boring when you can't speak local language.' Stanley settled back into the driver's seat and, almost talking to himself, said, 'Oh, what a beautiful car this is t' drive. 'Tis nearly brand new an't model only came out a year or so ago. Look at lines and bonnet's so long. I 'ave never driv'n an open top car before and on a day like this, it's bloomin' marvellous. It won everything at Nürburgring racetrack in two-litre class. I don't understand Germany at all. Instead of makin' tanks and marchin' in great rallies, they should focus on makin' cars like these. They would kick our arses up street and put t' Americans out of business. Now let's see what this little beauty can do. Two litres, we mus' be able to go over a hundred and fifty kilometres t' hour. Riga here we come.'

The roadside trees, with their bases painted white, were narrowly spaced and, as the roadster gathered pace, the white trunks merged in a blur. Resting back in his seat, thankful that further chatting was impossible over the noise of the engine and wind, Rupert thought of the evening ahead. He wondered where to take Irēne and how he might contact her to arrange their meeting. Rupert watched the scenery whip past the window and smiled. It would surely be a wonderful evening.

Three kilometres ahead of the speeding car and just around a hidden bend, a cow wandered out of a field and ambled along the main road to Riga.

Second City Hospital

Darkness, complete, pitch-black, utter darkness. So dark and dense it compresses. Bubbles from far below raise him up, up and up but towards what? Or, are they suspending him in this dark void for eternity? Noises far off in the distance: Rupert thinks it is the sound of swans. No, it is human voices and they are calling his name, 'Rupert, Rupert wake up.' *Is this Matron?* ; *she is a tyrant for not letting children sleep in.* But, something is not right; *does Matron speak German?* If he doesn't get up though, he will miss matins and then won't be allowed to play football. A distant voice, 'Rupert, we are going now.' *'Thank God,'* he thought, *'I can get some sleep.'*

In the murky depths of a deep darkness, Rupert saw a distant light, like the nascent dawn. Too tired and drained to open his eyes, he listened for clues as to where he was. He had a sense he wasn't at home or at his aunt's house but, beyond that, he had no idea as to his situation. The light was becoming intense through his closed eyes and suddenly he felt scared. With what seemed to him like superhuman endeavour, he cracked open a heavy, leaden eyelid and the unease increased. Everything was bright white and shafts of powerful light radiated in. He closed his eye and was aware of the pounding in his chest. *Can I be dead and still have a beating heart?*

Gradually, he half opened his right eye and a painful glare seared through to the back of his head. To his right there was a dark patch, which, after a brief while, he could see was the misty outline of a photograph on a table. He tentatively turned his head by a few degrees and swivelled his eyes to get a better look but the effort made him feel like he had just got off a fairground waltzer. After struggling again to look at the photograph, he realised it was of two people in something like a wedding photo. He was confused as he recognised the couple but, at the same time, did not know who they were. He closed his eyes, rested his head and drifted back into darkness.

When he opened his eyes again, he squinted hard to see if this would make the gentle rotation of the room stop. He noted the high ceiling and double window through which the light streamed in. He also looked down at the brown painted, wooden floor and understood that this was not The Manchester Royal Infirmary with which he was familiar.

Out of the pale wall a smudged, buttery coloured figure emerged and a hazy, rosy hue coalesced into a red cross on a cap. The figure stood over him and asked, '*Kā tev iet?*' Rupert understood the question but did not recognise the language. Confused, he tried to form the words of a response, but his mouth was too dry to speak. Soft, milk coloured hands lifted his head, brought a cup to his lips and tipped a few drops of water into his mouth. He noted his tongue felt too long and it was unusually furry but he was able to utter, 'Thank you, please, where am I?' The figure didn't respond to his question.

The nurse disappeared and soon came back with a doctor, who peered over Rupert and began speaking in German, 'Good morning Mr Lockart, it is good to see you awake.'

'Where am I?' Rupert repeated his question, this time in German.

'You are in the Second City Hospital.' The doctor explained and then asked, 'Do you remember what happened to you?' Rupert was unable to make sense of the question; everything was spinning and, after waiting for a reply, the doctor continued. 'You have been involved in a very serious car crash and are badly hurt. You have been sleeping for a long time. The good news is you survived.'

'Please, can I see my mother?' The effort tired him and he drifted back into unconsciousness.

Gradually the periods of wakefulness grew into minutes. In one episode, he looked again at the blurred, pulsing picture on the bedside and, despite feeling he knew whom the people were, he couldn't quite place them. He was struggling to work out who these people were, when a different man in a white coat came into the room wearing a blue polka dot bow tie. He announced himself as Doctor Berzins and, in a very businesslike manner, said, 'Mr. Lockart, you have badly broken your right leg in two places and I have had to operate to realign the bones. You have sustained other injuries as well, including a broken wrist and four broken ribs.'

'Huh.' Rupert hardly registered the news and the doctor looked into his eyes.

'Mr. Lockart...'

'My father... No... I'm Rupert.'

'Rupert, what year is it and how old are you?' He struggled to answer; everything about his life seemed to be just out of reach of his grasping mind.

'I'm not sure of the year, but I am twelve.' A quizzical expression fleetingly appeared on the doctor's face.

'We are giving you something for your pain but if it gets worse please let us know. Please don't try to turn over as your leg is in plaster.' Then, after checking Rupert's pulse, he left the room.

Night and day merged as Rupert drifted in and out of sleep. He could clearly remember coming home from school, his mother welcoming him with a hug, a kiss on the cheek and the offer of a freshly baked scone. He could almost smell it and its melting butter but he knew, somehow, this wasn't his most recent experience. Very tentatively, and with great effort, he moved his un-bandaged hand to his face and stroked his chin. He was surprised to find it was sharp and bristly and then he drifted back into a deep, concussed sleep.

When Doctor Berzins returned, Rupert was awake and was asked, 'How are you feeling?'

'Terrible... and I can't remember anything about recent times.' The doctor brought his head closer.

'Rupert,' his tone was confidential, 'you lost a lot of blood and you have had a nasty blow to the head. Don't be alarmed, you will start to recall things. I am sure you will be fine given time.'

When the doctor left, Rupert turned his head with great effort and studied the photograph again. He suddenly had a shock that made him flinch, sending a pain through his chest as he realised the man in the photograph was himself. A strange feeling came over him. He was conscious of memories slowly returning as if they were being drip fed from the bottle connected by a tube to his arm. With a gentle wave washing over him, he again drifted off to sleep.

Waking with a start, he realised that a memory of setting off with Stanley from the summerhouse had returned. He rang the buzzer, conveniently placed on the bed and when the nurse arrived he asked for Doctor Berzins.

With the arrival of the doctor, Rupert tried to lift his head but the doctor put his hand gently on his shoulder and suggested that he rest back on the pillow. Looking up at the doctor, Rupert asked, 'How is Stanley?'

'Mr. Billings did not survive the accident. I am very sorry.' The reply made Rupert shudder. After a pause, the doctor began again, 'The British Ambassador persuaded Mr. Billings' wife to return on the ship the following day and his body will be transported to England when it is safe.'

'Safe... how do you mean?' Rupert asked.

'You need to rest now.'

'Please tell me what you mean.'

'I am afraid your country and France have declared war on Germany.' Rupert's eyes grew wide. 'Germany will defend herself with the use of U-boats protecting the coast. As such, the Baltic Sea will be a very dangerous area for British ships. Safe passage cannot be guaranteed. There will be time to talk about this; the British Ambassador has asked to be informed when you are ready for visitors, so you will have the opportunity to speak to him in due course. Now rest.'

Unable to rest, Rupert tried to take in the news about the state of his injuries, the accident, Stanley's death and the declaration of war, which sounded in the words of the doctor like an act of aggression. Eventually, he went to sleep and when he awoke the sun was low in the window indicating it was evening, but he had no idea as to the day or how long he had been asleep.

When the doctor returned, Rupert enquired, 'Is there anything more you can tell me about what happened? I've no recollection at all of the accident.' The doctor shook his head.

'I am afraid there's not much I can tell you. The accident was on a very quiet road. The car must have hit a tree. By the time an ambulance got to the scene, Mr. Billings was dead.'

'Oh dear.'

'He was in the driver's seat and you were found ten metres from the car. Quite honestly, you are lucky to be alive as

44

you lost a lot of blood. Your memory may come back about the accident over time, but for now, I would like you to have some soup, as you haven't eaten anything for many days.'

A nurse arrived with soup and, by propping his head up on the pillow, fed him a few spoonfuls. He soon felt sick and motioned the nurse to stop. Despite her encouragement, he did not eat any more although he felt guilty as if he were behaving like a spoilt child.

His head felt as heavy as lead and his chest was tight. Gently he explored his body. He moved his hand under the bedclothes to feel the bandages that cocooned him from his throat to his thorax. He looked down the bed; the white sheets reminded him of a ski slope as they gently rose towards the end, covering his raised right leg. He suddenly felt very vulnerable, alone and a long way from home.

The next day, after swallowing a small amount of porridge for breakfast, Rupert used the bedpan, a process he found to be painful and embarrassing. For the rest of the day, he lay back and looked at the high ceiling as if his former life were projected on it. Memories bumped and barged their way into his consciousness and certainly did not form a neat, orderly and chronological queue. Occasionally, a few images came to mind that were so unfamiliar he was unsure as to whether they had ever taken place. He began to think there had been a mix up in the Memory Department of the hospital and that by accident he had been given a few memories that belonged to another patient. The idea amused him and helped reduce the anxiety of being a stranger in a strange land.

With the food and drink he had managed to keep down, he felt a little stronger and could now turn his head a little further without the world violently rotating. When he looked at the photograph on his bedside it was clear this was of himself and Irēne and it was the one Walter had taken of them together at the theatre. Studying the faces he wondered why he wore a large grin, whilst Irēne had her eyes cast down and looked a little sad.

Rupert was trying to recall all of the details of the evening at the opera when the door opened and the nurse announced a visitor. Behind her was Irēne carrying a bunch of bigheaded yellow dahlias and a package. Suddenly, his spirits soared and he wanted to jump out of bed to greet her, but all he could do was raise his bandaged hand. '*Labdien* Rupert.' Irēne came over and gave him a kiss on the cheek, clearly not put off by his badly blackened right eye and the multi-colored bruising to his forehead, which had begun to settle into a vivid yellow. He breathed in the fresh air that still surrounded her and the scent of the flowers and felt his heart pounding against the constraining bandage.

'Irēne, how lovely... please don't look too closely, especially as I haven't shaved.'

'You look very handsome, just like a sailor now with a beard.' Irēne brushed his unshaven chin.

'It sounds like I won't be doing much sailing for a while.'

Rupert looked at Irēne as she handed over the package wrapped in brown paper and tied with a bow made from a strip of patterned fabric. She wore a small, pale yellow, knitted cardigan over a linen dress, belted at the waist. *How simply perfect*, he thought. He showed his bandaged hand, indicating his inability to deal with the package, and she opened it to reveal a yellow scarf. 'I think you might need this as it seems yours has been lost on the way.'

'Oh that is lovely...' He was amazed that she had remembered his passing comment about the attire of Rupert Bear. 'But what about my check trousers?'

'You will be wearing those again very soon.' Irēne responded encouragingly.

'I'm not so sure.'

Pulling up the only chair in the room, Irēne said, 'I would have visited sooner, but was advised you were too poorly to be disturbed... Now, tell me, how are you feeling?'

'Never felt better.'

'And what do the doctors have to say?'

'Oh, a few broken bones here and there, nothing serious.' He wanted to keep their conversation light hearted but could not contain his feelings. 'Actually, I am worried about my memory. It is returning, but my memories are all mixed up and I don't know what is real and what I've dreamt. Images from different times and places are all jumbled up. It's like a box has been dropped and now I have the job of sorting through the contents and putting them back in order. But the problem is... I think some of the memories belong to another patient.'

'In that case, I do hope he had an interesting life.' Irēne said, her eyes twinkling. Rupert smiled. Some of his worry disappeared.

He told Irēne the extent of his injuries. 'What is really disturbing though - I can't feel my legs. There's not even any pain.' Irēne tried to reassure him that it was early days, after a dreadful accident and it would only be a question of time before everything recovered. He didn't voice his main worry, which was whether he had been paralysed. He tried to lighten the heavy mood beginning to settle on him. 'I'm sorry to have missed our date.'

'I imagined you wanted to stay on fishing.'

'Never!'

'But, when I read in the paper about the accident I knew it was you. I cannot tell you how shocked I was.'

'Do you know, I can't remember a thing about the crash. I recall thinking I needed to get a message to you and then there's nothing else... and to think Mrs. Billings had to go back with her husband laid out in the morgue. I'm only glad I wasn't driving. I don't think I could bear that on my conscience.' Silence fell for a moment. Rupert pictured Stanley, laughing, his broad, gentle face alight. Something leaden and cold dropped into Rupert's stomach and he shook his head to clear the image.

'Is there any good news?' he asked, 'What are you doing?'

'Oh, my small life is of no interest,' Irēne was uncharacteristically serious in her reply, 'especially as compared to what is happening elsewhere. Have the doctors told you Europe is at war?'

'Yes.'

'You might be a little bent but you are safe. The Baltic Sea is highly dangerous for British vessels, so it might be some time before you can set sail.' For the first time Rupert felt that, in being able to see more of Irēne, there was a benefit to be gained from his delayed departure. 'Now let me see if I can get a vase for these flowers.' Irēne stood up.

'Vase.' He repeated the word in her American style. 'There you go, Honey.' He laughed.

Returning with the dahlias, bright and cheery in a white porcelain vase, Irēne placed them on the side table just in Rupert's eye line. Then, picking up the photograph of the two of them at the opera, she asked, 'How did you get this?'

'Walter must have visited and brought it over whilst I was in a coma. The couple are very handsome I'd say. I think they were two very important people attending the premiere of Eugene Onegin.'

'Really,' exclaimed Irēne, 'and you, poor sailor, you know such people!' They both smiled. A nurse entered the room and suggested it was time for Rupert to rest. He tried to argue, but Irēne said she had better go and added, 'I need to visit my mother this Sunday, but I can call in to see you during the following weekend if you would like.'

'I'd like that very much.' He reached for her hand and brought it up to his lips. After Irēne had waved goodbye, he lay back smiling, then, as he relaxed, a shadow slid over his mind, as if cast by a cloud. He realised there was still a large gap in his memory.

Ruminations

Rupert ceased his pacing, sat down on the side of his cell's metal bed frame and covered his eyes with his palms. He tried to summon images of the accident but nothing came. He even tried to imagine the sounds of crunching metal and the car whirling through the air but this didn't bring back the real memories. He expected them to appear in his dreams but, whilst these were vivid, they never revealed the actual detail of the moments that changed the course of his life forever.

The lights were extinguished in his cell and he wished he could do the same to his thoughts; only sleep would take him away from his reality but that too was not at his command.

The phrase 'London is ablaze' kept coming back to him and he couldn't stop the idea creeping in that England was now the target of the Nazi bombers. He managed to take some comfort by thinking of the immensity of British industry, including Metropolitan Vickers; now, surely, every furnace, foundry and factory was focused on the war effort.

Recalling the massive cranes at Metropolitan Vickers dwarfing those who operated them, he imagined how the factory would now be gearing up to make the machinery of war. On the border of sleep, he heard the clanking of the crane calling forth the faithful to the cathedral space. In they cycled, in their boiler suits, bowing down, submitting to the god of production. And, as its mechanised heart beat faster, it began spitting out the bombs, guns, bullets and machinery of war. He twitched violently and fell into a dream-filled sleep in which German tanks rolled over the bluebells at Wythenshawe and churned up the grassy sward at the Hall.

He woke as usual before the klaxon, his head woozy from the disturbed sleep and back stiff from the hard bed. He didn't feel like undertaking his meditative walk and decided on a day off—a big mistake.

Instead of his thoughts being directed and controlled, they came randomly and in no pattern he understood. In the void of the cell and the vacuum of his mind his thoughts circled around and around in an ever-changing combination but were never corralled into coherent themes or arrived at a conclusion.

By the time the lights were switched out at the end of the day, Rupert was ready to choke on his own ruminations. He knew that days like this would see him being carted off to the psychiatric section, if the prison had such a thing, and vowed never again to simply let his mind wander wherever it pleased. If it did, he feared for the worst.

Visitors

The morning after Irēne's visit, Rupert asked a nurse, by the way of sign language, to help him shave as his beard was becoming unbearably itchy. She summoned another nurse over and, with care, they propped him up in bed. As they did so, he became aware of the massive force of gravity for the first time in his life as it bore down on his ribs and made his body feel heavier than if it were made of lead. He even said out loud, 'Now I understand how the moon's gravity can move the oceans.' The nurses looked at him and smiled, though they did not understand.

One of the nurses fetched a bowl and razor and carefully held his head. All the feelings that had been absent in his body since the accident seem to make their way to the nape of his neck and the sensitive skin on the back of his head. Despite the tightness in his ribs he felt close to ecstatic. The nurse drew the razor across his cheek in delicate sweeps. Although gently done, his skin smarted and tingled.

Later in the afternoon, with Rupert propped higher in the bed by pillows, Doctor Berzins entered and announced, 'The British Ambassador has come to see you.' Charles Orde, tall and elegantly dressed in a pinstriped, double-breasted suit, was ushered to the bedside carrying a small parcel under one arm. Doctor Berzins made his exit.

'Everyone insists on calling me Ambassador here; mind you, I can't blame them; Envoy Extraordinary and Minister-Plenipotentiary is a bit of a mouthful. Anyway, how are you old boy?' His jovial familiarity was disarming and Rupert, who had expected a formal visit, relaxed.

'Never felt better.'

'I'm very sorry to hear about the accident and, of course,

the passing of Stanley. It really is a great shame, especially considering you were both on your way home.'

'I still can't believe it.'

The ambassador put his parcel on the bed but refused Rupert's suggestion to pull up a chair. With a quick look around to make sure the door was closed he said in a hushed tone, 'You have heard, I'm sure, that we are at war.' Rupert nodded. 'On the 1st of September Germany invaded Poland and we had no alternative other than to help defend her sovereignty. Two days later, a German submarine sank the cruise ship Athenia and over one hundred people drowned. Britain and France have declared war on Germany and the RAF has already targeted German warships off their coast. I'm pleased to say that the Australians, Kiwis and South Africans have piled in to help - and the Canadians will join in as well. I don't want to say anything as crass as the war will be over by Christmas, but as there is a non-aggression pact between Russia and Germany, I think the war will soon become a stalemate with the end result being a few bites out of Poland.'

Whilst speculating that Andris might have a different view on the extent of the conflict, he nevertheless allowed the ambassador to continue without comment. 'The situation is highly volatile and many Brits are heading home, but it looks like you are best placed here for now while you recover from your injuries. I think Germany and Russia have bigger fish to fry than invading Latvia, so for a while we are safe. If this changes, we do have evacuation plans for Legation staff and British subjects. We will keep in touch but you must be ready to depart at a moment's notice.'

'I certainly will' Rupert had the sense of being caught in a magnetic field. Powerful forces were urging him home but, at the same time, he detected restraining ones. He couldn't fully analyse his sensations, as the ambassador continued.

'I will arrange for your clothes and personal items to be

brought here from your apartment, in readiness.'

The ambassador changed the subject and, in a louder voice, said, 'I thought that you might like some light reading. I have some old copies of the *Times* for you. Unfortunately, it doesn't look like we will be getting daily copies in the future. The library at the Legation is rather limited but my wife recommends *The Great Gatsby* and I've brought my favourite, *The Inimitable Jeeves.*' The ambassador put the parcel on the end of the bed and Rupert, given his bandaged hand and discomfort at sitting upright, wondered how long it would be before he was able to handle the awkwardly sized newspapers.

Thanking the ambassador for his visit and the books, Rupert then asked, 'Does my mother know of my accident?'

'A telegram has been sent to tell her of your delayed departure. We haven't said you are badly injured. There is a telephone in the Legation and when you are well enough I'm sure we can arrange for you to call England.'

'My mother hasn't got a telephone.... but we could ring Wytheshawe Hall; she works there.' Thinking he might not be visiting the Legation in the near future, he asked, 'But isn't there a telephone here in the hospital?'

'There is and you are more than welcome to try, but don't get your hopes up. As it won't be possible to route calls through Berlin, I think the chance of getting a good connection on a local line is slim. But, first you need to gain a little bit of strength and then you can have a go. If you don't get through soon and aren't well enough to come to the Legation, I will update your mother with another telegram.'

With the ambassador's departure, Rupert was pleased to slip into a more comfortable horizontal position and then slept for most of the rest of the day. That evening the doctor gave him something to help him sleep through the night, with limited success . Although awake, his thoughts were dreamlike and revolved around Stanley's grieving wife, his own imminent departure, German tanks rolling into Latvia and an image of Irene in her pale yellow knitted cardigan looking slim and beautiful.

The next morning he tried to read one of the books the ambassador had left, but with his bandaged left hand, found that he couldn't hold it properly. Instead, he lay back, listened to the sound of activity in the ward outside, tried to order his memories into the correct sequence and then fell into a doze.

When he next awoke, Andris's wide frame was at the door at first hiding Christa, his petite and slim wife. Rupert's first thought was the tangled wreck of the BMW and he was about to say sorry when Andris said, 'Rupert, we are so pleased you survived.' Christa appeared from behind Andris. *What is it about Latvian women?* he thought, *z all seem to be so well dressed without looking like they've tried.* He welcomed Christa in Latvian as he knew she didn't speak English or German, and she responded by brushing, with the lightest of touches, his still bruised forehead. Then he addressed Andris in German. 'I can't remember the accident, but by all accounts it must have been a really bad one. Your BMW is a wreck and I am sorry about that.' Andris was gracious.

'No matter; the car is only metal. We will buy another one,' and then added, 'well, after the war, and on further thought, I think we will have a British motorcar next time.'

Christa sat on the only seat and Andris, standing by the bed, asked 'How are you feeling now?' Rupert wondered about just saying, '*Fine,*' but decided to tell the truth.

'I feel confused at times and I am worried about not being able to feel my legs.'

'The anaesthetic will take time to wear off.' Andris tried to sound reassuring, but Rupert noticed that he had involuntarily raised his eyebrows. 'When you are feeling a bit better, how about a game of chess?'

'I will have to consult my secretary to see if I've time in my busy schedule... but yes, anytime.' After a little more chatting, and a promise to return with a chess set in the near future, Andris and Christa said their goodbyes. When they had departed, the anxiety Rupert felt earlier returned as he realised he knew how to play chess but had no recollection of where and when he had learnt the game.

The next few days crawled by for him in a mixture of sleep, wakefulness, dozing, eating and cleaning, accompanied by an increasing level of anxiety about his physical well being and lack of memory.

He wasn't sure what day it was when suddenly he had a sharp pain in the leg that had been operated upon. Rather than calling for the nurse, he lay back on his pillow and thought, *Pain is good. Pain is sensation and sensation surely means hope.* The following night passed seemingly without end. In the middle of it, he asked for something to help ease the throbbing pain that had started in his leg. By the morning, he felt more tired than he had ever felt in his life; too tired even for sleep. That afternoon, he was feeling wretched, his leg ached incessantly and his neck seemed to have become stiffer. Whilst he experienced a sense of relief that he might not be completely paralysed, he could not mask his fear that there were many things he should know that were just beyond the reach of his memory.

In a continuing state of disorientation, he wasn't sure of the day or date when Irēne surprised and delighted him by appearing at the door of his room. Carrying a large brown handbag, she wore a fawn coloured cardigan together with a long floaty skirt and he thought, *Beautiful, simple and elegant.* She came close, gently pressed his hand and asked, 'What has happened to the sailor who was here?' She then brushed his newly shaven cheek and asked, 'How is the patient today?'

'I have started to feel my leg again.'

'That is great news.'

'Yes, but the constant ache is difficult to ignore. And to cap it all I have an itch under the plaster that is driving me mad.' The humour hid the real thought that, although he had started to feel his leg again, he might remain a cripple.

Looking over to the side table, Irēne saw the books and said, 'I am so pleased you have something to take your mind off the itch, but I have brought you something as well.' She put a manuscript booklet on the bed. 'I thought you might like to see Brecht's latest work.' Rupert involuntarily frowned when he read the front cover, *The Life of Galileo, by Bertolt Brecht*. He tentatively opened it.

'It's signed, *From Bertolt with Love*, but surely it's not for me!'

'No, I got it from a friend of my mother's, the actress Asja Lācis. As you will see, it is a play and Brecht sent it to Asja as he wants her to be in it.'

Rupert laid the manuscript on the bed without flicking through it and was quiet. Irēne asked him whether he was feeling alright and he explained that he was anxious and confused. He added, 'I'm aware we talked about Brecht at the opera, but now I've no recollection of his work or how I came to know of him. There is a big chunk of my memory still missing. I know my memory is a mixed up jigsaw puzzle, but it is very worrying to find important parts missing.'

'You had a really serious accident and it will take time for everything to heal.' Irēne took his hand and in a soothing voice continued. 'But I am here and will help you physically and mentally as much as I can. When you are rested, let us just talk, without any stress, and let us see what memories come back. But do not trouble yourself now, I can tell you about my visit to the opera this week, if you would like to hear of it?'

'Thank you.' He squeezed her hand and his anxiety began to melt away.

Drawing up a chair, Irēne started to recall her visit to see *Faust* at the National Opera. 'You know the story do you not? It is based on Goethe's book about an old man who trades his soul for youth.'

'I've a vague recollection, but I have no idea where I heard the story.' Rupert looked puzzled.

'Do not to struggle; I will retell the tale for you.' He listened intently and watched her lips, burnished with a discrete coral colour. He was amazed at her ability to recount a story as if she was reading from a text. After telling the story, she asked, 'If Mephistopheles came to you, what would you trade your soul for?' He looked at Irēne and thought, *A kiss*, but as he was lying back, possibly paralysed, his worry prevented him from speaking his mind.

'Oh I'm not sure – maybe a proper cup of tea.'

'You are easily bought.'

Rupert smiled, thanked Irēne for diverting him from his worries and asked about her mother. Irēne looked at him, hesitated as if unsure of what to tell him, and gave a vague answer about her needing a lot of attention. He wanted to know more, but feeling her response meant that she wasn't keen to talk, he carried on.

'Talking about mothers, mine must be very worried. The ambassador said that there's a telephone in the hospital and we could try to get through to her.'

'I am sure she would love to hear from you.'

'Would you mind finding out where it is and how I could get to it?'

'It is probably in the Hospital Director's office which, I think, is on the top floor. To get there we would need to wheel you out and get you up there somehow?' Irène could see his face had saddened and she added, 'But let me have a word with the doctor and perhaps next weekend, when you are feeling stronger, we can try to call your mother.'

That evening, Rupert sat in his bed thinking of *Faust*. He realised that he knew the story, but he didn't know how he knew it. He recognised the name of Goethe but, again, didn't know where he had come across this author. He felt his chest tighten and tried to relax by breathing slowly and deeply. It was late into the night when he eventually felt like sleeping and, after pulling up the sheets and settling back into the large pillow, he wondered again about the question Irène had asked him. He went to sleep thinking, *I definitely would trade my soul for a kiss.*

The Intrusion of the Erotic

Rupert sat looking at the markings on the pad of paper and calculated how long he had languished in prison. 'Surely,' he thought, 'I should have been released by now. How long can they keep a British subject in prison without charge or reason?' When he saw the Lieutenant again he would try to be more assertive and demand he be able to, at least, write to the Embassy, or, better still, his patron, Lord Simon, in England.

He imagined the scene playing out of him puffing out his chest and blustering about being a British subject and how he demanded to inform the authorities of his plight. He then remembered a saying his father had often used and said aloud, 'That'll butter no parsnips.'

Letting his mind wander to Wythenshawe, Rupert went to his mother's warm and cosy house. This image provided no succour. It just emphasised his inadequacy; for where was he when his mother needed protecting the most, especially if the Germans had invaded and swarmed over the country.

Feeling on the verge of slipping into a state of utter despair, he tried to create some ideal, some hope to cling to, and then realised such efforts would be like building a straw house ahead of an impending tornado.

A slip into a dead end of madness seemed to be drawing nearer as his dreams became graphic and often frightening. Rupert understood that the only thing that stood between him and, at best, a deep, persistent melancholia were his recollections of Irēne. Thinking of her at night brought a familiar ache of desire but in his solitary confinement, he didn't want to dwell on the erotic. In order to distract himself from musing on the bliss of intimacy and resulting sensual reflections, he thought back to when he was a boarder at the cathedral choir school. He remembered how one of the masters had been especially vigilant at night ensuring the choristers slept in their own beds with all hands above the blankets.

For some reason, his memories turned to his aunt's house. He remembered when he first went there he was scared of the place. Even as an adult, it could still send the odd shiver down his spine in the dark. The door from the street opened into a long, narrow hallway and from there, a steep staircase led to a dark landing. Rupert recalled there being a heavy chain on the door. At Wythenshawe no one locked their doors, even at the Hall, but in his aunty's house he wondered, as a young child, what monsters this chain was trying to keep out.

Strangely, the memories of his aunty's house and the erotic recollections about Irēne coincided with the thought, 'I used to think the intimate parts of the female anatomy were scarier than my aunt's hallway. How changed I am as a man.'

Lying on his prison bed, conscious of his inflamed desire, he understood that the longing for physical touch and recollections of Irēne in this way not good for his mental wellbeing. However, he could not take his mind off her, 'What was she doing now, what was she wearing?'

It was well into the early hours of the morning before he finally drifted into a fitful slumber full of erotic images.

Rupert returned to a Mayfair apartment where he sat on a velvet banquette, the colour of old blood, a crystal glass in his hand diffracting the yellow candlelight. He heard the Count's voice, 'More champagne, more champagne,' an order rather than a question. 'I'd like you to meet Sophie and Chloe.' But he couldn't tell them apart, both blondes with blue eyes, long legs and deep cleavages. 'Rupert, fill the girls' glasses, more champagne, more champagne.' Jazz melodies, swaying bodies, intense, cloying perfume and soft breasts pressing against his jacket. 'More champagne, more champagne.'

Crisp white bed linen, satin brocade, silky skin. 'Is that the music pounding in my ears or the sound of my own blood?' He wondered. Lace, clasps, unrolling stockings over legs that don't stop.

Higher and higher the car ascends ratcheting, inch by inch, up the steep rollercoaster incline. Tension, load, force, pull, energy, potential. The moment of no return. How exhilarating, how steep the drop, how quickly back. Release, safety, regret. The Count's voice half laughing, 'Consider it a birthday present.'

Rupert awoke with a violent jolt and the thought that Irēne was pregnant. 'How wonderful!' He mouthed and then instantly followed it with, 'How terrible.' He didn't know how unmarried mothers would be treated by the Soviets but he suspected it would be with the same shame they faced in England.

He wasn't able to go back to sleep as he mulled this possibility over. The more he dwelt on it, the more agitated he became. He recalled that Irēne had said to him she wanted to have seven children. His last thought, before sleep's beckoning finger called him to slumber, was, *How lovely... how dreadful, for what sort of world would I be bringing them in to?*

Telephoning Home

With helping hands from two nurses, Rupert inched up his bed and, supported by thick pillows, found he was in a comfortable enough position to start to read *The Inimitable Jeeves*. He propped the book on a cushion one of the nurses had brought to him and managed to clumsily turn the pages with his un-bandaged hand. He had read the book before but he still laughed out loud, much to the distress of his lower ribs. He found he could only read a few pages at a time, however, before having to stop and relax his aching neck. After reading a few chapters, he lay back in hopeful anticipation of a visit from Irēne.

At the very beginning of the permitted visiting hours, Irēne entered the ward carrying a small fabric handbag and wearing a flowered skirt and a light, sleeveless top, evidence that Riga was experiencing an Indian summer. Rupert noticed her before she had got to his door, and watched her as she walked with poise and elegance to his room. He waved, smiled and called out, '*Sveici*', which Irēne repeated. He noticed how brown and healthy looking her slender arms were as she extended her hand to gently squeeze his un-bandaged one.

'Are you now speaking the local language?' Irēne asked.

'It seems the bang on the head hasn't given me any miraculous powers, but lying here provides an opportunity to learn the language, especially as the nurses don't speak English.'

'And are very pretty.'

He could see, by her smile, that she was only teasing him. 'I am pleased your forehead is no longer the colour of your check trousers,' she joked. He laughed but stifled this because of a sharp pain in his ribs. 'How are you feeling?' She asked.

'Much better physically, but I'm still anxious about my memory recall. However, my biggest concern is about my mother. She will be terribly worried. I don't know what she has been told, but I must be on her mind all of the time.'

'Yes, she must be worried.' Irēne replied.

'Can you find out if it is possible for me to telephone from the director's office? Even if I don't manage to talk to her personally, it would help if I managed to speak to someone who can pass on a message.'

'Of course.' With that she left the room.

On returning, Doctor Berzins accompanied her. 'You are still very weak,' he said, ' You need to rest, but Irēne has explained how important it is for you to speak with your mother. There is a telephone in the director's office on the top floor of the hospital. I will arrange for porters to push the bed through the ward to the lift and then take you up to the director's office where you can try to make an international call.'

The doctor departed, and whilst they were waiting for the porters, Irēne took out a comb from her bag and lightly combed Rupert's hair. 'If you are going to speak to your mother you need to look your best.' He was transported back in time and space to when his mother used to brush his hair before he left for school. He felt the tension in his shoulders ease a little.

Two porters arrived, together with Doctor Berzins, and wheeled the large, heavy bed out into the general ward. Looking towards the open area, which was used as a patients' lounge, Rupert resisted an urge to wave to those who watched him trundle past as if he were royalty in a horse-drawn carriage. The lift whirred and clattered its way to meet them at the lift entrance on the third floor. The porters dragged open the large, latticed metal doors and wheeled him inside.

The lift ascended together with his hopes. It seemed that Wythenshawe was almost at touching point, simply a telephone call away. In the director's long, low, gloomy office, Doctor Berzins talked to the operator and then passed the huge Bakelite receiver to Rupert who, with some effort, held it to his ear. The Russian operator passed on the call and the new operator sounded muffled and the number and volume of clicks on the line increased. By the time the call had been relayed yet again, the voice of the operator then handling the connection was almost inaudible. With every distracting click and buzz on the line, the sense of distance increased. Then the line went dead. Home was as far away as the moon.

When Rupert returned in the lift, his mood plummeted beyond the third floor, past disappointment and into the basement where it settled on despondency.

Remaining quiet for a short while, Rupert then asked Irēne, 'Would you mind calling in at the British Legation one lunch time to ask the ambassador to send a telegram from me to my mother reassuring her that I'm fine and will write soon? Telegrams, I understand, can get through on a piece of string.'

'Sure, I will tomorrow.' After a pause, she added, 'If the accident had not happened you would be home now. Would it help to talk of home?' He thought about it for a short while.

'Actually it would help, and I'd like you to know a bit more about me and my family.'

Irēne pulled up the chair and came close so that he could speak without strain. After painfully easing himself a little more upright he began hesitantly. 'Where do I start?' He paused, then, as he felt that his life was almost inseparable from the Hall his parents worked at, he continued with a flourish. 'My father worked for Thomas Egerton Tatton at Wythenshawe Hall. Of

65

course, you won't have heard of the Tattons or the Hall but Mr. Tatton was a very important man and the Hall was part of a grand estate near Manchester. The Tattons owned the estate for over six hundred years. It comprises a large area of land covering four parishes. The main house is beautiful and as a child I roamed around the whole of the Estate.'

'Quite a playground.'

'It certainly was. Father was Head of the Kitchen Garden and my mother and I lived on the estate in a tied cottage.' Irēne repeated the word *tied* and he explained. 'It's a house given to estate workers to live in, but only whilst they remain employed on the estate. They have to give it up when they stop working or if they change their employer.'

Rupert paused, wondering what next to say, and Irēne asked, 'What are your parents' names?'

'My mother's name is Catherine and my father's name is Peter although he's dead now. He died when I was thirteen.'

'Oh, I'm sorry to hear that and at such a young age... What happened to your father?'

He had never before been asked by anyone to talk about his father's death. It was as if this incident had been brushed under the carpet and he had to gather himself before continuing. 'Father scratched his face badly on a climbing rose, which had come undone from the walled garden, and that he was helping to reattach. The scratch didn't heal quickly, but we didn't think much of it at first. Then, the wound opened up and started to look sore. His collapse was very swift and he was taken into hospital - The Manchester Royal Infirmary. The last time I saw my father there was a tube draining liquid from his cheek and one eye had completely closed over. The next time I went, I wasn't allowed to see him; Mother said it would be too distressing. Actually, it was too distressing not to be able to see him. He died within weeks of being scratched and I never said goodbye.'

'And you were only thirteen; that is no age at which to lose a parent.'

He swallowed. Talking of home was proving harder than he had anticipated. 'It hit me hard, I admit, but I tried to be strong for my mother. Mr. Tatton said I was now the man of the house.'

'Yes, sometimes we have to bury our thoughts or emotions as they can become too much for us... and it sounds like you had to be brave for your mother's sake.'

'It was difficult for my mother with the cottage being tied to my father's job. She feared that we would have to move away. But luck, and the goodwill of a benefactor, was on our side.'

'Benefactor?'

'This was a man who looked after my mother and me after my father's death. I'm sorry if I am confusing you, but I probably need to tell you about the recent history of the Estate to make things clear. Are you interested?'

'Yes. Of course.'

Rupert was happy to provide Irēne with a history of the Tatton family and the Wythenshawe Estate. At the end of the rather long description of the family tree, Irēne reminded him that he had talked of a benefactor. He replied, 'Sorry, I was getting carried away. A past Lord Mayor of Manchester, Ernest Simon, or rather, Lord Simon of Wythenshawe as he is known today, bought Wythenshawe Hall together with two hundred and fifty acres of land. He then donated the Hall and land to Manchester Corporation to be used for the public good.'

'This Ernest gave away the house and land he bought!'

'Yes, I suppose it is surprising. He is an industrialist and public servant with a social conscience. He was our benefactor and he later became rather like a father figure to me and has acted as a patron. The sale of the estate was in progress at the time my father died and Lord Simon arranged for the Corporation to employ my mother to help run the Hall and we were allowed to keep our cottage.' He went on to explain how a trust fund set up by Ernest Simon to educate the children of workers on the Wythenshawe Hall Estate had funded him going to Manchester Grammar School and then on to university to study languages.

Turning to the subject that had been on his mind for a while, Rupert, in a serious tone, said, 'Talking of languages, I think I remember winning a scholarship to study French and German at Pembroke College, Cambridge, which was Lord Simon's alma mater. But, Irēne,' he looked directly in her eyes, 'I can't remember going there or, in fact, anything about the place or people. I'm worried about it. Not just that it might have been a waste of three year's education.'

'Rupert,' Irēne's voice was soothing, 'you have already recovered a great deal and, with time, everything will come back.'

'You see, it is a question of identity.' He wasn't convinced that his memory would return, 'Who am I? What did I achieve? We are defined by our experience, but if I can't remember....' He trailed off and she squeezed his hand.

Laying his head back on the pillow, he suddenly felt he was very young, very small and very immature. He wished that he hadn't started talking about his father. Now, he wanted to move away from his story altogether and asked, 'Can you tell me something about your family?'

68

'I think I have already told you my father's name is also Peter or Pēteris as we say in Latvia'.

'Well I know he is a handsome chap and young-looking.' Rupert remembered the time he had seen Irēne walking arm in arm with her father.

The bell for the end of visiting time sounded and Rupert, still holding Irēne's hand, said, 'Although you may not have guessed it from what I've been saying, you have lifted my spirits. Can you come often? I'd love to see you again soon.'

'Of course, I will come back as soon as I can but visiting hours are rather limited and you can see they are quite strict about it. I work until six o'clock - sometimes later and the Second City Hospital is quite a journey for me. At the weekends, I must also see my mother. But I would hate you to think I am making excuses.' She brought her face to his and gently kissed him on the cheek. He breathed in a scent that, together with the touch of cheek on cheek, made him feel joyous.

The scent of Irēne's perfume lingered after she had made her exit and Rupert placed it as the aroma of the Wythenshawe woods in spring, on a warm and windless afternoon when the scent of bluebells pooled to intoxicate the awed onlooker with its blue haze. In remembering Wythenshawe, he suddenly felt exhausted. He hadn't talked to anyone like this about his father's death and now worried he had been too serious with Irēne. He grew quite melancholic as he began to think about his situation and of his need to see Irēne. His final thought before drifting off to sleep was, *My memory is broken, my body is broken, I might even be a cripple. What is she going to see in me?*

69

Contrast

As Rupert lay on his bed waiting for the lights to be extinguished and listening to the sounds of the prison, he could not help contrasting this to his experience of being in the hospital.

In hospital, as evening turned into nighttime, the soft soled shuffles of nurses mixed with the sonorous snoring and gentle wheezing from the main ward. It was the very sound of safety and security.

From his cell, he caught the distant sounds of metal tipped boots and the odd inhuman grunt. His hospital bed, with its crisp, clean, white sheets seemed a world away from the hard and grubby prison bed on which he now lay.

He thought of the attentive nurses who had been so diligent and hard working yet always had a smile for him. He remembered, and then felt ashamed, how he, on occasion, had felt irritated by them, sometimes for their heinous crime of being too cheerful. His thoughts turned to his guards. He was amazed that he didn't feel anger towards them individually but he knew he did feel angry about his incarceration. He channeled some of it towards home; perhaps, somehow, Lord Simon had let him down. After all, where was the help from this powerful man with the ear of the establishment when it was needed?

Rupert looked forward to his meditative walk but his routine the next day was disturbed by the unexpected arrival of a guard who ordered him to gather his blanket and escorted him away from his cell. They walked past the cells with which Rupert had become familiar and, with the locking and unlocking of heavy iron gates, a cloak of anxiety settled on his shoulders. He was bundled into a room with hair scattered on the floor in such drifts it immediately brought an image to his mind of a badger's sett.

Ordered to sit, Rupert perched on a stool and in strode a huge, bald headed man in a grey uniform whose features had been made lopsided by a large scar running from the corner of his right eye to the edge of his thin-lipped mouth. Agitation turned to dread. A huge and clumsy looking fist, the knuckles of which bore crude tattoos, grasped a cutthroat razor.

As Rupert's head was shoved unceremoniously back to open his vulnerable neck to the sweep of the blade, he closed his eyes and just felt the tear of whiskers and the stab of pain as the barber carelessly nicked his skin. After that, he was allowed the use of a blunt pair of scissors to cut his nails as best he could. Then he was escorted into the wash area to take a lukewarm shower, shake out his blanket and rinse his underwear, which then had to be dried on the end of his bed.

In his cell, Rupert commenced his long walk and returned to the hospital. His thoughts were seemingly so realistic, he could almost smell the distinctive mixture of disinfectant and coal tar soap. He remembered the tenderness with which the nurses had shaved him at Second City and wondered if it could be categorised as quite the same activity.

Remembering Irēne's hospital visits put Rupert into a more positive frame of mind and, by the evening, he had decided that the only way to survive his imprisonment was to maintain and readily employ a sense of humour. When the hatch in the cell was opened for the meal to be passed through, he said, 'Put the cup of tea on the table by my bed would you old sport?' After the hatch had been banged shut, Rupert continued. 'Aaghhh, just right as usual, not too hot and not too sweet, not too weak, not too strong, a most amazing cove. But I fear you have forgotten the milk and saucer, something awry with the old grey matter Jeeves?'

The next morning he kept up the one-way banter with the guard enroute to the exercise yard. 'I say Jeeves, a man I met at the

Drones last night told me to put my shirt on Privateer for the two o' clock this afternoon. How about it? And, whilst we are on the subject of shirts, could you bring me my mauve one. This one is becoming awfully putrid.' When the breakfast arrived, he addressed the departing guard, 'Jeeves, I'd like three teaspoons of sugar but please don't stir it, I don't like it too sweet.' The guard slammed down the hatch and shouted at the top of his voice in Russian, 'Shut up you worthless piece of shit or you will be put on charge.'

After a day of walking to and fro in his cell and, as sleep crept up on him, Rupert imagined walking beneath the rocks at Staburags with Irēne. In his mind she wore a flowery dress and posed for his photographs by the old ruined castle. As he submerged beneath the waves of sleep washing over him, he felt cold water around his ankles as the River Daugava rose at an alarming rate because of the newly built dam upstream. With a violent jolt he awoke from this powerful dream just as the surging water was about to carry them both away.

Rupert's seven-step walk and turn routine staved off the mental chaos of having too little to do during the day but he realised he could not control, in the same manner, his dreams. Falling asleep had always been a pleasure until entering prison. He had enjoyed the fading of consciousness, where cause and effect held sway, and the imperceptible step into a magical dimension. Now, he feared that this realm could easily turn towards the dark and dangerous and even the demonic.

Tea Viz Milk

After spending over six weeks in his single room at the hospital, ahead of Irēne's expected visit, Rupert asked a doctor whether his bed could be wheeled out into the patients' lounge, which was an open area with seats and tables at the end of the general ward.

Before visiting time was due, Rupert had been washed and transferred to the lounge where a few patients gathered to listen to the radio and play board games together. From his bed he could see out of the window to the top of a nearby maple tree. Some of its leaves had already been shed, but those remaining were of a rich yellow colour that glowed in the autumn light. He imagined the headscarfed, old ladies, who were such a familiar sight throughout the city, bending to sweep and tidy away the falling leaves, keeping Riga in its doll's house neatness.

The radio was tuned to a station on which unknown people spoke an unknown language. Although he knew a few Latvian words and phrases, he found he could not follow the dialogue at all on the radio. Instead of trying to read he let the burble of the radio, and the gentle tap tap of the pieces of an unknown game being placed on its board, wash over him. It felt alien and foreign, but at the same time it was also strangely familiar and homely.

The tick of the clock on the wall heralded visiting time, but to him, in his anticipation of the arrival of Irēne, time seemed to have stalled. A man sleeping in an armchair near by him, and two patients in their dressing gowns sitting, almost immobile, silently, either side of their board game, added to this sense of ennui. Rain dripped down the large windows and he wondered whether this would deter Irēne from making the trek to the hospital. He looked down at his now un-bandaged hands, studying his palms like a fortune teller might look at them, *The scabs and scratches tell me of my recent past but what of the future...?*

His speculations were interrupted as, just behind the first visitor to arrive, he saw Irēne walk into the main ward and head towards his room. Waving to attract her attention, she pivoted around lightly as if she were a trained ballerina. He suddenly felt the day had sprung into life. Still caught up in the Jeeves story he had just finished reading, he said, 'My butler will take those from you shortly.' Irēne took off her coat and felt hat and put them on a stand by the door. Summer, it seemed, was drawing to an end. She then drew up a chair and took his hand.

'How is the patient today?'

'Better for seeing you, but I'm developing a flat bottom, which requires a nurse's attention on a regular basis. If I ever feel that I'm unlucky, I only have to think about the poor nurses who have to treat my rear end.'

'Well, what an interesting subject,' Irēne laughed, 'and I anticipated we would start with the weather.'

Irēne and Rupert chatted about the weather and then moved onto the subject of hospital food. He talked about his diet and the delicious meals that were served, including the best bread pudding he had ever eaten. 'It is completely different from the bread pudding my mother makes, but I like the malty taste of the Latvian version. In fact, I love all the desserts here.' Irēne immediately repeated the word *dessert.*

'I cannot help thinking of the Sahara when I hear this word.' He laughed at her comment.

'Desert and dessert.' Rupert pronounced both words over again. 'Oh, I see how similar they would sound to a foreign ear.'

Irēne fetched a glass of water and, insisting Rupert drink some, she passed it to him. He enjoyed the caress of her fingers. After a few sips, he asked, 'Did you manage to get a telegram sent to my mother?'

Irēne reported that she had and then added, 'I really enjoyed hearing about your family last week, can you tell me some more? What is your earliest memory?'

'Now let me think.' He laid his head back on the pillow and closed his eyes briefly. 'It's difficult to separate my own memories from details in the stories I've been told about myself. But my clearest early memories are of being in church.'

'Ah ha, I knew you were an angel.'

'An angel in pyjamas... but I'm an imposter.' They both smiled.

Taking a moment to let images of the church at Wythenshawe flood back into his mind, Rupert then talked about how he had enjoyed singing there and how Mrs. Tatton had helped his family to send him to Manchester Cathedral as a chorister. Rupert felt energised by being able to recall his early life with such clarity and said, 'I went to school at the cathedral until my voice broke when I was thirteen. Then I went to Manchester Grammar School, which is next door to the Cathedral.'

'And then to Cambridge if I have understood correctly.' In a gentle, caring voice, she added, 'But do not worry and do not strain to remember. I am sure, with time, it will all come back.'

Gazing around the room, Rupert noted that the patient sitting next to him in a large armchair appeared to be still asleep and asked encouragingly, 'I've told you a little about me, now it is your turn, if you are willing?'

Drawing up her chair and in a kind of confidential whisper Irēne asked, 'What do you think about Jews?' Rupert widened his eyes in surprise.

'What a strange question to ask!' Even before he had finished the statement, the image of the orthodox Jews he had seen one day emerging from the Synagogue on Gogoļa Street in Riga sprung into his mind along with older memories of similar sights in Manchester.

'Many people have strange ideas about Jews... I am part Jewish.' She paused to see if this had any effect on his face and obviously reassured that he appeared unmoved, then continued. 'My grandfather is a Russian Jew who had to flee from Odessa after Jews were blamed for the assassination of Tsar Alexander II.'

'I take it from what you say that Jews weren't behind the assassination.'

'Jews have a history of being blamed for anything bad.' Her voice initially had a hard edge to it, but then softened. 'After the assassination, many Jews were killed in Odessa and my grandfather fled to Latvia, where Jews were more tolerated. He settled in Liepāja and carried on the family tradition of working in the textile business. He began importing fine textiles from all over the world, maybe even from your Manchester, and soon had a thriving business. He is still alive and is the owner of three shops in the city.'

Rupert commented that Irēne's grandfather must have worked hard to establish a business in a completely different country and Irēne continued. 'He was only nineteen when he met and fell in love with my grandmother, Marta. I have seen photographs of her at the time and she was really beautiful. They married within a year of meeting. It was quite unusual because Grandmother is a Lutheran and not many of them marry Jews. My mother,

Rebecca was their only child and she was sent to Riga to attend the German School.'

'Was attending German schools common in those days?'

'As you have probably understood by now, German is the language of the intelligentsia. My mother speaks German very well and talked to me in German at home.' Irēne paused, as if wondering what to say next, and then added, 'My grandparents had high hopes for their daughter. Only, it seems her gifts were for acting - and seducing men!'

Rupert raised his eyebrows. 'Oh, tell me more.'

Irēne looked around the lounge as if to check who was listening to their conversation. Meanwhile, the patient next to them continued to slumber in his chair. She continued, 'My mother's first real conquest was a young man called Pēteris. I say man, but they were still both at school. Even so, that did not stop my mother from having what she desired, which was Pēteris as a husband. I am told that Pēteris' parents were set against the marriage. I believe they did not like the idea of their son marrying a girl with Jewish blood, especially one who wanted to be an actress. But my mother tends to get what she wants. They married and I was born when my mother was only nineteen.'

'And what about your father?'

'My mother broke his heart by going off to Moscow to study at a theatre studio, and there she fell in love with the famous poet and playwright, Linards Liepa. They returned to Riga and my father was, of course, very angry. I was too young to remember my father then, and I never saw him again – until a few years ago.'

Rupert was interested in Irēne's reunion with her father, but felt that asking about this would break the thread of the story of her early life, so he asked, 'Did Liepa become your father then? I mean, did he look after you?'

'I spent time in his company but he wasn't interested in me. He had an eye for the ladies and, as he was a bit of a hero figure to some, he had constant visitors.'

'What had he done to be a hero?'

'He was a revolutionary and wrote about Latvian independence and the need to break away from Russia - something Russia was not at all willing to tolerate. It seems it is deep in the Russian psyche that the Baltic countries are part of Russia and so writing about independence was a serious crime. He participated in the uprising of 1905 in Riga and after that he had to flee to Finland. When he came back to Riga, he was arrested and put in prison for a while. After being released, Liepa's work took him to Moscow, where he met my mother. When they came back to Riga, mother used to star in his plays and even do some provocative street theatre.'

Irēne paused and then, in a dismissive tone, added, 'I am not sure my mother had any real political interest, she was just happy getting attention. And when Liepa paid more attention to his other admirers, Mother packed her bags, with me in them, and we headed for Berlin. I was six at the time.'

Although keen to hear of Irēne's experience in Berlin, Rupert asked, 'What happened to Liepa?'

'Liepa became a member of Riga City Council and a member of parliament. He kept up his interest in writing and often travelled to the Soviet Union, but five years ago, under the, so called, National Operations, he was arrested and shot. He is buried in a mass grave in Moscow.'

Rupert could not prevent himself from blanching. 'Wow...

I don't know what to say... How do you feel about that?'

'I was very young and have some fond memories, but I quickly moved on in my affection.' Irēne carried on without a hint of emotion. 'I think there is something of my mother in me too. Of course I was saddened by his death. Mother had a more tough-minded approach; she said, *he is a revolutionary playwright, he had a fitting end.*'

Unused to hearing such powerful personal histories, it struck Rupert as odd that Irēne could recount this without upset or that her mother could be quite so cold. 'Sorry, I interrupted you, what happened in Berlin?' He asked.

'It was not long before Mother found a new lover, a theatre director.' The patient in the chair near to them stirred and Irēne stopped talking. Instead, she looked at the clock and asked if there was anything she could get for Rupert as time was moving on, adding, 'Now, I can see it is getting late. I need to go but, if you would like, I will visit again soon.'

'I would like that very much indeed.'

The door swung closed behind her, scattering the handful of autumn leaves that had made their way in from outside. Rupert mulled over what she had told him and why she had left in such a rapid manner. Perhaps he had imposed too much on her by asking her to talk about her family. It seemed only natural to want to find out more about her, but he was perplexed by her behaviour. Irēne was warm and caring towards him, but when talking about her family it seemed that she was rather cool and distant. He felt very close to her, but he recognised she was a woman he hardly knew.

Interrupting his thoughts, a nurse came into the lounge pushing a large trolley complete with an urn and began asking patients if they wanted tea or coffee. It had become standard practice for the nurses to address Rupert in English with the phrase, 'Tea viz milk,' even though milk wasn't offered. This time he became a little annoyed even though he was sure it was said in jest. He thought, *We are a nation that has given the world the blueprint for democracy, founded the industrial revolution and invented wondrous machines; is "tea viz milk" the only thing we will be remembered for?*

Rupert stifled his less than charitable feelings towards the nurses, guilt reminding him that they cared for him very well. The hush of the lounge was so complete that Rupert jumped when the old man in the chair next to him requested, in a low, tired voice, a cup of tea. He had long grey hair, a full beard, a long nose, rheumy eyes and a thick protruding lower lip.

When the nurses had left, the old man surprised Rupert by addressing him in heavily accented English. 'I listening to you talking with your girlfriend. Sorry – it is hard not hearing even whispered conversations when we are so close and do not worry, I only hear start.' Rupert was so taken aback by being addressed in English, and having Irēne referring to as his girlfriend, that he didn't respond at all and the man continued. 'Sorry, I surprise you. Forgive me, my name is Menachem. If not clear, I am Jew. Your girlfriend talks of Jews and assassination of Tsar Alexander. Are you interest in what happened?'

'My name is Rupert, pleased to meet you and yes, of course, I am interested.'

Menacham started to talk, but his voice was weak and Rupert had to strain to hear it. 'Jews not kill Tsar. *Narodnaya Volya* is behind assassination but when emotions running high, truth is first casualty. After assassination there is great anti-Semitism and many violence.' Rupert admitted to having never heard of *Narodnaya Volya* and Menachem informed him, '*Narodnaya Volya* or Peoples Will is revolutionary group set against Tsar. They for violent means to bring in socialism. They blow up Tsar in Petrograd but it not ending Romanov's rule. In fact, it firing back.'

Apologising for his poor knowledge of Russian history, Rupert asked the man to explain further and Menachem continued. 'Well, Tsar is simply replaced and reform taking back step. Murdered Tsar is given name Alexander Liberator as he letting serfs go free but Alexander III is old fashioned. One of his first acts is to bring in May Laws. These restricting right of Jews within Pale of Settlement.'

'Sorry, what is this pale?' Menachem laughed gently.

'Your teachers missing out much in your history lessons. The Pale of Settlement is area to western region of Imperial Russia where Jews allowing to settle. That means they were actively stopping from other parts but frequent pogroms showing, even in Pale, Jews not welcome.'

'Pogrom?'

'Now you are hanging noodles from my ear.' Rupert was amused by the expression he took to mean, "you are pulling my leg".

'No, I've never heard the word before.' Looking directly at Rupert, Menachem softened his tone. 'Pogrom is violent act of persecution, but is now associated with attacks on Jews in Pale of Settlement. Although, of course, anti-Semitism is not limited to Pale, it goes beyond and is widespread across Russia and Germany too.'

Talking seemed to tire Menachem as he stopped and slumped back in his chair. Rupert wasn't sure what to say and waited to see if the man would address him again. Eventually, Menachem cleared his throat. 'You can see that I am old. With a weak heart I not have long to live. My only wish is to die in Jerusalem.'

Whilst understanding that many religious people wanted to visit Jerusalem, Rupert, nevertheless, wondered why anyone would want to die in a foreign land. He asked, 'Why would you not want to die here in Latvia?' Menachem's answer surprised him.

'I was born and raised here but this is not home. The war changed everything. Latvians got their own country and we Jews became just tolerated inhabitants. Before war, that was different. Latvians, Jews, we had the same land to live and provide for us. At these times when Germans and Russians were ruling Latvia, the oppressed usually stick together. Now, I am not considered Latvian, only Jew. Jerusalem is home.'

Rupert didn't know what to say but eventually Menacham started again. 'I know there is a war on, but it must be possible to getting there still, with the right connections. I have money, actually many money and will give it all to get to Jerusalem. Jerusalem is under British Protectorate. Will you speak with your ambassador? I have seen him here before.'

'I will see.' Rupert wasn't brought up to say no to requests for help and, to change the subject, he asked Menachem where he learned English. He was surprised by the response and wondered how anybody could learn a foreign language simply by listening to the radio.

Soon after the conversation, the nurses came to push Rupert back to his room. Alone, he remembered what Irēne had told him and what he had learnt from Menachem. Rupert compared Irēne's early childhood with that of his own. Never for a moment, could he remember feeling unwelcome at the Hall or in friends' houses and certainly not at home. Unlike him, it seemed that Irēne hadn't had a stable family background and may have faced religious persecution. He dwelt on what Menachem had told him about the pogroms and contrasted this with his knowledge of the Jews he had seen on the streets of Manchester. *Different they are but they are not beaten or exiled. Nor are they persecuted for their beliefs.* Then he again contrasted his upbringing with that of Irēne. *Her family and even perhaps her religion is so different to mine, yet, somehow, I feel very connected to her.*

The week ahead seemed to stretch ahead like a desert to be crossed, with the only incentive to keep going being an oasis next Sunday when he would see Irēne again. Rupert changed the pronunciation in his head of desert to dessert and laughed, thinking of Irēne's politely furrowed brow.

Later that night, as the ward was settling into hushed somnolence, he heard something of a commotion in the ward outside, but the disturbance was short-lived and he drifted back to sleep. The next morning he saw that Menachem's bed was empty. He felt a pang of sadness for the old man, who would now never visit Jerusalem.

Interrogation

Having just returned from his brief solitary exercise in the yard, Rupert was about to begin his pacing when he heard the click of heels marching along the corridor, then the clatter of a key in his cell door. This unusual break to his routine made him feel ill at ease and this was compounded when a guard entered and ordered him to put on his jacket and leave the cell.

Escorted along the corridor between two guards, a rising apprehension turned into fear, his hands shaking as they carried on into what Rupert remembered as the area where he had been so roughly treated on arrival. Non-descript doors loomed and disappeared until they reached one where he was ordered to halt. A guard opened the unlocked door and another bundled Rupert in as if delivering an unwanted package. He was told to stand to attention by a wall. One of the guards remained inside posted by the door.

Having been starved of novelty for such a long time, Rupert tried to dampen his dread and looked around the room with uncommon interest.

To his right, by an inner door, stood a coat stand burdened with thick military coats and hats. Despite his nerves, Rupert devoured the sight. He looked at the folds of the cloth and the fine mist of water covering one of them. Blue bands surrounded the caps and on one he could see a badge with the hammer and sickle on it. In a world that had ceased to have colour, the red and silver of the badge was as striking as any jewel he had ever seen.

'Eyes forward.' the guard snapped and Rupert looked up to faced a picture of Stalin hanging on the wall. Stalin was smiling but his eyes seem to look directly at Rupert with a cruel, cold stare.

Standing to attention, his gaze restricted to the front of the room, Rupert watched the rain against the four sections of double windowpanes which faced into a courtyard. Drops coalesced into drips that ran down the windows and temporarily stopped at the lip of the frame before, eventually, plopping to the ground. He watched the drips forming and made a game of predicting when they would fall. He tried, with a ridiculously high level of excitement, to guess exactly when each drip would slip groundwards, but they always either dropped immediately or remained in place longer than anticipated. The longer he stared at the drips the more convinced he became that some of the drips actually defied gravity to move up the windowpanes. His poor performance in a sport of his own invention amused him and he persevered in order to avoid thinking about the reason for his summons.

Eventually, the inner door was opened and Rupert was ordered through. He found himself standing in front of a table together with a spare chair. Behind the table was the now familiar figure of Lieutenant Kuznetsov and two other officers he didn't recognise. A pile of papers lay on the desk. The lieutenant rose as if by way of introduction but his words were not those of welcome. 'Sit.' Rupert complied. Kuznetsov came around the desk and loomed over him. He said, 'I could shoot you for spying.' Rupert's mouth went dry and he swallowed. *Shoot him?* A sudden burst of adrenaline produced a tremor he prayed the lieutenant missed.

Kuznetsov continued, 'Metropolitan Vickers. My report on you has thrown up some interesting details.' He visibly puffed out his chest, 'Never has one country managed to turn itself so quickly from growing potatoes to building dams, canals and tractors in such numbers. It is miracle. We are envy of world and Westerners want to learn how we do it – and of course wreck our future progress. Metropolitan Vickers tried to do just that. Maybe you want to finish this particular story.'

Rupert knew the lieutenant was referring to the incident when employees of his firm were accused of being wreckers and spies but he knew no details and thought it best not to reply. The lieutenant broke the silence. 'No? Let me remind you. Not long after arrival of your colleagues there was series of sudden and regularly recurring breakdowns at big power stations in Moscow, Cheliabinsk, Zuevka and Zlatoust. Investigation by NKVD showed these were result of employees of your firm working with group of criminal elements in People's Commissariat of Heavy Industry. Together with foreign spies, this group made it their object to destroy power stations of USSR, which of course put out of commission State factories.'

Kuznetsov paused then jabbed a finger towards Rupert. 'One of your associates, Leslie Charles Thornton signed remarkably detailed confession saying they were drawn into spying operations under direction of C S Richards who was, supposedly, Managing Director of Metropolitan Vickers Electrical Export Company. Do you know Allen Monkhouse?' Rupert shook his head and the lieutenant added, 'He said he had been well cared for in Soviet prisons. You see, he was quite right about our hospitality.' The hairs on the back of Rupert's arm prickled. These were dangerous associations. 'Now,' the lieutenant fixed Rupert with a hard stare, 'What do you know of these men? Think carefully.'

Rupert licked his lips to try and moisten them so that he could reply. 'I have never met them and, as far as I know, they no longer work for Metropolitan Vickers.' A queasy feeling started in his stomach and tongue felt like it was covered in glue. He had already started to lie.

His mind flew to the last he had heard about those employees of Metropolitan Vickers who had been accused of spying. Peggie Benton, a representative of the British Legation, had informed him, almost as a passing comment, that she had recently met Leslie Thornton after his sudden departure from Warsaw. He wondered whether Leslie had indeed been a spy and, if he had, how dangerous this tenuous link to Rupert might prove to be. The interrogation seemed to go on forever, with the questions circling around the same topics.

Back in his cell, Rupert recapitulated every question asked and every answer given, He began to torture himself further as he turned it over and over in his head, desperate to find the mistake that would surely cost him his life.

For the rest of the day, he could concentrate on nothing else. The same thoughts kept flickering through his mind; *what do they know, what did he say, what must he say next time?* Tightening spirals of fear worked up his spine and then constricted his throat. *Had he been asked about Irēne? Had he said anything about her? Had he mentioned or incriminated her in any way?*

If he had and it led to her interrogation, imprisonment or worse, Rupert doubted whether he could ever forgive himself.

A Chill Wind

On Saturday, Rupert was pushed into the lounge area as usual but his spirits were low.

He looked out of the double window. Raindrops, sluggish with the cold, slid down the outer panes and the sky was a restless grey. He had a note from Irēne, handed to him earlier in the week tucked in the pocket of his dressing gown and, taking it out, he unfolded it.

Dearest Rupert, I look forward to the times when we can be together but, unfortunately, this weekend I am not able to visit you. There is family business I need to attend to and that takes me out of Riga. I will be away for some days, but I plan to visit you on the following weekend.

It is good to see your steady improvement and I am sure soon your memory will fully recover. The best thing is not to worry. Just as your body is healing itself from the trauma, so will your mind. I look forward to hearing more of your life in Manchester and your early years in idyllic Wythenshawe. When you are ready, I want to hear of your times in Cambridge.

Soon the doctors will get you out of bed and I will be there to help you regain your strength. It will not be long before we can take a stroll around the hospital, although I do not recommend you walk outside yet. Winter has come early, wet snow has already fallen.

I have a friend who is good at predicting the weather and she says that we are set for a very cold winter. The swans and geese have flown south over Latvia early this year and they have a sense for such things. Also the rowan trees are laden with berries. So, stay warm and continue to get better.

I look forward to my next visit.

Yours lovingly

Irēne

Studying Irēne's neat, German-style handwriting, Rupert wondered, What family business can this be? I don't imagine this is an excuse for having a weekend off, although I wouldn't blame her. Visiting someone who is bed ridden must be a real chore. He looked again at the ending, Yours lovingly and wondered what this might say about their relationship. Is this sincere or simply a friendly gesture?

Rupert thought about Irēne's previous visit and of her present. He had been reluctant to read the play given to him but he thought he had better try before he saw her again. He picked up the heavy manuscript and turned the page. It were as if in turning this, the bed lurched over too. He even grasped the edge to steady himself. A queasy feeling came over him as if he were heading into a rolling sea. He put the manuscript down and realised that memories of learning about Brecht were part of a hidden life that was still behind a locked door.

Rupert was in the middle of thinking about whether memories of his time at university would ever return when the wide frame of Andris appeared in the lounge carrying a chess board and box. Rupert shouted, 'Good afternoon Andris,' delighted to see his friend.

'I thought you might like to have a game?' Andris said.

Rupert had an inbuilt aversion to saying no but answered truthfully. 'Andris, would you mind if we left it a while?' Andris cocked an eyebrow with apparent concern. Rupert elaborated. 'I'm suffering from partial memory loss. There are three years that are just out of reach. These are the times when I was at university and learnt to play chess. Now, being asked to exercise a skill and not knowing how I acquired it is very stressful. I'm not sure I can concentrate fully.'

'In that case, this may be the only time I can beat you. But I understand... On the subject of chess, I'm going to the Latvian Chess Championship later in the month. Of course, I am not playing but it will be a great opportunity to see the luxurious sanatorium at Kemeri and to pick up a few tips from the chess masters.' Andris looked askance at Rupert. 'In return, I will give them your instruction that a well-positioned pawn, played with skill, possesses more strength than the bishop moved in a way that lacks strategy!' Andris's eyes twinkled.

Rupert groaned. 'Now I'm really embarrassed I offered you such obvious advice!'

Relinquishing the chess set, Andris settled in the chair at the end of the bed and said, 'I suppose you've heard that the Soviet Union invaded eastern Poland.'

'I picked up on some news but have no detail.'

'It is reported in the Russian press this is to protect Belorussian and Ukrainian nationals from Polish persecution. What good hearted people the Russians are to think of others in this way.' Andris gave a short ironic laugh. 'So, it is clear; the Molotov-Ribbentrop Pact included a deal between Stalin and Hitler to carve up Eastern Europe between them. It seems the biggest loser is going to be Poland – as always. Clearly, Hitler had the green light to invade the western part of Poland, whilst Stalin was given a free hand to annex the rest of the country. The state of Poland will, once again, be wiped off the map.'

There was a brief silence before Rupert said, 'There seems to be lots of excitement here with patients glued to the radio. I understand from the doctor there are reports of Russia wanting to protect itself from the possibility of invasion from Finland. It sounds bizarre; can it be true?'

'Of course not!' Andris snorted. 'People are picking up on Russian propaganda, which is entirely false. It's clear that what we're fed in the papers and hear on the radio is far from the reality of what's happening.'

'What is happening?'

'You may have heard, or been told, that the Soviet Union invited a Finnish delegation to Moscow for negotiations. Negotiations!' He added 'Pah,' with such force it made Rupert flinch. 'What are they talking about? The Finns were, in reality, summoned to Moscow where the Soviets demanded they cede substantial border territories. They claim this is for security reasons... Leningrad, as you might know, is thirty two kilometres from the Finnish border and they say this poses a defence risk to their city.'

'You say in reality,' Rupert cocked his head to one side and looked Andris in the eyes. 'It sounds like you have some inside information.'

Andris' eyes darted around the ward and, even though there was no one near, he dropped his voice to little more than a whisper, 'You know my father is high up in Government, well, he knows the Latvian Foreign Minister, Vilhelms Munters. They went to school together and are still loyal drinking partners. Vilhelms regularly stops by for a nightcap after a long day in the ministry.' Andris fixed Rupert with a searching look, and Rupert nodded. He understood. This was a highly confidential source. It would go no further than his hospital bed. Andris leant back in his chair, satisfied.

'Maybe the Russians have a right to be nervous?' Rupert asked.

'Who is going to attack them?' Andris raised his voice to his usual, commanding level. 'Not Finland for sure and Germany has said they will not attack Russia. No, this is a ruse to enable the Soviets to take over the rest of Finland. You can tell this from what they are demanding.'

'Which is?'

Dropping his voice once again, Andris detailed the Soviet demands that included moving the border north, leasing land and establishing military bases. Rupert enquired, 'If it is a negotiation, what are the Soviets offering?' Andris was struggling to keep his voice low and his emotions under control.

'I have told you, it is not a negotiation; it is political posturing to make it look like the Finns have a choice.' He stopped, took a breath, and restarted in a more measured tone. 'The Soviet Union would, graciously, cede two municipalities with twice the territory demanded from Finland, but this territory of mud, swamp and mosquitoes has no strategic benefit. If the Finns accept this, so called, offer the Soviets could stroll through to Helsinki at any time thereafter. Mark my words; this is a prelude to an invasion.'

Thanking Andris for the explanation, Rupert admitted, 'After the accident my world has closed in somewhat. I'm so focused on myself, my injuries and the worry of what my mother must be thinking, that all this talk of war seems so far away, so alien.'

'I understand but I'm not simply trying to distract you with foreign news. There is another reason for everyone's keen interest in these political machinations, and this will also have a personal impact on you. Finland and Latvia, in fact all of the Baltic States, have a common experience of being under Russian domination. As such, what happens to Finland will herald the same fate for all of us. We are in the same boat as your English saying puts it.'

'Really!'

'Just like us, Finland was a semi-autonomous state within the Russian Empire. The outbreak of the Great War, and the later collapse of the Russian Empire during the revolution and civil war, provided Finland with the opportunity to become independent. They seized the moment – as we did.' Andris puffed out his chest. 'But, it appears that Stalin wants to re-establish the old order and regain the provinces of Tsarist Russia lost at a time of chaos. It looks like Stalin is starting with Finland. Good luck to the plucky Finns for our fate is held in their hands. If they resist, we will have time to prepare our defences.'

Andris was just about to make his departure when the tall, bespectacled figure of Walter Zapp entered the room. Rupert smiled because it seemed that with the passing of time and with his big forehead and glasses Walter more and more epitomised a boffin. Rupert waved him over with a grin. After a cursory introduction Andris excused himself, leaving Rupert and Walter together. Rupert thanked Walter for the picture that now stood at his bedside and asked, 'How are things with the Minox.'

'Sales are good.' Walter handed over the box he had been carrying and Rupert saw it contained a VEF Minox sub-miniature camera. Rupert took it out of its box and case and, holding the thin, sleek, cold object in the palm of his hand, studied the dials.

'It is a thing of pure beauty.' Rupert said. Walter demonstrated how to use it and talked rapidly through its features.

'Minimum shooting distance twenty centimetres, shutter exposure from half to one thousandth of a second, depth of field from twenty centimetres to infinity, focus readjustment and luminous capacity three point five.' Rupert nodded his head, giving the impression of understanding more than he actually did. Walter carried on, 'This is not a simple act of selfless giving. I'd like you to get to know the camera and maybe you would be interested in helping me? The market is small here and it would be good to sell this in England. We have a distributor but we need a trusted representative there.'

'I am honoured. I would love to help when back in England.'

'By the way, I have used some of the film but there is plenty left. When you have finished the roll, send it back and I'll develop it for you and replace it with a new one'

After Walter had departed, Rupert replayed the conversations earlier in the day and concluded, *Andris is surely overstating the case. The Scandinavians are unlikely to stand back and see a neighbour invaded without doing anything.*

He tried to put from his mind all thoughts of war by studying the German version of the camera's instructions and accidentally took two photographs — one of his foot and one of the tea trolley. The more he considered Walter's request, the more he warmed to the idea of helping Walter. *He will change the shape of the camera forever and I can be a part of that.* Later, he dozed and, imagining himself back in England as the representative of Minox, wondered: *How do you get in touch with the British Secret Service?*

The next day, Rupert again dwelt on the long period before Irène's next visit. In an effort to distract himself from falling into a state of melancholia, he decided to persevere with *The Great Gatsby,* which he had started a few days before. Initially he had been intrigued with the story. Then, as he went on, he became annoyed with the characters, especially the narrator. Now, reaching the end of the book, he put it down and uttered, 'Unbelievable'.

Rupert sat back and started to analyse why the book, which he knew to be a best seller, hadn't appealed to him. *Firstly*, he thought, *it is written from the perspective of Nick Carraway, yet this active participant tells of things he'd have no knowledge of. This is a flaw in the narration, but surely it's not the reason for me to feel like I do?* By going over the story, he realised he was annoyed with Gatsby. *Here is a man who has everything, he is handsome and wealthy and knows how to throw good parties. Yet his life is centred around winning back an old girlfriend, whom he seemed to know only fleetingly at a time long before he became rich. It's an unbelievable story!*

Later that evening, Rupert again returned to the book. He wanted to dismiss it as over-rated, but could not stop thinking of Gatsby's continued infatuation. He wondered whether it was possible to maintain a desire for a person you hardly know. Then, he understood that if his life was to suddenly change, so that he was miraculously transported back to England on his own, he'd be tormented by thoughts of Irēne and the unanswered question of what might have been. He even uttered out loud, 'Surely, this is the worst question of all.'

In a rather serious mood, Rupert started to worry that Irēne had sent the note about not visiting as a means of letting him down gently. His heart thumped so hard he feared it would leap out of his chest. And why would she come? He was almost a cripple and had memory problems: hardly a good prospect. His sleep was uneasy.

Summoned Again

The sound of unexpected footsteps approaching his cell brought Rupert out in a cold sweat. He was frogmarched to a dull, bare anteroom and left standing alone. An hour passed. Then two. Rupert understood that this was part of a 'softening up' process, a tiring of the body and the mind. *So I am to be interrogated again,* he thought. The wooden floor was laid in an interesting pattern and he inwardly traced around it, tracking its tessellations, providing himself no mental space to fear what was coming.

Rupert's legs had grown stiff by the time he was ushered into the interrogation room. The lieutenant, who sat between two unfamiliar officers, eyed Rupert coldly and pointed to the lone chair. Rupert sat.

One of the officers was poised to make notes. The other turned a pale, bony face to Rupert and demanded, 'And what of Orlonsky?' Rupert was taken aback and looked blankly at the officer. He remembered telling the lieutenant at the sanatorium that he had learnt Russian from his university friend. *Why on earth are they interested in Orlonsky?* The dark, protruding eyes of the officer, searchlights behind thick, magnifying lenses, told Rupert he ought to tread carefully. His silence prompted a grimace, the man's fishy lips twisted with impatience. *Surely,* Rupert speculated, *here is face that must have provoked merciless bullying at school.'* He had hesitated too long.

'Answer me.' the man snapped, flecking his chin with spittle. Rupert flinched.

'I went to Cambridge University with him,' he stammered, 'I haven't seen him since.' He already started to lie. Rupert felt his heart thumping against his ribs. He had seen Orlonsky in London after graduating.

'Do you know anything of Orlonsky's grandfather?' Rupert looked surprised. The officer leant forward.

'Orlonsky never mentioned his Grandfather.' His pulse was now throbbing in his temples. He felt his throat bob. The lieutenant smiled, his lip curling.

'Even he was embarrassed by his family's past.' He rose to his feet, clasped his hands behind his back and began to pace. Chin raised, he spoke to the ceiling 'I was nine years of age when Tsar abdicated from train in sidings at Pskov - and I was there. My family lived in Pskov and my friends told me Royal Train was nearby. Of course we went to investigate. At that exact time I did not know what was happening in Petrograd; we were simply there to see Tsar. Large crowd formed and we were in jovial mood. Some of adults brought food, which they shared with us, and men drank beer. It was party. We saw man arrive early on and someone in crowd said it was physician. We all believed Tsar must be sick and some of the women said prayers for him. We stayed all day and into evening. Eventually Tsar appeared. We did not know he had just abdicated.'

Maintaining his steely voice, the lieutenant continued, 'To my shame, I clapped and joined in singing of *God Save Tsar* that started spontaneously. I say shame, but I didn't know at time that old bastard deserved everything coming his way.' He spat as if trying to get rid of a flake of tobacco on his lip. 'I was there at moment of history.... If only that was end of story. Unfortunately, provisional government were tainted elite that had already helped us get into mess. Tsar had abdicated but who took over? Prince – sort of man Russian peasants suffered under for centuries. Prince Lvov.' It briefly crossed Rupert's mind that the lieutenant was drunk as he wondered why he was providing this personal history.

Drawing close to Rupert, the lieutenant looked him in the eyes and sneered, 'Did you know, your so-called friend Orlonsky is the bastard descendent of Prime Minister of Russia, Prince Lvov?' Rupert froze.

The intent behind their questions was suddenly clear. Yet another unlikely, dangerous connection. *Yet another bar on my cell window,* Rupert thought, *or, worse still, yet another nail in my coffin.* He swallowed and did his best to hold the lieutenant's gaze. He had a horrible feeling that man's next move might be to pull out his revolver. He breathed a sigh of relief when the lieutenant continued.

'Orlonsky, his bastard descendent, even now is worming his way into soft underbelly of British life. Lvov and his crony, Kerensky, were happy to send more and more brave, but ill-equipped, soldiers to their death and for what? Yes, to prop up French and British Empires. And what did these, so called, allies do for us at end of war when Russia was throwing off shackles of Romanov dynasty? They got together in huddle with others happy to kick Russia when she is wounded and supported creation of independent states – including this, our Latvia. At least we have our land back now.' The lieutenant clenched his fist, his chest heaving. Rupert sensed the man's anger rising and feared the consequences.

'Did your *friend* tell you Lvov and his co-conspirator Kerensky kept us in bloody war, whilst any attack on Germans only ended in heavy losses and withdrawal? I could go on but my trigger finger is already itching.'

The lieutenant shook his head slightly and seemed to calm himself. 'Kerensky is probably writing his memoirs on some beach. Lvov's offspring are enjoying the fruits of the bourgeoisie. But they, their children and their children's children, have blood on their hands. You see,' he said, bringing his face close to Rupert's ear so that his breath lifted the hair on the back of Rupert's neck, 'it is not what you know but whom you know. And whom you know is very dangerous.'

'Tell us what you know.' The haddock-faced officer's voice was clipped and business-like, but Rupert felt the cold gravity of threat behind it. With a wet-lipped smile the man added, 'Think very carefully before you answer. If you are lying, we have well practised manicure procedures here. It is amazing how boiling water softens fingernails and allows them to be plucked out. Imagine how difficult it will be to scratch your insect bites without nails.' Rupert felt his stomach lurch.

The haddock-faced officer stood up and pushed a pile of photographs towards Rupert. Rupert noted the waxy texture of his yellowing skin. On the top there was a picture of a tall elegant man in a dark overcoat with a fur collar. The officer came around the desk bringing with him a stale, salty smell and, jabbing his finger on the photo, demanded, 'Who is this?'

'I have no idea.' Rupert replied truthfully. He had never seen the man before.

'Oh dear, so soon.' The officer's voice was pitiless and his smile widened. 'This was on your camera. Now, who is he?' The officer spread out the photos so that Rupert could see more of the others and immediately recognised these as the ones he had taken with his Minox.

Rupert remembered that Walter had said that some of the film had already been used. Then, with a flood of panic that set his nerves singing, he realised that in this pile of photos there were sure to be images of Irēne.

The officer spread more of the photos out and for the first time since arriving in the prison, Rupert thought how lucky he was. There were no images of Irēne in the photographs displayed in front of him. He remembered her reluctance to be photographed and breathed a sigh of relief. He even wanted to laugh a little as there were a few photographs comprising just sky or legs. Operator error had saved him from having to explain who Irēne was and his relationship to her.

The rest of the interrogation followed the same pattern as before; seemingly endless and repetitious questions that circled around his friends and acquaintances.

Alone in his cell Rupert watched the light fading at the window and thought about Orlonsky. He wondered why he had not mentioned his family connection to Prince Lvov. *Surely,* he thought, *he's not embarrassed about his illegitimate status?'* Rupert couldn't seem to get the sound of the officer's scratching pen out of his head, nor the sight of his nose bent over the page as he scribbled constantly. *What could he possibly have to write down? Why had I to repeat the same thing over and over? Why are they interested in Orlonsky and his friends? Surely, they are no threat now to the Soviets?*

That night the bed bugs seemed to be more active than usual and as he scratched his leg and bottom, he thought about the haddock-faced officer's threat. He knew that he must not lie or divulge information about Irène. Was there anything he could say regarding Orlonsky and his friends that his interrogators would find valuable? Anything that might content them? He wracked his brains. *I must produce something,* he thought, *if only to soften the blow in the event that their methods turned towards manicure.* Rupert shuddered at the idea and, turning his back to the room, sought sleep.

Mac The Knife

Rupert recognised the familiar signs that preceded the likely arrival of Irēne. He could not concentrate on anything and, as the minute hand crawled up the incline towards visiting time, every time someone appeared at the door of the ward he looked up in hopeful anticipation even though he knew she wouldn't be allowed in until after two o'clock.

It had been two weeks since Irēne's last visit and Rupert felt particularly agitated; his worries about being let down gently had resurfaced. By a quarter past two, he had convinced himself she wasn't coming. He found himself beginning to sink into a state never experienced before: a disconcerting combination of sadness, loneliness and frustration. This frustration wasn't directed at Irēne but at the world in general.

When Irēne appeared in the doorway of the ward, the heavy, depressing fog settling on Rupert evaporated and, greeting her with a broad, spontaneous smile, he said, 'The last fifteen minutes have felt like a fortnight. I got it into my head you weren't coming and I'm so pleased you're here.' Irēne furrowed her brow and Rupert, worrying that he was seen to be complaining about her being late, continued by asking '*Kā tev iet?*' *How are you?*'

'*Labi, paldies.*' Irēne said, *well, thank you.* How are your lessons going?'

'*Labi... paldies!*' Rupert said, frowning with concentration. Irēne laughed.

She was wearing a dark blue blazer, the lapels edged in cream brocade and the nautical effect immediately put Rupert in mind of Gatsby's yacht. Irēne took Rupert's hand and, gesturing to the lounge around them, said, 'I see you have been on your travels again?'

'Indeed. I've just returned from New York.'

'Oh, how was it?'

'I didn't like the place and I didn't like the people, especially Gatsby.'

'What is wrong with Gatsby?'

'I'm not quite sure, though I think he might be a bit too much like me.' He said. He was yet to find the root of his distaste for the man, fictional though he was.

'He cannot be so handsome.' Irēne said, with such conviction that Rupert felt his cheeks flush a little as he laughed.

Drawing up the chair up to the bed, Irēne asked, 'How are you feeling?'

'Fine, I had the chest bandages taken off on Friday, which is a relief, although my ribs are still sore. Please don't make me laugh too much... now I am just bored. I've run out of things to read. It's the second time I have read *Jeeves* and I can't face *Great Gatsby* again. Would you have anything that might be suitable in English or German?'

'I will take a look at home, but have you not started Brecht's play yet?'

'Actually, I haven't and it's because every time I think about it, I come over with a feeling of great anxiety. My heart races and I can't focus properly. I'm assuming it's because Brecht is part of my hidden life. When my memory returns, then I'll be able to read it'

'That must be distressing. I will find something that is light to read and you can save Brecht for now'

Rupert wondered whether his memory would ever return. *After all, I doubt whether I will ever fully recover physically, why should it be any different with my memory?* He decided not to voice his negativity. Instead, he said something to Irēne, which sounded vaguely Latvian, and she pulled a quizzical face. Realising he hadn't been understood, he took out a piece of paper, on which a long sentence in Latvian had been handwritten and passed it to her.

'Who has given you this?' Irēne asked.

'The nurses are helping me learn Latvian by correcting my pronunciation.'

'I think they might be having a little joke with you.' Irēne smiled.

'This says, *The sad young man from the far off land is amongst all of his pretty helpers, but he has only eyes for the beautiful princess.* I can imagine they were enjoying how you said these difficult Latvian words. And by the way, who is this beautiful princess?'

Enjoying the joke, Rupert smiled and said, 'The princess is someone you know well... but honestly, I'm frustrated by not being able to quickly learn the language. I try to speak with other patients, but they come and go so fast there is no opportunity to settle into a pattern, and the doctors and nurses are too busy. I imagined that my knowing Russian and German would help me learn Latvian, but I'm struggling.'

'Perhaps an introduction to Latvian will help.' Irēne sat up straight and struck a schoolmarmish pose, looking down her nose and raising a forefinger. 'It is an inflective language and there are two grammatical genders with a single and plural.

103

Nouns decline into seven cases and there are six declensions. There are no articles.'

'Now I understand why it is so hard to pick up,' Rupert laughed and then added, 'but I've built a Latvian vocabulary that includes: plate, knife, fork, spoon and X-Ray machine.'

'What is X-Ray machine in Latvian? Irēne enquired.

'That's easy, X-Rays *machina!*'

Rupert asked, 'Are there no books on learning Latvian?'

'The only books, I have seen on learning Latvian are in Latvian, which, to my mind, will be as useless as listening to the radio.' After scratching her chin with her thumb and forefinger, Irēne smiled and added, 'Maybe you have to learn like a child learns... I will bring in some fairytales and I will read them to you, explain what they mean and then maybe you can read them to me?'

'That's an excellent idea.'

Moving off the topic of languages, Rupert asked, 'When is your birthday and name day?'

'My birthday is on the 11th of November and my name day is on the 13th May.' He briefly thought about the dates and then smiled.

'Your date of birth is linked to that of the signing of the Armistice – and mine coincides with the declaration of war on the 28th of July 1914.

'Are we like war and peace?'

'I hope we're not opposites at all... or, if we are, maybe we're just two sides of the same coin.'

'Well, you know what they say about opposites!'

Changing the subject, Irēne said she was a few minutes later than normal because her flatmate had been delayed at work and she needed to see her before leaving for the hospital. Rupert asked, 'Just so I've a better image of where and how you live, could you describe your apartment and flatmate to me?'

'Oh, there is not much to say about the apartment. It is cosy with only two rooms together with a kitchen and bathroom. Katerīna and I have to share a bedroom but that is not a problem as we get on very well. Katerīna is far more interesting. She is Russian, very pretty and very intelligent. She works as a research chemist in the Technical University. Her family live in Yekaterinburg.'

'Isn't that where the Tsar and his family were exiled after the Russian Revolution?'

'Not just exiled, it is clear they were executed there too – in the Inpatiev House where they were held. The Bolsheviks have not admitted it, but they were butchered and their remains were tipped down a well. But all those from Yekaterinburg, or should I now say Sverdlovsk, know the truth.'

Both were quiet for a few moments. Rupert felt sickened by the idea of the royal family being executed. To lighten the atmosphere Irēne eventually said, 'Can you believe it, but she is one of ten children?'

'I'm an only child and can't imagine where we would have put an extra nine bodies in our small house. But there are families of that size in Manchester and they often live in houses like ours.'

'I would lose track of everybody's birthday and name days, but think of the number of parties! Talking of which, I have been thinking about name days and we need to find one for you. We don't have a name day for Rupert, but what about Roberts?' Rupert laughed.

'Oh, I better not change my name to Robert.'

'Why is that?'

'Robert Bruce Lockhart tried to kill Lenin.'

'Did he?'

Interrupted by a nurse bringing around the tea trolley and, in the way that had become customary, Rupert turned to her and said, '*Ja*, tea viz milk,' and then rolled his eyes at Irēne. The nurse offered Irēne a cup of tea and then smiled at her response. Rupert, intrigued, asked Irēne what she had said and she replied, 'I simply asked for tea with two sugars, but not stirred as I do not like it too sweet.' He thought about her response for a moment, then burst out laughing.

Tea in hand, Rupert provided a rather long account of how Robert Bruce Lockhart, a British diplomat working in Moscow, had been accused of enlisting the help of a revolutionary called Fanny Kaplan to murder Lenin. To finish off he said, 'Lockhart was dragged from his bed, arrested and taken to the Lubyanka. I'm told he was confronted with a terrified Fanny Kaplan. After a month in the Lubyanka, London exchanged him for a high-ranking Soviet diplomat. On his return, there was one last news report in the papers. Apparently, Kaplan was shot in the back of head and burned in a barrel. If true, Russian justice doesn't operate in a way I understand.'

'No remains - no martyr. Standard practice. Russia and justice are two words that do not often go together.'

'Hmm,' was all Rupert could think to say by way of response and then added, 'It is funny what I can remember.

These events all happened when I was very young and Mr. Tatton called me the Little Diplomat for a while because of the national interest in the story. Stanley even commented on our similar names. Stanley reminded me about it last year. I wish I could so easily recall my time at Cambridge.'

Irēne looked into his face with concern and Rupert, in an attempt to describe his plight said, 'It's as if I'm an obsessive librarian who comes across a large empty area in the shelving. I know the books are missing but I've lost the inventory and now can't sleep for worrying.' A wave of exhaustion had begun to build, as if it took physical energy, rather like building a dam, to hold back his memories.

Irēne must have detected the change of mood as she said, 'Don't worry, tell me about what you do remember.' Rupert was pleased to focus on what he could recall.

'The library resumes its orderly structure at *M* for Metropolitan Vickers. Although times were tough for many, I joined the firm as a trainee in the contracts department.' Irēne encouraged him to say more and he continued, 'I used to ride on my bike to the factory with some twenty thousand other workers. You should have seen us; a tide of bikes flowing in and out, each one pedalled by a labourer, craftsman or office worker of some sort. If only I could show you the turbine department building. It is grand. It even has a religious quality at times; everything is on such an epic scale. I would even liken it to a cathedral; only there they worship technology.'

Remembering the Minox in the pocket of his dressing gown, Rupert took it out. After explaining that Walter had visited and left him the camera, he said, 'Now, let me take a picture of you.'

'Oh no, I do not like my picture being taken.' Irēne's reaction surprised him. Nevertheless, he held the camera up and she turned away. 'No, I mean it. If you insist I will only pull a sad looking face.' He realised now why Irēne looked a little glum in the picture that had been taken of them at the opera.

'How strange, I thought everyone liked having their photograph taken.' He put the camera down.

'I have become a little superstitious.' Irēne shrugged her shoulders. 'Mother always wanted to be in front of the camera, but somehow I think that every image taken removes a little of our soul.'

Her face was solemn and, not wanting to belittle her concerns, Rupert set the camera down and changed the subject. He commented on the sudden change in the Latvian menu from summer to winter fare. He compared this to Manchester, 'Our mild summer rain gives way in autumn to a cooler variety of the same substance and the food only gradually moves from salad to cabbage.'

'You might reconsider whether the quick change of season is a good thing, as the winter can go on a long time here.' She emphasised her statement with an exaggerated shiver.

Irēne drew Rupert's attention to the burbling of a radio in the background and said, 'The announcer just mentioned the name of Bertolt Brecht.' Rupert had forgotten that there was a radio on in the background; as he didn't understand Latvian, he had long ago tuned out the sound. Irēne informed him that the announcer was talking of Brecht's play, *The Threepenny Opera*. She rose, went over to the radio and, as the lounge was empty, turned up the volume. As soon as the music of *Mac the Knife* began, Irēne started to accompany the male singer in his German rendition. She had a lovely, tuneful voice, which masked the dirge-like quality of the voice on the radio.

Oh, the shark has pretty teeth, dear,
And he shows them pearly white;

Irēne bared her teeth.

Just a jack-knife has Macheath, dear,
And he keeps it out of sight!

She pretended to open her blazer to show a knife hidden there.

When the shark bites with his teeth, dear,
Scarlet billows start to spread;
Fancy gloves, though, wears Macheath, dear,
So there's not a trace of red!

Irēne came towards Rupert smoothing on pretend gloves.

On the sidewalk Sunday morning
Lies a body oozing life;
Someone sneaking 'round the corner;
Is the someone Mack the Knife?

Rupert clapped his good hand on the bed and Irēne took several bows. Sitting down next to him once more, she said, 'I know the singer, Kurt Gerron. This takes me back to when I watched the rehearsals of *The Threepenny Opera* at Theater am Schiffbauerdamm in Berlin.' A smile showed she was enjoying the reminiscence. 'This song was composed only a few days before the opening production. Harold Paulsen played the part of London's most notorious criminal. He wanted something to set the scene and show how big a fish he was in the criminal world, so Brecht and his songwriter, Kurt Weill sat down and ran off the words and music to satisfy their star. The ballad became a big hit, although, to my mind, it could be more jazzy and less like a German folk song.'

Rupert gave no reply. Irēne looked at him at leapt to her feet up in alarm as his head dropped back on the pillow, the colour draining from his face. 'Rupert,' she said insistently, 'are you alright?' Rupert did not respond and, gripping his hand, Irēne was turning to call for a nurse when he faintly replied, 'I feel terribly faint and dizzy...'

Irēne rushed off to fetch a nurse and by the time they both returned, Rupert was unconscious.

A distant, fuzzy celestial light disturbed an infinite darkness. It grew in intensity and coalesced into a moon and penumbra. Slowly the penumbra shrank and the image transformed itself into a light bulb. Rupert realised he was in his hospital room and was looking at the nightlight on the far wall. As he regained consciousness he had a feeling he could only liken to a warm tide flowing into a shallow inlet.'

Sharing Histories

Irēne had hardly taken off her coat before Rupert said, 'I'm sorry for being so rude last week when you were talking to me about Brecht. I had a very woozy feeling and then passed out. I studied the lyrics of *The Threepenny Opera* for one of my modern German classes at Cambridge and it somehow affected me. By the way, thank you for phoning to see how I was, I got a message the next day'

'I was so pleased to hear that you had recovered.'

'A weight has been lifted.' Rupert said and meant it. It seemed as though he felt lighter and could draw himself upright with ease. 'Mac the Knife started something. At first it was just a small hole in the dam holding back my memory and a few fragments trickled out. Then, when I awoke, I could remember more and more of my time at Cambridge. I'm so thankful to you and Brecht for unlocking those years for me.'

'Well I am pleased that some good has come of the song. Hitler described it as degenerate music and banned it in Germany.'

Keen to make amends for his untimely collapse, Rupert asked Irēne to repeat what she had said about her time in Berlin, but she replied, 'Now the university years have reappeared I'd like to hear of these first. Did you like being at Cambridge?'

'Parts I did... I liked playing chess with the Count.'

'He was the man you mentioned when we were at the opera?'

'Yes. His name is Fyodor Orlonsky; we called him Count Orlonsky because he said he could trace his family tree back to Catherine the Great although he never spoke of them. We had struck up an easy relationship from the moment we first met and in the dark days of winter he taught me Russian and how to play chess. He must have been a good language teacher, because by the third year, I was fluent and we had long conversations in Russian deep into the night.'

Irēne asked Rupert to say more about his time at Cambridge and he talked of the autumn rains that soaked students on the way to lectures, cold mornings, the frost that sometimes formed on the inside of the windows of his rooms, the lighting of fires even in spring to ward off the bone-numbing cold and of the brief summer on the lawns. Irēne listened intently and then said, 'It is true then, the British do only talk about the weather.' Rupert smiled and then added other anecdotes about singing in the choir and punting on the Cam.

As the memories flowed, Rupert wondered where these had been hiding and concluded, 'I am enjoying remembering these scenes from Cambridge but some of them still appear as an outline; recounting them helps me fill in the detail and the colours. It does make me wonder whether our memories can ever be accurate records of what actually happened.' Rupert pulled out the Minox from his dressing gown's pocket. 'At least I can now take a visual record.'

'The more I see you play with that miniature camera, the more I think you would make a good spy.'

Irēne asked about what Rupert hadn't liked at Cambridge and, after a brief contemplation, he said, 'There's nothing in particular, only I felt I didn't quite fit in.'

'How was that?' She enquired.
'Most of the students were richer than me and from privileged families: they were from a different social class, as we would say in England. And many were keen to let me know it.' Irēne wrinkled her brow and Rupert understood she couldn't see

a problem, so he added, 'Although I'm from a working class background, I don't feel working class. Too much of the Tattons and Wythenshawe Hall has rubbed off on me to be able to play the role of a hard-bitten, take-me-as-you-find-me, working man. Instead I tried to portray a kind of natural gentility; the correct and elegant thing, I felt, was to have good manners even if no money. Strangely, I think that attitude made me appear rather aloof and distant and possibly superior.'

'Is class so important in your country?'

'As soon as you open your mouth your accent categorises you in England. The box you are placed in determines who you can mix with and what work you can do. Your life's chances are almost pre-ordained.'

He surprised himself by how vehement he was and, thinking he had better change the subject, said, 'Thanks to Brecht my memory has returned, and now I've been able to read the play you gave me.'

'I was hoping a Cambridge scholar would provide an interesting summary.' Irēne replied.

'I don't know about being a scholar, but I can talk to you about the *Life of Galileo* if you'd like.'

'Yes please.'

Sitting up a little straighter and grimacing as his ribs complained, Rupert tried to emulate the way Irēne recounted stories. In a dramatic voice he told her of Galileo's inquisition for supporting the heretical ideas that the earth goes around the sun. When he had finished the outline of the play, Rupert said, 'The really interesting thing for me is that, despite the efforts of the Catholic Church, the idea that the sun is the centre of our universe has come to be the orthodox view.' Then, he asked, 'It seems that, eventually, truth prevails, and I wonder if that goes for love too? Against all the forces of darkness that seem to set out to thwart it, can love eventually triumph?'

'I am optimist and a romantic, so my answer is yes.' Irēne's response made Rupert's heart flutter in his chest.

Towards the end of visiting time, Irēne dug into her large handbag, fetched out a book and exclaimed, 'I almost forgot, here is something to help your Latvian. It's a book of fairytales. I know you will not be able to read them, but I will enjoy reciting them to you. You can read them to me when you know what they are about. In no time, you will be as fluent as a five year old!' Rupert turned the pages of the beautifully illustrated book and stopped at one illustrated with a picture of fish swimming in the sea. The story was only a page long.

'What is this one about?' Irēne took hold of the book and smiled.
'This explains how the sea is salty.'

'Well, I never! I look forward to learning more.' He wanted to hear more, if only to listen to Irēne's melodic voice and her curious accent; a blend of German and Latvian with a hint of American.

After Irēne had dressed to leave she came over to Rupert, bent down and brought her face to his as if to give the customary goodbye with a hug and a kiss on the cheek, but, instead, planted a kiss on his lips. To Rupert this was the sweetest of all sensations and he immediately raised his head and kissed her back, her mouth soft and her scent sweet and floral.

'I've sold my soul to the devil.' He said, recalling their conversation about *Faust*.

'You really are easily bought.'

Lying on his bed after the evening meal, Rupert started to compile a list of the things he liked about Irēne and then realised that he liked everything. He liked her flowered dress and the necklace that somehow highlighted a discreet but definite décolletage. He liked the way she was able to turn broad, general subjects into being personal. More than anything, he liked the feel of her lips on his. Her birthday was fast approaching and Rupert began to wonder what present he could give to her on her next visit.

The next time Rupert was waiting in the patients' lounge for Irēne, he had been trundled through in a wheelchair instead of being in the hospital bed. Manoeuvring into the wheelchair had been an awkward and painful exercise but once seated, Rupert delighted in the sense of freedom it gave him. Sitting in his dressing gown with a knitted blanket covering the cast on his leg, he looked out of the window and was aware of how winter was tightening its icy grip. The clear skies of autumn had been replaced by, what appeared to be, a heavy grey blanket pressing down on the leafless trees. Even the red roofs of the nearby buildings took on a muddy brown hue. Between the panes of glass in the double windows, the outer of which was covered by slowly congealing raindrops, was a thermometer. Its crimson thread had shortened. It was close to freezing outside.

It was Remembrance Sunday and, to help pass time, Rupert lost himself in memories of lit candles and the rustle of his chorister's cassock in the pews. This year's service in Manchester Cathedral would be all the more poignant now that Britain was once again at war. Rupert felt a twinge of sadness and beneath it, a bitter splinter of fear.

Rupert was keen to surprise Irēne; not only with his being seated rather than bed-bound, but also with the birthday present he had bought her. This sat wrapped in brown paper on the table next to him. When she arrived, it was with a broad smile. 'Rupert, how wonderful! You look very regal in your chair.'

'I'm pleased to be out of bed, but I have to admit it took two porters and a nurse to get me into the wheelchair. Anyhow the most important thing is *Daudz laimes dzimšanas dienā.*' Rupert, passed on the Happy Birthday greeting he had been practicing and handed her the present.

'Have you been out to get it? Irēne asked. 'If so, you really have done well.'

Irēne took off her thick winter coat, fine snow crystals on the floral relief of its self-embossed collar testament to the winter conditions, before unwrapping the present. After carefully removing the paper, she held in her hands a copy of Oscar Wilde's, *The Happy Prince and Other Tales.* 'How wonderful and such a coincidence. I love Oscar Wilde.' She bent down and gave Rupert a hug and a kiss, holding her face close to his long enough for him to inhale her bluebell fragrance. 'How did you manage to find such a book?' He explained how he had asked Doctor Berzins to buy an English language book from the Army Economic Store when he next visited.

Flicking through the book, Irēne said, 'I love fairytales; I'll read this quickly and we can swap stories. How are you getting on with your fairy stories?'
    'Oh it is in my room! I have been trying to read it and I've noticed that most of the stories start in the same way even though I have yet to understand the meaning.'

'Yes, most of the stories start with the line, a man has three sons, two are clever and the third is a fool. The interesting thing is that normally the ending is the same too; the fool ends up marrying the princess and together they live in a golden palace.'

'Is there a story in the book that starts, a man has a son who is clever and sets off to a foreign land?'

'Yes there is such a fairytale.' Irēne smiled and added, 'It is not in this book though.' He asked about the ending and she enigmatically replied, 'Ah, we will have to wait and see.'

Rupert smiled and then asked, 'As it is your birthday, will you be seeing your mother and having a party?

'Mother is not so interested in parties these days.'

'Oh, I thought she would like a celebration! ...Anyhow, I am interested to hear about your life with her in Berlin.

'I was a young girl at the time and my memory is rather patchy... Do you really want to hear of my Berlin years?'

'Most definitely.' Irēne settled herself on her chair and then began.

'We arrived in Berlin in February 1924 and mother immediately started looking for work. To her surprise, she found a job at the first theatre she went to. The director, Erich Hesse, who produced most of Brecht's plays, had been let down by one of the leading actresses. He gave her an audition there and then and Mother's ability to speak German, her good looks and much flirting got her the part.'

Irēne paused and looked at Rupert, uncertainty in her face. He nodded his head for her to continue. 'It seemed we had hardly settled into Berlin, when Erich and his entourage, between productions, set off for Capri. Erich clearly enjoyed the company of glamorous women and he invited my mother – with me as, quite possibly, an unwelcome accessory.'

Rupert had an image of a flamboyant and arty group setting out on their adventures. It seemed almost comical but Irēne was contemplative, her brows smooth and her eyes unfocused and Rupert let her continue. 'I have the recollection of being very happy and free in Capri. For the first time in my life, I played with other children. Can you believe it, I had spent my time entirely in the company of grown ups?'

'Our upbringings are very different I think. I was constantly in the company of other children, especially boys. Sorry, I interrupted you.'

'Are all Englishmen so polite? When we returned to Berlin, I was back in the company of adults but I didn't mind, especially as I spent a lot of time with Alexandra Fischer. Fischer looked after me as if she was my aunty and I came to love her.'

'She sounds like she's very special.'

'I certainly think she is. Fischer had come to Berlin to escape a career as a teacher. In those days, can you believe it, to be a teacher required a woman to be celibate? Even though I was only six or seven, I knew she liked men. I would stay in her company for hours, whilst Mother was rehearsing, and she would tell me in English what she was working on.'

'And what was she working on?' Rupert enquired.

'Well, one thing that is particularly relevant. She helped Hesse stage the play that would restore your memory.'

'*The Threepenny Opera*! How bizarre and how wonderful you were there when it was being performed.'

Unable to detect any signs that Irēne's unconventional upbringing had created any negative consequences, Rupert realised she hadn't mentioned anything about her education and asked, 'Didn't you go to school?'

'Not until I was fifteen!' She responded with a triumphant note in her voice. 'I was free and never bored. I had the best teachers. Firstly there was my mother, she has her faults, but she taught me to read, and with Fischer I read like crazy.' Old Manachem who had learnt English from listening to the radio had amazed Rupert, and he was equally stunned that Irēne, although missing so much formal schooling, could be so well educated.

Wondering what his hours in the classrooms of Manchester Grammar had actually taught him, Rupert commented. 'I really enjoy hearing about your life. It is so different to mine.'

'When I eventually returned to Latvia I did go to school and, with a bit of extra help on history and geography, I graduated with flying colours – all the teachers were shocked.' Rupert just shook his head and Irēne concluded, 'Anyway, that summarises my Berlin years.'

They moved on to talk about the week ahead and Irēne informed him that she had to visit her mother during the forthcoming weekend. As soon she had told him this, it was as if an iridescent bubble rising inside him had been burst and reduced to its constituent drop of water. Despite the pain in his ribs from stretching, Rupert levered himself up using the armrests of his chair, took hold of Irēne's hand, brought her forward for his lips to meet hers. It was a sweet kiss that provided some comfort, because two weeks without a visit from Irēne would be a long time.

After the evening meal, Rupert thought about the Remembrance Day evening services taking place in England and that one of these would be broadcast on the radio. As it was just around seven o' clock he asked the nurse to arrange for him, this once, to be pushed to the radio in the patients' lounge in what he thought was a forlorn hope of finding the BBC.

Leaning forward from his wheelchair at full stretch and with his ribs screaming to sit back, Rupert twiddled the dial on the big radio. Foreign voices came and went and then suddenly there was the sound of an English presenter. He could not believe he had found the BBC and his jaw momentarily dropped when the presenter announced, 'And now we go to Manchester Cathedral for a special Remembrance Day evening service.' The music and song faded in and out but Rupert was transported to the candlelit quire, wearing a chorister's gown. He sang silently along with the music and, at the end, thinking that he was a long, long way from home, he wiped away a large tear that had welled up and run down his face.

Rupert returned to his hospital bed but couldn't easily fall asleep. He thought, *Irēne had such a different childhood to mine – yet it seems that we have so much in common.* In thinking about how they connected with each other, he knew it wasn't just about listening to another person's very different life story, but their conversations opened windows into a realm of feeling and emotion— a realm of vulnerability and trust.

The last conscious thought Rupert had before falling asleep was, *Remembrance Sunday 1939 will always have a special meaning for me from now on; it is the day I fell in love for the first time in my life.*

Sympathy For His Captors

The prison was filling up and Rupert began to hear the sounds of half-humanity. Grunts, shouts and expletives were becoming more common and, in his twice daily visits to the washroom, he was accompanied by grey apparitions, but was ordered not to speak to them.

He was also aware of the taps and clicks on the pipes and radiators that ran through the building and understood this was some sort of code. Although it was comforting to know that people were communicating with each other, he felt even more cut off and lonely.

The back of Rupert's notepad now held a sea of lines marking his incarceration, days that now ran into months. *Even the man who might have tried to kill Lenin was released quickly,* he thought. It began to dawn on him that far from being dangerous, he was, at best, insignificant, his only value his nationality. He would never be traded for some Soviet diplomat or spy. His release would not come, perhaps for years. He would simply sit here and decay in mind and body until the war was ended and the victor dispensed with the remnants. The thought hollowed out Rupert's stomach and drew a black cloud over his mind.

The days were shortening and the nights were getting colder. The cool nights meant, in the sport of fly catching, the odds had moved in Rupert's favour. However, the first frosts took all the fun out of the game. The flies that came into his cell were dried up and slow and seemingly startled by their own buzzing. They would remain in one place for hours until they revived one last time. Then they would fly off madly and hit the wall without Rupert's sweep of the hand.

Rupert replayed the jumbled memories of his years in Cambridge, with Orlonsky in his mind as he lay, shivering beneath his ragged blanket. Though much of it seemed blurred into cobbled streets, dark, wood-panelled rooms and honey coloured stone, he remembered his first day with startling clarity.

He recalled how he had put on his academic gown and mortarboard and was making his way to visit his college tutor when he nearly collided with Orlonsky who was struggling to get his arms through his gown. His first words to Rupert were, 'What is it about the British and weird theatricals?' They introduced themselves to each other and found that they had the same tutor. After meeting with him, they went back to Orlonsky's rooms, which happened to be opposite Rupert's. Rupert remembered Orlonsky spending much of the time complaining about the cold, a strange preoccupation, he thought, for a Russian.

Orlonsky's rooms had been the setting of many late-night fireside discussions. In particular he remembered when Orlonsky asked his friend, Tristan, to justify the bestial terror sanctioned by Lenin and Stalin, the torture houses, the blood-spattered walls and the forced exile of thousands.

Rupert's thoughts returned to the interrogation but couldn't remember exactly what he had said about Orlonsky or his friends. Instead, a snippet of conversation with Irène came back to him so vividly he imagined he could also smell the hospital ward where it had taken place.

'Yes,' Rupert said, 'we took ourselves very seriously sitting in Orlonsky's room... especially one of them; a man called Tristan. Tristan was a beanpole...'

'Beanpole?' Irène enquired.

'Sorry, I mean he was a tall man who had an annoying habit of chewing the end of his pipe before giving an answer to any question, however simple. More annoying than that, he was an old Etonian, young socialist. Have you heard of Eton?' Irēne shook her head and Rupert continued, 'It's one of the oldest public schools in England. Socialism and the types that go to Eton are strange bedfellows.'

'It is difficult to see what the motivation is of such a man. After all, he risks losing his privileged position.'

'Certainly, Tristan's motivation didn't come from love, especially a love of the working class. In fact, he'd be revolted rather than attracted by them... I should've invited him to my part of Manchester to have tea with the locals.'

'Does everything revolve around tea?'

'In this case tea refers to more than the drink. Sorry for the confusion. Certainly, Tristan could no more copy their habits and leave the milk bottle on the table, put pieces of meat into his mouth with the point of a knife, sit indoors with his cap on or drink tea out of a saucer than he could stick hot needles in his eyes.'

'Is that how you eat in England?' Irēne asked playfully.

'God forbid! I make no apology for this; I'm quite a snob too,'

'Good to know... What is Tristan doing now?'

'He has gone into politics.'

'That shows his motivation is for power.'

Rupert smiled at this recollection and then frowned as he wondered if his interrogation had been more about finding powerful friends to aid the Russians than worrying about what

Orlonsky was up to. An image came to mind of Tristan meeting some Russian spy in a seedy location.

Alone, he verbalised, 'I never considered that Lenin or Stalin would have any real impact on my life. But now I am myself imprisoned... well. Suddenly it's not an intellectual exercise. It is very real and deeply personal; life and death.' He now better understood why Orlonsky had become agitated after hearing Tristan's mutterings. He recalled Orlonsky's strident affirmation that Tristan and Cambridge graduates, and all students for that matter, would be destroyed by Stalin's regime as quickly as rabbits are by ferrets. The recollection was so clear that, for a moment, he believed that Orlonsky was in the cell with him. He smiled at the irony, 'Well, Count,' he murmured, 'It seems you were right. Here I am.'

The lieutenant's portrayal of the Petrograd uprising and his father's death had been vivid and Rupert imagined himself responding to the man: *Do you believe me when I say I understand? I would be angry if I had lost my father in this way. I know because, when I was a child, I was angry when my father died from an infection caused by a scratch to his face. I couldn't direct my anger at the government, it was not their fault, so I blamed God.* In Rupert's mind's eye, the lieutenant stiffened but then relaxed.

No, it is never easy to lose parent when you are young. He imaged the reply to be.

'I really understand things had to change,' Rupert said aloud, 'but does the future have to be built on hatred and fear?'

Speaking aloud with imaginary captors, I must truly be descending into madness, Rupert thought, but he could not help but defend the shred of sympathy he felt for the lieutenant. *We are all only human.*

In the gloom of his prison cell, Rupert wondered how Gatsby

would have coped with being held in a Russian prison. An image of the man in his tuxedo sipping champagne cocktails brought in by the guard made him smile and it lifted some of the melancholia that had settled with the cold into his bones.

Another fly roused itself from some crevice and veered drowsily into the wall, dropping to the floor with a final stuttering buzz. Rupert watched it twitch and grow still and wondered, not for the first time, how long it would be until he, too, folded his wings for good.

Innocence

Rupert had begun to dread Mondays, as the days immediately after Irēne's visit seemed to drag more than most. The day after Remembrance Sunday was no exception.

Listening to the service had summoned Rupert's thoughts back home, *How is Mum, what preparations are being made for war, what is happening further afield?* Even as a partial cripple, he felt he should be home and doing something to defend his family and country. He was beginning to feel both trapped and guilt ridden.

In the absence of any news of serious fighting involving Britain, Rupert concluded that perhaps the ambassador's prediction would hold true and hostilities would indeed result in a stalemate – with Finland's border with Russia moved back a bit and Poland being the only serious casualty. If the conflict did not escalate, it was comforting to think that life would remain relatively undisturbed. If he could not return home, perhaps he and Irēne would be able to get to know each other further, grow closer, become something. His heart rose. Then he recalled the conversation with Andris and shuddered as an image came to mind of the Red Army sweeping across the Baltic countries. *Surely not,* he thought, and he put it from his mind.

After lunch, Rupert was wheeled out to the patient's lounge and was placed near to a chair occupied by a tall, rather aristocratic looking man, with a splendid beard and moustache in the style of the Tsar and George V. He had a fine-boned, handsome face, but there was something stiff and haughty about the way he titled his chin and his thin mouth bore a self-congratulatory curl at the edges.

The man looked at Rupert and introduced himself without pause in German, 'Good afternoon. Otto Grunveld. I would stand, but my knees and toes are painful.'

'Rupert Lockart. Pleased to meet you.'

'I have difficulty walking. I don't think they can do much for me, but I need to be checked over as I'm due to leave Latvia in a few days.'

'Where are you going?'

'Poland.' Rupert's face registered surprise. Otto's smug smile widened and he folded his hands delicately on his chest.

'Yes, didn't you know, Herr Hitler has issued a call home to Baltic Germans to come and repopulate what was Prussia. Landowners will have estates similar to their own, businessmen will take over Polish firms and shopkeepers can carry on their trades. The same with doctors and lawyers, it is all organised. It will be a return to the good times before President Ulmanis decided to dispossess us Balts and dubiously redistribute the ill-gotten gains to the uneducated Lats.'

Rupert looked around the lounge to see who else was in the room as he wasn't sure everyone would welcome these comments. Otto continued. 'President Ulmanis has said good riddance but this is only posturing. He really knows who the power is behind the government, and they will be asking us to return soon enough when the country falls into chaos – if it is not overridden by the Russians before then.' Otto rounded off with a resounding, 'Either way, it is ruined.'

'Ruined?' replied Rupert instinctively, regretting his invitation for further unsavoury comment.
'The Baltic Germans have brought trade and wealth to Latvia since the time of the Hanseatic League. Even as part of the Russian Empire Baltic Germans were essential to the Tsar. We had large estates, that's true, but we imposed good governance

and order.' Otto stroked his beard and twiddled the end of his moustache. 'We gave the Tsar no cause to interfere with the tradition of regional government. Yes, there were a few troubles in 1905, but once the Russian Government had dealt with the problem and the Tsar had wisely reconsidered the benefits of reform, the old order was rebuilt.'

Wondering briefly what the 'old order' actually referred to, Rupert decided not to enquire further. Instead, he brought Otto back to the present day by asking, 'What is happening to the ethnic Poles if their land is being taken?'

'The Poles are a thin Germanic layer with dreadful material underneath. The Jews are even worse. Their towns are covered in dirt and everything is lice-ridden and depraved. Only a purposeful government can rule there. The Jews will be the first to go and we Germans will help to create cleanliness and order.' Otto's answer took Rupert's breath away. He was dumfounded and could not compose himself to reply. Otto continued, 'Jews! You wait to see how they behave when the Russians invade here; the Jews will grab the opportunity to pay back the Latvians, to go with the strongest, even if it is a strange and unacceptable power.'

After a few moments of silence, Rupert wheeled himself off to another part of the lounge. He was shocked by the blatant racism and anti Semitism. He wondered how widespread Otto's thinking and views might be amongst other Germans. It seemed this war had grown deeper, darker roots than he had imagined.

At visiting time Rupert was still sitting in the lounge when Andris came in looking for him. He congratulated Rupert on being out of bed and told him that he had brought a chess set on the off chance that he had regained his memory. Rupert was only too happy to agree and they soon found a suitable chair and table and laid out the chess set.

They started the game and at first Rupert was engrossed in thinking about his moves. However, he was soon distracted by his conversation with Otto Grunveld. Andris took his rook. Then, a mere minute later, one of his bishops. 'What is troubling you my friend? You are playing like you do not know the game.' Andris looked concerned. 'If your memory is not yet-'

'No, no,' Rupert said, 'It's not that. Sorry Andris, I have been shaken by a rather disturbing conversation.' He described his encounter with Otto. 'I think he is the first person in my life I genuinely disliked from the first instance.'

'You have lived a sheltered life haven't you?' Andris smiled. He reset Rupert's pieces.

'What do you think will happen to those Baltic Germans who leave for Poland? Do you really think they will be given the estates promised?' Andris turned down the corners of his mouth and shook his head.

'Eleven German ships have arrived in the Port of Riga and are moored in a double bank awaiting their cargo. It is said only the sick will have cabins and the rest must travel in the hold. The grass is never greener on the other side. It is a sign of things to come for them.'

Countering Rupert's next move, Andris said, 'In one way, the Baltic Germans are wise to leave. Munters stopped by recently and told us that Latvia has given the soviets permission to build special airfields and granted them the right of stationing thirty thousand military personnel. So, it seems we have already invited the Red Army into our home, why don't we just give them our beds now?'

'Maybe Uncle Joseph doesn't trust his friend Adolf after all, and needs the bases just in case Germany decides to invade.' Rupert knew he was in for a stern reply.

'Don't tell me that the Soviets are here to protect us from the Germans! Just because I look like a cabbage doesn't make me green.' He then looked around the lounge and, when he saw it was empty, he lowered his voice and continued. 'Remember, similar demands were sent to Finland and they have refused. I bet those plucky Finns put up a fight.'

Rupert asked Andris if he had any news about Britain's involvement in the war. Andris replied, 'I haven't heard a great deal. I know that British soldiers are posted on the Belgian border to support the defences of the French army, but I wouldn't like to be in the way of the German Panzer divisions if they decide to head to Paris. Apart from that, I think it is quiet... Rupert was pleased to hear that British soldiers were helping defend France and was sure that, however well equipped they were, the Germans couldn't simply stroll into Paris as if on a day out.

'What do you think your Metropolitan Vickers will be doing now overseas contracts must be limited?' Andris asked.

'That's an interesting question... I am sure British engineers will rise to the challenge of war.' Rupert imagined his uncle sitting at his draughtsboard helping design engines and other equipment for war. He said out loud, 'It might even be an exciting time to be an inventor or engineer.'

Both men were quiet for a while as they studied the board. Rupert made his move and, after Andris had responded, he ventured, 'When we were at your summerhouse, you asked about my chess tactics. I've had plenty of time to reflect on these, do you want to hear my thoughts?'

'Certainly.'

'We are taught that the key to playing chess successfully is to control the centre squares, specifically the four in the very middle. Obviously, this is because you can attack anywhere from the centre of the board and this allows you to control the pace and direction of the game.' Andris nodded. Rupert paused for dramatic effect. 'But, what if you control the middle by not being there?' He let the question hang in the air for a while before continuing. 'You will see that my rooks, queen, and knights are all on the perimeter controlling the squares leading to the centre, making it impossible for you to move into the middle without being taken.'

'I will pay close attention.'

Both settled down to concentrate on the game, which soon came to a characteristic end. 'Checkmate.' Rupert declared.

'You came into the centre after all.' Andris raised his voice in mock anger. Rupert looked at him out of the corner of his eyes with a smile on his face.

'Always keep your opponent guessing.' Andris turned down the corner of his mouth in an exaggerated way.

'If you weren't already in hospital...'

After the evening meal, Rupert asked if he could again listen to the radio before going to sleep. The nurse agreed and helped him to the lounge but, however carefully he moved the knob of the radio, the long waves of the BBC did not break, that night, on the Latvian shore. Listening to the buzz, crackle and high-pitched noise of the empty airwaves, it seemed to Rupert the concert he had heard from Manchester had been brought over on the wings of angels. *Perhaps they have deserted me,* he thought as he watched the sky darkening over Riga; *now, as the tide of war draws in.*

Better One Russian Dies

One night the taps on the pipes were feverish and incessant. It was obvious there was urgent news to be heard but Rupert was not privy to it.

As usual, after breakfast, Rupert was escorted to the toilet block joining other prisoners in their silent ablutions. But something felt different. Ablutions were customarily quick and economical, in order to finish in the allotted time. Today, as always, no one made eye contact, but the men were going about their washing with unnaturally slow, deliberate motion. The hairs on the back of Rupert's head prickled.

No sooner had Rupert squatted over one of the holes in the floor than there was a commotion. A broad shouldered man, whose bare torso was almost deathly pale, bellowed at another prisoner who was standing under the high, grilled window by the far end of the room. The guard at the door shouted for silence and stepped further into the toilet block. Taking no notice, the broad shouldered man swore at his adversary and went over and pushed him in the chest. The guard raised his gun so that he could use the butt to good effect and shouted, 'No talking,' striding towards what looked like the beginning of a brawl. Rupert stood up waiting for the thwack of rifle butt on unprotected bones.

As soon as the guard was well inside the room, one of the prisoners peeled away from the basin he had been standing at. There was the flash of a blade in the man's hand, before he stabbed the guard in his side, retracted the blade and stabbed him again. The guard stumbled and then crumpled on the floor, a terrible gargling sound bubbling from his throat.

A shot rang out so loud it seemed to split the room in two. He clapped his hands over his ears. The victim spun around and

Rupert saw, seemingly in slow motion, the splatter of blood shoot up, droplet by droplet from his left shoulder. In that, almost eternal, instant Rupert was surprised how strikingly red it was. A guard by the door swung his smoking gun around, shouting for the prisoners to get down. Rupert went to his knees, his own blood roaring in his ringing ears.

A moment's quiet was followed by the wail of a siren. Guards poured into the toilet block. The one who fired the shot rushed up to the guard's assailant, who was prostrate clutching his shoulder, and hit him with the butt of his rifle, producing an elemental moan. He disappeared in a crowd of kicking boots as the guards struck him again and again. When they pulled back, the prisoner turned a bloodied head and spat out a tooth. Two other guards pulled their wounded colleague out of the room but his body had gone limp and the gurgling sound had turned into a low rattle.

'Stay down, don't move.'

Rupert's stomach had shrunk into a tight, churning ball. He had no intention of shifting from the floor, nor, it seemed, did anyone else. He barely dared to breathe. The urine covering the floor began to soak into his trousers as he knelt.

Standing over the assailant, the guard pointed the muzzle of his gun at his head and Rupert turned his face away, bracing himself for the gunshot that would dispense summary justice, but the guard simply demanded that he stand. Clutching his wounded shoulder, the assailant obeyed, his bloody face etched with pain and defiance. Ordered out at gunpoint, he turned onto the prison landing and Rupert heard him shout out in Russian, 'Better one Russian dies than I live'. There was another terrible crack and the sound of a body hitting the floor.

Rupert remained knelt, huddled on the floor long after his legs had gone numb.

A guard watched over them, eyes darting from one possible assailant to another, until the arrival of a senior officer. The two men who had begun the original altercation were identified and they were ordered out, clearly under the suspicion of being co-conspirators. Eventually a guard came in and barked, 'Out you filth. Sleep well for your last night.' Then they were roughly escorted back to their cells. This time there was no shouting, nor banging of the railings. The prisoners moved in silence. On the walkway outside the bathroom, a pool of blood congealed slowly on the floor.

Rupert lay on his bed and stared at the ceiling. His mind was blank, in shock. His experience of violence had been limited to a few minor scuffles at school and although he had read of atrocities, and even taken part in an enactment of the Peterloo Massacre with his fellow choristers at Manchester Cathedral, he had never encountered violence like this.

Gradually, the churning nausea subsided and his mind started to work again. Later, he remembered Irēne telling him about how she had witnessed a bloodbath in Berlin when Nazis broke up a communist rally. Again, he realised how much more worldly-wise she was than him.

The violence he had seen made him wonder what ordinary life was like for the inhabitants of Riga. He thought of Irēne and his stomach lurched once more. *Will she see such violence as this?*

That night the prison was deathly quiet. Rupert could not sleep and paced his seven steps. He waited for the key to turn in his cell door and to be escorted to the interrogation room where he would surely be forced to reveal his part in the plot to kill the guard.

The window was open and Rupert listened out for the familiar grunts and groans of men sleeping badly, but all he could hear was silence. The hairs on the back of his arms stood up. He recognised this silence. He had heard it once before, many years ago at Wythenshawe when a tree had been felled in the woods beside his home. He lay, reliving the silence of the forest, that intake of breath, before the terrible rending crash. It fell in the wrong direction, bringing down a neighbouring tree that killed two of the onlookers. If Rupert had been standing ten yards nearer, he would have shared the same fate. 'Yes,' he thought, 'the silence before the tree came down is the same – full of foreboding. Full of death.'

Before the claxon sounded, Rupert was disturbed by a bang on the cell door and the appearance of a guard by his bedside. Ordered to leave, he was unable to even put on his jacket before he was pushed along the corridor. His typical morning drowsiness vanished. He was painfully aware of the guard's metal tipped boots on the floor, the sound echoing steadily around the black, vaulted roof like a tolling bell.

Stumbling into the exercise yard, Rupert hardly felt the chill of the cold, early morning air but he recognised a few of the faces of the men who had been with him in the toilet block. Of the eight men standing in a line in front of a pockmarked wall, two of them had nasty gashes with congealed blood on their cheeks. Their faces and exposed skin were the same colour as their grey trousers and grubby shirts in the semi darkness. Rupert's mouth went dry.

Less than twenty feet away an unkindness of soldiers stood to attention with rifles planted by their sides. With their greatcoats, black Ushanka hats and breath condensing in the icy morning air, they looked like thin, black chimneys.

With the butt of his rifle, the guard directed Rupert to join the men along the wall. His knees threatened to give way as he staggered towards the wall, the gaping bullet-holes across its surface seemed to open like mouths.

Rupert noticed the haddock-faced officer standing by the men. Images flashed before him as if sent from the flashbulbs of an attending press pack; Wythenshawe church, father in the kitchen garden, the conductor of the choir raising his batten, Orlonsky sitting by the fire, mother by the gate, Irene by his bed. He heard, 'Present Arms,' and experienced what can only be likened to a slowing of a film. Irene, standing before him, stretched her arms out and then slowly metamorphosed into the massive statue of Christ the Redeemer.

The officer barked an order. Rupert was grabbed by the arm and pulled from the row.

He looked towards the officer whose fishy eyes and lips gave no clue as to his emotions within. 'Take aim... Fire.' A volley of shots rang out and echoed from the surrounding walls. Rupert dropped to his knees and cried out — he could feel the bullets tearing into him, he was shot, surely he must die? Silence fell.

Rupert felt the breath sawing in and out of his lungs, the air cold and blissfully real. The floor beneath his palms was rough and solid. He ran his hands over his body, clutching, searching, but there were no wounds. He was unharmed. Dragged back upright, he looked towards the men but only saw what seemed to be a heap of bloodied rags lying by the wall. His mind went blank and was only vaguely aware of being pushed back to his cell.

The combination of bone chilling cold and the shock produced a violent shake in Rupert and as he lay on his bed it creaked and vibrated. Days passed without him recalling a single thought. Then he wondered, *Why save me? Why did I not die?* Then he felt angry, intensely so. *Why was I subjected to this terrible ordeal?*

Rupert brought the haddock-faced officer to mind and realised that if he was ever to meet him with the tables reversed, he would have no more qualm about dispatching this man than he would have about hitting a fish over the head he had caught from the River Mersey.

Unexpected Post

Drawing up a chair in the hospital lounge next to Rupert, Irēne said, 'It looks like Doctor Berzins has been rather busy this week with you. I see that your cast has been removed?'

'Having the cast off was wonderful as I can, at last, scratch that terrible itch that's been going on forever. But I am shocked to see how thin my leg is.' Rupert was going to reveal the scar on his leg to Irēne when into the lounge came Doctor Berzins together with two burly looking porters, one of whom carried a crutch.

'Good afternoon,' Dr Berzins inclined his head to Irēne. 'I thought we would take advantage of your visit to help Rupert take a few steps. It is time for him to exercise his legs.'

'Oh wonderful, how can I help?' Irēne asked.

'Just move a few metres away. We will lift Rupert out of his chair and get him to walk to you.'

Rupert was used to being transferred from his bed to the wheelchair but he was not used to straightening his leg. With the porters supporting him under the arms he tried to do that and it felt like he was unfolding centuries old, un-oiled leather. Stretching his tendons to what felt like breaking point, he grimaced and placed his weight on the weakened leg. Without the support of the porters it would surely have given way.

Irene stretched out her arms and hands and, with a porter either side to steady him, Rupert took five or six wobbly steps and then clutched Irēne. 'Well done.' She said triumphantly and kissed his forehead already covered with perspiration.

Doctor Berzins congratulated Rupert and then said, 'You don't look that pleased with yourself.'

Rupert was quiet, gazing down at his legs with a pinched expression. 'I didn't think walking would ever be that difficult. Will I ever fully recover?'

'Step by step.' Doctor Berzins answered. Rupert felt a delayed sense of elation. He had harboured the fear that he was crippled and now it was clear he was not. Yet there was a long road ahead.

Not wanting to voice that he'd been fearful, he said, 'In the past, I simply put one foot in front of the other. Now, it seems to involve so much more and my upper body is as stiff as a board.' Doctor Berzins presented him with a crutch that he immediately placed under his arm and said, 'If you know who Long John Silver is, you'll soon see I do quite a good impression of him.'

'Yes, I have read *Treasure Island*; I will bring in a parrot on my next visit.' Irēne replied

Once Doctor Berzins and the porters had vacated the lounge, and Rupert was seated once more, he told Irēne that he had missed her and asked how the visit to her mother had gone the weekend before. 'It was short but successful.' She replied, but did not offer any further details and he decided not to press her. Instead, he gave her his good news.

'I had unexpected letters from my mother and aunt this week. They were sent before my accident and they have taken more than four months to reach here.'

Taking the letters out of his dressing gown pocket, Rupert looked at the date stamp, ran his thumb over the raised stamp and recalled the feelings the receipt of these had induced. Whilst it had been lovely to look at the familiar handwriting, the fact that the letters had taken so long to arrive and had travelled such a circuitous route emphasised just how far home was away. He passed them over.

'They have more postmarks on them than an explorer's passport and have come via Denmark, Sweden, Finland and Estonia. It's amazing they have arrived at all.' Irēne remarked, returning them.

'Actually it is difficult for me to read because Mum writes about how much she is looking forward to my return. However, there's some news about Wythenshawe, would you like me to read some of it out?'

'Yes, that would be lovely.'

Rupert began with a brief introduction. 'You remember I told you that most of the land on Wythenshawe Estate had been sold to Manchester Corporation?' Irēne nodded. 'It was about two thousand five hundred acres and it was designated for housing ahead of slum clearance in the city centre.'

'I do not know what an acre is but it sounds like a lot of land.'

'And beautiful too, considering how close it is to Manchester. Well, Mum writes about this; she isn't very impressed.' He read an extract from the letter.

'You will see many changes when you come home. The houses they are building are coming closer to the Hall.

Slum clearance seems to mean scooping out the centre of the town and plonking it on the outskirts. This is all very well in a way but, considering the poor conditions in which they used to live, the new residents do a lot of complaining. They complain that 'out in the country' they are freezing and there are moans about restrictions in Corporation houses. They are not allowed to keep their houses and gardens as they want to, which, in the case of most, is full of poultry and pigeons. The biggest complaint is that there are too few pubs on the estate.'

Turning the pages of the letter, Rupert said, 'There is plenty of news about how they are turning the old Hall into an administrative centre and are setting up an art gallery there. Then, Mum hints at a surprise for me when I'm home. You can read the letter if you like?'

'But first, can you tell me something of your mother?' This was the first time Rupert had ever been asked to describe his mother and, his first thought was that he found it difficult to separate her from the house and her activities.

'Well, she is Mother; loving, kind and patient.'

Pausing, he wondered whether he sounded too much like a doting son but started again. 'First, let's start with the facts. My Mother, Catherine, works in the Hall on the Wythenshawe Estate. She lives in a lovely cottage there. Just two bedrooms, a parlour and scullery, but it's home, at least it is for my mother. During the week, I live with my aunt in Manchester, which is conveniently located for my work at Metro Vicks. My mother is about your height, has gingery blonde, curly hair and is slim. I think she is quite pretty and Dad definitely knew so, as he used to say, *your mother is the most beautiful woman in the world.* Said just within her earshot, of course. Mum always seems to be busy either cleaning or cooking and, even when sitting down in the evening will always be doing something like darning socks.'

Rupert concluded, 'I don't know what else to say to be honest.... I need more warning if you ask me such difficult questions.' Irēne smiled.

'I have a few more difficult questions but these can wait. In the meantime, can you tell me more about the cottage?'

'Now we are on easier ground. Mum's cottage is on the remains of the old Wythenshawe Estate. It's semi-detached, meaning that it has an adjoining neighbour, and it has its own garden. Ours is full of apple trees and there is a pear tree that grows against one of the walls. I can almost hear my mother calling, 'Rupe, can you pick some apples off the tree for me?"

'I am sure she has a lovely voice.'

'Yes, she has a very pleasant Cheshire accent. Above the front door is a beautiful stained glass window, which, interestingly, marks the seasonal shifts. From almost the exact time of the spring equinox the evening sun falls on the window flooding coloured light in to the hall and parlour. Contrastingly, after the autumn equinox, when the evening sun quickly falls below the line of the shed roof, the stained glass doesn't glow in the same way. But, there are other compensations such as cosy winter evenings. I seem to remember they always ended with Mum chasing me up the stairs saying, 'Fee, Fie, Foe Fum, I smell the blood of an Englishman. Be he 'live or be he dead, I'll grind his bones to make my bread'.

'That sounds scary.'
The afternoon progressed with the sharing of thoughts on the books exchanged and read in the intervening weeks. Rupert admitted to still finding it impossible to make any sense of the fairytales and said, 'It's apt to say that I shouldn't try to run before I can walk,' and asked, 'can you bring me a book for two to three year olds?'

'Of course... I will enjoy reading it to you. Now, would you like me to tell you the story of the *Happy Prince?*' Rupert nodded and she recounted the story of how a faithful swallow had given up its own life to be with his friend, the statue. He was amazed at the detail with which she could conjure a story. It was enthralling to watch and listen to her speak.

After Rupert had hugged Irēne and kissed her goodbye, he wondered whether he was the Happy Prince who had been befriended, ahead of winter, by the most wonderful of creatures. But he did not pursue the analogy — the outcome of the story was far from happy.

In the following week, the days leading up to Irēne's next visit seemed to extend in length. Time decelerated as the weekend crawled closer. He occupied himself by undertaking long walks around the ward and reading a novel, which he had picked out from the small, battered selection of donated books which sat on a worn wooden trolley in the patients' lounge.

When Irēne arrived at visiting time, Rupert was in the middle of one of his walks and called out, 'Aargh, Jim Lad, I'm the pirate we were speakin' of.'

'A pirate in a dressing gown, how unusual and with two legs as well.' Irēne said and Rupert, hobbling closer, gave her a kiss before asking her to put the crutches by the wall.

'Would you like to have a look at my pirate's scar?' Without waiting for an answer, he rolled up the trouser leg of his pyjamas as high as he could and pointed to a long scar running up his right leg from his knee. 'I got that off the coast of Jamaica.' Irēne studied the well-healed wound.

'The pirates must have access to the best of medical help for the scar to be so neat.'

'Pieces of eight, pieces of eight.'

The conversation was interrupted by the unexpected arrival of Andris. Introducing his visitors to each other, Rupert felt a great sense of pride when he said, 'Andris, this is Irēne.' Irēne informed him they had already met though the dam project.

Rupert eased himself into a chair and both visitors sat near to him. Andris said, 'I won't stay long, I just wanted to make sure you weren't too isolated here from news of the outside world.'

'Chamberlain is sending me personal updates on the progress of the war.' Rupert beamed at Irēne.

'Well, in that case, you've probably heard that the Soviets have invaded Finland. What did I say? Did your Prime Minister tell you that they intend to conquer all of Finland and that this is just the start of them reclaiming all of the old Tsarist lands?'

'Yes I did hear Finland has been invaded.'

Rupert stopped smiling and, realising that especially in the company of Andris he needed be serious, he asked for details of the invasion. Andris was happy to oblige. 'The Soviets possess more than three times as many soldiers as the Finns, thirty times as many aircraft, and a hundred times as many tanks. It won't be long before the Red Army enjoys the Helsinki nightlife.'

'How did it start?'

'The Russians have played the old trick of bombing themselves to make it look like they have been attacked and using this as a pretext to going on the offensive.'

'They bombed themselves!' Andris gave a sideways glance, which Rupert read as, 'How naïve.'

'Last Sunday a Soviet border post was shelled resulting, according to Soviet reports, in the deaths of four border guards and injuries to nine others. Of course, Finland had nothing to do with the attack, denied it and rejected demands to move the border. The Soviet Union claimed that the Finnish response was hostile, renounced the non-aggression pact and severed diplomatic relations with Finland on Wednesday.'

'I can hardly believe a country would bomb its own people.'

'You'd better toughen up and quickly.' Andris was quite sharp in his reply. 'Russia doesn't play cricket you know.'

Looking at Irēne, Rupert wondered if he was being made to look weak and ineffective in her eyes. Andris continued, 'With this little bit of theatre providing an opening, three days ago Soviet forces invaded Finland with full force. They bombed Helsinki inflicting substantial damage and civilian casualties. Can you believe this; Molotov told the rest of the world that they were dropping bread to the starving Finns.' Andris gave an explosive 'Pah!' and carried on. 'The Soviet attack, without a declaration of war, violated three different non-aggression pacts. But, it seems that, if you are prepared to sacrifice a few border guards, you can get away with anything.'

Rising from his chair, Andris informed them he had to leave and, once he had put on his coat and wished Irēne a safe journey home, he spoke in confidential tone to Rupert. 'I wish you a speedy recovery because when Finland falls we will all be running for our lives.'

With the departure of Andris, Rupert turned towards Irēne and said, 'Running for our lives. The Russians had better not come now as I can hardly walk! Anyway, maybe that's enough world news for today. Have you any local news?

'The mouse is still safe.' Rupert looked at her, his eyebrows furrowing, and she took out of her bag a small illustrated book, with a friendly looking, little brown mouse on the cover. 'Here is your next week's reading.' With that she reached over and tickled him under the chin. Rupert flicked through the small book, illustrated with a mouse being chased by a cat and the mouse then hiding away, eating cheese in his cosy home.

'I look forward to chatting like a three year old some day soon.'

After taking out a letter from his dressing gown, Rupert said, 'I didn't get around to telling you about the letter from my aunt. There is plenty in it about my anticipated return home. Apparently, aunty has made my uncle paint the outside privy in my honour, so I'm to be given a hero's welcome.'

'Do all the women in your life spoil you?'

'Absolutely,' He smiled, 'and it's very much appreciated.'

'What are the names of your aunt and uncle?'

'Well, Aunty is Margaret, but everyone calls her Peggie, and Uncle is George, but everyone calls him Nobby.'

'How very strange the English are.' Irēne smiled. 'I have heard of the name Peggie before but never Nobby.'

'I suppose it is strange. Every man with the surname Clark is given the name Nobby; don't ask me why!' Irēne said she knew why and the reason was that the English were completely mad.

As the end of visiting time drew near, Rupert asked Irēne to fetch the crutches. When she had done so he asked her to help him to his feet, which she did by placing a hand around his waist. He steadied himself.

'I only did that so I could have you close.' he said. He drew Irēne in and gave her a lingering kiss. It felt like being enclosed in warm velvet.

Distant Wythenshawe

Rupert had a feeling the meal was due to be delivered and ceased his seven steps with a turn. The fare was nothing much to look forward to but, at least, it broke up the day a little.

Sitting waiting for the familiar clank of the spy hole and the scrape and shove of the tray, Rupert began to think about the advice he had given Andris on playing chess, both before his accident and at the hospital. Having always assumed chess was a game that mirrored life, he now pondered, *'n this case how much of this so-called insight, which I so earnestly passed on to Andris, can be related to my own position?'* The arrival of his meal temporarily interrupted this train of thought.

After eating the thin soup of grey peas and the shred of pork fat, Rupert recalled he had once said to Andris that his success was down to handling what he didn't know better than his opponent. Now, he felt he had been arrogant and began to make a list of all the things he didn't know: whether he'd ever walk again without a limp, whether his mother was well and how she was coping without any proper contact from her son, whether he'd ever get home, whether Irēne would be waiting for him if he ever got out of prison? He wondered to himself, *And how am I handling these things? With the focus and finesse of an accomplished chess player? No. With sleeplessness and constant worrying.*

Rupert continued his self-analysis. *As for my advice about being able to control things without actually being there, well that was completely wrong. I'm not in complete control of anything, not even my own memory and certainly not my life. I might have a gift for chess, but I really don't know much about life.*

An image of the men shot by the firing squad came to mind and his skin crawled. He thought, *Why did we line up without at least an attempt to run at the soldiers and grab a rifle or overwhelm them?* Then he realised how futile such an act would have been and how, in the face of overwhelming force, you have to accept whatever the more powerful demand, even if it is merely standing to attention whilst they riddle you with bullets.

Deep into the night, Rupert turned the phrase 'London is ablaze' over and over in his mind. The facts, as far as he knew them, about the progress of the war swirled around his skull. For a moment, he thought of Europe as a giant chessboard, the pieces set. He shuddered. *I'm not even a pawn in the game and, even if I was, pawns are sacrificed for a greater goal.*

Rupert turned his mind from the image and sought solace in the wandering of Wythenshawe Hall. Moving methodically through the familiar rooms, he remembered the portrait of Robert Henry Grenville Tatton with his dog that hung in the hallway, a present from the tenant farmers on his coming of age. Rupert pondered on the nature of the relationship between the rich landowner, Robert, and the poor, but contented, tenant farmers. He thought, *This may have been a brief lull in the ebb and flow of power between the rich and the poor, Crown and State or maybe I was born in a perfect bubble, but this was my world.*

Rupert's mind drifted out of the Hall, towards the memorial dedicated to those estate workers who had given their lives in the Great War, which stood, cool and grey in the courtyard. He knew several more had died from Spanish Influenza. He spiralled around the memorial, heavy with a sense of loss, loss born of war. War had come, too, to Wythenshawe and now it might come again. It seemed to have already taken him. He imagined his own name, engraved in the smooth stone cross, the letters painted black. His leg gave a spasm of pain, as if in sympathy with Rupert's realisation of what had already changed and how the vestiges of what remained might be swept away forever.

The photograph of Robert Henry Grenville Tatton hanging in the library swam into view. He wore the tunic of a captain in the Oxford and Buckinghamshire Light Infantry, every inch an officer and hero. Rupert felt a dull pang of guilt as he thought of himself, cowering in his protected hovel of a foreign prison instead of being at home defending his mother and his home.

Unable to sleep, Rupert got out of bed, turned the bucket over, stood on it and managed to look out of the barred window. It was as if he hoped to see, over the top of the adjoining block, the distant woods of Wythenshawe or the small bell tower on the apex of the Hall's roof.

He speculated about being with Irēne and wondered what their life might be like if they lived in England. He thought of his aunt's life, which was dominated by looking after the house in Manchester. He couldn't see Irēne conforming to the traditional role of a British housewife; polishing the outside step, preparing meals, cleaning and waiting for her man to return from work.

The image of the stained glass window above his mother's front door created a picture of a rosy future. He swapped his parents for himself and Irēne and imagined them living together in the cottage on the estate. In this bucolic fantasy, Irēne would work in the Hall for Mrs. Egerton Tatton and he'd do his father's old job. There would always be fresh vegetables and, in the long evenings of winter, they could talk about the books they'd read. In the summer they could walk through the woods as far as Northenden and pick wild flowers along the banks of the River Mersey.

He was absorbed by his daydream when he remembered that this life could no longer exist. If he was to live in Wythenshawe, it would have to be in one of the Manchester Corporation houses. He couldn't see either of them being happy stuck on a corporation estate. Irēne was a city girl who was accustomed to going to the cinema, theatre, concert hall or opera whenever she wanted and, by the sound of it, Wythenshawe lacked even pubs.

Rupert stepped off the bucket and returned to his meagre world, his consciousness clinging to the only spark of light and life that seemed left to him: Irēne.

Men!

Visiting time rolled around once more and Rupert was sitting in the patients' lounge enrobed in his dressing gown, reading a copy of the *London Times*.

'Welcome to my club.', he called to an approaching Irēne, who bent down to give him a kiss. Feeling the winter's cold on her coat and skin, Rupert added, 'It must be well below zero outside.'

'I have never experienced anything like it before Christmas. Sometimes the temperature in January and February can be very low but this year the worst of the cold weather has arrived early.'

'In that case, old bean,' said Rupert, engaging his best Wooster bluster, 'pull up your chair by the fire, I'll get Jeeves to bring a warming rum and we can sit here reading the papers.' When she had taken off her coat, gloves and scarf and sat down, he said, 'I had forgotten about the newspapers the ambassador gave me when he first visited. I couldn't handle them properly at the time and they got put into the cupboard. Now, I've gone through one of them in some detail. Not terribly heartening, I must say.'

Conversation was cut short when two adults, followed by a large group of smartly dressed children, all in complimentary formal outfits, entered the room. Rupert counted the children as they passed him on their way to visiting an older looking man, who sat further along the lounge. He whispered to Irēne, 'Seven!'

'That is my favourite number.'

'Does that go for the number of children you want?' As soon as the words left his mouth, he felt his cheeks redden. He wondered whether he had inadvertently implied, *With me.*

'Actually I love children.' Irēne paused and then her tone changed as she continued. 'But boys grow into men and I am not sure about these at all.'

'What have men done to deserve such mistrust?'

'I suppose that my view has been formed by my experiences of the men my mother has been involved with. It is difficult to put the blame on any one man in particular, but Erich Hesse has definitely had a major influence. He mistreated women.' Rupert's eyes widened.

'He didn't physically touch you did he?'

'No, not at all. I was only a young girl and was ignored by him, but he did mistreat the women in his life and there were many.' Irēne continued. 'When he wanted to, Erich could really charm people. I noticed that he changed from being intense and opinionated to, that rarest of commodities, an attentive listener.'

'I'm told I am a good listener.' Rupert said, then, catching sight of Irēne's raised eyebrow, he felt a rush of embarrassment and added, 'Oh yes, I can listen to myself all day. Sorry, that was flippant of me, do go on, I shan't interrupt."

'He was a man who liked to be admired and loved by women, but when he got bored with them, he ruthlessly cast them off. If they worked for him, he criticised their work and was rude to them in public.'

Pausing, Irēne looked at Rupert with narrowed eyes, and asked, 'Are you such a man with a need to be liked by all women?' Rupert felt like he had been jabbed in the stomach. He wasn't used to answering such personal questions and took time to compose an answer.

'Well, that's a good question. I hope not. Of course, I like to be liked but women are a mystery to me. I suppose my going to boys' schools hasn't helped, and also most of the students at Cambridge were male.'

'Have you ever had a girlfriend?' This was the direct question he had been dreading, but he answered it truthfully.

'Never.'

Rupert wished she would change the subject. In his mind the question could easily have been, 'Are you a virgin?'. His first visit to London, the night out with Orlonsky that ended at a Mayfair club, flickered in his head. He'd resolved never tell anyone about that, even if he were subjected to torture.

Tearing himself away from the lurking memory of Mayfair, Rupert said, 'Women in England seem to be from a different planet or speak a different language or something, so I find it hard to get to know any of them. In any case, I was too working class to attract any eligible lady I might have come across at Cambridge and now, I'm seen as too upper class by the girls I meet at work. No, that's probably unfair. I think they see me as too serious, I know I can come across in that way at times. That probably means that they also find me to be boring. In a nutshell, I have always been hopelessly embarrassed in the presence of girls and ladies.'

'You do not seem to be hopelessly embarrassed with me.'

'I feel comfortable with you.'

'Like a slipper?'

'No, not at all. But it seems I've known you a long time.' He knew he wasn't handling this well and added, 'That is, I feel very close to you.' He placed both hands on the arms of his chair and hoisted himself up to a standing position. Irène moved

153

closer to steady him and he took hold of her, brought her close and kissed her fully and deeply 'Even if it is in front of the children,' he murmured.

The kiss dissipated some of his inner tension, but Rupert knew that he might be more like Erich Hesse than he cared to admit. He turned the conversation aside, asking Irēne whether she had managed to see any films or even gone to the opera.

'You are good at changing the subject,' she said. She gave him a searching look but didn't press him anymore. Instead, she told him she had been to see *Madame Butterfly* with Katerīna. She gasped when Rupert wryly admitted that he didn't know the story and recounted it for him. 'It is a story of betrayal,' she said, 'Lieutenant Pinkerton marries the beautiful Cho Cho San but later leaves her with a baby.' She went into detail and Rupert sat in rapt attention. When she had finished, she said, 'So, we did not quite change the subject,' and, with exaggerated disgust in her voice, concluded, 'Men!'

Rupert wanted to drop the subject, even with a tacit admission that he was 'guilty as charged'. He was able to distract Irēne by saying, 'Have a look at these papers. See here, this is the issue printed on the day of my accident. It's interesting to know what the rest of the world was doing whilst I was getting my bump on the head.'

'And what were they doing?' He took hold of the newspaper dated 25th August 1939.

'Well, the strange thing is that there is no big news about the upcoming war. It is as if everyone wanted to believe that life would go on forever, just as it was. Look here.' He passed the paper and pointed out the advert for the Cunard White Star Line:

Express Service to New York from Southampton/Cherbourg. Queen Mary sails again Wednesday Aug 31.

'We could've visited Gatsby.' Rupert said.

'You said you didn't like him.' Irēne commented and added, 'You do have funny papers in England. There are no headlines; only adverts and notices of births and deaths.'

'For some, birth and death is big news.' He then pointed to an article about how a lawn tennis competition at Budleigh Salterton had proceeded at a merry pace despite a lingering mist.

Rupert was enjoying this sharing of news articles. Not only was it amusing, it also reminded him of the happy times with his parents, who had a similar habit. He recalled that his father always preceded the sharing of a news article with, 'Mother, you are never going to believe this'. He resisted the urge to use this phraseology when he talked to Irēne about Herr Hitler's reply to a letter from the French Premier about German intentions towards Poland. He read out an extract of the text in the paper dated 26th August.

'Herr Prime Minister, I understand the misgivings which you express. I too have never overlooked the high obligation which is laid on those who are placed over the fate of nations. As an old front soldier myself I know, as you do, the horrors of war....'

'He means to take the land corridor in Poland. You know I think he truly believes it to be rightfully his. He writes in a very appeasing manner and sounds sincere, but he ruins it with the most terrible threats. Look what he says at the end. *That our two people shall enter into a new and bloody extermination over the question is very distressing.* Extermination! What a word to use. It's amazing what a difference a day makes. In your paper there is hardly a word about the war. In this one it's all about cancellation of air and sea services, mobilisation and emergency powers, so, clearly, everyone believes Hitler is going to invade Poland.'

'I lived in Berlin during at the time when Hitler was rising to power.' Irēne looked grave. 'It was clear to everyone that he had no intention of appeasing anyone. Not wanting to hear the truth may have cost the rest of the world a great deal.'

Rupert agreed with Irēne and remained silent for a while, pondering the impact of Britain's lack of preparation for war on its outcome. 'It is not all bad news.' He tried to lighten the tone. 'The weather is nice in the health resorts. It is seventy two degrees in Morecambe, the nearest resort to Manchester - although it does report drizzle.'

'Seventy-two degrees! But I thought England was cool in climate? That sounds like it is close to literally boiling.'

Rupert laughed, 'Sorry, I slipped into my old ways; seventy-two degrees Fahrenheit is about twenty-two degrees Celsius.' He laughed a little more at the thought of holidaymakers sizzling like sausages on the promenade.

That night Rupert's sleep was disturbed, his leg ached and his conscience pricked him. Irēne's question rang in his ears: 'Are you such a man?' He wondered, *What sort of man am I? Not a bold one for sure; it took Irēne to initiate the first proper kiss. Certainly not the sort to handle any real hardship with aplomb.*

Men

Seated at the small desk in his prison cell, Rupert reflected on the accuracy of his own recollection of his time in hospital. The desk reminded him of being at Wythenshawe School and he was sure that his teacher, the strict Miss West, would not have awarded a gold star for his recall skills. Already, memories were fading; he couldn't even accurately bring the level of pain he experienced after the accident to mind. However, he recalled with absolute clarity the reading of the papers together in hospital. How strange that, of all things, this act of domestic simplicity remained so clearly and brought with it such contentment.

In the dead of night the claxon blared and there were distant shouts. Disturbed and fully awake, Rupert could not go back to sleep and sat thinking about the oppressive prison regime. Manchester had its Strangeways Prison and Rupert knew it accommodated some particularly nasty and dangerous characters. He wondered whether his fellow prisoners had done anything wrong or were just, like himself, guilty of being at the wrong place at the wrong time?

Irène's exclamation, 'Men!', seemed to float through the dark window and Rupert, dwelling on the type of man who was prepared to carry out atrocities in the name of Stalin, grimaced. He recalled one or two masters at the cathedral school who were over zealous with their use of the cane but, however hard he tried, he failed to understand the motivation of the men who were in charge of Russian justice. Perhaps they simply enjoyed cruelty.

Rupert remembered a conversation he had once had with a fellow patient whilst in the Second City Hospital. The man, named Vladimir, was elderly and had the look of the old Tolstoy about him with his grey hair and long beard.

Vladimir was originally from Russia although he had retired to a small homestead deep in the Latvian countryside with his Latvian wife. Rupert enjoyed getting to know him over the week he was in hospital recovering from a deep wound to his thigh delivered by a wild boar. They swapped experiences, Vladimir talking about his work on the Russian railways and Rupert telling of life at Metropolitan Vickers. Yet not all of Valdimir's stories had been pleasant.

'I met American military officers and their translators when I was senior controller on Russian State Railway.' Vladimir had said. He had explained that after the Great War there was mass starvation in the villages even though the Americans had sent huge amounts of wheat and medical supplies to help avert a disaster. The poor state of the rolling stock had meant these could not easily be moved once delivered to Moscow. In addition, vital people, accused of being wreckers, were removed from their posts and soon nobody was left who cared.

Rupert was increasingly fascinated by Russia; a strange land that had seemed so distant but was now his neighbour.

Vladimir had said, 'It all came to head at Baloshov Junction where there was such congestion that trains could not come or go.' He stopped, though Rupert could tell the story was not yet at an end.

'What happened next?' Rupert asked.

Vladimir did not immediately respond, as if weighing up what he could say. 'I was summoned to attend meeting in Moscow,' he said, slowly, 'and was surprised to find that Felix Dzerzhinsky headed it. He was meeting Colonel Haskell, an American officer who was in charge of aid convoys. At this meeting Haskell was angry and direct. Translator said that American people had not contributed money to buy food and shipment to Russia to have it sit in sidings at desolate railway station. Haskell demanded

Dzerzhinsky arrange for convoys to be moved even if it meant sending last working locomotive there. If it wasn't done, Haskell told Dzerzhinsky he would immediately cable America ordering all further supplies to be stopped. I do not think Dzerzhinsky had ever been talked to like that before.'

Vladimir dropped his voice to that of a confidential whisper. 'Dzerzhinsky looked at American Colonel for short time and I really thought he was going to tell him to go to hell but he ushered us out of meeting without saying word to him. Dzerzhinsky turned to me and said, *You know of limited time there is to carry out details. These trains will move and if you fail - supreme punishment is waiting you. That is all. Go.* There was not even flicker of emotion on his face.'

'Sorry for my ignorance but who is this Felix Dzerzhinsky? Rupert enquired.

'You have never heard of him? Well, let's hope you never experience results of his legacy. He was founder of Cheka. When Dzerzhinsky faced me, I looked into his eyes for brief moment. They were grey, cloudy and melancholy. Cold. They revealed secret of his soul. The eyes of a man happy to send thousands of people to their deaths. He is dead now but we have his shadow hanging over us.'

Rupert thought of the dead eyes of the haddock-faced officer and realised that he could no more understand the mind of a man like Dzerzhinsky, or even that of his interrogator, than he could fully appreciate how evolutionary forces over aeons could have resulted in something as exquisitely expressive as the human eye.

He turned his mind away in search of good men, of the men he knew best. He thought of his father who had served in the Cheshire Regiment and had never spoken of his efforts on the Western Front, who had diligently tended the kitchen gardens at the Hall, had been so gentle and calm. He thought about Lord Simon, who was so generous, honest and welcoming. He remembered walking with him in the grounds of the Hall, around the manicured lawns.

He remembered that Lord Simon, sporting his familiar tweed suit, had once asked of him what his philosophy of life was; then apologised for asking such a broad question when Rupert stumbled for a clear response. Then, without lecturing, Lord Simon began to talk to him about his own philosophy. He could hear his voice with its light Cheshire accent as if Lord Simon were seated at his prison desk, not four feet from him. 'Whilst I can imagine, and promote, a new way of living for thousands of impoverished people, I lack the imagination to fully understand why some people are able to combine personal happiness with unconcern for the welfare of others. My religion, if you can call it that, is wanting to leave the world better than I found it.'

Yes, Lord Simon was a good man. His words struck a telling contrast to the 'end justifies the means' philosophy Rupert now understood to underpin the Soviet system.

Rupert recalled that Irēne had on one occasion compared him to Lord Simon and accused them both of being naïve. Now, in the darkness, he felt the slithering of a bitter desire, '*If I want to leave the world a better place, I could start by killing that haddock-faced officer who slaughtered those men.*' As soon as the thought had seeped into his mind, Rupert shot out of bed and brushed himself down as if trying to rid himself of some filth that clung to him. *What monstrosity is this?* He thought, appalled, *Can I truly be thinking such things?* His stomach turned over. *When this is over, who will I be? Will I be so changed that I will not settle to anything? Will I be so changed I can no longer love-- like a husband?* Irēne's face rose in his mind, soft and full of light. *No*, he thought, *that could never be possible.*

Christmas 1940

Rupert marked off the days and although his repetitive routines had robbed time of its relevance, he knew Christmas was drawing near. The festive period brought no changes to the monotonous prison regime or its diet. On the 24th of December, the evening meal was the same grey cabbage stew as always. With his fork, Rupert found a measly piece of pork nestling at the bottom of the aluminium bowl and, popping this into his mouth, he tried to savour it. His stomach twinged as he thought of his magnificent goose cooked each year by his mother. In a rush, Christmas at Wythenshawe filled his mind.

He remembered the shivery thrill of Christmas morning; waking early, full of excitement, in the knowledge that, after the morning services, he'd return to Wythenshawe and his decorated home to open Christmas presents. He recalled his donning the chorister's gown, with the ruched collar pushing up against his chin. The boys would joke and jostle with each other in the vestry and then follow the choirmaster out into the quire as if obedient angels. He felt the vibration of the organ and the harmonics of his fellow singers. He mouthed the words of a Psalm he had sung many times in Manchester.

My God, my God, why hast thou forsaken me? Why art thou so far from helping me, and from the words of my roaring?
O my God, I cry in the day time, but thou hearest not; and in the night season, and am not silent.

The organ stopped. Rupert felt the hum dissipate. He opened his eyes to the gloom of a Russian prison. He wondered if he was going mad. His blood began to boil and without any clear intention he took the chair, moved it to the barred window and climbed on it to see out.

All he could see was a gloomy leaden sky and the roof of the adjoining block. He felt a churning in his stomach and, addressing the nothingness outside, spoke in a whisper. 'Why did You wake me from my slumber? Why am I still alive? Did Death visit me and You told him it wasn't my time? Did You want to test your little chorister by letting him fall in love and then snatching that joy away? In so doing, and incarcerating me here, did you want me to rise above myself, to become a man and move closer to the divine truth?'

Rupert's voice gradually rose in volume. 'Did You want a new person to emerge from this living hell of continual silence, a finer man capable of forgiving those who trespass against us? Did You choose me to bear pain, anguish and loss so that I could emerge stronger and nobler than before? Well, I can tell you, you failed. Did You do all of this so that I should learn what anger is?' Rupert suddenly shouted, 'Well You succeeded. I have an anger of such intensity it will consume me long before it burns those responsible for my pain.' Then, he screamed out of the cell window, 'I am so fucking angry,' stepped down, moved to his bed and lay on it, spent.

The next day, Rupert felt submerged under the weight of self-recrimination. In bitter frustration, he thought about the opportunities to escape this terrible incarceration he had missed. Then after a full-blown assault upon himself, he suddenly stopped the onslaught as if he was fighting a beaten opponent. *This helplessness,* he thought, *it began last Christmas. That's when I lost control, truly, for the first time.*

Christmas 1939

Rupert's spirits were low as he waited for visiting time. It was Sunday 17th December, barely a week before Christmas. He didn't want to dwell on this being Irēne's last visit until New Year's Eve. Therefore, he turned his thoughts towards Wythenshawe, his mother and the cottage, which would be cosily decorated ready for Christmas. *God knows how she is.* He hated to think of her alone. Andris's warning about the Russian intention to reclaim its lost territories came to mind. *Just like the incoming tide,* he thought, *it's a force that can't be resisted.'* Rupert remembered the British Ambassador talking about evacuation plans and he hoped that, if there were an invasion, he'd be plucked out of path of the incoming tide just in time.

The arrival of Irēne, and the receipt of a kiss in greeting, immediately dissipated his low spirits. She carried a slim, wrapped box and handed to Rupert with the words, 'Look what Saint Nicholas has brought you.'

'I have a present for you too.' He said and picked up a small parcel from the table beside his chair and passed it to Irēne

'Let's open them now, you first.'

Irēne's gift, neatly wrapped and tied with simple string, was a box containing three red silk handkerchiefs. 'These are from my Grandfather's shop; have you seen the monogram?' She asked and Rupert, closely examining one of the handkerchiefs, rubbed his thumb over the raised initials, RL, embroidered in one corner.

'These are so special that I'd hate to use them, other than for dressing my jacket pocket at the opera.'

'You will look such a dandy that Bertie Wooster would be proud of you.' On opening her present, Irēne found it was a framed photograph of Rupert overlooking the Daugava River. He explained, 'I managed to get a message to Walter; he took a lot of pictures on our expedition up the river valley and he was happy to give me a copy of this one. I hope you don't think it an arrogant gift' Irēne studied the photograph.

'Not at all! With your shirt half undone, you look like a real explorer and very handsome I might add.' She grasped his hand, 'It is a perfect gift. It will be good to take something of you home with me, at least, in a way.' Rupert felt the colour rise to his cheeks. He dropped his gaze to the photograph.

'Those happy, carefree days seem a long time ago.'

'They will return, you are already beginning to walk again.'

Irēne spoke about her plans to go to her Grandparents' house and described what the festivities would be like there. Rupert was intrigued that they followed the traditions of eating goose on Christmas Eve and marking the birth of Christ even though her grandfather was Jewish. Then, they chatted idly for a while, avoiding the subject of the New Year and the fact that this would inevitably bring big changes. They could look forward to Rupert leaving hospital, but otherwise the future was clouded in uncertainty. When it was time to depart, they clung to each other at the door, locked in a tight embrace. Rupert kissed Irēne tenderly, willing himself to hold on to the sensation of her mouth against his and the smell of her skin. At length, they drew apart, their fingertips lingering together. The lift doors clanked shut in front of Irēne and Rupert experienced a physical pain in his chest as if he had been caught between the closing doors. He felt that his close connection to Irēne had been severed and, with it, his sense of belonging in the Latvia.

Returning to the patients' lounge and, noting the absence of Christmas decorations, Rupert felt that it looked bleak and unhomelike. He had been told earlier that it was the hospital's custom to put up decorations only on Christmas Eve and now he imagined his mother's house adorned with its well decorated Christmas tree, homemade paper chains and a huge holly wreath burdened with berries on the front door. Rupert felt sad and alone and, wondering how his mother must feel without him at Christmas for the second year running, he felt a churning sensation in his stomach and a desperate need to be home again.

The arrival of Christmas Day tightened a constriction that had been developing around Rupert's throat. Just before the serving of a Christmas meal to the few patients remaining on the ward, and sitting by the window, looking out into a grey, upon grey sky, he listened to the muffled tolling of a single, distant church bell. Recalling the majestic and sonorous sound of Manchester Cathedral's ten magnificent bells change ringing, the comparison only amplified a feeling that he was a foreigner in a foreign land, far from home and far from safety. By the time the meal was served, it was as if someone's thumbs were digging into his windpipe and he doubted whether he could eat even a mouthful of the festive fare.

A week later, on New Year's Eve, dozing after lunch, Rupert sat in the patients' lounge next to the sparsely decorated Christmas tree, the only festive addition to the ward. His mind had wandered to the New Year's Eve Party at Wythenshawe Hall that had been an annual tradition, but his reminiscence was broken by sharp footsteps approaching the doorway and looked up to see the British Ambassador.

Giving a quick wave to Rupert, before brushing the snow off his arms and depositing his Crombie coat, cashmere scarf and trilby on the stand by the door, the ambassador made his way over to Rupert, who was now out of his chair. The ambassador wished him, 'Seasons Greetings,' and added, 'I'm pleased to see you look fit and well. Hospital food seems to suit you.' Rupert briefly wondered whether the ambassador was insinuating he was getting fat, but had no chance to formulate a suitable response as the ambassador moved on. 'I'm afraid I don't have much time for pleasantries today. Evacuation plans are in place and we need to execute them now.'

Indicating that Rupert should sit down, the ambassador pulled up a chair for himself before continuing in a hushed tone, 'I can't give you any specific details, but you will know, I'm sure, that the Russians have invaded Finland. Britain and France are trying to arrange some military support for the Finns, but, quite frankly, the Swedes and Norwegians are blocking every move, and it is highly likely Finland will soon succumb to the overwhelming force of the Soviet army. Don't ask me why the Scandinavians are proving to be less than united. If Finland falls, then the Russians might not stop until they have their hands firmly on the Swedish iron ore deposits.' He glanced at Rupert, who was doing his best to arrange his in what he hoped was a look of solemn understanding. The ambassador seemed unconvinced. He continued. 'Anyway, before the Russians make life more complicated than it is already, it's time to depart. I am sure you must be desperate to get back to England to do your bit.' Rupert felt a tightening in his stomach. The ambassador's words brought half-submerged thoughts about his duty to his country to the forefront of his mind.

The ambassador continued, 'There's an opportunity to fly out via a safe route avoiding the Luftwaffe. We are waiting for the right weather conditions, but the evacuation is imminent.' Rupert immediately thought of his mother and the welcome he would receive on returning to Wythenshawe. 'I've informed the director here; once you get word to proceed, he will arrange an ambulance to get you to our point of departure. Don't be late, as the plane won't be hanging around.' Rupert asked whether they might depart later that day and the ambassador replied, 'With the weather so miserable at the moment, it is unlikely we will be flying in the next few days, so enjoy your last New Year's Eve party in Latvia. When the weather improves and settles into a decent spell, expect a call.'

Before the ambassador left, he reminded Rupert to bring his passport and then, after the slightest of hesitations, said, 'Actually it would be best if I took it now as it will save time registering you as a passenger with the Latvian authorities.' Rupert told him that his passport was in the bottom of his bedside cupboard and asked if he wouldn't mind waiting a few minutes whilst he fetched it. The ambassador insisted that he fetch it himself. With Rupert's passport safely in his pocket, Charles Orde bade him farewell. Thanking the ambassador for coming to see him personally, Rupert wished him, 'Happy New Year'. Just before the ambassador reached the door he turned and said, 'Remember, as soon as you get the note, get a move on and don't be late.'

Rupert was left feeling shaken and dizzy. His heart was racing and he sat back in his chair and breathed deeply as the anxiety rose in him like water. The imminent flight was of no concern, for he had no fear of flying. But to leave Irēne? He pulled himself to his feet and paced back and forth across the lounge. He was oblivious to the pain in his leg and that his crutch nearly swept all before it each time he turned sharply around. Rupert thought about 'doing his bit' and realised that a huge enlistment campaign must be underway back at home, but not for long could he drag his mind away from contemplating the potential loss of Irēne.

When she came through to the patients' lounge Rupert limped to her side, hugged her tightly and helped her off with her heavy woollen coat, damp from melted snow. Before she had sat down he told her about the ambassador's visit and exclaimed, 'I have to be ready to leave at any time. They will send a message and I must be at the rendezvous at the time they give.'

'That is good news.' Irēne took his hand and, clearly

noticing his anxious expression, asked, 'Is it not?'

'I don't want to leave; that is, of course, I want to go home and see my mother, and help with the war effort, but... I don't want to leave you.' Irēne gently squeezed Rupert's hand.

'That is lovely of you to say. I do not want you to go either...' Both were silent for a while before Irēne continued. 'But you need to go. England is your home and is being threatened and your mother has been waiting a long time for your return. And if there is an invasion, this is the worst place to be a lone Englishman without any rights or protection.'

Rupert sat taking this in before saying, 'What if you came with me and I explained to the ambassador about us; that we have met and...' He wanted to say, 'fallen in love,' but did not, as he was only sure that it was he who was in love. Then he added, 'Maybe I could persuade him to take you too?'

'For a Cambridge graduate and intelligent chess player you really are a *dummkopf.*' Irēne's voice was soft and gentle. 'When it comes to an evacuation, plans will have been put in place and seats allocated; they will only take those who are on the list. No, when the message arrives you must leave immediately and without hesitation.'

'I cannot leave,' Rupert said, getting to his feet and seizing her hands. He realised what he should have asked Irēne before, 'That is I cannot leave without taking you with me, at least in my heart...' Indeed his heart felt like it might burst from his throat, but Rupert knew the words must come. He looked into her face.

'Irēne, will you marry me?'

Her wide eyes filled with light and she drew him to her. They gripped each other. Rupert hardly dared to breathe. 'The answer is yes. Yes, I will.' She whispered in his ear.

The joy filled Rupert like electricity, tempered only by the dull, icy knowledge that he would be separated from his new fiancé within the next few days. Taking both of Rupert's hands in hers, Irēne said, 'You do not need to marry me to keep me in your heart. And anyway, is there time? Maybe you will be summoned tonight?'

'No, not tonight, the weather is too bad. But it will take place within a few days as soon as the weather settles... At least we are engaged and can pick up our lives as soon as this madness has finished.'

'I know the British are crazy but I see they are lovable too.'

As it was New Year's Eve, visiting time had been extended and at nine o' clock the Hospital Director, looking happy and flushed, arrived in the ward with a bottle of champagne, together with a small entourage of nurses. One of them carried a tray of glasses; the director poured champagne into these for the small number of patients who had remained in the ward over the Christmas period and in Latvian and German wished them, 'Happy New Year.'

As the flutes were passed around, Rupert said that he had an announcement to make and duly told the small group that Irēne had accepted his proposal of marriage. The director immediately said, 'Congratulations,' and once everyone had a glass he toasted the couple. He then burst into song, surprising Rupert who wondered how many glasses of champagne the director had already consumed before visiting the ward.

The director had a good bass-baritone voice and Irēne, recognising the song, began to accompany him. Rupert soon picked up the melody and began to hum along. Once a few other people had joined in, there was quite a chorus. Everyone laughed and clapped as the director made a final flourish at the end of the song and, clearly enjoying himself, he launched into another. This proved even more popular and by the end of it, all in the ward, including the nurses, were in full voice.

Drawing the Minox camera out of his dressing gown's pocket, Rupert announced, 'Such a splendid occasion needs to be recorded for posterity.' He looked over to Irēne to see if she'd object, but she gave no hint of disapproval. The director was intrigued by the camera and, after brief instructions, took charge, commanding the nurses to line up behind the betrothed.

The nurses stood in a regimented line with all the seriousness of people attending an identity parade. There was a brief holdup, as the director tried to look through the lens window rather than the viewfinder. Finally, he was ready to take the picture and did so with a clumsy prod of the shutter release button. Rupert had his hand around Irēne's waist and, as he heard the shutter click, he had the distinct impression that Irēne had pulled a sad face. With the nurses also striking a serious pose, he wondered how he was going to explain why he was the only one smiling in the photograph, whilst being surrounded by pretty but glum looking women.

At ten o' clock visiting time ended and Rupert felt a sudden mood shift from elation to trepidation. He didn't want to leave Irēne but consoled himself by saying, 'It will take time for the weather to settle, so I look forward to seeing you before I leave.' They had agreed that she would return in two day's time, as she had to work late the next day. After a drawn-out departure, Rupert walked back to his room. He tried to hang onto the beautiful sensation of his lips meeting Irēne's and of embracing her. He was acutely aware of his enflamed desire.

Spilve Aerodrome

When Rupert awoke the next day he could see there was still low cloud and, from the movement of the branches outside, it seemed a strong wind was still blowing; certainly these were not ideal flying conditions. He was looking forward to leaving the hospital and going home, but he didn't want the good weather to arrive so quickly that he was called before he was able to see Irēne once more. He was anxious that, because of the war, there would potentially be many months, a year or, God forbid, even longer, before he'd see Irēne again. *And in war,* he thought, *who knows if indeed we will see each other again.* He didn't want to think about the implications of the Russians invading Latvia. Fervently, he hoped that the Finns were teaching the Soviets that they couldn't simply walk into neighbouring countries.

The previous night he had gone to bed as happy as he could ever remember. Now, he felt increasingly agitated and the day dragged on as if it was a fortnight. *Let me see her one more time please!*

During the day, a fellow patient had recounted his experience of witnessing a terrible crush, when huge crowds had gathered at Khodynka Field in Moscow to celebrate the coronation of the new Tsar. That night Rupert was restless and his dreams were disturbing. Elegant men with beards and women in flowing white dresses danced gracefully together under sunlit marquees. Then, the scene changed. He was in the midst of a vast crowd pouring down the side of a huge depression to catch a glimpse of the Tsar with his new bride, Princess Alexandra of Hesse. The ground rose steeply on the other side of the depression and the grass was wet and sticky with mud. Many people could not clamber up this slope and there was a crush as the people following behind could not stop. Layers of heaving bodies built-up resulting in bone crunching compression, blue faces, vomiting, gasping for air...

Rupert awoke sweating with an uncomfortable sense that the dream foretold sudden change from perfection to disaster. He shook his head to remove the association. When the dawn broke he was pleased to see that the sky was again cloudy and the wind hadn't abated. *Not today.* He looked forward to seeing Irēne that evening.

Rupert shaved well and changed into his outdoor clothes, more in the way of a practice run than in any real expectation of the Legation informing him he was to meet up with the other evacuees. It felt strange to him to put on trousers and a shirt. Indeed the process of dressing took a considerable time, and was not without pain, as he had to lie on his bed and somehow pull on the trousers without being able to fully bend his right leg.

Once dressed, he could neither read nor rest, so he paced up and down the ward, looking up at the doorway as soon as anyone came into the ward, although he knew that Irēne wouldn't come until after she finished work. The morning and early afternoon passed without any news or visit. Then, shortly after lunch, Doctor Berzins burst through the ward doors and ran towards Rupert, a letter clutched in his hand. Rupert took it. Attn; R B Lockart, c/o Second City Hospital. His surname was badly smudged. He tore open the envelope and read the short note enclosed.

Dear Mr. Lockart,

As informed of recent evacuation procedures, it is urgent you meet us at 2.00pm sharp today at Spilve Aerodrome.

Bring this letter and show it to the guard on the gate.

Yours Faithfully

Reginald Perkins
Representative

Letting out a strangled cry, Rupert looked up at the clock that showed the time as one-fifty in the afternoon. He shouted, 'What is this, how has this happened?' He looked around for the small bag that he was to take to the airport before crying out, 'Please! My plane leaves at two!'

Grabbing Rupert's bag, Doctor Berzins said, 'There will be an ambulance at the front. Now hurry put on your warm coat and scarf, it's minus fifteen degrees outside.' Rupert rushed as best he could to his room, threw on his coat, grabbed his crutches and hurried to the lift. Much to his frustration, this clanked and whirred and stopped and started at its own pace.

Outside, the cold assaulted Rupert just as physically as if he had run into plate glass. He took short breaths and was aware of a prickling in his throat, but he did not have time to dwell on the extreme temperature. It was already two o'clock by the time that he had been helped into the ambulance. Doctor Berzins shouted for the driver to go, as fast as he could, to Spilve Aerodrome, which Rupert knew to be on the other side of the city.

The first bump in the road sent a shock wave of pain up Rupert's leg and he had to bend double in an attempt to prevent it running up his entire body. Gritting his teeth, he asked Doctor Berzins, 'Why wasn't this delivered sooner?' Doctor Berzins fiddled with his bow tie.

'It was handed in a few hours ago at reception, but the lady there doesn't speak English and knew that we don't have a patient by the apparent name on the envelope.' He spelt out ATTN and continued. 'The lady decided to leave it until I arrived.'

'If I miss the plane because of this, the Gods must really be against me.' He looked accusingly at Doctor Berzins.

Rupert hadn't been out of the hospital for over four months and the brightness of the sun on the reflected snow made him screw up his eyes. But he gave no consideration to this, as his heart raced in the frantic hope they would somehow arrive in time for take off. The ambulance driver went as fast as he dared over the cobbles of *Vienibas Gatve* and then down past the frozen ponds in *Arkadijas Parcs*. Rupert almost boiled up in frustration and said, 'Bloody hell, why didn't this Reginald Perkins ask for me and hand me the note or just take me to the airfield himself?'

In his first winter abroad, Rupert had liked to see the horse-drawn sleighs on the streets of Riga. Now, approaching the centre of the city, their slow progress was incredibly frustrating, as the ambulance could not overtake them due to the snow piled in the middle of the road. On the main road, he looked over the River Daugava and saw the pontoon bridge encased in ice. He noted that people had forged paths across the frozen river, but he didn't even look towards the spires and domes of the old town beyond, which would normally have attracted his attention. Away from the centre, the ambulance was able to shoot through the outskirts of Riga at considerable speed. Rupert continued to double up in pain with every jolt and cursed under his breath in growing panic.

The small collection of hangars and buildings that comprised Spilve Aerodrome came into sight. Rupert saw what he took to be smoke trails dissipating in the light breeze. He let out an audible groan. The ambulance stopped at a checkpoint at the entrance to the aerodrome. Doctor Berzins said, 'I will talk to the soldier on duty.' When he opened the door, all the warm air in the ambulance was sucked out and immediately replaced by an arctic chill. Rupert shivered and looked out towards the runway. This had been cleared but was deserted except for a huddle of biplanes at the far end, fat and heavy beneath the piled snow that covered their wings and fuselages.

Doctor Berzins got back in to the ambulance after a short

conversation with the sentry and explained that a British plane had landed, embarked passengers and left in a very quick turnaround. He suggested that they drive to the British Legation in the centre of Riga, to see if there was any backup plan. Rupert agreed but did not have high hopes. He had missed the plane and that, he suspected, was probably that.

Setting off at a more sedate pace, the ambulance headed towards the city centre. Rupert remembered Riga as quite a bustling city, but even though it was still mid afternoon, it seemed deadened, with far fewer cars than usual and very few sleighs. He was deep in thought when the ambulance arrived at the lemon-yellow and white painted Legation. Doctor Berzins got out and spoke to the man at the gate, but he soon came back and told Rupert that the ambassador and his British staff had all left earlier in the day and would not be returning. Rupert put his head in his hands and when the doctor said that there were still some local staff at the Legation who they could address questions to, he responded curtly in English, 'Yes, I have a question, what the hell do I do now?'

On the way back to the hospital, Rupert imagined his mother waiting for him and then considered how rudely he had addressed the doctor. He apologised for his outburst and thanked him for his kindness and attentiveness over the last few months. Then, turning away to stare out of the window, he let the hot tears of frustration run down his face.

Fires

The cold of the Latvian winter seeped through the bricks of Rupert's cell and he struggled to focus on anything else. Only whilst walking could he forget about the chill.

One day, looking out of the prison window at the leaden sky, which foretold the arrival of more snow, he wondered, *Will this winter ever end?* Then he smiled as he remembered how he had once thought of the hospital as kind a prison. He even chuckled as he imagined himself in the warm patients' lounge railing at his uncaring and cruel gaolers, ice and snow. He now understood that the hospital, far from being a prison, was a blissful oasis, recollections of which softened his harsh present conditions.

Rupert managed to shut the window behind the metal bars but it made practically no difference to the temperature in his cell. He stood by the small radiator and attempted to absorb the faint murmur of warmth.

He knew he had a battle on his hands to both keep warm and stay sane. At the best of times, little in the way of natural light entered his cell, but in January this minimal nourishment was withheld and he began to wish he were somewhere else, anywhere. Even if he were in a prisoners' work detail breaking stones on a northern fellside, or laying train tracks in America, or even in a trench waiting to go over the top he would see other faces, hear other voices, but here he remained alone with his thoughts, and often these were not the best of company. He had tired himself on his walk and now his thoughts wandered from topic to topic.

He thought that being in the depths of Siberia might be preferable to his drab cell and his mind flickered to a conversation he had once with Irēne.

Rupert had told Irēne about Orlonsky's rosy view of pre-Lenin Russian. Her reply had been sharp and swift.

'Your friend forgot to tell you that exile has been a means of dealing with dissenters for centuries and Siberia has always needed slave labour. So, in the past many people were sent there for such minor things as felling oak trees and begging with false distress.'

'Really! Begging with false distress; I've never heard of the offence but it sounds very serious.'

'Well, it was on the same level as recklessly driving a cart without the use of reins, and that could also lead you straight to a sentence in Siberia.' Irēne said. 'Yes, the serious offenders, such as murderers and rapists, were literally branded before they were banished. Can you believe it? They were treated like cattle. Before the Trans Siberian Railway was built it took the prisoners three years to walk to the remotest points of exile – and their sentence only started once they got there!'

Involuntarily, Rupert touched the scar on his leg and understood that he, for one, would not have withstood such an ordeal.

Turning his thoughts to his first year at university and the lighting of fires, he said out loud, 'Actually, Orlonsky was right about the cold. Manchester is wet but doesn't have the sort of damp, nasty, bone numbing cold that drifts in off the Fens.' He recalled how he had suffered with the cold at Cambridge during the winter. In the morning, there was often a thin layer of ice on the surface of the washstand jug, which he used to break with his toothbrush. Now, frequently falling into the habit of talking to himself he said, 'Getting up was no fun at all. I can still feel the frost rimed on the inside of the windowpane and seeping into my bones. I remember the bleakness of the morning walk to the baths.' He joked with himself by saying, 'Honestly, I was right in what I said to the lieutenant; maybe if I hadn't gone to

Cambridge, I wouldn't have been so prepared for prison life.'

The rooms at Pembroke comprised a bedroom and study, which were quite large but had bare walls and were sparsely furnished. Unless a fire was blazing, they felt cold most of the year. He recalled that on the first day they met, Orlonsky hadn't managed to light the fire in his study and it was freezing in there. Rupert presumed that this was not a task he had to do for himself in Russia and he set about showing him what to do. Firstly, he laid some pieces of coal over kindling and when this was alight, spread a sheet of newspaper over the smoking black mouth of the fireplace to draw the flames and light the coals.

Sitting back on his prison bed, he remembered the enjoyment he got from the simple process of lighting fires – something he must have done hundreds of time at home and at his aunty's. He particularly liked it when the newspaper over the face of the fire started to hum and became as tight as parchment as it was drawn into what was beginning to sound like an inferno in the mouth of the fire.

His recollections of the first fire he set in Orlonsky's rooms were very specific. An orange spot appeared in the middle of the sheet and highlighted the report in the *London Times* of Benito Mussolini freeing sixteen thousand prisoners. He concluded, 'It is funny what you remember.'

His thoughts now jumped to the fireside discussions he had with Orlonsky and how his friend would often repeat in these early days at Cambridge that before the revolution the country possessed a legislation of which many Western democracies might be proud with its widely read liberal journals, all shades of political thought and fearless and independent judges. He tried to mimic the accent of the Eton-educated friend who had sat, incredulous, with them at the time, 'Oh I say, now you are really pulling our leg.'

Thinking of fires, Rupert remembered the first sound he heard in the morning at his aunty's was the clatter of the firegrate being cleaned by his aunt – even in summer. Then there was the clink, clink of milk bottles being delivered to the doorstep, followed by the clack, clack of the clogs along the cobbled street as chatty young women made their way to the tobacco factory to start the early shift.

Thinking of fires did not make him any warmer. At night, huddled under the blanket, he could not warm the ice blocks that were his feet.

He was becoming sleepy and in the melding of reality and dreams he was pleased to welcome Irēne to his home. 'How lovely to see you, you look so sun-tanned and healthy, and I'm so pleased you have come home. Look how the fire glows in the open range and the flames' dance is reflected off the painted wainscoting that stretches half way up the wall. There is Father in his shirt sleeves, sitting in the rocking chair on one side of the fire reading, and Mother sits on the other side with her sewing and I'm happy sitting in my dressing gown, studying evensong verses whilst our dog, Scruffy stretches himself on the rug. And the smell is very specific; coal, kippers, strong tea and warm dog. Yes, as you say, it is *gemütlich*. No Mother, I've a guest here, I cannot go to bed so soon.'

Understanding that when he started to speculate he became worried and fretful, Rupert realised that it was best to stick to remembering reality, rather than courting possibilities of past and future alike. The gaping blankness of his future repelled him and so, in an effort to drive away the constant gnawing of the cold, Rupert drifted once again into the past. In his mind, the ambulance bore him away from the aborted flight and wove its way towards wedding planning, thunderstorms and, Rupert shivered, towards the wide, dark eyes of Irēne's mother.

Mothers

After returning to the hospital from Spilve Aerodrome Rupert was sore and felt utterly exhausted. He couldn't think clearly about anything and, when visiting time came, he was lying on his bed rather than seated in his usual place in the patients' lounge. Irēne greeted him with, 'Rupert this is unusual...'

'The plane...' There was a catch in his throat. 'The plane left without me.' Irēne embraced him as he tried to get his emotions under control.

Eventually, he managed to tell her about the panicky dash to the aerodrome, of being too late to be evacuated, and of his thwarted hopes of getting home. He ended angrily, 'What utter stupidity to come all the way to the hospital to leave a note as important as that with a lady on reception. I can't remember feeling so cross about anything before'. Then, he softened his tone, 'But mostly I feel sad for my mother. Hopefully, she didn't know about me being flown home but, nevertheless, she must be frantic with worry by now.'

Irēne pulled up a chair and waited patiently. Eventually, he spoke again. 'I'm sorry, I'm feeling tremendously tired. It is amazing how such a panic can rob you of a sense of peace. Only last night I was thinking about our New Year's Eve party and how very happy and contented I felt. Of course, there's a consolation in not going home and that is I am here with you...' and willing himself into a positive attitude added, 'and we have a wedding to prepare for!'

'I am pleased to be able to see you, but I can imagine how you were so much looking forward to going home and seeing your mother again.'

Rupert could feel a lump reappearing in his throat. 'I am sorry for my melancholy state. Maybe instead of talking, we can walk up and down the ward.' He paused, then, trying to improve his mood, added, 'I will show you the sights on the way.' Much of the visiting time was spent walking in silence and, before leaving, Irēne promised to return the next day.

The following day, Rupert dwelt on the ambassador's remark about being desperate to get home to do his bit. *How strange,* he thought, *I've given no serious consideration to actually fighting in the war.* He remembered the old soldiers who had returned to Wythenshawe after the Great War with limbs missing and permanent lung damage. He thought about the increasing mechanical capability of Metro Vicks and other engineering companies and realised that conflict would be even more mechanised and deadly. *If it is asked of me, of course I will join up. Yet my desire to return lies in comforting my mother, in home itself.* Yet equally he longed to stay in Latvia with Irēne. *I am being torn in two,* he thought.

As the day progressed, the weather worsened and Rupert noted that the red vein of the thermometer had contracted to a point far lower than he had seen before. When Irēne arrived, he hugged her and found that her coat was stiff with frost. He tried to warm her up with a big hug and a kiss on her icy red nose.

After they had settled in the patients' lounge, he updated Irēne with some news relayed to him before lunch. He began, 'Doctor Berzins came to see me earlier and said that he had spoken to representatives at the British Legation. Apparently, not all the British have left and, contrary to what the gatekeeper said, the ambassador is still there, which is good news, not least because he has my passport. He was assured that I haven't been forgotten and that if there's a further evacuation of the legation I will be included.'

Irēne smiled, stood up, gave Rupert a kiss and said, 'That is good.'

'You know the only reason I am going...' She didn't let him finish.

'Of course, you need to reassure your mother you are well.'

'The Doctor tells me Metro Vicks has agreed to underwrite any further treatment costs and that in a few weeks I'm going to be transferred to a sanatorium at a place called Kemeri. Actually, the use of the word sanatorium was a bit of a worry but apparently, here, it means health resort.'

'I know of the place. You are lucky, it opened just a few years ago to cater for rich foreign tourists, but as they no longer come, due to the declaration of war, you could have the place to yourself.'

Imagining lounging around in a luxurious bathrobe, Rupert asked, 'Is the regime cold showers and vegetarian meals or warm baths, massage and grapes?'

'Oh, it is all about being pampered - especially if you like sitting in mud baths and drinking sulphurated water.'

'Hmm - sounds lovely... Yes, Doctor Berzins said they would provide a recuperative exercise regime and he thinks in six months I'll be completely recovered.'

'Let us drink to that,' and added, 'tea viz milk,' as the nurse pushed in the trolley.

After taking a few sips of her drink, Irēne said, 'You seem to be much calmer than yesterday. I was wondering if you would like to talk about your mother? I have gained a sense of her character and what she looks like, but I am interested to hear more and maybe it would be good for you to talk about her.' He welcomed the suggestion but wondered how to start.

'Well... it's difficult to separate my mother from our home and family life. I can only say that my mother must be the polar opposite of yours. Not in terms of looks, I hasten to add, as I think she's rather pretty, but in terms of temperament. She has a girlish charm and I can't imagine her intentionally flirting with the Tattons for instance.' Rupert looked up at Irēne and, wondering whether he had been rude in the way he had compared his mother with Irēne's, added, 'I'm sorry if I have presumed too much about your mother.'

'No, my mother took flirting to the realms of high art.'

Irēne laughed gently and asked Rupert to continue. 'Mother has a clear belief that the most important people in the world are family and friends and she'd do anything to help those she cares for. This genuine care and interest in others gives her a remarkable ability to put people at their ease. People always come first and, whilst she is always busy, she never uses this as an excuse for not being available.'

'She does sound like a wonderful lady and mother.' Then she added, 'I can imagine you are the apple of her eye.'

Rupert sat back and smiled in the knowledge that he had a special relationship with his mother. 'Indeed,' he responded, 'but I think that as an only child this is natural and after my father died we became even closer. Her biggest wish was for me to have a good education. Even when I felt a little unwell, or had a sniffle, I was packed off to school.'

'Your mother's disciplined approach to education has served you well.'

'It wasn't that she wanted my head filled with facts. Far from it, she was keen that in all things I tried my hardest and was polite at all times, especially to my elders and anyone in authority. For my mother, there is a natural pecking order and education isn't designed to break this, only to help you fit in better.'

'And why would you want to break it anyway; as you have described it, life in Wythenshawe sounds idyllic.'

'Let the Lords and Ladies have their big houses for ours was far cosier.' He had a slight choke to his voice. 'I'm sorry but I am becoming quite homesick.'

'Of course you are and that is only right. You love your mother and it is time for you to see her.'

They were quiet for a while and then he said, 'Sorry, I am being sentimental. My mother believes it isn't the cards you are dealt in life that's important, it's how you play them. And talking of cards, I think you are the highest card I've ever been dealt; and I am still with you... so all is not lost.'

Moving over to Irēne, Rupert kissed her forehead and asked, 'Can you tell me more about your mother?'

'My mother could captivate a whole room.' Irēne settled back in her seat. 'She was really beautiful and had an infectious laugh. She was charming, fresh, original, humorous and witty, and she had an extraordinary sense of fashion. She always projected a coordinated look with hat, gloves and shoes matching her outfit, even though she never had a large wardrobe.'

'It seems you have inherited her fashion sense.' She gave him a sideways glance and then took a purse out of her bag and, from this, extracted a photograph, which she passed over to him.

The picture was of Rebecca wearing a summer dress in an elegant park. 'Yes, I can see she is beautiful and has a lovely smile. Where was this taken?' Rupert asked.

'Berlin.'

'Can you tell me more about your time together there?'

'I have wonderfully happy memories of being with her. We lived in Fasanenstrasse, which is an elegant street in a fashionable part of Berlin. I remember that light came streaming into the apartment, even in winter, and this seemed to set the scene for our life. My early memories are of mother smiling and laughing a great deal. Living with her was great fun. In her company, the world was filled with pleasure and promise. She was curious about almost everything and able to describe with delight, and in such an original way, the beauties of the natural world. A raindrop was never just a raindrop, or a cloud just a cloud or a snowflake just a snowflake.'

Intrigued as to how anyone could make these everyday aspects interesting Rupert asked, 'In what way?'

'Well, as an example, raindrops were jewels and clouds told us stories from foreign lands. Everything was unique but oddly connected. Her enthusiasm was infectious and would encompass everything. Singing filled the house. Wonderful new pieces of material appeared and I would be enthralled listening to all the plans for new fashionable articles to be made from it.'

'Did she make her own clothes?'

'Yes, and mine too. She used to be able to combine different garments to amazing effect. Different colours and patterns next to each other seemed to work effortlessly when my mother put them together.'

'As I say, this is a skill you have inherited,' He wondered whether, for a moment, Irēne's features hadn't hardened.

Having not before heard Irēne being so talkative about her life and, enjoying the experience of listening to her, Rupert asked her to continue. 'Mother was very creative, with intensity, power and magic she was able to leap between different activities and subjects. Not only did she make these seem related, but also, made them appear to contain, to my young mind at least, some essential key to the weave of the universe. The happiest times were the periods when she was rehearsing for new plays. She found memorising her lines and learning new songs easy and I liked testing her.' Irēne smiled. 'I enjoyed these times with my mother, it felt like I was being carried high by her positive energy.'

'It sounds like it was fun to be in your mother's company.'

'Mostly.' Irēne said in a quiet voice. 'She had such a vivid imagination and she could make up amusing stories to tell me without effort.'

'Do you remember any?'

Smiling, Irēne recounted a story of her mother pretending to be a spy trailing two men across the Volkspark because she said they were secret agents. She suddenly stopped smiling and said, 'Life was mostly fun.' After that, she fell silent signalling that she had finished talking about her time in Berlin.

Only when he was sure she had finished did Rupert gently voice a sense that had developed as Irēne described her mother.

'I have the idea of her not being here anymore. You use the past tense quite a lot.'

'No. No, that is my poor English. She is here. I am only talking about past times.' She then changed the subject to talk about how cold it was outside.

They chatted a little about Irēne's flatmate before Rupert brought the conversation back to Rebecca, 'You mentioned that mostly life with your mother was fun. *Mostly*. Were there times that were not?'

'Talking of that incident in the park reminded me she could take things too far.'

'In what way?'

'It was funny, but mother reacted strangely, obsessively really. She said one of the men had reminded her of a character in a book she had just read. With a great sense of urgency, she almost dragged me to the library and immediately found a copy of it. One association led to another. Eventually, the librarian asked us to leave as books were scattered everywhere.'

Rupert nodded encouragingly for Irēne to continue. 'This was a characteristic of my mother that became more pronounced over time; one thing would immediately lead to three other things. Her mind would begin to dart here and there, bubbling with plans and enthusiasms and getting immersed in her plays. From the lofty heights, my mother would climb further. Her mind would go faster and faster. Ideas with only the slightest of connections spilled from her. Her thoughts tumbled out so quickly I could not follow them. In this state she could not keep still and, if she had nothing to occupy her hands or mind, she had to get out. Once, she shoplifted a blouse because she could not wait another second to be served by the sloppy sales girl.'

Rupert remembered a rare visit he made as a young boy with his mother to Kendals department store in Manchester and how they waited patiently for assistance. 'That must have been difficult for you.' He commented.

'I was uplifted by my mother's wit, charm, intensity and imagination when her moods were good, but when her moods changed,' Irēne's voice flattened, 'I often felt tense when she became overly positive.'

Sitting in bed that night, and thinking over the conversation with Irēne, Rupert speculated again about her use of the past tense when talking of her mother and wondered, *What has happened to her?*

Repeating the phrase, *apple of her eye,* he wondered if Irēne saw him as being too much of a mother's boy. He pondered, *All this sentimentality about going home and I've not expressed the same level of feeling about leaving Irēne. She must really think I will leave without shedding a tear or having any concern for her very uncertain future.*

He did not fall asleep easily that night but gained a sense of relief that the aeroplane had left without him. Now, having partially recovered, be able to spend time with his future wife. They would, together, face whatever the world had to throw at them.

Sisu

Andris paid an unexpected visit on Saturday, 13th January. He shook his head as Rupert told him about the late delivery of the note, the missed aeroplane and his now confirmed position as an exile.

'But, it is not all terrible news,' Rupert said. He told Andris about his engagement to Irēne.

'Congratulations my friend!' Andris, grasped Rupert's hand and shook it with vigour, a wide smile on his face, 'And what are to be your wedding arrangements?' Rupert surprised himself when he realised he had none. 'All in good time, do not worry!' Said Andris with a wink.

As usual, Andris had brought his chess set and a challenge was soon offered and accepted. Andris informed Rupert that he had recently attended the Latvian Chess Championship, adding, 'So watch out for some new tactics!' After his opening move, Andris asked, 'Are you keeping up with the news of the fighting on the Finnish Front?' Without waiting for an answer, he continued. 'It is quite a surprise to many that the Finns are holding out so stubbornly, especially as they have to defend a frontier that's more than a thousand kilometres long.'

'And as I understand it, Finland has a population of less than four million.'

'Yes and little in the way of military capability. Munters says that the ammunition situation is alarming; stockpiles of cartridges, shells and fuel are only enough to last for three months at the most. But, in the Finns' favour is the terrain, the terrible cold of this winter and the fact they are well dug in along, what is being called, the Mannerheim Line. Above all though is *sisu*.'

'What is *sisu*?'

'It's Finnish for guts or spirit.'

Rupert completed his move and, after responding, Andris said, 'The Finns have learned that, at close range, logs and crowbars jammed into a tank's bogie wheels can immobilise it. They have also fielded a homemade weapon, the Molotov cocktail.'

'What's that?' Rupert was envisaging Finnish soldiers raising Gatsby-esque crystal tumblers, complete with olives on cocktail sticks, as the tanks rumbled past. Andris's answer swiftly dissipated the image.

'It's a glass bottle filled with flammable liquids with a simple hand-lit fuse. The name's an ironic reference to the bombs that were dropped by the Russians on Helsinki. The Finns dubbed these Molotov's breadbaskets because the Russians claimed that they were dropping food parcels. Hurling one of these makeshift incendiaries into the small crevice between a tank and its gun turret, the Finns cry, *here is the drink to go with the food.*'

'In that case it may be wise to watch what you ask for when out drinking with the Finns. Seriously though, the Finns must have a lot of *sisu* if they can jump out of their trenches to storm tanks.'

'Plenty. Even the women are getting involved. Many are joining the *Lotta Svärd* and some are even fighting alongside the men.'

The game continued and each time it was Rupert's turn, Andris spoke about the war at length. At one point, Andris detailed the heavy losses the small Finnish army was inflicting on the mighty Red Army.

Rupert commented, 'It's amazing what a well placed pawn can do to a poorly moved bishop!' Andris raised a wiry eyebrow and Rupert carried on. 'I can't imagine that Stalin is very pleased with the efforts of his army.'

Rupert took his next move and Andris, after silent consideration, placed his queen into an attacking position. 'I can just imagine his big moustache twitching away as he hears how the Red Army is being humiliated. But, Stalin has done what he is good at, he has blamed others. I really pray for the Finns to win, but God may not be on their side. Stalin is a pragmatist and realises that, however good Finnish tactics are, miracles beyond turning water into wine are required to keep back the swarm of the Red Army. The Baltic Sea might not have much of a tide, but the Red Army's wash across Finland is as irresistible as the pull of the moon.'

Rupert's hand hovered over one of his pieces, 'Andris, talking of tactics, what are yours?'

'Distraction.' Andris laughed. 'Is it working?'

'Not quite... check!' The game finished soon after with Rupert dislodging his opponent's bishop, with a well-placed pawn, to produce a checkmate.

'Would you like me to prepare you a Molotov cocktail?' Andris gave a twisted smile.

Rupert was more pleased than usual to see Irēne on the following Sunday. Once she had taken off her coat, jumpers, scarves, gloves and hat, which together had only partially succeeded in keeping out the terrible cold, and settled into a chair in the patients' lounge, he was quick to apologise for his self-centredness. Sitting opposite her, taking hold of her still cold hands, he explained, 'I think I've acted like a small child who is clinging to his mother's apron... but I have experienced such a lot over the last few weeks. I've been taken up with my own situation as if I'm the only person with troubles to contend with. I have been angry and sad and I've felt guilty about leaving you. It is a great deal to cope with, especially for an Englishman who has been taught to keep his emotions under control.'

Irēne smiled and said, 'Welcome to the human race. We all have the gift of being able to want two things that are incompatible at the same time and, anyway, have you not the right to be angry?'

'Strangely, I've not felt angry about the accident. Of course, I could be angry as I was badly injured and I'm not sure I will ever get rid of this limp. But my overriding feeling is one of being lucky. I could have died, so despite everything, I'm living a life I could so easily have been denied. But the other day I did feel anger; no, more than that, rage at the stupidity of the man who delivered the note to the hospital. Now I want to write a thank you letter to him.'

'Why is that?'

'Because I am here with you.' He looked into Irēne's eyes and she smiled. Then he added, 'By the way, Andris visited me yesterday and I told him that we are engaged. It reminded me that we need to think about our wedding.'

Rupert told Irēne all about Andris's visit and said, 'He's trying to strike fear into me about the arrival of the Russians. But whatever he says is blunted by the fact that I have a rather benign view of the country. This is despite what Orlonsky used to tell me.'

'Why is that?'

'I think I mentioned my patron, Ernest Simon.' She nodded and he continued. 'Lord Simon was the man who made it possible for me to go to Cambridge.'

'Isn't he the one making your mother's life difficult with all those new homes in Wythenshawe?'

'Well...' He began defensively, 'Ernest had a vision of improving people's lives by moving them from the slums to new houses, built further away from the city centre on quiet roads that don't go anywhere.'

'I wouldn't like to live on a road that doesn't go anywhere.'

'Yes, put like that! But he once told me he had engaged the best planners and that there would be schools, clinics and playgrounds.'

'If I were you, I'd be angry with Lord Simon. Once beauty is gone, it is gone forever.'

He was again struck by how Irēne was able to challenge, in a subtle, loving way, his preconceptions. He continued, 'The reason I've a rather benign view of the Russians is that Ernest, his wife and three other academics went to Russia three years ago to study the city government of Moscow. They were impressed and the end result was a book entitled *Moscow in the Making*.'

'It must have been a best seller!' Irēne said, her eyes twinkling.

Rupert smiled at the recollection of the sparsely attended lecture at the Manchester Philosophical and Literature Society. He recounted the lecture and how both Lord Simon and his wife, Shena, had spoken in positive terms of the benefits of state control when it came to urban planning and promoting equality of educational opportunity. He ended by saying, 'Ernest was inspired by the designs for the Moscow suburbs where the apartment blocks being built are angled to make the most of the sunlight.'

'Ah, the Moscow light!'

Rupert heard the heavy irony in Irēne's tone, but he simply said, 'That's right... Anyway, all in all, I probably have the mistaken belief that if the Russians invade they will bring the benefits of urban town planning and a good educational system.'

'I think that Ernest may be somewhat naïve... and that goes for you too.' He felt that he had just received a well-deserved poke in the ribs.

Rupert turned to the subject that had been on his mind all week and said, 'Let's talk about our wedding. We can focus on the plans now.'

'That is something to look forward to,' Irēne replied with excitement in her voice and then changed her tone, 'but are you sure Rupert? What about your mother? Surely you would want her to be at our wedding?'

'Ideally, yes, but if I return home with a beautiful wife, Mum will be happy for me. In any case, we can have a blessing in the chapel at Wythenshawe.' To indicate that this was the problem solved in his mind, he cheerily asked, 'When shall we have the ceremony? I was thinking of next week.'

'I like it you are so keen but arrangements will take a little longer than that.' Then tentatively, she asked, 'Would you mind if we left it until later in the year? I have told my grandparents all about us and I would like them to attend the ceremony. However Grandfather is busy with his shops until the holiday period and Grandmother doesn't travel well as she has bad hips.'

'Do you think we can wait until then? Everyone seems to

think the Red Army will invade and soon.' For him, summer seemed far off and he had assumed that by then, somehow, he would be back in England. He also wondered whether he could possibly wait such a long time for other, physical, reasons. Irēne nodded, as if she understood his compelling urgency.

'Of course the Red Army are a law unto themselves, but they are busy in Finland. It will take them time to finish the job there.'

Rupert realised there had been no discussion about religion, so he asked, 'Are your grandparents fine with a Protestant wedding?'

'Yes, my father is a Lutheran and mother married him in a church. Also Grandmother is a Lutheran, although she did marry in a synagogue, and Grandfather is not worried about where we marry. He is just pleased I have found a good man.'

Rupert imagined a church full of people. He could almost smell the scent of summer and breathed a sigh of relief. 'What about our honeymoon?' He asked.

'Well, if we can't go to your idyllic Wythenshawe, then we can go to my idyllic Pāvilosta, near Liepāja, where my grandparents have a summerhouse. It is a traditional wooden cottage just on the edge of the village and there will be flowers blooming in the lovely garden.'

'It sounds perfect.'

'It is really pretty, especially in the summer, although even in the winter, there is desolate beauty. It is a proper fishing village, well sheltered behind an inlet. From there, we can walk along the white sands of the Baltic coast.'

Later that evening Rupert reflected on their difference. He

understood that Irēne had both spirit and resilience otherwise she wouldn't have been able to cope with her mother's lifestyle and moods. He also knew that he had a naïve and trusting nature; qualities that were ever likely to lead to problems. A question arose in his mind, was he mentally tough enough to handle the many problems that might realistically be heading his way?

Rebecca

The next week passed in the same manner as the previous ones; with soul-destroying monotony. Rupert distracted himself by exercising as best he could, reading and having infrequent conversations with fellow patients if they could speak either German or Russian. His attention often turned to his potential mother-in-law. *I don't know much about Rebecca, not even where she lives.* He resolved to find out more about her, when Irēne visited next.

Irēne found Rupert perambulating along the ward with only a walking stick. He kissed and was shocked at how cold her nose was. Then, he helped her remove her stiff and near-frozen coat. It smelt strongly of some kind of animal, a thick, heady musk, but he didn't make any comment.

Irēne's eyelashes wore a silver coating of frost and had stuck together, and Rupert took her hands and rubbed them before saying, 'If the temperature drops any lower, you'd better not risk coming over.' Irēne shrugged her shoulders.

'Actually, I have had a little adventure. With the cold, I decided to take a sleigh. My driver had a flaming red beard and, bulked out by two bearskin coats and a fur hat, he looked a wonderful sight, and the horse, hung with its sleigh bells, made a beautiful sound. I was wrapped in bearskin rugs and was much warmer than if I had come by tram.' Rupert realised that it was the odour of bear he had detected on Irēne's coat and smiled. He suggested that they sit in the lounge and, as he followed Irēne, he looked appreciatively at her shapely calves, well insulated with thick stockings.

Keen to update Irēne about his physical progress, he informed her that he had begun to walk up the stairs of the hospital to strengthen his legs and added, 'I can now manage a whole flight, although it is very tiring as I have to drag my right leg up after me... but as you can see I am improving.'

'If you lived in my apartment,' she replied, 'you would have some real daily exercise as there are three, very steep, flights of stairs.' The image of climbing the stairs to her apartment sprang to his mind. He thought of the bed waiting at the top and knew what exercise he'd like to take there.

After chatting a little, Rupert brought the conversation around to Rebecca. 'I was thinking about you and your mother and how she'd become overly active and positive. Can anyone behave like that all of the time? It sounds like it would be too draining.' Irēne looked at him and was silent for such a long while that Rupert considered he had better turn the conversation to another topic.

'No.' Irēne eventually replied and then, after another lengthy pause, added, 'There is a dark side to such high flying emotions.'

'Are you able to describe this to me? I am sorry, I don't mean to pry.'

' No, no, it is alright.' Irēne took a breath, 'Once a play opened, and after long weeks of flying high on her success and sleeping little, her energy would completely disappear.'

Rupert didn't comment and let Irēne fill the silence. 'At times she lost all her willpower, was unable to get out of bed and profoundly pessimistic about every aspect of her life and future. She would become extremely negative about the play she was in; her character in it, how she was playing her role and the quality of the other actors. Not only did she slow down, in fact, she would come to a grinding halt. If she opened a book, she would read the same passage over and over without understanding a single word. She would stare out of the window and looked like she had no idea at all about what was going on.'

'After the fun times you had together, these periods must have been a great contrast and trial.'

Irēne looked out of the window for a while before answering. 'In the period after the positive wave had risen and crashed, Mother came to be like a baby and would ask in a childlike voice, *Mummy is very tired, can Mummy have a cup of tea or can Mummy sleep in your bed tonight?*' The sense of infantile need made Rupert uncomfortable and he tried to keep it from his face. Irēne continued, 'Eventually her energy gradually returned, but I was left with the feeling, somehow, it was my fault, that if she did not have me to look after she would cope better.'

Rupert knew Irēne wouldn't have talked much about her mother in this way before, if at all, and was conscious he should not press her too much. However, after a pause, he gently asked, 'Did these downward spirals happen often?'

'Yes, but mostly they were soon over and I had the positive mother back in my life almost before I knew it.' Rupert expected this to end the matter and her to change the subject, but she continued, 'However, towards the end of our stay in Berlin her thoughts took terrible, dark a downward turn.'

'Did anything happen in particular?'

'Just the old problem – men!'

Rupert repeated, 'Men,' and let Irēne restart.

'It really came out after Erich Hesse married his leading lady in a quiet civil ceremony.' Rupert wondered what the director's marriage had to do with the downward spiral of Rebecca when Irēne explained, 'I was shocked that my mother was also badly shaken. Until then, I had not realised that she was one of his women. Soon after the wedding, Erich came to meet my mother at our flat, which was the first time I had seen him there - but he probably knew it quite well. He carried a bouquet of flowers and although I was bundled into the bedroom, I heard him explain that the marriage did not mean a thing. At least my mother had the courage to push him out of the door and throw the flowers after his retreating back.'

Irēne, her reluctance gone, carried on with her recollections at quite a pace as though the dam holding back her past had burst. 'Then, later on, she showed me a letter Erich had written her in which he begged for her understanding. After this there were days when Mother would not come out of her room saying that she felt tired and sat at the mirror looking at herself, twisting a piece of hair, lost in thought.'

Irēne raised a hand to her own hair, tucking a loose strand behind her ear with intent.

'It took forever for her to get out of bed in the morning and she wore the same clothes day after day and went to great lengths to avoid other people. Her thoughts were about how beauty soon fades and that her career was over. She was clear that her looks, rather than her acting talent, were the reason for being chosen in the past. But, somehow she dragged herself to the theatre for her performances. She was able to hide from others her negative outlook and maybe no one, other than me, knew just how much Erich had hurt her.'

Wanting to hear more, Rupert asked, 'What happened after that?'

'When her mood lifted slightly, Mother just wanted to get away and she quickly decided to go to Capri. I do not know where she got the funds – maybe Erich gave it to us to lessen the complications in his life?'

'You had been to Capri before hadn't you?'
'Capri had good memories for me and I was happy to be

back and, away from Berlin, Mother slowly improved for a while.' She looked up at Rupert and gave a small smile that did not reach her eyes, which remained wide and glossed with sadness.

'Of course my mother is unable to live without a man and she took another lover. This time it was a Russian philosopher, full of Marxist theory by the name of Borya and he was quick to point out that this meant battle, war or fight. Mother found him fascinating. He was young, handsome and rich. Mother has always been attracted to revolutionaries, but to me he was a charlatan.'

Rupert took an instant dislike to Borya and then asked, 'In what way was he a charlatan?' Irēne was quick to respond with an edge in her voice that Rupert had not heard before.

'What sort of revolutionary suns himself all over in the isolated coves of Capri?'

'Was your mother able to recover there?'

'Well... well my mother saw Borya trying to kiss me one day.' Rupert's head shot back and his eyes opened wide. 'Yes, I can see I have shocked you. I was on the beach and had just come out of the sea when he came by, grabbed my hand, and pulled me towards a small cove saying that he had something to show me. When we got there he pushed me against the rocks and kissed me. I tried to move him away but he was strong. Suddenly my mother was standing close by. She had seen Borya take me by the hand and rushed along the beach. I am not sure quite what would have happened if she had not been there.'

Rupert didn't want to think what might have happened. He felt a bubble of rage rise and burst in his chest. His hand twitched and he felt a simultaneous urge to seize Irēne and hold her close and to strike the table with his fist. He said with some force, 'It was a good job I wasn't there. I would have done something

201

violent.'

'You would have had to be very careful as he is also a fencing champion.' Irēne was regarding Rupert with her head on one side. She seemed to have softened at the sight of his anger. Rupert relaxed.

'Ah, well. In that case I'd have stabbed him in the chest with some well-aimed rude names.'

They both smiled and Rupert asked, 'How did you feel about the incident?'

'I was only thirteen and it was shocking to be roughly kissed by an older man, his breath smelt dusty and sour. But, it affected Mother more; she took it very badly. Afterwards, she spent a great deal of time telling me never to get involved with men and that I must not trust them. Then she became distant and plunged into despair. It was a darkness from which she never truly recovered.'

'Oh dear... How is she now?'

Irēne did not answer the question; instead her whole body became stock still as if waiting for something calamitous to happen. She looked at Rupert, bit her lip, and started speaking, 'I really find this hard to say....' then stopped. He did not say anything but nodded gently. She took a small, sharp breath and spoke fast. 'People have very odd ideas on the subject I am struggling to talk about... My mother is in a mental institute suffering from severe depression and delusions. I doubt she will ever return to a normal life.' She finished with an emphatic, 'There, I have said it.'

Rupert simply reached for her hand and asked, 'You say that people have odd ideas about this type of illness; what strange ideas do you think I have?'

'Well, many people think madness runs in the family. You even think fashion sense is inherited!' Then, in a strident, almost accusatory voice, she added, 'Maybe you think I am like my mother in more ways than simply her taste in clothes?' He understood now why she had given him a strange look when he had complimented her on having a similar fashion sense to that of her mother.

Rupert looked into her face with gentle conviction 'The woman you have described is not at all like the Irēne I know. While I am certain you are alike and different in many ways, you are not Rebecca. You are Irēne and you are unique.' Rupert paused. 'Well — there is one way in which you are alike. You are both very beautiful.' He smiled, stood up, helped Irēne to her feet and hugged her. On pulling apart, he saw her eyes first misting over and then brimming with tears.

'I was so afraid that, when you found out my mother was in a mental institute, you would not want to marry me.' Irēne tried to stifle a sob, 'I did not know how an Englishman would see such things.'

'You thought I'd desert you?'

Irēne looked at Rupert and, for a brief moment, he wasn't sure how she was going to react. Then she smiled and asked, 'Desert or dessert?' He kissed her passionately. His rising caused him to pull away in embarrassment.

They sat. To Rupert's surprise, Irēne wanted to continue with her story. She seemed lighter, buoyed by her unburdening and Rupert's acceptance.

'After this, Mother's utterances turned towards the subjects of death and decay, she'd say things like, 'I am going to die, what difference does it make anyway? Life's run is only a short and meaningless one, why live? Everything is born to die, best die now and save the pain of waiting.' Her despair was punctuated by periods of horrible restlessness; at times she was in a screaming rage, which would fill me with terror. Once disturbed, she could not get back to sleep and would pace like a caged tiger back and forwards across the tiny space of my bedroom. I waited and waited for the return of the laughter and high moods and enthusiasm. However, except for rare glimpses of her old self, there was only anger, despair and emotional withdrawal.'

Rupert wanted to sympathise with Irēne, but found himself groping for words that would not come. He was disappointed in himself when he simply asked, 'What happened then?'

'Mother soon wanted to return to what she called her beloved Latvia. However, when we came back – the train trip through Italy, Switzerland, Germany Poland and Lithuania was tortuous - her mind finally span out of control.'

'Span out of control!'

'Yes, we went to live with my grandparents in Liepāja and, soon after we arrived, Mother went to a local chemist and asked to buy snakebite antidote. When she found they did not sell it she repeatedly shrieked, *Do you not understand that snakes are beginning to cover Europe?*'

Looking down and shaking her head, Irēne's voice was soft and slow as she continued. 'Mother completely fell apart.' She told Rupert about how she barricaded herself in her room and even took a local doctor hostage for a short while. She finished off by saying, 'Words spilled out without order or sense. The doctor had to arrange for her to be admitted to a hospital.'

Having sat almost spellbound, Rupert, with tears welling in his eyes, said 'My love, what a terrible ordeal for you. What are your feelings now about her now?'

'I still love her but...'

'But?'

'I am left with the question, which of these contrasting sets of characteristics is my mother? The wild impulsive, chaotic and energetic one? Or the shy, withdrawn, desperate, doomed, tired and crazy one? Both or neither? When I visit her, she sometimes recognises me but... these are rare days.'

Instead of saying anything, Rupert took Irēne's hand and let her continue. 'After all of that, I got in touch with my father, Pēteris and it was he who helped me get a job as an interpreter at the Ministry of Interior Affairs. Now, I think, I have told you more than you wish to know about my mother.'

Rupert had never felt so moved and he struggled to keep back his compassionate tears. He wanted to protect Irēne, care for her, soothe her and he was surprised by his physical reaction. His blood rose and becoming aware of a tingling tumescence, he realised that, most of all, he wanted to make love to her. Instead of reaching for Irēne, he dampened his physical reaction by concentrating on formulating a sensitive reply.

'Thank you,' he said. 'Thank you for being so brave in telling me something so painful. Your trust means a great deal to me.'

That evening, Rupert turned to the erotic charge that had suffused his body. He wondered if he was some monster who could easily have taken advantage of his loved one in her distress. Lying in bed, he thought, *How inappropriate, how selfish.* Later, he was kinder to himself, *I just felt so close to her and longed to be closer, to make her feel that she was loved. That she was not alone.*' but his conscience prickled and he was loathe to trust his motives. *'Men'* he heard Irēne say in his head. *Am I such a man as Borya?* he thought, *Driven by desire and covetous of beauty for my own selfish pleasures? No, I cannot be so. Yet now is not the time to think of these things.* He turned guiltily from carnal thoughts. Instead, he considered the subject of inheritance. He always found it odd that he had a few of his father's features but was generally told he looked like his mother. He looked at his hands and saw a younger, less calloused version of his father's hands. Then, he slipped his feet out from under the bedclothes and looked at the bony bump on each foot, similar to those on his father's feet. *Surely,* he thought, *how we think, the machinations of our minds, can't be passed on in the same way?*

Rupert reflected on what he had been told about Rebecca's descent into madness. Before he went to sleep, imagining snuggling up to Irène, he concluded, *There might be a silver lining. When it comes to departing for England, she may not be too saddened by leaving her mother.* The thought prompted another pang of guilt as he considered leaving his own mother and he shook himself. *Rebecca is to be my family. Her care is to be as much my responsibility as Irène's. I must meet her.'*

The background noises on the ward became muffled and soporific and he began to doze off. In the twilight between sleep and wakefulness, he could smell bear and then imagined being whisked off into the countryside, borne away on a sledge driven by a wild man with a flaming beard, whilst snuggling up to Irène under the fur cover.

A Brush With Madness

When Rupert saw Irēne arrive he forgot about the icy weather outside the hospital. As she approached him, already removing her thick knitted scarf, he said, 'Here is my sunshine,' and gave her a brief kiss on the lips, which, if other patients hadn't been watching, he'd have turned into something more substantial.

Rupert reported on what Doctor Berzins had told him the previous day. He was to be moved to Kemeri Sanatorium on the 12th of March and, as it was still frozen outside, they were arranging to transport him by ambulance to better protect his leg. He added, 'But, I think I'm fit and able enough to come into Riga before I leave. There are two very important things I need to do. The first is to retrieve my passport.' He paused long enough for Irēne to ask the obvious question.

'And the second thing?'

'To buy you a ring.'

'Oh that is not important at all,' She smiled and then added, 'I agree with the doctor; conditions are treacherous. Everyday, I see people slip and slide on the cobbled streets. There is no sign of this long winter ending and the last thing we need is you breaking another leg! We can wait until the weather is better and then have a day out in Riga.'

'Going to see a film or even the opera would be lovely.' Rupert commented.

'Yes, I would love to go back to the National Opera with you and we have never been to the cinema together. Did you ever go to the Splendid Palace in Riga?'

'No, I know where it is though.'

'That is a shame. It does not matter what film is on, it is always a treat to go inside. When you are better and the weather has warmed up, I am sure you will be allowed out of Kemeri, at weekends, to go to the cinema. And there is, I am told, a great film on at the moment called the *Fisherman's Son*. Katerīna went to see it and she said there was a standing ovation at the end.'

Changing the subject, Irēne asked, 'If you weren't here, what would you be doing in Manchester at the weekend?'

'Oh, I rarely venture out at the weekend at home.' Irēne wrinkled her brow in exaggerated surprise.

'And what about on Saturday nights, dancing and such like?'

'Occasionally, I have gone to dances at Stretford Town Hall organised by the social club at the factory. But I was uncomfortable as I didn't dance well and was unsure of the etiquette. Whenever I got up courage to ask a girl for a dance, some other rotter would get there first. Most of the men from the factory were either great dancers or great drinkers and I didn't fit into either category.'

'I love to dance. I want you to promise that you will take me dancing when we are next in Riga together.' Rupert took Irēne's hand and ceremoniously shook it.

'Very well!' he laughed, 'On your own head— or rather feet— be it!'

They turned to the subject of their wedding and after chatting for a bit, Rupert said, 'Can you believe this? On the wedding day of Robert Egerton Tatton, the staff and tenants of the estate of Wythenshawe Hall donated a gold bracelet to the bride and a canteen of silver cutlery to the groom. With what has happened in Russia between workers and their ex-bosses, it is strange to think that the poor workers on the Wythenshawe Estate voluntarily scrimped and saved to buy expensive presents for people who were already very wealthy.'

'It certainly sounds odd.'

'But the Tattons were good to their dependants, there was a caring relationship between the haves and the have-nots. If the Tattons still owned the Hall they would definitely have let us use the chapel and one of the side rooms for our reception. It wouldn't have been as grand as the Tatton's own wedding, but for a day, we would have felt like landed gentry.'

'Let's hope you don't get given a set of silver cutlery, where would we put it?'

The task of finding a place for wedding gifts triggered Rupert to ask, 'Where are we going to live?'

'I have spoken to Katerīna and she has kindly agreed that she will find another room to rent. So, if you like, you can come to live with me?'

'I'd love to.' He leaned over to Irēne and gave her a lingering kiss.

When it was time to leave, Rupert escorted Irēne down the flights of stairs to the foyer. But, instead of letting her leave, he directed her into a small alcove furnished with chairs and a table. Sitting down, he said, 'I'm strong enough to walk quite a way now and I am feeling like this place is becoming more of a prison every day. Next week, if she is not too far away, I think we should go and see your mother. If the Legation do organize another evacuation, it might be the last time I have the opportunity to meet her.'

Irēne bit her lip. 'Are you sure,' she began 'It is not easy', but Rupert cupped her cheek in his hand.

'I am sure' he said. Irēne nodded.

'She is in Jūrmala, not far away but let me have a think about it.'

Rupert lent forward and their lips met. He felt a kind of electric current surge from his head to his feet when their tongues touched. It was a passionate kiss, but short lived as he broke the embrace when he heard footsteps approaching. As soon as he did so, he chastised himself for his self-conscious English ways, what was wrong with a man kissing his betrothed?

Reviewing the day, Rupert knew he was burying his head in the sand. All this talk of living with Irene was fantasy and, in reality, he would be heading back to England. Nevertheless, the fantasy was attractive and he let it play out in his mind.

Over the course of the next week, the most exciting pastime for Rupert was watching a slow but steady ascent of the thermometer's red vein.

A few days of milder weather had made the footpaths treacherous; ice had reformed over the top of melt-water puddles. As Rupert hobbled out of the Second City Hospital and along *Apsu iela* towards the tram stop, he wondered whether he had made a terrible mistake insisting that they should visit Irēne's mother. Even with the support of his stick and with Irēne's arm drawn tightly through his, progress was slow and uncertain. The street was as slippery as an ice-rink and he knew that an awkward, uncontrolled fall could jar his injured leg and put his recovery back significantly.

It was a short walk from the hospital to the nearest stop for the number ten tram. Once he had stepped on board, with the help of Irēne pushing him up from behind, Rupert began to feel a sense of newfound freedom. He had always enjoyed travelling on the trams, but after so many months cooped-up in hospital, this was a doubly welcome adventure. He began to whistle contentedly, he could not help himself, as the tram rocked along *Vienibas Gatve* and then down past the beautiful, and aptly named, *Arkadijas Parcs.*

The pathway from the tram stop to the Central Railway Station was clear of snow and Rupert said, 'Even Bertie Wooster, walking down Piccadilly, couldn't have felt as free as I do now.' On entering the concourse, its grand scale was almost overwhelming to him after the confines of the hospital ward. He stood looking up at the high roof as if he had just walked into a medieval cathedral. The click, clack of the automated departure board caught his attention and he was surprised to see the details for a train to Berlin. This added to his sense that the war was confined to the margins of Europe and that life was carrying on as normal for most.

After buying train tickets, there was time to visit the *kafejnīca* and Rupert went to the counter to try out his Latvian. He was disappointed the lady serving him didn't use the abacus on the counter to tot up the bill. He remembered seeing these beads on wire frames in all the shops in Riga and was fascinated this children's toy was used so effortlessly to total up the costs of long lists of provisions. He paid the bill and sat down next to Irēne saying, 'Now let's see what we get.' He was thankful that two hot coffees promptly arrived at their table.

'You must speak like a native.'

'*Paldies.* Now that has been safely negotiated, how has your week been?'

'There was one highlight. I went to listen to Prokofiev's *Romeo and Juliet* at the National Opera on Thursday.' He felt himself stiffen. He relaxed when she explained that she had gone with Katerīna and added, 'It was lovely to think of my own Romeo.' Understanding he had felt a little pang of jealousy, or even fear, that Irēne had gone to the theatre with another man, he, for a moment, did not want to think of her having a life away from his own.

After finishing their coffees they walked to the platform designated for their train where a massive mechanical beast, hissing steam and spitting sparks, greeted them. As they walked past the locomotive, it announced its readiness to depart with a massive whistle. Rupert said, 'Latvia may be a small country, but you can tell that it's part of a huge continent by the size of the trains. British ones are toy-like in comparison.'

'Do the British try to be different from the rest of the world just for effect? Irēne commented and Rupert smiled.

The slatted wooden seats were surprisingly comfortable and, once the train had clanked and rattled out of the station, they chit-chatted about Rupert's home, Cambridge and Irēne's daily life. Later they talked about what response to expect from Rebecca and Irēne warned that her mother might not even recognise her. She finished by adding,
'On the other hand, she is always different when men pay attention to her so who knows...'

The pair fell silent for a while as they watched the last scattered vestiges of Riga's suburbs disappear. Under a clear blue sky, the birch trees shimmered and their bare branches provided a purplish veil to the dramatic winter landscape. The train made its way over the frozen Lielupe River and Rupert was both amazed and horrified to see a few hardy individuals ice fishing in the sub-zero temperatures. The fishermen were sitting stock still by their rods as if also frozen, waiting patiently for the drowsy fish to bite. He commented on the joys of travelling away from home with an ice-cold bottle of vodka for company and they both smiled.

Irēne asked Rupert whether he had ever seen Riga Bay when it was frozen. When he said that he hadn't, she suggested that they make a quick detour to the sea before heading to see her mother.

Disembarking at Dzintari, they made their way to the front of the impressive station and found a lone horse sleigh cab. The dispirited horse was shivering and clomping its hooves to keep warm. Irēne spoke to the cabbie and they climbed aboard and huddled under an animal skin, which Rupert took to be bear as it bore the same musky odour that had clung to Irēne when she had travelled to the hospital by sleigh. The cabbie gave a quick tug of the reigns and they set off towards the seafront. Rupert was delighted. He had never ridden in a sleigh before and was amazed at the speed and comfort of the ride. From their cosy capsule he marvelled at the fabulous, fretted eves of the expensive looking, temporarily uninhabited summerhouses lining the streets of this seaside resort.

From the edge of the esplanade, Rupert could see out to Riga Bay and what he saw was like a vision from a frozen planet. Sunlight coruscated across the bay. Underneath a few shredded clouds, that were being chased by their shadows, the silvery sea sparkled as if encrusted with millions of tiny diamonds. In the bay, about forty yards from the seashore, a line of huge ice blocks seemed to totter precariously. It was a scene that Rupert wanted to fully appreciate, and he asked Irēne to tell the cabbie to pull up for a while.

Irēne explained that due to the severe winter weather, the whole bay had frozen over and the blocks had been formed through wave action at the start of the freeze. Rupert took out his Minox camera, which he now always carried with him, and took a picture.

The whole scene was so otherworldly and unreal looking, so beautiful that Rupert could not help asking, 'Do you believe in God?'

'I think I told you about Latvian Goddesses.' Irēne replied, 'Scratch a Latvian and underneath we are pure pagan. I certainly believe in the power of Mother Nature... Do you believe?' Rupert hesitated.

'I used to believe in God but the death of my dad changed that.' Irēne encouraged him to say more. 'As a chorister I grew up believing in the power of prayer – after all we said prayers for the King every day and he kept well - but despite all my efforts to communicate directly with God, he decided to let my father suffer in a way that only a cruel, unloving God would allow.' He felt himself becoming emotional, 'Sorry, I don't want to sound bitter, but if you'd seen the garden at Wythenshawe Hall you would have believed you were in the Garden of Eden. For something so unjust and unnecessary... and horrible to happen there. Well...'

'I understand.' Irēne had already taken hold of his hand and now gently squeezed it.

On Irēne's instruction, the cabbie gave a tug of the reigns and the horse set off in the direction of the mental institute. Rupert hadn't fully pictured what the building would be like, but the word 'institute' had conjured up images of a drab, forbidding, Victorian pile. Rebecca's home could not have been more different. It was a large two-storey, wooden house painted light blue. Each gulley was swollen with snow and the garden had its own white eiderdown reflecting light into the cosy-looking, glass-covered veranda.

Stepping inside, Rupert inhaled a familiar scent. At Manchester Royal Infirmary, he had walked through a ward full of old people and here was the same aroma, the sweet and sour smell of human decay.

The receptionist welcomed Irēne as if she were an old friend. After they had put their coats in the cloakroom, she showed them into a large lounge inhabited by bodies seated in various contortions. At the far end, sitting upright and striking a regal pose was a woman who looked young and fresh, as if she were a visitor. 'Mamma.' Irēne called over and her mother looked up and smiled. Rupert could see that Irēne and her mother shared the same high cheekbones and thick, lustrous hair. Rebecca was still a good-looking woman.

Rupert walked over and offered Rebecca his hand. He looked at her eyes, which, whilst blue-grey like Irēne's, did not have the same sparkle. Indeed, to him, they seemed to be sad and distant. Instead of shaking his hand, Rebecca took it and held it fast whilst she spoke to him in Latvian. Irēne told her that he did not speak Latvian and she immediately began to speak in German, 'You are a very young, handsome man but why are you using a walking stick?'

'Mama, I told you about Rupert's accident.' Irēne's comment seemed to jog her memory.

'Of course, Irēne has told me about you. Now sit here and tell me more about yourself.' Rupert hadn't known what to expect but it wasn't quite this.

Sitting down next to Rebecca, Rupert talked about his home, the Hall and his mother. When he had finished speaking, Rebecca said, 'I already like you. You are kind to your mother and that says a lot about a man. You will make a good husband.' Irēne looked at Rupert opened her eyes wide and raised her eyes. Then Rebecca added, 'I can only offer some small advice; don't try to control Irēne. She is a free spirit – just like her mother.'

'Don't go putting him off me.' Irēne commented.

Struck by Rebecca's lucidity and attentive gaze, Rupert wondered whether Irēne had exaggerated her mother's condition. She appeared to be a completely normal person.

After a short while Irēne excused herself, saying that she had to see the administrator, and when she had left the lounge Rupert said to Rebecca, 'I understand you are an actress and starred in some of Brecht's plays.' Rebecca's response of looking away surprised him and he feared he had strayed onto the wrong subject. Rebecca stared out of the window for some time. When she looked back towards Rupert, it wasn't at him but through him. She took hold of his hand and, with a fearful, voice asked, 'What is the sound coming from over there in that distant sand dune?'

Rupert, realising that Rebecca had gone into herself, put his hands up to stop her. Rebecca paid no heed and carried on. 'It is as if a giant brush is gently sweeping the sand, but there is no wind. Has a cloud passing overhead darkened the earth? No, surely not, not... not snakes.' She shrieked and Rupert recoiled. 'Black, dark, deathly black. They are covering Europe. Run, run, but the sand is so deep it is stopping me and the sweeping sound is increasing.' Rupert stood up looking for Irēne or a nurse. 'No, don't look back, oh there are so many hunters, I said don't look back. They are quick and hunt in packs. Slithering, sliding, coiling. Oh how they writhe and wriggle, twisting and contorting.' Rebecca coiled her arms around her head and body. 'Hissing and flicking their forked tongues, their bright swastika eyes.' Rupert wanted to run for help as Rebecca raised herself from her seat and shouted, 'I'm being covered, bound, weighted down.'

Irēne, together with a nurse, rushed into the lounge. She then calmly took hold of Rebecca and settled her back in her seat. Rupert remained standing in a kind of shock.

That evening, Rupert lay in bed feeling dreadfully tired. He wondered if this was due to the physical effort involved in walking so far that day or the mental shock of finding out how deeply disturbed Rebecca was. Her vision of snakes covering Europe had been far more frightening than anything Andris had talked about. The image had shocked him into realising he had been living in cloud cuckoo land, completely oblivious to the reality of what was happening elsewhere. He couldn't help but feel that Rebecca was closer to the truth than she knew. *Instead of making wedding plans*, he thought, *I should be contacting the ambassador. I must return home.*

The next day, Rupert obtained permission to use the director's phone to contact the British Legation. After a long wait he was put through to a Peggie Benton, who he had met briefly at the Legation's Christmas party at Schwarz's, more than a year ago. She reassured him that the legation knew where he was and of the plans to move him to Kemeri Sanatorium. She ended by saying, 'In the event of the Legation being evacuated I will contact you personally.' Rupert sincerely hoped she would. Surely, his next chance would be his last.

Kemeri Sanatorium

On the morning of March 12th, Rupert sat waiting for the ambulance to transport him to the sanatorium at Kemeri. It hadn't taken him long to put the few things used in the hospital into his trunk that the ambassador had arranged to be delivered from Rupert's apartment. He looked around the ward that had been his home for the last six months. Despite the excellent care, he was not sorry to be leaving.

To Rupert, the minute hand moved even slower than normal around the face of the wall clock. He watched every jolt and vibration, heard every tick and was surprised with each successive movement of the minute hand. He had fallen into a kind of reverie and when he heard his name called and jolted upright.

Rupert let the porter manhandle the trunk, whilst he said goodbye to the nurses on the ward. Each came up to him to give him a hug and wish him well. He suddenly felt tearful despite his need to escape.

With walking stick in hand, he followed the porter outside, where he breathed in deeply, gulping in lungfuls of fresh air. Dressed in a thick overcoat and intricately patterned mittens, the accompanying doctor said, 'You can smell spring in the air.' Rupert nodded. He was unable to detect spring, but he liked the idea that winter was finally loosening its icy grip.

The ambulance set off on a bumpy, measured journey to Kemeri. Rupert fell into conversation with the doctor who started by saying, 'I am envious of your sojourn at the sanatorium. The healing properties of the mud found there means that it is used to treat all sorts of problems, especially skin complaints.'

'Well, my bottom would welcome some treatment as I have done nothing but sit on it for six months.' Both laughed.

'And you will be away from all this talk of war.'

Rupert doubted that there was anywhere cocooned from the news of war and said, 'It is surprising how long it is taking the Red Army to defeat the Finns.'

'You're right. The Red Army is suffering from Stalin's purge of its officers. It is said that over thirty thousand officers have been executed or imprisoned. Bureaucrats and amateurs must now be in charge of it.' The doctor talked more about the war and of the harshness of the conditions on the front line. He surprised Rupert by saying. 'As I'm a doctor, maybe you would expect me to be sorry for the poor Soviet soldier. But no, not at all. I say let them rot or freeze on the front line.'

Passing what looked like a frozen bog, with reeds poking through the snow-covered surface, the ambulance carried on through birch trees standing in scattered clumps with their thin, vein-like white trunks set against a purple wash of bare twigs. Rupert was enjoying the trip as much as any he could remember.

The ambulance eventually turned off the main road and proceeded down a side street populated by small, well-tended cottages dotted along either side. What appeared to be a giant cruise-liner trapped in pack ice came into view; so large, so bright, so magnificent that Rupert couldn't help but exclaim, 'By jingo, that is something else.' Kemeri Sanatorium came into full view as the ambulance wended its way along the approach road passing yellow coloured outbuildings, which the doctor explained were the bathhouses. Immediately the ambulance came to a stop at the main door, a doorman emerged, giving the impression this was a grand hotel rather than a health resort and certainly not a hospital.

Rupert's leg had stiffened during the journey and as he walked awkwardly into the huge foyer, he was met by a stooped man, wearing a formal, dark suit who, after welcoming Rupert in

German, introduced himself as Herr Kocke, the manager. After the doctor had handed over Rupert's medical file and bid them both goodbyes, Herr Kocke escorted Rupert towards his room. Rupert looked around the foyer as they waited for the lift. Everything was grey, but rather than appearing sombre, the many different muted shades somehow combined to create a tone that immediately made him feel at ease. Looking up he saw a magnificent chandelier that would have dwarfed anything found in a Cambridge college.

Rupert's bedroom was comfortably furnished and decorated in muted tones complementing those in the foyer. The doorman had already carried the luggage upstairs and Rupert unpacked. He was amazed to find, behind one of the doors, a vast porcelain bath and he decided to try this out once he had explored the rest of the sanatorium.

Back on the ground floor, Rupert went into the guests' lounge. It was furnished with deeply upholstered chairs and settees and decorated with bright, modern paintings. On one wall was a huge mural depicting a pastoral scene overlooking a wide river with Latvian peasants in the foreground wearing their smocks embroidered with intricate motifs. Next door, was a vast dining room, filled with a surprising number of pristine white tables and elegant chairs. Rupert wondered how many guests the sanatorium expected to host. Returning through the lounge, he turned into the library and noticed an old lady sitting, fast asleep, in the depths of one of several armchairs.

Walking over to one of the well-stocked bookcases, Rupert looked at some of the titles. Most were in Latvian but there was a fair selection of German books and some in Russian. He couldn't see any in English and thought, *No matter, it is a good job I like German literature.* He retraced his steps and examined the pillars holding up the wide ceiling. Each pillar was decorated with a flourish of palm fronds at its capital. His overall impression was one of luxury; it was clear that the sanatorium had been built to cater for Europe's wealthiest clients. He mused, *The owners, who ever they are, must be feeling the financial blow now hardly anyone is here.*

Deciding to leave exploration of the grounds until the following day, Rupert returned to his room to take the bath he had promised himself. It was a couple of hours later, after a long, luxurious soak in the biggest bath he had ever been in, when he re-entered the lounge. To his surprise and delight, he saw Andris talking to a tall, thin, middle-aged man who appeared to be wearing somebody else's suit. The jacket hung off his shoulders and looked like it could accommodate at least one more person.

Andris stood up, waved Rupert over to him, and said, 'Rupert, I came to see how you liked your new abode and guess who I have found here? Let me introduce Fricis Apšenieks. Fricis, this is Rupert Lockart from England. Fricis is a Latvian chess champion.' The men shook hands and Andris turned to Fricis, 'I believe you won in 1926 and 1934, if I'm not mistaken. Fricis, Rupert is a good player, maybe you two would like a game some time?' Rupert commented that he was a simple amateur but would like the opportunity to learn from a chess champion.

Andris was keen Rupert heard more about the Latvian chess champion. 'Fricis has been to England. Fricis, can you remind me of your wins there?' Fricis replied in English, which impressed Rupert.

'Yes, I in England been, twice. Bromley and Folkestone. Both trips I very happy. I play well and enjoy English hospitality. Bromley go in 1925 but World Amateur Championship I not win. I tie in third place. Eight years after I go in summer of 1933 to Chess Olympiad in Folkestone where I fifth. But I play best games of chess. I play Gideon Stahlberg of Sweden and used Slav Defense. We still talk about game.'

Rupert congratulated Fricis on his English and Andris continued the conversation in German. 'Rupert, it's a pity you were in hospital as this was the venue for the Latvian championship late last year.'

'Let's not speak about the result here.' Fricis interjected, also speaking in German, 'I did though have the opportunity to watch Salo Flohr, who won the competition, in action. What a player and I have picked up a few of his moves. I especially like his variation of the Queen's Gambit.'

'I look forward to being soundly beaten by it.' Rupert replied.

The three men had been standing until this point, and as they sat themselves down Andris took an opportunity to change the subject. 'Talking of being soundly beaten, despite the heroic efforts of the plucky Finns, the Red wave has washed over them. They have been forced to sign a peace treaty.'

'What brought their resistance to an end?' Rupert asked.

'It is clear the Russian bear gets very angry when its will is challenged.' Andris waved his big hand in front of him as if it were the paw of a huge bear sweeping all before it. He talked about the weight of the Soviet firepower directed at the ill-equipped Finns and the lack of promised support. It seems that Norway and Sweden denied transit rights to Britain and France to avoid angering the Soviets.

Remembering what he had previously been told about the heroic Finns, Rupert felt sorry that all of their efforts seemed to be coming to nothing. He said, 'I suppose once the Mannerheim line was breached the game was up.'

'Yes, the Finnish military situation on the Karelian Isthmus was dire with its troops experiencing heavy casualties. With the Swedes cutting off supplies, the Finns had little choice but to accept the Soviet terms for a peace deal.

'What sort of deal?'

'A humiliating one. Now, as well as burying their dead, the Finns have to re-house nearly half a million people who lived in the lands of Karelia that have been ceded to the Russians. It is a bitter harvest from an unprovoked war. A cease-fire took effect yesterday at noon Leningrad time and the formal peace treaty is being signed today in Moscow.'

Rupert was surprised that the doctor he had travelled with hadn't spoken about the cease-fire, but put this down to either him being too busy to keep himself informed, or the news being carefully controlled. Breathing deeply, Andris, in a deep, ominous voice, continued. 'Now, surely the Soviets will take breath, regroup, re-amour and come our way. Remember this day; 12th March was the day our fate was sealed. The Finns put up a brave fight but at what cost? Also, they had the winter conditions and Finnish terrain on their side. What do we have? Nothing to help us for sure, but plenty to aid the oncoming Russians. We have roadlinks and railway infrastructure that will allow them to arrive in comfort. Not that I'm saying we should give up without a fight.'

Andris changed the subject and the men chatted for a while longer until Andris told the others that he had only called in en-route to another meeting and must now depart. They shook hands and, when Andris had left, Rupert turned to Fricis and asked in English, 'Did you like England?' Fricis smiled and began again in English.

'I like walking down Bromley Main Street and look at shops and shopkeepers, such a variety. I thinking Latvians like hats until I go England but English have so many. Railway man's is different to stationmaster and milkman's is different to baker's. I liked Bobby's hats and bank manager's, how you say, bowler. Hats for all professions! And one other thing, I like English public toilets. I know it is strange to say. Such good

223

architecture and tiled interiors. Clean and bright, they are mark of civilised society.'

Rupert smiled and thought, *Tea with milk and model public toilets; what a contribution we have made to the world!* Fricis continued. 'In Folkestone, I like gardens of houses and public spaces. Such neatness! World is safe and ordered place when roses grow over door and border flowers rise in steps to huge dahlias.' Rupert wasn't sure roses growing up walls was at all a mark of safety but did not comment on this.

'What didn't you like?' Rupert asked.

'I like everything, even food! Only I have one complaint; English measures for whisky can be larger.' They both laughed.

Later, the two men left the lounge to go upstairs and get ready for the evening meal. When Rupert returned, he was surprised the tables for dinner were specifically allocated even though the dining room was almost empty. He sat at the table that bore his name card. It was set with table mats, cutlery, lead crystal glasses and napkins threaded through monogrammed rings, all laid on a crisp white tablecloth. The only oddities, to his eye, were the table mats. On the main one in front of him was an alpine scene with the legend, 'The Eagle's Nest' printed in German on the bottom right-hand corner. He wondered if this was a hint as to the nationality or political leanings of the owners of the sanatorium.

Nodding to the lady he had seen sleeping in the library earlier in the day, Rupert said, '*Labvakar*' to an elderly couple sitting at a table close by. He wasn't unhappy to be eating alone and after ordering from a menu presented to him by a waiter, he sat back thinking that even Thomas Egerton Tatton could not have had an easier life. The first course arrived, fresh and delicious and Rupert addressed the waiter, who wore a white jacket buttoned to the collar. 'If you have any, I would like some Chateau Yquem

'13 to go with the fish.'

The waiter smiled and commented, 'I am sorry sir, it is a rule in the sanatorium that no alcohol is served, although I admire your choice.' Rupert took the opportunity to introduce himself. The waiter responded by saying that his name was Uldis and then returned to the kitchen. It seemed clear to Rupert that another house rule was not to fraternise with the guests.

Back in his room, later that evening, Rupert looked out of the window and was surprised to see that it was snowing. A silver light from the obscured moon filtered through the gently falling flakes, and snow had already blurred every contour of the landscape. He watched large clumps of snow fall noiselessly from the fir trees that edged the garden and considered how fortunate he was to have been transferred to the sanatorium. *It really is beautiful,* he thought.

In bed, he realised he hadn't once used his walking stick that day and wondered whether he'd soon be found out as a malingerer. Looking forward to the arrival of Irēne at the weekend, at length he drifted into an erotic slumber thinking of her in his wide, comfortable bed.

Chess Lesson

On coming down to breakfast, Rupert was surprised to find he was the only person in the dining room and, returning to his table, thought, *My table; how quickly we appropriate things and call them our own.* Waiting for him was a breakfast menu and a list of the day's activities. He decided upon one of the many egg-based dishes offered on the menu and turned his attention to the activities. He found that these mostly involved mud in one sort of treatment or another. Finding that cross-country skiing was also listed, he wondered whether he'd be able to attempt this with Irēne when she visited. The thought of sweeping elegantly across the snow with Irēne by his side sounded idyllic.

During the course of Rupert's breakfast only one other guest, a bearded man with a severe stoop, made an appearance and he acknowledged him with a nod of the head. Rupert wondered where the other guests were he had seen the night before.

After breakfast, he returned to his bedroom. Climbing the stairs was challenging and he took his time, his leg stiff and sore. His lack of muscle tone displeased him and he hoped his stay at the sanatorium would offer the chance to correct this. Retrieving his PG Wodehouse novel, he then made his way to the library and placed his book on the shelves before taking down a copy of *The Notebooks of Malte Laurids Brigge* by Rainer Maria Rilke. Out of one of the pages a pressed rosebud fluttered to the floor and Rupert thought, *I might not be able to smell spring, but at least here is a clear message that it'll come.* He looked at the page from which the flower had fallen and read the words *The woman who loves always surpasses the man who is loved.* Intrigued by the line, he tucked the book beneath his arm.

After identifying a comfortable armchair, Rupert turned it to look out over the snow-covered grounds. As he did so, he noticed that the longcase clock against the wall was showing eleven-thirty.

He wondered what time Irēne would arrive the following day. Visiting times were not restricted, so he hoped he wouldn't have to wait until the afternoon before she came to see him.

Settling himself into the seat, he studied the snowy expanse of the garden, which had taken on a pale reflection of the leaden sky. He mused that, with the largely grey interior mirroring the grey shades of the outside, he might well be in a cloud; admittedly a jolly comfy one. He began to read and was surprised at how quickly he was absorbed. The ticking of the clock and the muffled silence of the snow cocooned Rupert in the comfort of the library and he was on the verge of falling asleep when footsteps roused him. Fricis came into the room. Rupert rose to greet him, setting the book aside. Fricis pulled up another chair and, as if by magic, Uldis appeared and they ordered two coffees.

Rupert asked Fricis why he was staying at the Sanatorium and, as if answering the question, he started to cough. Turning from Rupert, he dug into his baggy trousers and brought out a handkerchief to cover his mouth, muffling the hacking sound. Eventually, after the coughing had ceased, Fricis explained that over the previous two months he had felt very tired and had completely lost his appetite, adding, 'I think I have been playing too much chess and I decided a few days of rest would do me good.' Rupert understood that, with his ill-fitting suit, Fricis must have lost a good deal of weight.

'I'm sorry to hear that... especially as I was going to suggest we have a game.'

'Of course we can have a game. It's not chess that's the problem; only, when it's your profession there is the need to keep on winning and that can be stressful. And this is my last day here, so we will not have another opportunity.'

After drinking their coffees, Fricis directed them to the games room. The lights suspended above a billiard table had been left on and they cast a green hue across the room producing a curious effect of giving the snowy scene outside a purple tinge. Besides the billiard table, there was a bagatelle board and a number of card tables. Piled on shelves were boxes of chess pieces that Rupert assumed must have been left over from the chess championship.

They set up a chessboard on a table close to large French windows. In the summer, these would give easy access to a terrace and what Rupert assumed to be lawns under the snowy covering.

They had not been playing long before Rupert knew he was up against a different quality of opponent than he was used to. Even though Rupert tried to maintain control by preventing Fricis dominating the centre ground, he soon found his options had been skilfully closed down. Retreating wasn't possible and after a short, ineffective counter attack, Rupert could foresee his inevitable collapse.

Before the game ended, Rupert looked at Fricis and noticed that, whilst he had very pale, even waxy skin, his intelligent eyes shone with curious light. After Fricis declared, 'Checkmate,' Rupert smiled and said, 'I'm pleased you won. I was beginning to think I was invincible and that's probably not a good thing.' They reset the board.

Rupert opened the game and, to his way of thinking, Fricis soon made an unwise counter allowing Rupert to capture his pawn without ceding any apparent gain. Rupert hoped Fricis had lost concentration.

In the first game, Rupert had been silent but now, in the knowledge that he was likely to be soundly beaten, let his thoughts wander to a subject he had often considered, and asked, 'You are clearly a great strategist. Tell me, why aren't you running the government or, for that matter, why aren't chess masters - masters of the world?' Rupert paused to let Fricis appreciate the scope of the question and then added, 'Surely, the skills of being able to develop a strategy, make predictions and outwit the moves of an opponent must be highly relevant in all areas?'

Fricis threw back his head and laughed. 'Oh dear, what a thought! Chess is a game; it's not real life. Real life throws up so much more than can be encountered with thirty-two pieces on a chequered board.' Rupert wondered whether Fricis was going to leave his response at that but, after a brief pause, he continued. 'If it shows you anything, it shows how difficult it is to come up with a winning strategy and to make predictions. In chess, we have two people playing within a very clearly defined set of rules. Yet, even here, in a very narrow field, predictions are often wrong. Anyway, I don't try and think too many moves ahead. My game is largely based on the tactics of knowing which plays will create the greatest opportunities.'

The game continued for a while and after making a move, Rupert said, 'Maybe it's just my ego, but I was rather hoping a world run by chess players would be rather benign.' Fricis smiled.

'It's clear you've never been to a world chess tournament. It is full of backstabbing, squabbling and even cheating.' Rupert admitted to being surprised. Fricis concluded with, 'Chess masters should be left where they are.'

As the game progressed, Rupert felt there was an opportunity to go on the offensive and moved his bishop to begin an attack. Having made his move, he reflected on what Fricis had said about the difficulty of making predictions and contrasted this with the ordered routine of his day. Rupert asked, 'Is it that hard to make predictions?' Fricis soon countered Rupert's move.

'It's not hard to make predictions, we do this all the time, but making predictions that turn out to be right is another matter.' Fricis paused briefly and then added, 'If a prediction does turn out to be right, it still might only have been a lucky guess. Real life, taken over the course of years, is entirely unpredictable.'

'Entirely?'

Fricis waited for Rupert to make a move before responding. 'Yes, entirely. Who would have predicted that an ill-organised, ragbag of murderous Bolsheviks would seize power in Russia? Who would have predicted the reign of terror that was to follow? Who would have predicted that out of the chaos of the Great War, Latvia would become an independent nation? Prediction is impossible because history turns on the smallest, and seemingly insignificant, of events. What if the Germans, for instance, hadn't smuggled Lenin into Russia in a covered train as if he were a deadly bacillus ready to infect a nation?'

'Who'd have predicted the plane would leave without me...' Rupert murmured. Fricis furrowed his brow and Rupert smiled, 'Sorry, I will tell you about that another time.'

After a brief pause, Rupert continued. 'There is so much talk of inevitability. I have come to believe that the arrow of time is flying in a particular direction and is predetermined to hit a specified target.' Fricis, who seemed to be concentrating more on the conversation than the game, moved a piece without any apparent consideration and said, 'Luckily, nothing is inevitable. Firstly, time's arrow doesn't fly in a straight line because time is not linear; time in the social realm is circular.' Rupert drew his eyebrows together and pursed his lips.

Returning his attention to the board, Rupert pondered on how to build his offensive. After a while he moved his rook and, with some satisfaction, took one of Fricis' pawns before addressing his opponent. 'I'm not sure I can quite get my head around the idea that time is circular.'

'One day you may.' Then, after apologising for sounding enigmatic, Fricis added, 'The important thing to realise is this; there are very different laws that apply in the social realm compared to the physical realm.'

'How are they different?'

'Natural scientists tease apart the underlying cause and effect relationships in the physical world and this has given us the power to predict important matters.'

Demonstrating what he meant, Fricis picked up one of his pawns and knocked over one of Rupert's, adding, 'Cause – mine moves, effect – yours removed.' Rupert was happy to sacrifice a pawn to help him dominate the centre and maintain his attack. Fricis carried on. 'As such, much of what used to be in the province of the gods has been dragged into the realm of mere mortals. Scientists and engineers have made massive progress and improved our lives – would you not agree?'

Rupert thought of Metropolitan Vickers and how it worked to turn still water into power, by damming a river and then converting the kinetic energy of falling water into mechanical energy before converting the mechanical energy through a generator into electrical energy. 'Yes,' he agreed, 'we are learning to exploit the laws of the universe.'

'Scientists are learning to predict the outcome of physical events, and I wish them success, but cause and effect do not operate in the same way in the social world.'

'Don't they?'

Fricis didn't immediately respond to Rupert's question, but after Rupert had taken his move he sat back, as if offering a break from the game, and said, 'In the physical realm there are actions

231

and reactions, stimuli and responses; one thing causes another thing to happen. However, in the social realm, nothing is as simple as that. No organism simply responds to a stimulus, we respond to what we interpret the stimulus to be and this, in turn, is a function of our intentions or the goals that we have.'

'I like the sound of that even if I don't fully understand it.'

'All living creatures act intentionally. Intention enables us to operate one step ahead of our learnt behaviours and our evolutionary specified responses and, in anticipating the future, we beat the world to the punch.'

'All living creatures?' questioned Rupert.

'Yes, all living creatures and I will go one step further; all living organisms.'

Without any apparent forethought, Fricis moved his rook to what Rupert considered to be a defensive position and then continued. 'We are all, from amoeba to man, goal-oriented and are continually asking, if I do this, then that will happen, or will it? That is always the question, whether or not we can say it out loud. The question is sometimes easy to answer, sometimes difficult to answer without further work, and sometimes impossible to work out at all.'

'And, even if it is impossible, we seem to be able to make choices anyway.'

'Exactly, you are a quick learner. We are free to choose. That is for sure... and it is necessary. Nothing ever quite repeats. Contrary to what the physicists tell us, there is randomness and without exercising free choice, we wouldn't be able to cope with the gaps in knowledge that life throws at us.'

Returning their attention to the board, both men remained silent allowing Rupert to study his attacking position. He had a foretaste of the glory that would be his in beating a chess champion. Then he laughed at his own vanity when he realised the stealth with which he had been surrounded. How bold he had felt only a few moves before, how sure he was that Fricis was distracted. Now it was clear to him that if he made a queen he'd be immediately taken by the bishop. He ran though the options and understood that even if, after another move, he was in a position to check Fricis with a knight he'd then have to retreat and, after that, would end up losing. In the knowledge he was now on the slippery slope to defeat, Rupert nevertheless, moved his pawn and promoted it to a queen.

Fricis immediately took the newly promoted piece by moving his bishop and recommenced the conversation. 'We are free to choose, but we are not in control. No one person is in control of the future, be he chess master, dictator or president. The future comes to be through the interactions of multiple choosing beings and is different to how any one person sees it to be.' Rupert was sure this applied to him in both chess and life in general. An image of being caught in a web came to mind.

'We're not in control of our destiny; that, it seems, is clear, but aren't Stalin and Hitler in control?' Fricis snorted ironically at the question.

'No, in the battle to win territory and exercise power, even these two aren't in control. No one can predict the future. No one knows the consequences of Stalin's and Hitler's bids to create golden empires – not even them.'

Reflecting on how he felt about leaders being out of control, just like the rest of the population, Rupert was quiet for a while and then said, 'I suppose to be masters of our own destiny we would need the power to go back in time to unpick the consequences of poor choices and not even these two are time travellers.'

'Thank God for that.'

The end of the game unfolded as Rupert had envisaged and, after declaring, 'Checkmate,' Fricis said, 'I hope you liked Flohr's variation of the Queen's Gambit.'

'I don't know what the variation is; all I know is that I've been well and truly thrashed.'

After packing away the chess set and returning the box to the shelf, Rupert thanked Fricis for the interesting conversation and then said, 'I take my hat off to you as a chess player but I think I can beat you at bagatelle.' Fricis looked at Rupert blankly and Rupert, realising he hadn't been understood, went over to the game.

'I see, but we call that Russian billiards.'

It was clear that Fricis wasn't a well man and Rupert was concerned about tiring him, but he had one burning question to ask, 'If you were a betting man, would you put any money on Latvia remaining independent?'

'In a world that is entirely unpredictable, it would seem sensible not to bet at all.' Rupert felt stupid as this was just what Fricis had been talking about, but after a pause, Fricis continued, 'However, there are some common themes that help us to make an educated guess. In the social world one of these themes concerns the nature of power.' Fricis paused long enough for Rupert to cock his head in anticipation and then concluded. 'The strong dominate the weak.'

'Go on.' Rupert was intrigued.

'Latvia, as part of the Russian Empire, was weak. Latvia as an independent nation is weaker still, militarily. The Government has declared neutrality in the current conflict as if this, miraculously, will keep it out of the war. But it has no defences, worthy of talking about, to prevent the big powers ignoring its declared neutrality and invading, which they surely will.'

Fricis started to cough and it was a few minutes before he had brought the deep rattle under control. 'Could you stay a while longer to fully recover?' Rupert enquired and Fricis replied that he had chess commitments to be honoured and would have to leave in the morning.

Fricis then excused himself and the two men, after shaking hands, bade each other farewell.

Rupert watched Fricis' thin frame disappear out of the games room and, replaying in his mind one of his phrases, thought, *The only way I'm going to beat the world to the punch is by getting home and taking Irene with me. But how on earth do I do that?*

History Turns on the Smallest of Things

Rupert huddled under his prison blanket and wondered whether the occupation of Latvia had opened up the possibility of Fricis becoming a Soviet chess champion. An image entered his head of himself being back at Metro Vicks and talking to his colleagues. He imagined himself saying, 'I once knew the great Soviet Chess Master, Fricis Apšenieks.' He then realised that, if Fricis was right, the future wouldn't be how he imagined it to be.

With what felt like superhuman effort, he replayed in his mind the games of chess he had played with Fricis. He was pleased that, for this short period, he could dislodge the unwelcome swirling, chattering whirlpool of his thoughts which surged whenever he stopped pacing. Rupert tried to play chess against himself. He visually set the board in his mind but wasn't able to hold the sequences for long and the changing image of the board pieces.

Frustrated, Rupert's mind scattered the pieces and he jumped up from the bed berating himself, *Why have I taken so long to come up with such a simple idea.* At the desk, and with trembling hands, he tore out two pages from the note pad. On one he marked out sixty-four small squares and, on the other, he drew thirty-two figures representing the chess pieces.

He was pleased with his work. It took him a long time to carefully fill in the alternate squares and draw and tear out the chess pieces, so he decided to save the pleasure of having his first game until the next day.

Rupert enjoyed the process of making the chess set but when he sat to play the game he found there was an insoluble problem. He realised that the attraction of chess was guessing the strategies of the opponent and thwarting them. His one brain was incapable of simultaneously knowing something and not knowing it at the same time. He soon found he couldn't think even two moves ahead as he normally would have done. *How can I,* he thought, *as I already know the possible moves of my opponent.* In the end, he said to himself, *This way madness lies. To do this well, I'll have to create two distinct personalities. This is absurd, like trying to jump over your own shadow.*

Rupert felt tired and ill at ease. To try to settle himself he compiled a list of things that he missed from England: Pears soap, Golden Syrup on morning porridge, Eccles cakes, sweat pea plants, the excitement of the football pools being checked by his uncle, Raleigh bikes, Brooks saddles, Morecambe Bay shrimps and the shipping forecast announced on the radio.

He remembered Irēne had once said, 'The only thing that I have had from England, other than books, is Colman's Mustard. Fiery but fantastic on a frankfurter.' He added mustard to his list. With a clunk, the lights went out in the cell.

Rupert had begun to dread going to sleep. His dreams were growing darker and ever more frightening. He thought once more of the shipping forecast and wondered if he might recall each of the sea areas. *Perhaps,* he thought, *this almost meditative recitation will help me have a good night's sleep. Tyne, Forth, Cromarty, Dogger, Forties, Viking, Fair Isle...* By the time he reached Dover, Thames and Heligoland, he had drifted softly out to sea.

How quickly the second hand moves over a massive clock face. Jerkily not smooth at all and not tick-tock but click-clack. Ten minutes past. Pull myself up to sit on the cold metal hand. What a view from up here. But, is there a way off? Do I have to wait until the hand reaches twelve and climb through the cuckoo's hole, surely not? I can see the Hall from here and yes my house too. What a sight, how beautiful, green and pleasant, the Head Gardner is waving to Dad. What? Surely not, he wants him help tie the rose back up against the wall. There it is, the thick, barbed

237

branches spread out on the path like tentacles of a giant octopus to catch the passing sailor. No. Don't touch it. It is poisonous. Worse than that, more deadly than the serpent's bite. My voice, they can't hear me. It is being carried away and lost in the void of years. Twenty-five past. The slope of the hand is already too steep. I have to edge my foot against the bulbous end to stop me falling off. Any more and I will slide off and such a way to fall. Yes, I can see Stanley racing to my rescue. He's driving fast but that is good. He needs to reach me soon. No, it's too fast, better slow down!

Rupert woke shouting, 'No, Stanley, there is a cow in the road ahead. Brake!'

It took ten minutes before his heart rate settled and he was able to lie down. He avoided going back to sleep straight away, lest the theme began again, but something was different. *The cow.* 'Ah!' Rupert said aloud, his mind seizing hold of the memory at last. He remembered. Stanley had swerved to avoid the cow and hit one of the trees by the side of the road.

Rupert again considered what Fricis had said— that history turns on the smallest of things. He wondered what his life would be like now if the cow had not ventured into their path.

Acceptance

It was the day of Irēne's visit and Rupert could not settle to anything. He decided to finish *Notebooks of Malte Laurids Brigge* but every time he finished a paragraph, he looked up to see how far the clock's minute hand had moved, only to find it had stalled or, occasionally, seemingly moved back. He reread the paragraphs without seeing them.

Unable to make progress with the book, he stood and decided to walk, inspecting the ground floor of the sanatorium starting with the dining room on the east side of the building. The dining room was set for lunch but was empty of any guests. He looked towards his allocated table and anticipated sharing the delights of the sanatorium's kitchen in Irēne's company.

On re-entering the lounge, Rupert noticed the grey hair of the old lady, who he had seen on his first day, poking up behind the back of a winged chair. Her head was tilted forward and, assuming that she must be asleep, he did not disturb her. The lounge was both broad and long and had a high ceiling. The bright light coming though the windows from the reflected snow highlighted the thin green stripes in the mainly grey upholstered seating. It put Rupert in mind of the shoots of snowdrops that pierced the snow of the Wythenshawe gardens as spring approached.

The wide hallway lead to the foyer, dominated by a very grand, splendidly intricate, wrought iron balustrade encasing the wooden staircase. After walking along a corridor, his foot tapping on the patterned, well polished parquet flooring, he passed the games room and came to a door marked *Medicīnas Centrs*. He knocked; there was no response. He tried the door and, finding it unlocked, entered a large room painted white and furnished with a desk, examination table and a large picture of the human skeleton mounted on one of the walls. He thought, *What a strange place this is. Apart from a few elderly guests, there is virtually no one here and that includes employees. Yet, when I go to my room the bed is made and the dining room is reset in my absence.* Rupert crossed to the large closed door at the end of the room and opened it. He was met with a row of tables blank steel tables and a scrupulously clean, tiled floor. The room seemed unnaturally cold, the chill pressing against Rupert, bringing with it the faint whiff of formaldehyde.

Rupert felt himself shiver. *Is this Hotel Dieu? God's Hotel, where those at death's door take it into their heads they need to rest before finally checking out?*

'Can I help you?' The voice came from behind and Rupert's heart clenched. He hadn't heard anyone approach and he span around to see the stooped, black suited figure of Herr Koche. Rupert felt the blood rising to his cheeks.

'No, sorry, I was just exploring the hotel.' The manager remained looking at Rupert, his gaze pointed and cool.

'Guests are not permitted in this wing without accompanying medical staff. If you need to see the doctor, please book an appointment at reception.' With that, the manager turned and walked away leaving Rupert feeling like a naughty boy chastised for scrumping apples.

Returning to the lounge, Rupert tried to resume reading his book, but the sight of the morgue and Herr Kocke's admonishment had rattled him. He found himself watching the hands of the clock, willing them to leap forwards to Irēne's arrival, whenever that might be.

Rupert fidgeted. At long last, Irēne appeared at the lounge entrance. Rupert hurried over and wrapped his arms around her. He hugged her closely to him, before separating enough to plant a kiss on her lips still cold from the outside air. 'How I've been looking forward to seeing you,' he uttered, with a sense that he had hardly ever said anything quite so true.

'Glad to hear it and that is the same for me.' Irēne replied.

Rupert helped Irēne remove her coat and as he did so, she said, 'Spring really is in the air.' He wondered what it was she detected and then was reminded of his inability to identify the elusive fragrance others had described when sampling white wines from the cellar of Pembroke College.

'Is it a hint of grass?' He said, enigmatically. Without waiting for an answer, he asked whether she'd like a tour of the sanatorium before lunch. After hanging her coat in the lobby, he started off by taking her to the library and showing her the large selection of books. He reached up to one. 'We even have an English section.' He brought down *The Inimitable Jeeves,* which Irēne recognised as Rupert's own copy.

'You really are a strange egg.' They both laughed.

From the library, Rupert took Irēne along the hall to the games room. After picking up two cues, he offered one to Irēne, saying, 'Fancy a frame or two?'

'I do not know what end of the stick to use but I can offer you a game of Russian billiards.' Rupert put the billiard cues back.

'Before we do, let's have a look at the other games on offer.' They both stood looking at the boxes piled on the shelves in an alcove.

Rupert was surprised to find a game he did recognise, *Escalado,* which he had played a few times in the junior common room at Pembroke College. He took a painted lead horse out of the box

241

and smiled as he recalled, 'The last time I played this game, I beat Orlonsky and won a pint of beer on the winning horse.'

'Oh, you are a serious gambler.' Irēne exclaimed. Then, she uncovered another box and asked, 'Have you ever played *The Landlord's Game?*'

'Never even heard of it.'

'It is a game of buying real estate and making as much money as possible.'

'Real estate, you Americans are taking over.'

Standing close to Irēne, Rupert could feel the press of her right hip against his. Gently he put his arm around her waist before bringing his head forward and kissing her. Their tongues touched, then entwined and he felt himself becoming tense with excitement. There was a noise in the corridor and Rupert broke away from their embrace and looked up, half expecting to see Herr Kocke frowning from the doorway.

Deciding against showing Irēne the Medical Centre, Rupert, instead, asked whether she'd like to go over to the bathhouse and added, 'It means going back outside, but it should be interesting and I haven't visited it yet.' She agreed and sat down in the lounge to wait for Rupert whilst he went to fetch his coat. As he opened the door of his room he noticed the bed had been made. His blood rose as he imagined Irēne lying on the cream-coloured quilt.

Suitably attired, Rupert and Irēne left the side door of the sanatorium and headed across a path towards a group of yellow buildings, which comprised the boiler room and bathhouse. These were spread out under the shadow of a large chimney. The snow squeaked beneath their feet as they walked together, arm in arm. The touch of Irēne's arm in his reminded Rupert of their

242

visit to the opera. He took deep lungfuls of air. 'How do you feel?' Irēne asked.

'Never better.' He replied, with sincerity. It was a short walk to the bathhouse and, as they approached, they both commented on the smell of bad eggs, which became increasingly noticeable. Feeling a catch in his throat and the taste of sulphur on his tongue, he said, 'They don't tell you about this in the brochure.'

They entered the bathhouse and, once through the thick, double doors into the lobby, were immediately struck by it being strangely, cool and damp. Assailed by the now almost overpowering smell, Rupert went over to the desk and hit the bell to attract attention. He was surprised by the immediate appearance of a woman wearing a thick coat who greeted them in Latvian. Irēne had a brief conversation with the woman and reported that the mud baths and sauna needed to be booked in advance but skis were available for use.

At Cambridge, Rupert had known a few students who went to Klosters to ski at Christmas. It suddenly came into his mind that one of them had returned in the Lent term with his leg in plaster. Without a great deal of enthusiasm in his voice, Rupert said, 'If only I knew how to ski.'

'The skis will be for cross-country skiing. It is very simple and is just like walking - or sliding to be more accurate.'

'But what about my leg?'

'It is not as dangerous as walking on the cobbles in the city centre; at the moment the snow is thick enough to prevent injury if you fall and, anyway, we will not be going fast.'

'Sorry to sound like such a mouse, but it has always looked dangerous to me.' They went through the door marked

Slēpošana into a large room filled with skis and skiwear and picked out appropriate equipment and apparel. There were separate ladies' and gentlemen's changing areas and when Irēne emerged Rupert commented, 'How sporty you look,' and thought, *alluring too.*

Carrying the skis and sticks, they made their way towards a path of flattened snow and once there, Irēne swiftly clipped her boot tips onto her skis. She then gave Rupert a quick demonstration of how to slide along, lifting her back heel at the end of each projection. Afterwards, she suggested that he should try these movements himself. Under her watchful eye, he clipped his boots into the skis and stood up.

Despite the ground looking like it was flat, Rupert started to gently slide backward and then, with his legs separating like a chicken's wishbone, shouted out, 'Help!' Irēne' doubled over with laughter and only when Rupert began to descend into the splits did she compose herself enough to assist him. Back in an upright position with his feet together, Rupert gingerly set off, sliding one ski in front of another as Irēne had demonstrated. She came alongside and said encouragingly,

'There, you do well.'

Shortly afterwards they came to a dip in the path. Rupert automatically accelerated and, tucking his skis under his arms to exaggerate the sense of speed, he shouted, 'Whoosh.' Irēne used her sticks to come alongside him.

'Are you the famous downhill skier who we hear is holidaying in Kemeri?' Rupert smiled as he slowed to a standstill and noticed the sweat on his brow; nevertheless, he felt fit and strong. It wasn't long before the brief circuit around the grounds had been completed and, back at the bathhouse, he suggested that they go skiing again soon. She replied that this would have to be soon as spring was coming and the snow would quickly thaw.

After changing back into their own clothes and hanging up the skis and other equipment, they returned to the sanatorium where lunch was being served. Rupert had warned Uldis he'd have a guest and, when they reached his table, they found it already set for two.

At the table, Rupert remarked that this was their first proper meal together and they raised glasses of water to celebrate. He then recounted the conversation he had with Andris and Fricis, concluding, 'Andris is sure that the Russians are coming. Do you think we should bring the wedding forward? Who knows what barriers the Russians will impose if they take over the country.'

'The Russians are certainly coming, but somehow I think it unlikely they will arrive tomorrow or even in the next few months.' Rupert found Irēne's tone reassuring. 'The Baltic States are like plump, juicy grapes they can pluck at any time. They are busy in Poland and Finland. Maybe they will take their plunder only when it is clear to them what Germany's ambitions are further west.' Rupert must have looked like he needed reassuring, as Irēne added, 'However, I will have a word with the priest at the local church to see if, needs be, he could marry us in an emergency.'

Rupert nodded his head and then realised he was ravenous after his exercise. He asked about Katerīna and listened to Irēne's reply whilst demolishing the bread that accompanied the cream of vegetable soup. Then, he listened to Irēne talking about her week whilst he polished off the fish course. He wondered whether it was too early in their culinary relationship to ask Irēne if he could eat the remains of her leftover potatoes. He resisted the temptation.

'Are you having a desert?' Irēne asked.

'Desert? Too dry for my taste. Dessert, however' Rupert

teased and Irēne tutted and rapped his knuckles affectionately. Sitting back in his chair after finishing his meal, Rupert looked around the dining room, now empty except for Irēne and himself. The sense of emptiness, somehow, gave him the feeling that he owned the place. 'I don't even think that life at Wythenshawe Hall for the Tatton family could have been as good as this.' He uttered. He took Irēne's hand and kissed it before turning his face to hers, leaning forward and kissing her on the lips. He was conscious of a tightening of the muscles around his scrotum, as if he were being forcibly pulled towards his unspoken goal. He wanted to finish the tour by showing Irēne his bedroom but held back until she asked, 'Have we seen everything now?' Without replying to her question, he rose and, helping her to her feet by pulling back the heavy dining chair, took her hand and led her through the hall and up the staircase.

On the landing in front of his bedroom door, Rupert was conscious that his palms were unusually sweaty. He turned the handle of the door and pulled it open. The curtains fluttered as fresh air was drawn in through a slightly open window. He went over to it and drew the curtains across, darkening the room. Returning, he clasped Irēne tightly and kissed her, conscious of his developing erection. He waited for a signal or gesture to indicate that he should desist. There was none, his tongue explored hers and then, gently and cautiously he pulled her closer and pressed himself against her body.

Laying one hand on Irēne's neck, Rupert, softly and gently, let it travel with a stroking motion down her back and then under her blouse to the curve just above the waistband of her skirt. He felt her so-soft skin and the faintest of downy hair at the base of her spine. Breathing deeply to help settle his nervous tremble, he unbuttoned her white blouse and helped her out of it. Irēne stood in the shade of the room wearing a creamy bodice.

The afternoon sunlight through the closed curtains was still strong enough for Rupert to see her arms and the firm, welcoming roundness of her breasts underneath the silk top. With a quiver of exquisite pleasure, he covered her right breast with his hand and a universe of feeling passed through his palm as he felt the hardening nipple. He brought Irēne towards himself, desperate to enter her soft, accepting body. Sensing his urgency, Irēne said, 'Come.' Both paused to take off their lower garments and then she led him over to the bed, where she removed the cover and lay back on the feather soft mattress.

Irēne helped him enter her body, that of the woman he loved. After a few urgent, but gentle thrusts the activity was over, the climax all his. Together, the two of them lay still in a kind of sleep, Rupert on top with his arms round her body. After some time, shattering the perfect peace, he said, 'Thank you,' which he instantly regretted. He started to dis-entwine himself, but Irēne said, 'Shhh' and prevented him from moving so that they continued to lie together, content in a mysterious stillness, for a while longer.

Distant Drums

Outside the lounge window, a fine drizzle had set in. Water dripped off the fir trees and occasional clumps of snow crumpled to the ground. He was due to meet Irēne off the one o'clock train and, as he sat in the lounge wondering how he would kill a few hours, in strode Andris. Rupert stood up so suddenly he startled the old lady who was sitting close by.

Andris joined Rupert by the window and, with the instant appearance of Uldis, coffees were ordered. The conversation soon turned to the signing of the peace treaty between Finland and Russia. Rupert said, 'Maybe Finland has given the Soviets a salutary warning causing them to pause and think. They may reflect that taking over other small countries such as Estonia and Latvia will also present them with a few challenges.'

Rupert wondered whether his comments revealed a naivety that would anger his friend but Andris was measured in his response. 'Don't be lulled into a false sense of security. Firstly, Finland has agreed to cede more territory than originally demanded by the Soviet Union.' He then described how the Red Army had defeated the Japanese at Khalkin Gol under General Zhukov. He cautioned, 'Now the Japanese have been taught a lesson in the east, Stalin can concentrate on his plan of restoring the Russian Empire in the west.'

Reflecting on the months to come, Rupert felt a growing sense that his life would take a severe turn for the worse. Before he was able to voice these concerns, Andris said, 'I'll tell you why we need to be worried. Vilhelm Munters addressed an audience at the University of Latvia and told them that relations between Latvia and Russia were entirely satisfactory. Oh dear, Vilhelm can no more tell a convincing lie than hold his tongue after a few vodkas. Let's see how long it takes the Red Army to get here.'

Suddenly, the old lady, who Rupert had, so far, only acknowledged with a nod of his head, spoke in English, in a surprisingly strong voice. 'You call it Red Army or Soviet Army but it is Russian army. They come from Russia and they talk and sing in Russian, do they not? It is same army burn homesteads, kill Latvian men and rape Latvian women already one hundred years ago in time of Terrible Ivan - but no less terrible now. It is same Russian army shot Latvians under orders of Nicholas II after uprising in 1905. Same Russian army our fathers were forced to fight within during the Great War. Same Russian army was chased out of Latvia in 1919. And now beaten, and chased out army, is to march in again.'

Hearing the old lady talk in such a way left Rupert temporarily speechless and he was searching for a response when she continued. 'Karlis Ulmanis is weak man. He must stand against Russians like brave Finnish people. If no, we are *kaput*.' Rupert now recalled the British Military Attaché's unfavourable assessment of Latvia's forces in startling detail and asked, 'But, how long can a small, ill-equipped army oppose the might of Russia? How many people will die in an attempt to stop the incoming tide?'

'It is better than what is to come.' The old lady sounded strong and defiant. Rupert thanked her for her honesty and emotion and apologised for not having introduced himself. '

'Ana Weisman.' she said. 'I have seen tragedy at the hands of the Russians. I see it comes ever closer once again.' She got to her feet with difficulty and regarded Rupert with watery brown eyes. "You should leave this place, young man, while your life is still your own.' she said and hobbled from the room.

Conscious that Andris' English was poor, Rupert turned his attention back to him and asked in German, 'I don't know much about President Ulmanis; is he a fighter?' Andris gave a small laugh.

'He is charismatic and can tap into the hidden and unexpressed needs and desires of us Latvians. He managed to stage a bloodless coup and when he set up the Government of National Unity people didn't take to the streets. Yes, he took away the people's power to vote him out of office, but he gave them clarity of purpose and a sense of unity and national pride. The only problem with Ulmanis is that he is a most unusual animal; a trusting and naïve dictator. He thinks that the way of dealing with a mad dog is to stroke it. He will be bitten so badly I can imagine him dying of his wounds.'

An image of Stalin chomping down on the back of Ulmanis' neck came to mind and Rupert shook his head to dislodge the unsavoury association. He asked, 'And when the Russians do come, what can we expect? Will they allow us get on with life as before?'

'Life will become a great deal harsher. Stalin is systematically purging the intelligentsia and bourgeoisie in Russia, but as an independent nation we have escaped such atrocities. I suspect that now, it is only a question of time before we also suffer.'

'Maybe the worst excesses have passed?' Rupert was again concerned that he sounded naive and expected a sharper response, but again Andris was calm and measured in his reply.

'I would love to think so, but violence and cruelty are Communist Party policy. Lenin believed that human lives were expendable in the cause of building communism. And the most expendable are those with a vested interest in keeping things as they are. Marx wrote, no private property – no problem but Stalin has taken it a step further, no people - no problem.'

Rupert and Andris changed the subject. A short while later, Rupert waved Andris goodbye at the entrance to the sanatorium and, as there was a little time before he must head to the train station, he returned to his room.

Laying on his bed, he reflected that Andris' reports of war were like reading something from a newspaper, informative but not necessarily engaging. They elicited little fear. Yet when he heard news or views that came from the heart, even if it was imagined, as in the case of Rebecca, his immediate connection with it stirred a building sense of panic. Thinking about Ana Weisman's outburst and his own situation, he understood the drumbeats of war, once so distant, were growing louder.

The spring sunshine warmed Rupert's face whilst he waited for the arrival of Irēne's train. Looking around he was surprised how quickly the spring thaw had progressed. Much diminished and blackened remnants of snow, piled up by the station staff sweeping the platform, were the only visible reminders of the winter scene that had dominated only a few days before. Rupert looked through the trees surrounding the station to see if he could see any snowdrops but there was only crushed, brown grass. He recalled the bluebell woods in Wythenshawe and how the early shoots would already be showing, and of the secret glade in the garden where the early magnolia would be flowering.

In the distance, he heard the deep wheezing of the train. The sounds became louder as the train turned a bend in the track and came into view. It blew its whistle on the final approach and to Rupert, the toot-toot was as good as a cheery, 'What ho.' As it halted, he waved to Irēne, who already had her head out of the window and helped her get down from the high carriage by holding her waist to slow her descent as she jumped the last foot down to the very low platform. They kissed immediately and the train had chuffed away from the station before they separated. He detected a smell like burning grass and commented on this. He was surprised to find out that, as importing steam coal from Wales had been prevented by the threat of shipping being blown up by U-boats, the trains now ran on home-produced peat.

Having booked Irēne in for lunch at the sanatorium, they walked with haste as time was pressing. Rupert told Irēne of Andris' visit, but it wasn't until they were both seated comfortably in the restaurant that he recounted their conversation. Irēne listened attentively and then, after hearing him talk about the Russian leaders' attitude to their people, said, 'I had a lecture from Borya in Capri, who compared the present generation to the Jews whom Moses led through the wilderness. They must not only conquer a new world, they must also perish in order to make room for the people who are fit for a new world. I think those were his words. It was funny at the time as after delivering the lecture he cheerily ordered a second bottle of champagne. But, it is not funny at all.'

'I really do want to punch that man.' Rupert pulled an aggressive looking face.

'Safer to stick with calling him names.' They both smiled and further discussion was put on hold until the fish soup had been savoured.

Looking around the plush, light-filled dining room and thinking of his good fortune to be eating a splendid meal in the company of a beautiful woman, Rupert guiltily realised that the drum beat of war he had heard only a few hours earlier had again receded to the back of his mind. He lifted his glass and proposed a toast, 'To privilege.'

'To us.' Irēne said.

The toast prompted Rupert to say that he wanted to visit the British Legation in Riga as soon as possible. Irēne replied, 'Yes, your passport.'

'Not just my passport. With all this talk of war, I think we need to be more in charge of our own destiny. I want the Legation to arrange for you to come with me to England when there is another evacuation. Is that alright?'

'It is more than alright, but I doubt whether they will comply with your wishes. The British have a very strong reputation for following protocol and I don't think that a man taking his girlfriend home will be covered.'

'Oh, we aren't that stuffy.' Then thinking that Irēne might be right added, 'But, let's get married soon just in case.'

During the rest of the meal, they talked about the improvement in the weather and discussed what they could do for a day out in Riga. 'What about going to see the *The Fisherman's Son?*' Rupert asked and Irēne sniffed.

'I was misled by Katrina. Other people I have spoken to say that it is just a simple morality tale about how everything is better if there is cooperation. Anyway, it is in Latvian without subtitles. No, I'm sure there is something better we can do and, anyway, you promised we would go dancing. There are some great places where we can dance and listen to jazz.'

At the end of the meal, Rupert told Irēne he had arranged for them to use the sauna and have a mud treatment later in the afternoon. After they had sat and chatted for a while in the lounge, they put on their winter clothes for the short walk to the bathhouse. When they arrived, the lady at the desk in the foyer spoke to them in Latvian and Irēne relayed the instructions given. 'I'm told there is a male and female section and we are to have separate treatments. The lady will give each of us our own towels and we should arrange to meet back here.' Rupert's face dropped.

He hadn't envisaged the sauna being separate and had already imagined running his hand down Irēne's mud softened leg. He tried to hide his disappointment by saying, 'Well, let's meet here in an hour; don't go to sleep in the sauna.' He watched her being escorted to the ladies treatment area and couldn't help voicing, out loud, 'Damn.'

An hour or so later, Rupert, who had endured, rather than enjoyed, being coated with mud and left alone whilst it soaked into his skin, was waiting for Irēne's return at the entrance to the bathhouse. When he saw her reddened cheeks, he smiled and gave her a hug. 'Did you enjoy the experience?

'It was interesting.'

'Let's go back to my bedroom.' Rupert whispered.

'Has the sauna made you sleepy?' said Irēne, jabbing him playfully in the ribs.

When they walked into the lobby of the main building, there was no one to greet them. Rupert reached for Irēne's hand and escorted her to the lift and then along the wooden floored corridor to his bedroom. The bed had been made but the curtains, for some reason, were still pulled across as if to keep the sun out of a room in a hot country. Rupert helped Irēne take off her thick winter coat.

As if drugged by the heat of the sauna and the fumes from the sulphurous mud, Rupert and Irēne lay together, still and entwined, on the bed. Sensing her breath against his cheek, he gently turned towards her until their lips met. Slow, little kisses with puckered lips built into a luxurious melding.

Unbuttoning Irēne's blouse, Rupert helped her remove it and embracing her, enjoyed the feel of her silky bodice next to his skin. After he had removed his shirt and trousers, she said, 'I want to take this off too,' and gathering the thin bodice in her hands, she pulled it, with his assistance, over her head. As she sat there with bare shoulders and her firm, round breasts exposed, Rupert could feel his heart pounding.

He was surprised when she asked him to let the sun flood into the room. Carefully he got off the bed and pulled back the curtains, enjoying the sensation of being stark naked, straining out into the blueness of the day. *Have I ever felt quite so alive?*, he thought to himself. Becoming self-conscious, he was unable to turn around because of his arousal. He lifted his shirt off the floor and shielding himself with it, he returned to the bed. 'No,' Irēne said, preventing him from rejoining her, 'no, let me see you,' and she took the shirt out of his hands.

Reluctantly, Rupert stood still looking towards Irēne. The thin blue scar running up his leg seemed to point to the triumphant tower, rising rampant from the mat of mousy hair. He had never stood like this in front of anyone before and began to feel embarrassed. In his mind he was waiting for a shrieked rebuke from the Dormitory Master. Instead, he heard Irēne's soft voice, 'How strange! So purposeful.'

Rupert involuntarily tensed and his manhood nodded. They both laughed out loud and he rejoined her on the bed. 'So proud,' she murmured, 'Lord Wythenshawe! A bit frightening but lovely at the same time,' she said. Tuning towards him and rotating on to her knees, she drew near to him so that the firm globe of her right breast touched the tip of his erect phallus and caught a drop of its lubricant, which for a moment made a gloopy connection.

Pulling Rupert on top of her, she said, 'You know he is mine too, he is ours.' A shudder went through Rupert's body as his blood surged and he felt himself fill and rise and grow harder and bigger. 'Take him then.' He surprised himself with his sudden dominance. His hands traced her curves to where her hips flared and their tongues met in a passionate kiss.

This time Irēne did not need to guide Rupert and he felt her quiver at the moment of entry. Nor did he climax so quickly; his thrusts built into a powerful rhythm and the insistent beat left them hot and wet once the music had finished. Again, like the audience at the end of a great concert who were too much in awe to clap; they remained silent until his arm had deadened beneath her body and he needed to move it.

Rupert rolled away and Irēne reached for him saying, 'This is metamorphosis in reverse. Now he is a tiny, soft little chrysalis hiding in the undergrowth. You can hardly imagine the transformation! One minute meek and mild, the next dominant and demanding. Two sides of one man.' Sitting up, still naked, Rupert didn't really want to think too much about the nature of manhood, as he understood that man's darker side was leading inexorably to invasion and war.

A Visit to Riga

In anticipation of setting off to see Irēne in Riga, Rupert re-checked the contents of his small overnight bag. He didn't want to recall the last time he had packed his bag in this way, but images of his ill-fated return to the city with Stanley came back to him. He often wondered whether the last few minutes of the journey, and what they had said to each other prior to the accident, would ever resurface in his mind, but it seemed these memories were buried forever.

Looking out of the lounge window onto the garden and the bright, clear blue April sky above, Rupert was bemused by the fact winter had finished some weeks ago, but spring wasn't following directly in its footsteps. The grass remained brown and crushed as a reminder of winter's iron oppression. He recalled the previous year and remembered waiting a long time for spring to timidly venture forth. It seemed as if it were holding back until certain that the harsh winter wouldn't make an unpleasant return. 'The waiting season,' he said out loud, 'I know how it feels.' He strolled to the station.

Sitting by the window of the train carriage looking at the trees and small villages pass by through a haze of smoke and cinder, Rupert tried to identify how he was feeling. He knew he was excited to be seeing Irēne, but he also recognised an underlying feeling of fear. He imagined a convict, after a lengthy sentence, being released from prison and how he would be fearful about coping. He had heard stories of released prisoners who, used to all of their decisions being made for them, immediately reoffended so they could return to the world they knew. Facetiously, he hoped that he wouldn't break another leg to produce similar results.

At Dzintari station, two large, well-dressed men, carrying briefcases, got on the train and sat a few rows in front of Rupert.

When underway, they started talking loudly in German. The larger of the two took a newspaper out of his case and broadcast the leading article in a raised voice so everyone in the carriage could hear. 'This morning the German envoys in Oslo and Copenhagen presented the Norwegian and Danish governments with an ultimatum demanding they immediately accept the Protection of the Reich. Denmark immediately agreed and the country was under German occupation within six hours. The Norwegian Foreign Affairs Minister however, responded with the defiant words, *we will not submit voluntarily; the struggle is already underway.*' They broke into a deep, gloating laugh when the one reading the paper added, 'Such brave words. The entire Norwegian government, including King Haakon VII, fled the capital yesterday morning for the mountains in the north.'

Rupert tried to ignore the rest of this conversation, but he could not help dwelling on the news. He had hoped that German interests would have remained relatively local, perhaps consolidating gains in the Sudetanland and Poland, but with the potential occupation of Denmark and Norway, Germany seemed to be creeping up on the northern and eastern flanks of Britain. He hoped the British government had finally, fully woken to the threat clearly posed by German expansionism. He speculated on when the Legation would be contacting him regarding another evacuation. It was time to get home.

The old city came into view through the train window and as a result Rupert's spirit rose. He was pleased to see the welcoming tiers of St Peter's spire appearing and also to catch sight of the fat, round dome of the cathedral. Soon afterwards, the steam-belching train pulled into Riga station and Rupert spotted Irēne wearing a light coat at the far end of the platform. He clambered out of the carriage and hurried along the platform to meet her. The first thing she said was, 'Welcome home.'

'Yes, it does feel like I am returning to my hometown!' He said before hugging her.

They walked, hand in hand, towards the closest tram stop on the route to *Miera Iela* and Irēne's apartment. Rupert commented, 'The station seems emptier than I remember it.'

'Everything is quieter. It is as if everyone is holding their breath, waiting for something.'

'Not just for spring.' He added.

During the tram ride, Rupert did his best to hide his growing excitement. It wasn't long before the tram clacked and rocked its way to *Miera Iela* where they clambered down. After a short walk, they turned into a side street and stopped outside a four storey wooden building. Irēne announced, 'Here we are. Home'

'How lovely.' He exclaimed and meant it, as it looked homely with reddish paint and shuttered windows.

Irēne lived on the top floor and, once they had climbed the wooden staircase, they soon entered the apartment through two sets of double doors. Rupert looked at the small hallway and the pretty paintings that hung on its walls and said, 'Yes, *gemütlich.*' Irēne then directed him into the lounge where there was a wide, comfortable sofa, and scrubbed table and chairs. He noted that the photograph of him with his shirt half undone, which Walter had taken, had been given pride of place on a set of bookshelves crowded with Latvian and German books.

'Would you like a cup of tea?'

'Eh, me tongue's drier than a budgie's cage.' Rupert amused himself by coming out with one of his father's old expressions.

After hanging their coats in the hall, Rupert followed Irēne into a small, white tiled kitchen. She filled a kettle at a large enamel sink and put it on the stove to boil. She then took hold of his hand and, to finish the short tour, ushered him to the bedroom furnished with two single beds, neatly covered with patchwork quilts. He enquired, 'Which is mine?'

'You are on the sofa.'

They drank their tea and chatted about where Katerīna was spending the weekend. Then Rupert said that there was something he must do whilst in Riga. Irēne looked at him askance, 'Yes,' he said, 'I need to go to a jeweller's. There is someone very special who is owed a ring.' She protested that such a purchase was unnecessary, but he was insistent and they were soon back on *Miera Iela* located in a fashionable and artistic part of the city which boasted a few jewellers.

They entered the premises of Abrams Samuals, *Juvelieri Zeltkaļi un Sudrabkaļi* and Rupert asked what Irēne would like in the way of a gemstone. She said she had always liked emeralds, so the bearded shopkeeper, who Rupert presumed to be the owner, brought a tray of emerald rings out to them. It wasn't long before they both identified an exquisite ring cut in a way that seemed to accentuate the lustrous, deep green of the stone. Abrams Samuals commented on the good choice. When Rupert enquired about its price, he was disappointed that he had insufficient cash with him to cover the total cost. However, with a bit of haggling, and by throwing in his pocket watch in part exchange, the deal was done. Irēne left the shop wearing emerald ring on her slim finger and Rupert, wearing a large smile.

The purchase of the ring was celebrated with a late lunch at a local restaurant, which had the amusing title of *The Spinster's Cat*. Over the first course of sautéed chicken livers, they talked about how they could spend Rupert's remaining ten Lats and the rest of the day together. Irēne suggested, 'Let us go to the National Opera for some uplifting culture and then onto a jazz club that Katerīna says stays open late.'

'For almost a year, I've been in bed by half past ten, I can't wait to paint the town red.'

'I am not sure about your choice of colour, but let us go painting.'

'Let's go. But, before that, I need to visit the British Legation to pick up my passport.'

After finishing their coffee, which, now being a commodity in short supply, was supplemented by a generous helping of roasted barley, they went to catch a tram that would drop them close to the Legation. En route, the tram passed the Riga Post Office and Rupert remembered going in there for the first time and seeing a range of typewriters for public use. These included a row of machines with Hebrew typefaces, catering for the sizeable Jewish population.

A short tram ride later and they strolled through the Esplanade past the National Museum of Art where Rupert noticed that sandbags had been piled at the foot of the imposing steps leading up to the huge wooden doors dwarfed by Doric columns reaching to the domed roof. Two soldiers marched backwards and forwards along the building's frontage, rifles shouldered.

It wasn't long before, hand in hand, they arrived at the cream and yellow painted British Legation where there was a surprisingly long queue snaking its way out of the building. They tried to get through to the entrance but two men wearing kippahs blocked their way and they were told, unceremoniously, that queue jumping wasn't permitted. They made some enquiries and discovered that the queue was formed of Jewish people seeking permits to leave Riga for Palestine. Reluctantly, the couple joined the back of the queue.

As the queue edged forward, Rupert told Irēne of what he had heard on the train about the German invasion of Denmark and imminent invasion Norway. He then commented, 'Speaking of which, it's as if the National Musuem is expecting a flood, not an invasion. Shouldn't everything be better defended?' Sandbags and rifles are hardly going to stop the Russians, or Germans for that matter.'

'You can defend things too well you know.' Irēne responded. 'The Russians would destroy the city to capture it and then would rebuild it in their own image. I could not imagine such a terrible fate for such a beautiful city.' Once again, he realised the wisdom of her thinking.

Deciding to lighten the conversation, Rupert used the opportunity to tell Irēne he'd found out Uldis had once been a cameraman on the film, *Battleship Potemkin*. He added, 'Apparently, even the Nazis liked it. Their Minister of Propaganda, Joseph Goebbels, called it a marvellous film without equal in the cinema.' On mentioning the name of Goebbels, Irēne took a step back.

'Goebbels! I wonder if he is the same man I met?'

'If it is, how come?' He shot her a quizzical glance.

'Sometimes, Mother and I used to be taken out in Erich Hesse's big, open top Opel on drives to the west of Berlin and occasionally out as far as Potsdam. On the way back, we also used to go into his favourite restaurant; Schlichter's on Martin-Luther Strasse in Schöneberg. There, intellectual Berlin hung out. I was too young to follow the arguments, which did become heated at times, but I enjoyed the atmosphere and attention of the men – I am my mother's child after all. They were all friendly except for one - Joseph Goebbels. He was a doctor. He used to scare me and, if it is the same man, it seems I had good reason to be worried.' Rupert tilted his head.

'You.' He couldn't sum up his amazement, so just

brought her to him and gave her a hug.

Rupert returned to the subject of the film and whilst they were engrossed in conversation the queue shortened. Before they were tired with standing they found themselves inside the Legation and Rupert recognised a harassed looking woman dealing with the applications. It was Peggie Benton whom he had previously met and subsequently talked to over the telephone. She looked up in surprise when he greeted her in English and her face softened when he reminded her who he was. She turned to say something to a colleague at the next desk and then, to the obvious displeasure of those behind in the queue, she stood up and beckoned them to follow her through to an inner office. After she was introduced to Irēne, she offered them a cup of tea and Rupert was just about to say his usual teasing, 'Tea viz milk,' before he thought better of it and stopped himself.

Peggie explained that the Legation was inundated with Jewish people seeking to leave the country, adding, 'It has got to the point where only those with proven assets in Palestine can hope to obtain a visa and getting out of the country is becoming an ordeal.' Rupert wanted to say, 'Tell me about it,' but bit his lip. Instead, he brought the subject around to his passport.

Rupert felt as if someone had kicked him in the stomach when Peggie told him that his passport had been mistakenly taken by the Representative, Reginald Perkins, on to the aeroplane and was now back in England. She informed him that they had requested it be returned, but, as diplomatic bags were now few and far between and communications were largely limited to ciphered messages, it had yet to arrive.

Rupert was heartened, somewhat, when Peggie said, 'You haven't been forgotten about and I will personally contact you when we have new repatriation arrangements in place. Given what is happening, this might be soon. This time, don't be late getting to the rendezvous point. In the meantime, don't worry about your passport; if it is not returned, we will issue you with an emergency travel document that will let you out of the country and into Britain.'

He felt like a chastised schoolboy, but, trying to sound confident and in control, asked, 'I also want you to arrange for Irēne to be evacuated with me when the time comes.'

'Oh... are you married?'

'Engaged.'

'I am sorry but only spouses can be included.' Rupert shot a glance at Irēne.

'And if we were to get married soon...?'

'That would be a different matter.' Peggie smiled at them both encouragingly.

After waiting in the queue and the cup of tea, Rupert needed to use the toilet before he left and Peggie directed him to a lavatory on the first floor. He looked at the big porcelain WC with the name Dreadnought emblazoned on it and the roll of Bronco toilet paper. He felt a pang of homesickness and then laughed as he noticed on each sheet of the Bronco paper was printed the legend, *Property of HM Government.*

On returning, Peggie asked him to confirm his address in Latvia and for the names of guarantors who would have to underwrite the cost of his repatriation. Rupert was surprised that, at such a time, any citizen would have to pay the unexpected cost. He at first gave the name and address of Lord Simon, realising that his mother would never have the money to pay for such an expensive trip. He also suggested that Metropolitan Vickers should pick up the bill as his employer. Peggie made a note of this.

As Peggie escorted them towards the entrance door, she informed Rupert that she had recently met a colleague of his. Rupert was surprised to hear the name Leslie Thornton, one of the men involved in the Metropolitan Vickers espionage trial in Moscow. Peggie added, 'He turned up one day having bicycled two hundred miles from Warsaw where he has been working since his expulsion from the USSR.'

'He must have an interesting tale to tell.' Rupert decided not to make any further comment. Something told him that with the Russians knocking on Riga's door, admitting any connection to Leslie Thornton might prove more trouble than it was worth.

Outside the Legation, Rupert said, 'Stuffy bloody English. I'm sorry but this means only one thing.'

'What is that?'

'We need to get married quickly.'

'It won't be that quick if you have not got a passport. Latvians too have tough rules on such matters.' For the second time that day Rupert felt like he had been kicked in the stomach.

Later in the afternoon, Rupert and Irēne made their way to the National Opera for the evening performance of *Lady Macbeth of Mtsensk District* by Shostakovich. On the way there, Rupert stopped and turned to Irēne, 'Won't I be woefully under-dressed without a suit and bow tie?'

'No need to worry about that. Due to a lack of funding, the singers aren't performing the opera; only the orchestra is playing the music. It will be much more relaxed.'

'No butterfly required!'

Rupert was pleased to be back at the Opera House and, standing with Irēne where Walter had taken their photograph, it seemed to him that his previous visit had happened in a former lifetime. Not only did it feel like a long time had passed, but also he realised he wasn't the same man as the innocent abroad who had stood in the same place the year before. He sat holding hands with Irēne through the whole performance. Whilst enjoying the music, he could not help being anxious about the jazz club and his inability to dance.

Going outside into the chilly, April air after the performance, they walked, arm in arm, through the park past the hill of Bastejkalns and onto the Swedish Gate where the Jazz club was located. It was only ten o' clock when they entered the club reached by a narrow set of steps into the basement. A jazz record was playing at low volume and they found they were the only customers. Rupert commented, 'You take me to the wildest places!' They both smiled. A waiter approached and after a brief exchange with Irēne he showed them to a table, dimly lit by a red shaded light, facing a raised stage and close to the dance floor. She explained that the waiter had asked whether they were eating and she had said, 'Just a snack.'

After Irēne had explained the menu, they ordered some crispy pig's cheeks on a salad, some tongue on rye bread and a bottle of German Riesling. When the food arrived, the portions were huge. 'Just a snack?' Rupert said and Irēne laughed. He poured two large glasses of wine and they clinked their glasses together before looking into each other's eyes. 'Bottoms up.'

Rupert had drunk less than half a glass when he felt the alcohol create a tingling in his feet followed by a mild floating sensation. This was his first alcoholic drink since New Year's Eve and he was enjoying its unusually heightened effects. The wine added an edge to his appetite so that he tucked into the pig's cheeks with gusto. It also oiled his tongue so that his words, dammed too long during his stays in the hospital and the sanatorium, flowed easily and these included more than a few in Latvian. Irēne commented, 'Maybe wine is the secret ingredient to you talking like a local.' He immediately ordered a second bottle.

By the time the band was announced, the club had filled up and was quite noisy. After polite applause, a ragged looking group of musicians came on to the stage and began their performance. Immediately, Rupert started to tap his right foot and commented on the catchy rhythm. When a few couples got up to dance, Irēne took his hand and said, 'A promise is a promise.' Despite the benefits of the alcohol, he felt self-conscious. He recalled the last time he tried to foxtrot and had stood on his partner's toes generating a yelp and a look of extreme annoyance. Irēne must have sensed his unease. 'Do not worry, there are no steps. Just let the music take you.' She seemed to melt into his arms and he, in turn, became one with the music.

Rupert had no idea what time it was when a horse drawn cab pitched them out onto *Miera Iela.* He wasn't concerned, all he knew was he loved jazz, loved pig's cheeks, loved Irēne and loved the way the pavement gently swayed. With the earworm of the jazz rhythm still boring away, he tried to ascend the stairs up to Irēne's apartment in a musical manner but stumbled and she made a loud, 'Ssshhhing,' noise before laughing out loud.

After Irēne had clumsily unlocked the apartment, they stumbled inside and pushed the door to. They both fumbled with their clothing, scattering various items, as they moved unsteadily down the hallway into the bedroom. Finally naked, they flopped down together onto Irēne's bed. There was little foreplay before Rupert entered her willing body and for the second time that day, she said, 'Welcome home.'

Not wanting the evening to ever end and moving to a sedate jazz rhythm, Rupert stayed hard inside her and present, managing somehow to keep to the heady path between life and oblivion whilst the bed revolved gently around the room. Eventually, when the swaying became more pronounced and with the release of his seed, they drifted off into a post-coital slumber. Before this, Irēne whispered, 'Thank you darling for my beautiful ring. I love you.' Then she added, 'When the time comes, you will have to go home alone. You know that don't you.'

Later, Rupert awoke. It was warm in the room but he was shivering; he didn't want to think of leaving alone and decided that, somehow, they would find a way of marrying before he had to leave Latvia.

Zoumm, Zoumm

During breakfast times, Uldis often passed snippets of news he had heard on the radio to Rupert. On Sunday 12th of May, 1940, he informed Rupert that the British Prime Minister, Chamberlain, had resigned and had been replaced by Churchill. He also told him that the American child star, Shirley Temple, had retired from film acting at the age of eleven. Rupert was amused by the bizarre connection, but struggled digest the impact of the first piece of news.

Germany now occupied both Denmark and Norway, and his desire to return home became more urgent on hearing the news conveyed by Uldis. However, he understood that Russia's victories on its eastern and western borders were far more relevant to his situation. As for Shirley Temple, he just laughed and mouthed, 'Americans'.

Irēne was due to arrive later in the morning and, as it was her name-day on the following day, Rupert planned to pick some wild flowers for her. These were now coming through in an unstoppable rush, driven by the warm days that had characterised the early part of May. He put war, resignations and retirements to the back of his mind, and set off, well before the train was due to arrive, to pick flowers to make a bouquet.

Later, standing on the platform and listening out for the expected train, Rupert discovered that the cough and wheeze of a steam engine in the distance was one of the sweetest sounds imaginable. It was at least on a par with the skylarks that soared over Wythenshawe's summer cut fields. After he had handed Irēne an impressive collection of bluebells, wild garlic and a few flowers he didn't recognise, he couldn't contain himself and asked her whether she had been able to arrange a quick wedding. Her voice was soft as she replied, 'I am sorry Rupert, I have gone everywhere, but every priest needs to have proper documentation before performing a marriage ceremony. In your case, as a foreigner, the required documentation would be your passport and birth certificate. They all said that even a letter from the Legation would not be sufficient.'

'Hell.' He exclaimed.

They retraced Rupert's steps to the sanatorium, then, moving past the bathhouse, they walked on to the fountain, now ice-free and gushing with sulphurated water from the mouth of a carved lizard. From a distance, he had come to quite like the odour of bad eggs, but up close to the spring the smell was, almost, overpowering. Nevertheless, they bent down, cupped their hands and first sipped, then splashed their faces with the smelly water. He declared, 'Aargh, the devil's brew.'

From the fountain, they walked into the gardens of the sanatorium and sat on a bench in the sun sheltered from the cool breeze by a screen of conifers. In the sunshine, the garden seemed alive with insects and Irēne said, 'Look at all of those bees around the carpet of daisies. Zoumm, zoumm. Busy as bees; has there ever been a more apt expression?'

'What's this zoumm noise?' Rupert looked at her askance. 'Is that how Latvian bees sound?'

'That's how all bees sound - including those in England I am guessing.'

'Ah, well that's where you are wrong.' He laughed. 'It's a well-known fact English bees go buzz, buzz.'

Sitting up straight, Irēne turned to Rupert as if she were an inspector verifying a witness's statement. 'How very intriguing, I suppose that is because you are an island. It is said the English are very peculiar and not really European; maybe that is also true for the birds and the bees. But, let us check out some of your other animal noises. I suppose that English dogs do not guv, guv.'

'That's correct, they woof, woof.'

'Vuff, vuff indeed!' Irēne smiled. 'They would be laughed at here. And what of ducks, they must prak, prak?'

'Never!' He strained to hold back the laughter. 'They quack, quack.'

'Unbelievable. Surely pigs have a universal language with their rouk, rouk?' He began to laugh and it was a while before he could continue.

'It is clear that English pigs wouldn't travel well, for no one would understand their oink, oink.' Irēne, clapped her hands in a way an inspector would shut his notebook after an interview.

'That confirms what I suspected. The English are bizarre. I was told they drive on the left but I didn't believe it until now. Anything is possible.' They chuckled together as Irēne made a zoumming noise whilst watching the bees going about their business.

At one o' clock, they went inside for lunch and Uldis took the bunch of wild flowers from Irēne to put them in a vase. When they had finished the *karbonade* Rupert returned to their conversation about animal noises. 'It is really interesting how language shapes us. I'm told there is a native tribe in Africa that has no words for ownership. It's almost impossible to think how that would change your perceptions about the environment and family life.'

'Our comrades across the border are trying to relearn what ownership means, but I suspect it will come down to this;

what the state has, I own too and what I have is my own.'

'Too true.'

After lunch, they decided to make the most of the pleasant afternoon by exploring the nearby swamp, which had a boardwalk threading through it for visitors to walk on. On their way, Rupert recounted Uldis's news about Winston Churchill and Shirley Temple. Irēne replied, 'How interesting, but I have not heard of either of them before now.'

As they approached the swamp, a loud rasping sound could be heard that grew in intensity and then suddenly stopped. As they continued walking, the sound restarted and again increased in volume. It wasn't until they were close to the edge of the swamp, looking through reed beds to a large lake beyond, that they realised the sound was the simultaneous croaking of thousands of frogs. They noted and remarked upon the strange phenomenon of the frogs all beginning their croaking at the same time. The resulting noise built up to a crescendo, and then, presumably in response to some secret signal, all of the frogs stopped croaking and the noise immediately ceased.

Close to the boardwalk a rowing boat nestled against a small jetty amidst a gap in the reeds and there was a sign stating in German, Russian and Latvian, *For the Use of Guests Only.* The boat was nicely painted and appeared to be in good condition, so Rupert suggested they go for a trip. Irēne enquired, 'Do you know how to row?'

'I'm a Cambridge graduate, what a thing to ask!' Rupert replied with mock indignation in his voice and then admitted, 'Well actually no, I haven't rowed before but I have punted on the River Cam.'

'Punted?'

'Sorry, this is a means of navigating the river in a narrow boat with a long pole.'

'Two short poles should be easy in that case.' She nimbly dropped from the boardwalk down to the level of the boat and stepped aboard.

After a little shoving against the jetty with an oar, he succeeded in getting the vessel launched and then started to row. His first few strokes were fine, but he then had a lapse of concentration causing him to splash his passenger with his next stroke. He apologised, adding, 'I don't suppose there will be a tip for the driver at the end of this?'

Rupert carefully rowed out to the middle of the lake. There, he rested with the warm sun on his back and peered into the water. From the bank the water had looked dark grey. Now with the sunlight penetrating the water's depths the surface was a golden colour accentuated with flecks of amber. He said, 'This actually does remind me of being on the Cam with my friend Orlonsky. Not the view of course, but the tranquillity.'

Irēne, sitting at the back of the small rowing boat in her dress and cardigan, looked to Rupert more beautiful than any of the girls he had seen boating on the Cam. Those girls, to his mind, had been a little too keen to signal what a splendid time they were having. In contrast, whilst Irēne was not outwardly demonstrative, he was sure that she was genuinely happy. At this precise moment, Rupert knew that he was himself supremely content.

Irēne almost broke into his reverie when she asked, 'When you let your thoughts soar, what future do you see for yourself?' Rupert stopped rowing and laid the oars back in the boat to give this question the consideration it deserved. He decided not to voice the reality that he was likely to be redeployed onto work for the war effort or possibly conscripted into the forces.

'I really enjoyed working on the dam project, but I'm not an engineer or a designer. The best I can hope for with Metropolitan Vicars is to continue to work on contracts and agreements, but I'm not sure that is my future.' Wondering if what he was about to say sounded too fanciful, he paused before continuing. 'I'm not sure that my heart is in working on projects for damming beautiful rivers. Although I've only taken a few photographs with Walter's camera, in my wildest dreams I think I'd like to get involved with the Minox project. However, I am not an inventor, photographer or cameraman so I'm not sure how I can help. But, if I could find some job with Walter, then I would stay in Riga... and we could then live happily ever after.' He again paused before adding, 'Sorry, is that one of those Latvian fairytales you were going to translate for me?' They both laughed and then he added, 'Of course the war will intervene in this. For now, I must get home, but once the conflict is over, I think we can in some way realise this dream.'

Looking at Irēne sitting just in front of him with her hair curled characteristically against her cheek, Rupert asked, 'When you look into the crystal ball what do you see?'

'I try not plan too far in advance or predict what will happen. I learnt early on in my life that there are greater powers at play than our own motives and aspirations.'

'You have a wise head on a pair of young shoulders.'

A fresh breeze picked up, sweeping over the water and Rupert looked up to see ominous, dark clouds heading their way. He picked up the oars and, to try and outrun what looked like an incoming squall, started to row back towards the landing stage with strenuous strokes.

Approaching the bank, and having avoided the rain, Rupert was about to bring the boat into the jetty when a large frog launched itself from the nearby reeds and plopped into the vessel. This seemed to be the signal for a mass croak from its neighbours. Irēne raised her legs in surprise and the boat rocked. She said, in a voice that contained more than a hint of panic, 'Rupert, please get rid of the frog, I really am scared of them.' He lent forward but couldn't catch the frog and the boat rocked violently. Steadying the vessel, he calmly took one of the oars from its rowlock and used the blade to tip the frog into the water. Irēne said, 'My knight in shining armour. Thank you.'

After tying up the rowing boat as he had found it, Rupert helped Irēne clamber back onto the jetty. Once they were on the boardwalk, he took her in his arms and kissed her. They were holding each other fast together when large plops of rain struck his head. He looked up to see black clouds in the near distance and another squall scurrying across the lake.

They hadn't reached the cover of the trees when the heavy, cold rain caught up with them and began to drench them. They quickened their pace, but were thoroughly soaked by the time they reached the canopy of a large spreading oak. Rupert took off his wet shirt and Irēne gave a shriek as he pressed his chilled flesh against her body.

As their lips met, Rupert noticed there was now a faint mist forming around them. Whether or not it was having just saved Irēne from the dreadful frog, he suddenly felt powerful and elemental. Rain hissed around the canopy creating a sensation of them being in their own bubble. Delirious with desire, he touched Irēne's body and he felt her breasts through the sodden blouse.

Parting momentarily, Rupert unbuttoned his fly and then grabbed Irēne who lifted her skirt, jumped up and wrapped her legs around his waist, enabling a slippery entry. He wondered whether his leg was strong enough for this but, as his excitement heightened and his breath came in short sharp bursts, he ignored these concerns. He gathered her lovely, rounded cheeks, one in each hand, and pressed them towards himself as he impaled her. In the hissing silence he took her, short and sharp, against the trunk of the mighty oak and finished like a frenzied animal. Breathless, he kissed her and let her feet touch the ground.

Happy, sodden and sated they ran like gazelles back to the sanatorium.

That night Rupert lay back on the featherdown pillows with Irēne's head resting on his chest. She had just fallen asleep and was purring slightly. The window was open and he was listening for the nightingale that often sang at night.

How can I get Irēne evacuated with me when the call comes? Inspiration did not strike and, eventually, he turned aside from the darkening thought.

Vilis Lācis

Rupert sat forlornly in the lounge, wondering how to occupy himself. The week ahead was going to seem longer than normal without a visit from Irēne on the Sunday. He remembered he used to keep a diary and now wished he could write in it, *Thursday 13th June, 1940. Time drags. Irēne visits grandparents for a few days. Another ten days before I see her. Even paradise can be a prison.'*

Rupert's attention was drawn away from his musings as he saw a new guest passing the door of the lounge heading outside. He had the air of a Hollywood actor; he was handsome and wore a smart double-breasted jacket together with a fancy cravat. This man had eaten in the restaurant that morning but had buried himself in a book, studiously avoiding the social norms requiring, at least, a greeting or a farewell even if it was just with a nod of the head.

When Uldis brought him a mid-morning coffee, Rupert discovered that the new guest was the author, Vilis Lācis. Rupert expressed to Uldis an interest in meeting the man, saying that he would try to break the ice and initiate a conversation in due course. Uldis, rather formally, said, 'As you wish,' and then disappeared. After his coffee, Rupert strolled around the grounds and headed for one of his favourite spots, the pavilion, which nestled in a wood at the edge of the formal garden. It was painted in a warm, summer yellow, had a raised floor with a balustrade around it separating high columns and an open spiral staircase leading to an upper floor and domed roof.

After he climbed the steps to the upper floor, he found the new guest, jacket off, sitting in a seat close to the balustrade that he had himself intended to use. His immediate reaction was to become territorial, but he held his irritation in check. He greeted the man in Latvian with, *'Labrit.'* The man responded in Latvian and Rupert then apologised, in German, saying that he could not carry on in Latvian as he didn't speak the language. The man replied in Russian that he did not speak good German, so between them they settled on Russian as a common language.

Rupert introduced himself and Vilis reciprocated. Despite his seemingly unfriendly appearance at breakfast, Vilis asked Rupert to join him and pulled a second chair over to the balustrade, where the sun shone in the blue, spring sky.

Pleasantries aside, Rupert enquired after Vilis' visit to the sanatorium. Vilis explained that he was an author whose recent book, *The Fisherman's Son*, had been turned into a film. Rupert studied his companion and noted his handsome features including thick, slicked hair parted with scrupulous neatness. He judged that Vilis was in his late thirties and was intelligent, cultured and refined. Rupert asked Vilis how long he was staying at the sanatorium and found out that he was there for a short break of a few days only.

Rupert told Vilis that he had heard of the film, but lied when he said he hadn't yet had an opportunity to see it. He asked for a summary and Vilis obliged. 'Book describes life of Latvian fisher folk and their struggle for improvement of economic conditions. It centres around family of old Klava, his sons Oscar and Robert and his daughter Olga. Oscar comes to realise not all is as it should be in his native land and wants to break free of his father's rule and old ways. He doesn't fully comprehend true meaning of political struggle but understands shameless exploitation of fisherman's toil by middleman, Garoza, which becomes more evident every day. Oscar's endeavour to create cooperative is not only thwarted by Garoza but also by prejudices of darkened minds of toilers of sea. However, fisher folk could not return to their old life. There is also love and deceit and in film there are folksy songs.' It sounded, to Rupert, that Vilis had repeated this description many times before to the point of it becoming a boring chore.

Whilst his story was far from gripping, Rupert was intrigued by the man and asked Vilis when he had written the book. He replied, 'I finished it in 1934. I was manual labourer, working in port of Riga and writing in evenings and hungry days of unemployment.' Vilis smiled and added, 'When it was published, prominent fish dealer tried to sue me as he believed I had based Garoza on him!'

'I hope he didn't win any damages.'

'Not one centime.' Vilis said sternly. 'Because of book, I became favourite of Karlis Ulmanis and his government funded film adaptation of *Fisherman's Son*.'

Vilis then asked Rupert about himself and he briefly explained about his time in Riga, the accident and missing the plane home. He decided not to take up more of Vilis' time, especially as he had indicated at breakfast he didn't want company, and made his departure saying he looked forward to seeing the film when next in Riga.

Before lunch, Rupert returned to his room and, lying on the bed, he turned to wondering how Irēne was coping with her mother. The rest of the day was taken up eating, walking and reading a German version of *The Fisherman's Son,* which he had found in the library. He progressed well with it and reaching the part where Garoza, the cheating middleman, appears Rupert thought, 'He doesn't sound that scary.' He then put the book down and looked forward to talking with Vilis again, perhaps over dinner. At the evening meal, he tried to catch Vilis' eye but it was clear he was intent on eating in peace.

The next day, Rupert decided to go for a long walk to test his leg and to follow this up with a sauna. He set off after lunch and found that he could step out manfully without any discomfort. He walked through the trees, enjoying the dappled shade they provided and marvelling at the insect-eating pants and the huge variety of mosses, which he had never seen in England.

Feeling free, fit and full of hope, Rupert quickened his pace to test his stamina and strode on towards the lake where he decided to rest while watching the birdlife. As he sat on an old stump, variety of life around him and the tranquillity of the shimmering water amazed him. Watching the swaying reeds, he felt hypnotised by the aura of the countryside and its quiet, unfenced, unassuming beauty.

During years of walking in the woods at Wythenshawe, Rupert had become quite proficient at identifying birds, even some of the rarer ones. But by the lake, with the exception of a wagtail and green woodpecker, the many species of smaller birds he saw were unknown to him. In the distance he could make out the shape of a stork and, wanting to capture the scene, took out the Minox camera from his trouser pocket. He gave an involuntary whoop as he saw an eagle circling high above.

The eagle appeared to hang stationary in the azure sky, then it hurtled down pulling out of its deathly dive just before it seemed certain to hit the water and plucked out its meal with outstretched talons. Rupert flailed the camera around trying to match the trajectory of the bird's flight and hoped that he had at least captured the sight of the eagle leaving with its struggling prey. *One moment you are going about your daily life, the next you are dinner.* This caused him to shiver despite the day's warmth and he started back to the sanatorium and the sauna as if he were trying to outpace a stealthy pursuant.

When he opened the sauna door, he was surprised to see Vilis Lācis sitting, naked, in the place where he normally sat. Vilis moved his hand by way of welcome and Rubert joined him in the sauna. They sat absorbing the heat together; Rupert self-consciously clutching his towel around his waist, Vilis unclothed and confident that he had nothing to be ashamed of with his strong athletic body. Rupert was pleased to meet Vilis again. He was intrigued by the man and glad of the opportunity to learn more about him, his life and any new projects he was working on.

Rupert was about to ask a question about the film when Vilis spoke. 'Have you heard about disastrous evacuation of British troops at Dunkirk?' Rupert said he hadn't and Vilis continued in a light-hearted manner. 'I say disastrous... for you. War is going badly for English.' Rupert was surprised by the news and Vilis's tone and he decided to challenge Vilis by saying, 'Do I take it you are not displeased?'

'I am pleased.' Vilis responded in such a vehement way that Rupert wondered if this was the same gentleman he had chatted amiably with only the day before. 'Once England is defeated in Europe, next step will be for her to lose India to Bolshevism and then Asia will be swallowed before wave comes to Europe to flush out fascist opportunists.'

'And you think that this is good thing?' Rupert could only respond with incredulity.

'Of course.' Vilis almost spat out the words.

Vilis' eyes were dark and more menacing in the gloom of the sauna. He considered excusing himself, perhaps claiming excessive heat, but Vilis continued. 'I know the sort of people you have been talking to here. They are bound to have given you capitalist propaganda.' He fixed Rupert with a pointed stare. Rupert was acutely aware that they were alone and help was further away than he might have liked. He tried to countered his growing unease with civility.
'And what is the real story?'

Sitting back against the hot boards, Vilis replied. 'At beginning of Soviet era fisherman's son nearly starved as unable to take to his boat. Blockades by the Western powers strangled Russia's trade and investment. In addition, Britain's dirty tricks and support for wreckers caused unnecessary hardship. So, fisherman's son had to get rid of greedy middlemen and create his wealth in new way. Industrialisation had to be achieved by heroic efforts on part of workers and financed by confiscation of wealth from former privileged classes. First Five Year Plan set almost impossibly high targets and tough timetables in every sector of industry, yet Soviet people rose to challenge.'

Rupert wondered why this Latvian man was acting as a spokesman for the Soviet regime but did not interrupt.

'These plans achieved outstanding results. Output doubled and doubled again. Gigantic new industrial centres are being built out of almost nothing. Hydroelectric dam harnessed River Dnieper, powering factories employing half million people. Two hundred kilometre Belomor Canal linking White Sea to Baltic was built in record time. So too, construction of gargantuan blast furnaces at Magnitogorsk in Ural Mountains. I could go on.'

Vilis' voice trailed off and then he turned to Rupert and said in a sour, dismissive tone, 'You British failed to kill Lenin, but even if you had, the Soviet locomotive had already gathered speed. Our track to progress is laid on solid foundations. There is simple formula. No private property – no problem. But, do you think that can be achieved overnight? No. There are plenty of people with vested interests who want us to fail and return privileged elite to former positions.' Vilis looked at Rupert in a way that clearly included him in this category.

Requiring no prompts or questions to encourage him to continue, Vilis persisted with his monologue. 'You see there is inevitability to communism. That's because capitalism is flawed. Of course, it depends on people's continued greed to acquire luxuries beyond their needs and for privileged elite to draw unearned income from masses but, more importantly, it limits creativity and invention. Capitalists, and all Jews for that matter, don't complicate issue of investment by asking whether a particular action is conducive to wealth and well being of all. No, they simply ask whether it pays.

Vilis' voice rose to deliver what Rupert believed must be his conclusion. 'Fatal flaw in capitalism slows down progress. Any invention that doesn't promise immediate profits is ignored; some that threaten to reduce profits are ruthlessly suppressed. Remove profit motive and inventor will have free hand.' Vilis softened his voice and it became almost seductive. 'Mechanisation will be enormously accelerated. The socialist world is ordered world, efficient world, which unlocks creativity and, after all hard work to start revolution, will deliver comfortable life for Soviet people.' Rupert's head span.

'What about art?'

'Art!' Art. Artists and their bedmates, priests and philosophers, are there to trick us. I know because I tricked Ulmanis. He believed *Fisherman's Son* was cosy story of gritty Latvian characters and it described beautiful Latvian scenery.' Vilis gave an ironic sounding laugh and continued. 'He didn't understand it is allegory. I dared only speak under my breath as reactionary bourgeois hunted down slightest manifestation of progressive thought. Mostly, artists are capitalist lackeys who simply promote economic interests.'

An image of the painting depicting Christ being taken from the cross, which hung above the altar in the chapel of Pembroke College, came to Rupert's mind, but Vilis interrupted the train of thought,

'Artists disguise painful reality that whole of human history is history of class struggles. There will be time soon when fisherman's son is not exploited by Garozas of this world. There will be proper fishing fleets and proper facilities such as canning, storage and transport. What is more, everyone will get fair day's pay for fair day's work.' His words were bitter and harsh and Rupert felt decidedly unsettled by them.

Vilis sat looking into the middle distance for some time. Seriously overheated, Rupert was about to make his departure when Vilis started again. 'There are two great motivators of human progress, greed and fear. In England you have greed. This means one man acquires wealth that can take many future generations to squander at expense of majority. But, nasty side may even be masked to you, for you don't see rats unless you lift drains. If you enjoy little luxury in England it is because you are keeping tight hold of your empire. For you to live in comparative comfort, hundred million Indians must live on verge of starvation. Without empire, England would be cold and unimportant little island, where you would all have to work very hard and live on herrings and potatoes. Fear is needed to purge country of bourgeoisie and liberals who have vested interests in maintaining powerful elite. Those who still fear are those who have stolen land from others in past, or recoil at discomforts of revolutionary period before socialism is established.' Vilis struck his fist against the wooden boards, making Rupert, absorbed in the dramatic performance, jump.

Understanding Vilis truly believed in the future he had described, Rupert revised his view of the man and thought, 'He is both attractive and repellent but, on balance, I don't like him.' Hoping to elicit a more favourable discussion, he changed the subject.

'What will you do when you go home?'

'Prepare for government.' With that, Vilis said, 'Good afternoon,' stood up and walked from the sauna, leaving Rupert surprised and perplexed in the steamy gloom.

Although Rupert was now starting to feel faint from the heat, he remained sitting in the sauna until he heard Vilis leave the changing room. By the time he himself had changed and returned to his room, he felt his day had been ruined. He lay on his bed, still sweating and thought back to listening to the organ in Manchester Cathedral. He recalled that when the organ was in full cry he felt like he was vibrating in tune with the universe. He thought, *Vilis talks of order, of efficiency and mechanical progress, but he doesn't mention the human spirit or even freedom, liberty and justice.* An image of the gargantuan blast furnaces mentioned by Vilis came to his mind, *Will we not be enslaved to technology even if, as slaves, we eventually become well fed and contented?* The clock struck six and Rupert laughed softly as the dinner bell rang in the foyer below.

After eating his meal alone, Rupert straightaway retired to his room for the night, He could not get out of his head the lecture given by Vilis. He visualised the chapel at Pemboke College and looked up at the ornate plaster reliefs on the ceiling and at the painting of Christ by Barocci. He thought, *Is this magnificence simply a distraction to the reality that the rich and powerful have put one over on us? I very much doubt that. Surely there's nothing wrong with helping raise the human spirit above the humdrum of everyday existence?*

Rupert looked over to the upturned book, *The Fisherman's Son,* and decided he would not finish it.

As the evening faded into night, Rupert had a recurring image of the eagle swooping in and plucking its prey from the lake. He got up and paced about the room, trying to rid himself of an anxious feeling that was gathering in his chest, settling on his shoulders.

A breeze from the open window lifted his hair and Rupert had the strange conviction that the draught was result of the page of time, turning to reveal a new, more disturbing, chapter.

Tipping Point

On Saturday, Rupert returned to his room after breakfast and was lying on his bed, mulling over the news from Uldis that the Germans had arrived in Paris and marched full-strength down the Avenue des Champs-Élysées.

Recalling that in his early teens he had seen old newsreel at the pictures of the ragged and defeated German army. He now wondered how this broken and humiliated force could have regrouped and re-equipped so quickly to have taken France, especially when four years of stalemate in the Great War had resulted in the gain and loss of territory measured in miles, if not yards.

The news underscored that Britain, fighting Germany alone, was in peril. His thoughts were in turmoil; he needed to get home but was desperate to take Irène with him. He racked his brain but no solution presented itself.

The shrill bray of the telephone startled him, pulling him out of himself. It had not rung before and until that rather sudden moment, he had forgotten there even was one. On answering, he found it was the hotel manager, who announced that he had a visitor. He wasn't expecting Irène until the following weekend and he wondered who it could be. After briefly tidying himself up and combing his hair, he hurried down the stairs to find that the mystery visitor was Andris. Rupert could see that Andris was far from happy, his mouth downturned in a grimace and his eyes shadowed.

'Is there somewhere we can speak alone?' He asked Rupert, forgoing even a casual greeting.

Rupert was taken aback but nodded, 'Of course,' he said and he ushered him into the privacy of the library.

Andris looked about the room before he spoke in a hushed tone. 'It is clear Russia intends to invade. The Soviets watched the German Army march into Paris two days ago, and it looks like they have decided to collect their share of the plunder.'

Realising that things were now happening fast, Rupert felt his heart give an uncomfortable squeeze. The Red Army may already be on their way. He swallowed and asked, 'When do you think the Russians will be marching along *Brīvības Iela*?'

'It could be anytime. Yesterday, the Government issued emergency powers to the Latvian minister in London, Kārlis Reinholds Zarin and to the Latvian minister in Washington as his substitute. So, the government are prepared even though they are not sure when exactly the steamroller will arrive.'

'How dare they. I am getting married soon!' Rupert tried to make light of the news but the joke fell flat and the laughter died on his lips.

Andris, who Rupert knew to be serious at the best of times, sat looking at Rupert with a stern expression. Then, he said, 'Be ready to leave at anytime. I really mean it; it will be dangerous for you to stay. I know you won't want to leave without your fiancé so talk to her and have her pack a bag with as much warm clothing as is possible to carry.'

'Do you have plans? Where are we headed?'
'I can't tell you too much because I don't have all the details but we have a wealthy friend who owns a yacht and it is our intention to set sail to Sweden with him'

'Will the Russians just let us take off like that?'

'We intend to go before the Russians arrive.' Andris snorted and then added, 'And, in any case, we are not going to ask them. We will set off in the dead of night if need be. Have you sailed before?'

'No.' Rupert wondered how Irēne would feel about leaving her family and setting sail in such a manner.

Worried that he needed to get a message to Irēne, Rupert asked, 'When is the boat leaving?

'I'd like us to go tomorrow or the next day but my friend, who is a wealthy man, wants to get his finances in order before departing. It may be a week or so before we finally depart.' Uldis interrupted the conversation in order to ask whether they wanted coffee. After Uldis departed with the order, Rupert informed his friend that he had met and talked to Vilis Lācis at the sanatorium. Andris' angry response surprised him.

'Lācis,' he spat, 'he is a dangerous opportunist and womaniser. He is a known communist but, because he wrote a servant class book about rural Latvia, he has, somehow, become a national treasure. The only reason it was published in the first place was his bedding of the owner of the newspaper, Emily Benjamins, and it was her newspaper that first serialised it. When the Russians come, he will be the first to shake their hand.' Rupert recalled Vilis' handsome features and his parting words, *prepare for government.*

Before they had finished their coffee, Rupert offered Andris a game of chess, hoping to dispel the gravity of the meeting. Andris shook his head. 'I have my own affairs to settle. It will not be easy.' Seeing Rupert's unease, he smiled gently. 'But I look forward to a game with you in Sweden, my friend.'

Before Andris left, Rupert wrote out Irēne's address, gave it to him and asked, 'If the departure date is before Sunday week, would you call on Irēne, explain and make sure she comes here with you?'

'Take it as done.'

'Thank you Andris, you are a great friend.'

'*Lūdzu.*' With that, Andris departed.

For the rest of the day Rupert dwelt on the planned departure by yacht. He wondered how he and Irēne would be able to continue their journey to Britain from Sweden given the German presence in Denmark and Norway and their likely total control of the Skagerrak. In the end, he decided to cross that metaphorical bridge when faced with it.

Falling into a reverie, he pictured Irēne and himself arriving in Manchester by train and then taking the bus to Wythenshawe. Rupert had a clear image of his mother in the scullery being utterly surprised and delighted at his return. He heard his own voice saying, 'Mum, this is Irēne, my fiancée,' and realised he had said this out loud. A passing Uldis raised an eyebrow, but politely averted his gaze.

Rupert woke early the next day, excited by the prospect that Andris, Christa, Irēne and he would soon be setting sail to Sweden. When he went into the restaurant for breakfast, he found Uldis tuning in a radio. Uldis interrupted what he was doing to fetch Rupert's breakfast order, which had now settled on a favoured selection of the available items. When he returned, Uldis explained they were waiting for an important announcement later that day, but did not have any more information.

To avoid missing the announcement Rupert decided not to go for his usual long walk. Instead, he took some fresh air with a short, brisk walk to the village and then settled down in the lounge to read a book he had borrowed from the library. He found that the walk had rid him of some of his nervous energy and he was able to read it without too much distraction. Unusually, the radio burbled in the background, but as he only understood the odd word of Latvian, it did not put him off from his reading.

Just before lunch, there was a commotion as Uldis ushered in the workers and guests who weren't already in the lounge. Shortly afterwards, the Manager appeared and, stooping even more than normal, addressed them in an official sounding voice in German, 'I have just had a phone call from the Swiss Embassy who informed me that the Latvian Government have received an ultimatum. The Soviets demand that full access is granted to the Red Army. It is clear they are coming in force.'

At the end of this short speech, Rupert looked at the faces around him. Once Uldis had translated the news, the cook brought her hands to her mouth. Rupert turned to Herr Koche and asked, 'Are you not worried?'

'Not unduly, I am Swiss. Switzerland has declared its neutrality in this conflict and we are well represented by our Ambassador.'

'Lucky you.' Rupert surprised himself by saying this out loud.
He wondered whether he should now throw himself on the mercy of the British Legation, but with Andris's escape plan including a place for Irēne, he soon thought better of this idea.

Later that afternoon, as Rupert paced around the formal gardens in the forlorn hope that physical activity would lessen his anxiety, Uldis came running up to him and told him that an English lady was asking for him on the telephone in the manager's office. *Mother?* He thought, with a thrill of confusion, *Surely not?*. He raced to the phone.

Picking up the heavy receiver, he found the English lady was Peggie Benton, who came straight to the point, 'Rupert, you must report to the Legation at once. If not, I cannot be held responsible for what happens.'

'Peggie, can I ask again about Irēne?'

'I am sorry, but unless you have been able to marry then I am afraid it won't be possible to repatriate you both.' Rupert felt like a drowning swimmer who has been thrown a lifebuoy that landed too short.

Rupert thanked Peggie and informed her that he'd pack immediately, but, even before the receiver hit the cradle, he knew that he would again miss the plane, which he imagined was already on its way to save the British nationals from their uncertain future. Rupert could not leave Irēne and he consoled himself with the prospect that, together, they would somehow be able to make their own way home via Sweden.

The rest of the day was spent in a state of nervous anticipation. The rest of the guests were restless and fearful and a warm, persistent drizzle exacerbated the oppressive atmosphere.

Monday, June 17th 1940 began in much the same way as the previous day. Everyone's attention was given to the radio in the likelihood of an announcement being broadcast. They did not have to wait long. A sombre President Ulmanis followed the voice of the announcer. At the end of his speech, the cook and Ana Weisman burst into tears. Uldis explained. 'God help us. Ulmanis has ordered there to be no resistance to the Soviet Army and he said *I will remain in my place and you remain in yours.* I suppose he is trying to reassure us life will go on as before but, I can tell you, no one believes that.'

'It is happening,' cried Ana, tears pouring from her rheumy eyes and coursing down her cheeks, 'It is happening again. It over.' She hid her face in her hands.

Rupert considered jumping on the next train to Riga to see Irēne, but then decided against it as he reasoned that Andris might turn up at the Sanatorium with her at any moment and it was likely he would be stranded in Riga without money or passport when the Russians arrived. The urge to flee battled the urge to stand his ground. He had never felt so indecisive and torn.

In the late afternoon after Uldis informed him that the Soviets had entered the city. *Irēne, Irēne, Irēne,* was all his whirling mind could think. Rupert went to talk to the Manager. He rang the bell at reception for several minutes and prompted no response. After some time he sought out Uldis.

'Herr Koch is gone.' Uldis said, grimly.

'What!' Rupert felt his stomach lurch.

'He has packed and left. I understand he was going to the Swiss Embassy.'

Rupert slept badly that night. At three o' clock he was pacing backwards and forwards across his room, his head reeling. He could not hold onto a single train of thought, each half-formed idea would breakdown and a new idea would then start to coalesce. If there was a repeated image in his mind, it was of the back of Herr Koch disappearing into the Swiss Embassy for a glass of kirsch. By seven o' clock, he felt wretched, exhausted and useless, and on getting back into bed, he fell into a broken sleep. It was ten o' clock when he awoke with a sharp jerk, thinking he had missed a visit from Andris. By the time he had dressed, he had calmed down and tried to look forward to the arrival of Irēne in a few days time.

In the breakfast room, Rupert was greeted by Uldis who told him that the sanatorium was now effectively shut. It was news Rupert had expected and, before he could ask a question, Uldis carried on, 'However, there is no one pressing you to leave, only you will have to help with the duties now, which include harvesting the vegetables and preparing the food.' Rupert thanked Uldis and thought, *I wish I had been asked to do this before*. It would give him something on which to focus. His thoughts turned to memories of the walled garden in Wythenshawe where he had often helped his father sow seeds, tend the vegetables and harvest the summer berries.

Uldis interrupted Rupert's reminiscence with the offer of a coffee for breakfast and added, 'Just to help you to ease into being part of the proletariat.' They both smiled.

When Uldis brought in the coffee, Rupert asked him what would happen to the sanatorium and he answered with an authoritative nod. 'Kemeri is owned by foreign investors but now the Russians have arrived there is no way they can make use of their asset. It will become state property and I'm sure, very soon, it will be full of wounded Russian soldiers in need of convalescence. Meanwhile, we may have a few more weeks left to enjoy its charms. The chickens are doing well, there is plenty growing in the kitchen garden and the lake is full of fish. I suggest we make the most of it.' With that, Uldis disappeared back into the kitchens, leaving Rupert imagining the mess soldiers would make of the fine furniture and tablecloths.

Rupert was drinking his coffee when there were sharp footsteps and Irēne appeared, hurrying into the lounge. Rupert leapt to his feet in surprise and spilt half of his coffee down his shirt. He went over to her and, in giving her a prolonged hug, transferred a small, damp patch of coffee onto her cream blouse. He could hardly form the words but said, 'I've been so horribly worried and I'm so very pleased you are here.'

'It is terrible.' Irēne's eyes were full of tears.

'It is, but there is hope.' They sat down, and he told her about the call from the Legation.

Irēne's eyes widened and when she spoke she was adamant, 'But, you should have gone without me. I told you, you had to.' Then he recounted the visit from Andris and described the escape plan, sketchy as it was. Irēne gathered herself together, wiped her eyes and commented, 'I think that this is good news. At least we are taking our destiny into our own hands. If you stay, God knows what the Russians will do with a captured Englishman.'

Leaning over, Rupert kissed Irēne and apologised for the coffee stain that had now spread out into a sizeable patch. As they sat back, Irēne said, 'Yesterday, in the late afternoon, a Russian armoured truck stopped in the street opposite our block. No one got out of the truck for a long time and, eventually, a group of small boys came up to investigate. They soon ran off when other trucks arrived and then soldiers started to jump out of the backs of the trucks. They seemed small and dirty and poorly equipped to my eyes and very Asiatic looking. Everything seemed unreal. It is a strange invasion. There is no shooting and no panic and the trains are running although I had to show my passport before boarding the train to come here.'

Rupert raised the subject of the wedding, saying, 'I was looking forward to getting married. I know it's too late for the evacuation from the Legation, but let's do it anyway or at least have a blessing of some sort. I don't know why I feel the need, but somehow it seems appropriate. Let's get married here, quickly, before Andris's contact finishes getting his finances sorted out. Then, we can go yachting on our honeymoon.'

'You are a complete romantic. But I love the idea. I know a priest in Riga who will at least give us his blessing.'

'A blessing is simply perfect. It gives us the opportunity of having an official wedding at Wythenshawe. Can you arrange to get the priest to come here this Saturday?'

'Yes.'

The time that remained to them, before Irēne had to catch the train back to Riga, was taken up with plans for the wedding, which included inviting Andris and Christa. Then, Rupert walked Irēne back to the station; dusk had arrived and in the gloaming, he felt calm and happy. Rupert's worries about the Soviet invasion and a daredevil escape by yacht over the Baltic Sea were put to the back of his mind, to be dealt with after the service.

The train departed, carrying its precious cargo to the city. Rupert stood looking at the dissipating steam set against the rising moon and the pale sky and realised it made everything appear to be distant. Even the outlying landscape looked further away than normal, sketched in rather than solid. The whole scene looked like it had been painted in shades of grey upon silk. Its unreality made him suddenly anxious, as if, with a slip of the paintbrush, the artist creating the scene could over-paint him— puff, gone. He shuddered and made his way back to the sanatorium.

Marriage Blessing

When Irēne clambered off the train with her father, Rupert understood why, when he had seen them walking together arm in arm a year before, he had thought they must be a couple. Pēteris was tall, young and handsome and, after hugging Irēne, Rupert shook his hand and welcomed him to Kemeri in German. He apologised for not having officially asked him for his daughter's hand but Pēteris waved it away with an elegant hand and replied, 'I'm happy if Irēne is happy.'

Rupert took Irēne's bag and they set off to the sanatorium. Walking in step with Pēteris, Rupert wondered how he might feel about him whisking his daughter off to a foreign land and was pleased when Pēteris addressed him as if chatting to an old friend.

'On the way here, we saw a small group of people on *Brīvības Iela* carrying red flags and singing communist songs. The interesting thing was there were no policemen but plenty of photographers. To me, it looked staged. I'm sure tomorrow's newspapers will be telling the world Latvia welcomes the Russian Army.'

Rupert asked about life in Riga and Pēteris replied, 'Oh dear... The Soviets have roped off the Esplanade and turned it into a military camp. Rows of tanks are drawn up around the perimeter, and young children watch the scene with more enjoyment than a trip to the zoo... But today, let's not think of anything other than your wedding to my beautiful daughter. The sun is out, and you are going to have a very special day.' Rupert immediately recollected how the ladies in the park, with heads covered by scarves, kept it immaculate by sweeping up any fallen leaves. He could hardly bear to think about what it looked like now filled with kitchens, tents, boots, blankets and the other detritus of an army in the field.

Irēne explained that the priest was due to arrive at one o' clock with Katerīna, and she had managed to invite Andris and Christa. Rupert said, 'Excellent, we have plenty of time to set up the pavilion before the priest arrives.' There, cornflowers, daisies and poppies lay in a great pile on the floor gathered by Rupert from a nearby meadow earlier that morning.

Irēne set about arranging the multicoloured blooms artfully around the balustrade of the open sided pavilion and on a table that had been set up for the ceremony. After that, apart from changing their clothes and awaiting their other guests, they had nothing else to do, so Rupert and Irēne took the opportunity to show Pēteris around the grounds. Then, leaving Pēteris sitting in the garden, Irēne accompanied Rupert to his old bedroom to drop off her bag. He informed her that Uldis had moved them into the honeymoon suite for the night.

Rejoining Pēteris in the garden, Rupert told him about his happy times working on the damming project and about life in England. Pēteris talked about his job in the ministry as it used to be before the Russians arrived. He also explained how he was exceptionally busy renovating a traditional log cabin along the coast at Salkrasti. Rupert thought of the night he had spent at Andris' summerhouse on the coast near to Salkrasti and smiled. Then, he had anticipated only one more evening with Irēne, now he was about to embark on a lifetime with her.

'Will you be our photographer this afternoon?' Rupert asked, handing over the Minox. Peteris took it hesitantly.

'Of course, but, I am afraid I have not used a camera such as this before.'

Rupert smiled. 'Don't worry, it really is beautifully simple.' He demonstrated how to operate the Minox and Peteris pointed and clicked away at the surrounding trees, muttering 'Remarkable, remarkable!'. Rupert interrupted him before he used up the film.

Time seemed to race and soon Rupert and Irēne were headed back to the station to meet the priest and Katerīna. Upon the train's arrival, what appeared to be a huge, black mass squeezed itself out of the carriage door. For an instant, the train seemed diminished by the massive figure of the priest standing next to it. He had a reassuring solidity and, when he greeted Irēne, Rupert found this was matched by a deep, bass-baritone voice. Katerīna exited the train after the priest. She was wearing a cream dress with a pink ribbon around the waist and carried a bunch of flowers in one hand and a bag in the other. Rupert thought, *Irēne was right, she is beautiful,* and was surprised when Katerīna handed the bunch of flowers to him, saying in Russian, 'For the groom.'

Introductions over, they started to walk back to the sanatorium together but it wasn't long before there was a toot from a car horn, and Andris and Christa drew up alongside in a fiery red Peugeot. They offered everyone a lift, but it was clear that, with the priest's great bulk, they wouldn't all fit in the car. Rupert insisted that the priest and Katerīna go ahead in the car whilst he and Irēne followed them on foot. Rupert welcomed the opportunity to be alone with Irēne and, after the car had disappeared into the distance, he pulled her to him and kissed her.

On reaching the sanatorium, Katerīna was waiting for them at the entrance and, taking hold of Irēne's hand, the two of them went off together to Rupert's old room. Rupert retired to the honeymoon suite to wash, shave and get changed. After donning a dark pair of trousers and white shirt, he made his way to the pavilion; its cream and yellow paintwork shining under the azure sky. The beauty of the building had been enhanced by the draping of long ribbons from the centre of the ceiling, fanning out to the columns supporting the roof. The gentlest of breezes, soft and caressing, made the ribbons dance and shimmer in the warm sun. Andris, Christa, Uldis, the Cook and the Housekeeper together the few remaining sanatorium guests were seated in the pavilion whilst the priest stood by the table onto which he had placed a cross and two candles.

It wasn't long before the bride appeared and, escorted arm in arm by a beaming Pēteris and followed by Katerīna, she made her way over the lush, uncut grasses to the pavilion. Rupert watched her approach, his heart racing. She was radiantly beautiful in a white lace dress finished with a pink ribbon around the waist. A simple circlet of wild flowers adorned her head. Rupert felt tears well in his eyes, his chest full to bursting with pride and joy as he stood by the makeshift altar and waited for Irēne to be delivered to his side.

The blessing was conducted in Latvian. It made no difference to Rupert that he didn't understand the words, for he understood their meaning perfectly well. Above all else, he wanted to make this commitment to Irēne; for him, this blessing was as significant as an official wedding. He couldn't tear his eyes away from Irēne's, nor his fingers from hers. When instructed to kiss, Irēne offered her face to his and when their lips met the pavilion erupted with applause. Yet Rupert did not hear it. All he heard was Irēne's gentle sigh and the singing of his every nerve as he kissed her.

Drawing apart, Rupert became aware that Pēteris was holding up the Minox camera and that Irēne was smiling. The blessing ended with the singing of a traditional Latvian hymn, which filled the air with voices in harmonious song. Rupert felt the priest's bass baritone vibrate through him and at that moment he considered this to be better even than hearing the organ in Manchester Cathedral.

Uldis led the group back to the main building where the cook had laid on a feast of salads, pickled herring, sprats, tongue and boiled meats. Everyone tucked in, and Uldis brought out a case of champagne and a tray of glasses.

'The no-alcohol policy is henceforth, in light of current events, revoked!' he declared, raising a glass in a toast. 'To the bride and groom!' he said and the refrain was echoed in a musical mix of three languages.

Rupert coughed slightly to clear a lump in his throat, got to his feet and said, 'Thank you all for coming to our wedding, especially Pēteris for giving away his beloved daughter, Katerīna for being a beautiful bridesmaid, Andris and Christa for being great friends, Uldis and the Housekeeper for their hard work and our Cook for the lovely buffet.' Then, he turned to Irēne and said, 'Thank you for agreeing to spend the rest of your life with me'.

With the short speech out of the way, and the buffet eaten, everyone retired to the garden. Ana Weisman started the afternoon's entertainment by singing her favourite folk song and everyone, apart from Rupert, immediately joined in with the words. However, it didn't take him long to work out the melody and soon he was humming along. Song rose from the meadows, over the trees and through the golden afternoon light towards the grey mass of the city in the distance.

The afternoon turned into evening without any noticeable drop in temperature, and the group remained in the garden until Andris said that he and his wife had to start their journey back to Riga. It was agreed that they would take the Priest, Katerīna and Pēteris back with them.

On the way to the car, Andris took Rupert aside and said, 'The date for our departure is next Friday. We will be leaving here at three o' clock in the afternoon.' It was as if a dark cloud had descended after an endless series of sunny Sundays. An image came to Rupert of the Ambassador at the hospital saying *don't be late,* but he dismissed this. Such a wonderful day was not going to be spoiled by thinking of a perilous escape.

The Priest wedged himself into the front of the car with Andris, whilst Pēteris squashed into the back with the two ladies. The Priest, who continued to sing a variety of songs, was in a jolly mood, enhanced by his polishing off, almost single-handedly, the last bottle of champagne. Rupert had his arm around Irēne and they, together with the remaining guests, watched the car disappear into the gloom of the evening until neither the car nor the bass-baritone singing of the priest could be heard. Uldis then insisted that he'd clean up and tidy everything away, and that the newly married couple should retire to the honeymoon suite. Before going to their room, the newlyweds turned to look at the distant pine trees that cast a faint double shadow from the setting sun and rising moon.

The bridal suite was luminous in the late evening light. The light grey walls and cream linen bedspread covering the double bed provided a perfect canvas for the wild, kingfisher blue cornflowers displayed in a crystal vase, radiating blue fire. Rupert poured two large glasses of Rigas Balsam, given as a wedding present by Andris and Christa, and toasted their health, 'Uz vesilību, They layed together on the bed. Irēne laid her head on his arm. 'Such a lovely day.' She sighed.

'The very best.'

As the bitter essence of the balsam added to the effects of the champagne, they began to relax, and Irēne turned her face towards Rupert who kissed her deeply. Irēne became soft and wonderful in his arms and the fire and passion that had been gently burning inside him ignited into erotic love. All his blood vessels craved with intense, yet tender, desire, for her, for her softness, for her acceptance, for the reassurance and release she provided. As they lay back on the bed, he stroked the silky slopes of her calves underneath the wedding dress. Then up, up along her thighs, coming nearer and nearer to the welcoming place he yearned to enter.

The flame of desire grew and they helped each other out of their clothes. Irène laid back wearing a silk petticoat and Rupert traced his index finger down her décolletage and gently uncovered her firm, ripe breasts. Gently, he stroked the parabola of her femininity and felt the hard protuberance of her nipple. His need to be within her grew and Irène guided him gently towards her. Bearing his weight on his arms, he entered her. Then he moved his hands down her back behind the soft globes of her bottom.

Clinging to him, Irène's breath came deeply in a way that sounded, to Rupert, almost like terror. He moved in and out and, with each cycle of movement, he could feel an intensifying of sensation, which he had never experienced before. She wrapped her whole body around his aching phallus and he could feel the pulses that were running through her whole body. His world was hard, soft, eternal, exploding.

Shaking her head, Irène cried, '*Ne, ne!,*' He kissed her as if to consume her, to eat every morsel. As she moved to her climax, he heard the sounds of ecstasy beneath him and to him it was the sound of life. He listened in awe, understanding that love sprang from her moans. Conjoined in a moment of eternity, Irène's body suddenly buckled in a soft, shuddering convulsion. The wave, which had built and taken them far and high, now crashed. All was flotsam and jetsam, all was spent. Irène lay clinging to his chest, uttering inarticulate moans and murmuring, '*Mana mīla* - my love.' Rupert felt himself involuntarily withdrawing and contracting, coming to the terrible moment when he would slip out of her and they would be separate beings once more. Irène clung to him preventing their coming apart. 'It was so perfect.' She said. He held her close and she laid her head on his chest.

Rupert said nothing, he wondered what had happened and realised that he had almost scaled the highest of mountains but had let his climbing mate reach the summit alone. He held her tight and, to break the unfathomable silence, asked, 'What

happened? Speak to me. Say something to me... Describe it!'
Irēne took her time to respond and eventually whispered, 'It was more lovely than anything could be. Only that.' Irēne nestled up to him and, enfolded, they each fell into a deep, contented sleep.

As Rupert emerged from the depths of his slumber, the beech trees outside the sanatorium, with their sap rising, stood erect in the morning light. Turning towards Irēne, he lay watching her and stroked the edge of her breast with his fingers through the thin nightdress. *She is so womanly, so beautiful,* he thought, looking at her fine, long, delicate yet strong neck. As Irēne awoke and opened her blue-grey eyes, she smiled, and he greeted her with, 'Good morning Mrs. Lockart.'

On coming down from their room, they found a breakfast table in the restaurant laid for them. Uldis greeted them, Rupert said, 'This is like the old days.'

'It's your honeymoon; even the workers need a day off. Would you both like scrambled eggs?' They both said they would and Rupert thanked him for his kind attention. Looking outside towards the flower borders, now redolent with summer blooms, Rupert couldn't imagine a more perfect scene. The sun, which had chased off any lingering morning coolness, was suspended in a sapphire sky. Whilst waiting for their breakfast to be served, they chatted about the day ahead and decided to revisit the lake.

Making their way along the meandering path, enjoying the sun's warmth and occasionally swishing away a mosquito, Rupert pointed out the insect-eating plants with their strange bulbous bodies. When they stopped to sit on a felled tree overlooking the water, he talked about how he had seen an eagle come swooping down to pick up a large fish in its talons and plucked at Irēne's hand for dramatic effect. He also recalled his thoughts at the time and said, 'It makes you realise just how fragile life is. One moment we are enjoying the sunshine, but in the next moment a metaphorical claw can come and take us away.'

'Such thoughts are not the cheeriest to hear on a honeymoon.'

Deciding to avoid negative subjects, Rupert, instead, talked about Wythenshawe, the cottage garden, his parents and some of the characters at Metro Vicks. Irēne talked about Katerīna and some of the books she had recently read. As they alternately chatted and then fell silent, the sun rose to its zenith in a cloudless sky.

At the evening meal, Rupert informed Irēne of the timing of Andris' arrival and, to Rupert, it really did seem that they were making last minute arrangements for their honeymoon.

Later, they walked around the sanatorium's grounds. The fading sun moved towards the already risen moon and gradually dipped and set. It was in a state of bliss that they returned through the small orchard, where the apples were swelling and bees zoummed.

They made their way back to their suite and lay on the bed together, Rupert stroking Irēne's suntanned arm. Risking breaking the magical spell seemingly cast over them, he asked her when she needed to leave the next day. He knew that she had to get back to Riga and arrange to see her mother. She replied, 'There is no rush,' and so he changed the subject.

After making love, Rupert opened the bedroom window wide, and he saw the bright moon hovering over the outline of the distant trees. Everything was quiet and serene and at that moment, in a bubble of contentment, the world was perfect.

By the morning, fine rain had set in, reflecting a change in Rupert's mood. The short honeymoon was over, with Irēne returning to Riga later that day. He tried to keep positive by telling himself that she'd be back on Friday, ready for the voyage to Sweden.

The rain became heavy and persistent, preventing them from taking a walk. Irēne asked Rupert whether he would mind if she sat in the library to write a letter. He joined her and, although his mind wasn't on reading, he enjoyed sitting in the tranquillity of the room, daydreaming and occasionally watching Irēne. Finally, she finished writing and sealed the letter in an envelope that bore the address of the sanatorium on its reverse. On the front of the envelope, Irēne wrote Rupert's name and passed it to him with the words, 'Please open it later when I have gone.'

With a break in the incessant rain, they made their way to the station. Each step seemed to worsen Rupert's increasingly wretched mood. He didn't want to go back to the sanatorium by himself even though he knew he couldn't accompany Irēne to Riga. They talked about the plan for Friday and agreed that she would catch the early train, so they could spend the morning together and be well prepared before the arrival of Christa and Andris.

Just before the train pulled into the station, Rupert asked Irēne to take the film from the Minox to VEF for Walter to have it developed. Happy to oblige, she took hold of the small roll. When the train bore her away, he turned to walk back to the sanatorium and a tear welled up in his eye and rolled down his cheek. He rebuked himself, *Such a sentimental fool. Did yesterday teach you nothing? You weep at her leaving yet she is to spend the rest of her life at your side.*

Feeling that it was wrong to luxuriate in the honeymoon suite without Irēne, Rupert went back to his old bedroom and put the unopened letter on the chest of drawers. It was only later in the day that he took the envelope, broke the seal, unfolded the letter and read:

Dearest Rupert,

I am writing to you in German because my English is not up to

305

describing my feelings.

Until I met you and came to know you, deep within me there was fear. Fear of being lost, not heard, temporary, non-existent. A fear compounded by man, powerful, using and abusing man.

Yet, I am here, present, saved, alive through a man. A man! Through the life force of manhood upon me and within me.

You could have taken your sword and pierced my heart; that would be death. But you offered, in your slow and tender thrust, peace and a primordial connection.

You asked me to describe it but it is before and beyond the word, in the beginning and forever more.

I can only give a vague outline.

It starts with a strange melting sensation and slight buzz in my very being that gives no real portent as to what is to come. Then, there is a knotting in my stomach and rippling inside like a sea anemone under the tide, inviting you, no, clamouring for you. Soft, undulating, rippling, feathery waves run to points of exquisite iridescence as they wash up on the extremities of my skin, eyes and ears. Soft, yet at the same time powerful, waves of unvoiceable pleasure.

The waves grow in a strange rhythmic motion and there is nothing but rollers rising, shearing and falling in a great swell. I am Umwelt. I am Uberwelt. I am Dasein. Then, I plunge into the deepening whirlpools of sensation until I am one perfect floating essence in the vortex of pure feeling. As passion swirls around, the sensual current flows through me with a radiance such as no artist could portray. All liquid, all fire. One more oscillation and I would explode, die a marvellous death and be scattered as wind borne spume.

The man, with his trident, joined me in the very heart of the maelstrom and, in doing so, the deep organic fear, which lay submerged like a reef to catch the unwary, has disappeared; swept away by the sensual tide. As I dared to let go of everything, all myself including my fears, and be lost in the flood, I came powerfully alive. Absorbed, consumed, but not gone. Through the immersion, it is as if I have been reborn, naked and unashamed. I am a self, a being, a woman because I shared my ultimate nakedness with you; my love, my hope, my life.

I am counting every minute we are apart and cannot wait until our new life begins.

Yours forever and always

Irēne

Such a letter! Rupert wanted to keep it safe and placed it the centre of one of the thick German books he was trying to read.

That night the bed felt huge and empty.

Lieutenant Dmitri Kuznetsov, State Security

Two days had passed since Rupert had seen Irēne and, to him, it seemed like it could have been twenty. Even though he had settled into helping Uldis and the cook with domestic tasks, these didn't take his mind off the return of Irēne and the arrival of Andris and Christa.

As Rupert stood waiting for the early train two days later on Friday, each second seemed to stretch out for an eternity and he became increasingly tense. Then, there was the moment of release when he heard a distant whistle and the approaching chuffing of the engine.

As it came into full view, Rupert was surprised to see a red star painted onto the front of the train. He thought, *How quickly the Soviets appropriate things that they don't own.* He suddenly felt off balance, as if his world had stopped rotating on its axis. As the train came to a stop, he was breathing deeply but caught his breath when Irēne didn't appear from any of the carriages. His heart raced as the whistle sounded ahead of the train's departure, but there was still no sign of her. As the monster lurched and clanked back in to motion, Rupert shouted, 'Irēne!' and raced up and down the platform looking through the windows to see, without any real hope, whether she had forgotten to get off the train. He waited. The next train bore no sign of her and Rupert began to feel icy fear rising in his chest like water. *What has happened to her?*

He returned to the sanatorium and dialled Andris in desperation, but there was no reply. *Perhaps there has been a change of plan, perhaps she shall arrive with Andris, in the car.* Doing his best to convince himself of this, he settled down in the lounge to wait for them. His nervous energy could not be contained, however, and well before the anticipated arrival time of Andris's car, he moved outside to sit in the garden. From there, he had a good view of the road and would get advanced warning of any approaching cars. At three o' clock, he stood up, peered up the road, sat back down. Then he stood once more. He had repeated this activity several times before he heard the engine of a car and then caught sight of a red flash of hope approaching the sanatorium.

Rupert raced back through the building to meet Andris' car in the driveway. His heart sank. Irēne was not in the back seat. Andris and Christa got out and Andris's first words were, 'I am sorry Rupert.' Rupert's mind went blank and he hardly heard what Andris said next.

'There is no departure today. There is no yacht. Our friend, I say friend, has changed his mind.'

'Irēne,' Rupert said, insistently, 'Where is she?'

'I do not know,' Andris shook his head, 'She did not arrive?' Travel restrictions have been put in place. Maybe she wasn't allowed on the train?' He added, 'We would have tried to find her to bring with us if the yacht trip had been going ahead.' Rupert was suddenly pleased there was no yacht, as he wouldn't have left without Irēne.

Andris added, 'I am sorry to disappoint you; we are devastated. The wealthy man we know is the owner of a large building company. The Russians have talked to him about converting a large apartment block on the corner of *Stabu* and *Brivibes Iela* into Cheka headquarters and to work on extending Riga Central Prison. The man is a Jew and understands there is money to be made.' Then, with an ironic smile, he added, 'But I think he is a man who is going to end up in the gaol he built.' Rupert was shocked by his friend's tone. It seemed the pervading influence of antisemitism had reached even Riga.
Rupert thanked Andris and Christa for coming to tell him the news and, as they were getting back into the car, Andris said,

'We will make other plans and let you know. All the best for now.'

They shook hands and once the Peugeot had disappeared, Rupert said aloud, 'Hell, will I ever get out of this country?'

Rupert wondered if there were any people remaining at the British Legation. If there were, he knew he'd get a frosty reception after failing to arrive for a second evacuation, but perhaps they would help in any case. As the day wore on, he became increasingly annoyed with himself that he hadn't taken the opportunity to travel into Riga with Andris and Christa so that he could visit the British Legation. He sought out Uldis to talk to him about how he might best reach the city.

Rupert found Uldis smoking a cigarette at the kitchen door.

'You are still here?' Uldis said, 'Where are your friends?'

'I'm afraid our plan fell through.' Rupert said, his jaw clenched. Uldis took in his tense frame and pinched face and motioned for Rupert to sit with him on the pile of wooden vegetable crates.

'I am sorry. What will you do?' Rupert explained that Andris had gone away to arrange something else. He finished by asking,

'Now I need to get to the Legation and have neither passport nor money, can you help?'

Uldis sucked his teeth and shook his head. 'I don't advise that. You can't get on a train without a passport, and, even if it is open, Soviet soldiers will be guarding the Legation. You will be walking into a trap.'

'What about making a telephone call?'

'The Russians now operate the telephone system. If you were to ask for the Legation, this would immediately alert the authorities and it would bring a swift and unwelcome response. No, I think you can only wait for Andris to return with another plan.'

Rupert felt like a hand had been tightened around his throat.

Later in the day, as a distraction from the whirlpool of emotions that threatened to suck him into a vortex of despair, Rupert was weeding in the vegetable garden when he heard the sound of lorries in the distance, the growing rumble heading towards the sanatorium. He returned to the main building, washed his hands in the kitchen sink and then went into the hallway just as a group of soldiers barged their way in through the main door. They were led by an officer with a determined expression on his young face, who shouted, 'Papers!' Rupert's insides turned to ice.

The soldiers held back as the officer came up to Rupert. He looked down at Rupert and barked, 'Lieutenant Dmitri Kuznetsov, State Security.' He pushed his face close to Rupert's, 'I will not ask again. Papers.'

Rupert drew himself up and said, with as much confidence as he could muster, 'I am a British subject and my passport was taken by the British Ambassador, Charles Orde as I was due to leave by plane.'

'British? What is your name?' The Lieutenant's eyes narrowed.

'Rupert Lockart.'

'Lockart?'

Rupert blanched. He had guessed that his name would call to mind associations with the attempted assassination of Lenin and knew that this first meeting with a Russian official wasn't going well. A nervous tremor, increasing in amplitude, threatened to take control of his body.

'And you have no papers, Rupert Lockart?' The lieutenant said, his mouth curling into a nasty smile.

'No, sir.'

'No passport!' The lieutenant spat and turned on his heel to face the soldiers.

'Find the rest!' He jerked his head at Rupert, 'You! This way.' He led the way into the lounge. The lieutenant seemed entirely at home. He took off his cap and gestured for Rupert to sit at one of the tables as if he were inviting him for tea. Rupert, after looking at the lieutenant's features and his hair, which had a sun kissed streak in it similar to his own, guessed that the lieutenant was barely ten years older than himself.

He eyed Rupert coldly. 'Explain.'

Rupert tried to prevent his voice from trembling by increasing the volume and talking as confidently as he could about the damming project he had been working on, the accident, his recovery and missing the plane. He did not say anything about Irène. The lieutenant listened without interruption and, after Rupert had explained why he had been sent to the sanatorium, asked, 'Where did you learn your Russian?' He replied that his friend, Fyodor Orlonsky, had taught him whilst he was at Pembroke College in Cambridge University. The lieutenant repeated the name Orlonsky, took out a pad and made a note of it.

One of the soldiers entered and hurried over to the lieutenant. He had clearly searched Rupert's room. He handed over the Minox camera. The lieutenant studied the camera for some time and then enclosed his fist around it in such a manner that Rupert anticipated he was going to be struck with it.

'So you are a spy. What have you been taking photographs of?' Rupert had always considered the Minox as being ideal for espionage and cursed himself inwardly that he had not considered the risks of carrying it.

'It was given as a present.' Rupert was cut short by the lieutenant's intervention. His tone was brusque and threatening.

'And why is there no film in it?'

'I recently posted it to VEF for developing and was expecting a new film soon.' With this lie, a cold, clammy feeling spread over his entire body.

The lieutenant got up and walked from the lounge. Rupert heard occasional snatches of barked orders given to people rounded up by his soldiers. After a short while, he returned and said, 'Do not leave the building. My men will be posted at the doors. One step outside and you will be shot whilst trying to escape. I will be back.' Rupert watched the lieutenant detail five of the men for guard duty and then lead the rest of the soldiers out of the building.

Once the soldiers had left, Uldis came over to Rupert but they did not speak until they heard the lorry move off. Rupert was shaking. 'The lieutenant said he was from State Security, what is this?' he asked Uldis, whose mouth was set in a grim line.

'NKVD.' When he noticed Rupert's furrowed brow, he added, 'Cheka; it is the new name for the old firm.'

'How can you tell?'

'Well State Security is NKVD. It is also clear from the

markings on their shoulder boards and royal blue piping around the jacket and on the hats.'

'I understood the Cheka were secret police. It's not very secret if they wear uniforms.'

'State Security is like an iceberg, the ones with uniforms sit on the top but eighty percent are hidden.' Uldis then explained they had been ordered to stay within the grounds of the sanatorium and await further instructions. Rupert told him that he wasn't even allowed out of the building.

In bed that night, as Rupert tossed and turned and failed to get any sleep, he dwelt on why Irēne hadn't managed to come to the sanatorium. He concluded that the Soviets were strengthening their control over Latvia and that probably involved restricting the movement of people. He knew he had to get to Riga, but he realised that, with guards posted at the doors, he could not simply hop on the train. To take some comfort, here read Irēne's letter, which had remained undiscovered.

In the early hours, as he finally drifted off to sleep, he concluded that his seeing Irēne again really did depend upon Andris and Christa devising a new plan.

Over the next few days, Rupert found he could not concentrate and reading was beyond him. The only activity that helped pass the time was assisting the cook with preparing, which now had to stretch to feed the guards posted at the sanatorium. Peeling the potatoes was a relief to the boredom and worry about what was to come. Even though the cook only spoke Latvian, they seemed to get on well and his assistance was genuinely welcomed.

Despite the stress, Rupert took solace from sitting with the small group of remaining staff and patients in the evenings, eating together and talking quietly. After that he fell into the habit of playing billiards in the games room with Uldis. Neither was proficient at the game, but it provided a means of wiling away the evening hours. They talked about various subjects from filmmaking to fishing, but Rupert never voiced the slight resentment he had towards Uldis. *Surely, it would have been better to risk getting to the Legation after all, than sitting in house arrest, like a rat in a trap?*

Rupert wasn't sure how many days had passed when he heard the distinctive note of a returning lorry. Lieutenant Kuznetsov came into the sanatorium hallway with his escort and, as he breezed past, snapped his fingers for Rupert to follow him into the lounge. After both men had sat down, the lieutenant, with a cold edge to his voice, said, 'I could shoot you without qualm for being a spy. Believe me I'm tempted, but it seems live Englishman is worth more than dead one. Now, we invite you to rest here a while. Enjoy your prison. When we have fully prepared our Soviet prisons we may well invite you to change your accommodation. But, remember what I said about setting one foot outside.'

After the lieutenant had ordered his men out of the building, Rupert went to his room and, lying down on his bed, he tried to stop himself from shaking. He recalled his wedding and was astounded that it was less than a fortnight since the happiest day of his life. It seemed much longer ago. He wondered what Irēne was doing and in his imagination he transferred himself to being in her bed. As he stepped gently into the dream world, he heard a pop and thought, *The bubble has burst.*

The feeling of foreboding he'd been trying to stave off slipped over Rupert like an ill-fitting glove, so tightly he could barely breathe.

Dilemma

More than four weeks had passed without any contact from Irēne, Andris or Lieutenant Kuznetsov. This coincided with a period of intense summer heat that sucked all of the fresh air out of the sanatorium and took Rupert's energy with it. The sun was so fierce that its violence bruised the lawns and, often with the wind in a certain direction, Rupert imagined the smell of clinkered fumes and blasts of sulphur came from between the cracks of the patio slabs.

Rupert had added cleaning to his kitchen duties but, with so few rooms in use and only a handful of people to feed, the work did not consume much of the day. The elastic hour stretched much longer than its constituent sixty minutes and Rupert desperately tried to quicken the clock by keeping himself occupied. After exploring every nook and cranny of the building, he had discovered a small tower at the very top of the building. To him, this seemed like the bridge of a ship and it had become his favourite refuge. If there was a cooling breeze, it was to be found here.

From his vantage point, he was able to look down at the straw coloured lawns and over the forest and swamp to see the coastline of Riga Bay sweeping away from him in a shimmering arc, edged with a margin of white sand. He constantly scanned the horizon for Andris' car, willing it to appear, bringing some news of Irēne. The silence from her was deafening.

The guards were changed at regular intervals and each time a Soviet lorry approached Rupert broke out in a cold sweat, fearing the arrival of the lieutenant and news of his "new accommodation". The sanatorium had become a kind of prison, but he knew life here would seem laughably luxurious when he encountered the genuine article. He was under no illusion. Conditions would be harsh and no visitor, Irēne or otherwise, would be permitted.

Rupert had never felt so utterly helpless, even though he had recovered well and could now walk long distances without assistance. During the long, hot days, he spent most of the time dwelling on his options. While it was tempting, he knew he couldn't simply walk off and hide in the woods. Not only might he be shot whilst attempting to escape but, also, he realised that he didn't have the resources or skills necessary to last more than a few days alone. He couldn't get to Riga without papers and a telephone call would be monitored and, now he was suspected of espionage, have terrible consequences for caller and recipient alike. He understood he was at the mercy of world events and the actions of others, like his friend, Andris. Perhaps this invasion of an independent state would bring a swift counter from Britain and her allies? However, with Britain seemingly surrounded by enemy forces, he feared this was unlikely. Perhaps Andris was already on his way with a new plan and would bring Irēne with him? *Whatever Andris's escape plan may be, I cannot imagine it. I can only hope he has not already fled.*

On the thirty-third day of his house arrest, having been on the 'bridge' for a few hours, Rupert was overheated. The sun, high in the sky, beat down on the tiled floor and he began to fold his deckchair, intending to return to the shade of the building's interior. Ears constantly pricked to detect oncoming vehicles, he suddenly perceived the faint sound of a car engine in the distance. He looked over the parapet towards the station and, soon enough, a red ray of hope beamed in the distance. *Andris* he thought and then, with a rush of searing hope *Irēne!* Almost falling over the half-closed chair, Rupert clattered from the tower and ran down the stairs to the hall where a Russian soldier was on guard duty.

Rupert stopped. He could not simply run out of the building— the guard would shoot him the second he set foot outside. Instead, he made a commotion, pointed to the door and said to the shabby, confused soldier, 'Go! Strangers have arrived.' The soldier, gathering his gun, went to investigate and Rupert took the risk of following him outside, just in time to see the familiar red Peugeot turn into the driveway. His heart leapt. There, in the back seat, was Irēne.

The car hadn't quite stopped before Rupert, darting passed the nonplussed guard, flung open the door, lent in and kissed Irēne. He helped her out of the car and they embraced. All he could say was, 'Thank God, thank God.'

Reluctantly, he broke their embrace to welcome Andris, but when he looked up he saw that Andris was showing a document to the soldier. The soldier soon became aware he had let his prisoner out of the building and started to shout and wave his rifle in Rupert's direction. Calmly, Rupert took Irēne's hand and led her, Andris and Christa back into the sanatorium and through to the lounge.

Offering to make tea for his guests, Rupert disappeared into the kitchen but the cook took over the tea-making and insisted that he return to the lounge. Rejoining his visitors, he sat by Irēne and took her hand. Andris said, 'We have our things packed and are ready to escape. Whilst the tea is being prepared, let me tell you what has happened since we last met.' Rupert leaned forward as Andris explained, 'Jurmala, and this whole area by the coast, is now requisitioned by the Soviets. You can't come here unless you are a resident or have official papers allowing a visit or are authorised to carry out essential work. I have papers to show I am working on a building project... but we are not going back to Riga.'

The cook brought in a pot of tea together with cups and a plate of homemade biscuits. Irēne served the tea whilst Andris continued. 'Things have moved so fast. Only a few weeks ago a decree was issued announcing new elections. Latvian democratic parties attempted to participate under the National Committee but were stopped. Vilis Lācis, the Russian stooge, he is the Soviet-appointed Minister of Internal Affairs. Anyway, he ordered the National Committee to be shut down.' Rupert was surprised to hear Vilis's name mentioned.

Andris then said. 'How can people so quickly turn against their own? Last Saturday, Lācis removed Ulmanis from his post and two days ago he signed the authorisation to deport him along with Munters and other prominent leaders of the Republic of Latvia – including my father.'

Rupert uttered, 'Your father!' in disbelief but Andris did not dwell on it.

He went on. 'Ulmanis backed and supported Lācis and this is how he is to be repaid. God knows what will happen to them all now.'

Rupert squeezed Irēne's hand. He longed to simply take a walk with her in the garden; to ask her how she was feeling. He remained attentive to Andris, however, who continued, 'Then, we had the elections but to use the term is a joke. It was completely rigged. Only individuals on a pre-approved list of candidates were allowed to stand for election to the, so called, People's Parliament. The ballot had instructions; *Only votes for the Latvian Working People's Bloc must be deposited in ballot box.* The alleged voter turnout was over ninety-seven percent and, of those voting, ninety-four percent voted communist. But, I am impressed with Russian efficiency; the complete election results were published in Moscow twelve hours before the election closed!'

A bleak smile briefly crossed Andris' face. Then he continued in a low voice, 'If this is not bad enough, the *Saeima* met for the first time and the only agenda was a petition to join the Soviet Union. What a surprise, this was carried unanimously. Now, tribunals have been set up to punish, so called, traitors to the people.'

Rupert repeated the last phrase and then asked, 'What does this mean?'

'We are told tribunals will punish those who have fallen short of their, so called, political duty of supporting Latvia's inclusion within the USSR. Orders have been given for those who fail to convince the authorities of their commitment to be shot in the back of the head.'

The word 'shot' seemed to reverberate around the lounge like the report of a pistol. Then, looking directly at Rupert, Andris continued. 'You may think we are rushing away too soon. Many are saying they have done nothing wrong and, with a clean conscience, they sleep easy, unafraid of the knock at the door in the night. But, I have not told you about the experience of my father who used to visit Moscow on business in the time of the Red Terror. He had that knock on his hotel door and, although not killed, was tortured terribly. With the disappearance of my father, it is clear that what is happening now is a repeat of those dark days in Russia. You need to remember that they are not interested in you, the individual. They want to eradicate a whole class of people. We need to leave now whilst there is still the opportunity.'

Rupert wanted to say something, even if it was only to sympathise with the disappearance of Andris's father, but could not immediately find the words. After a pause, Andris again spoke. 'The plunder of Latvia has started. Empty trains have rolled into Riga bearing the slogan, *Bread for Famine Victims in Latvia* and have returned to Russia full of Latvian grain and other products. Now, we have two choices, stay and, at best, be shackled to the Soviet state, or at worst, shot in the back of the head as a traitor to the people. Or we can try to get out. We have chosen Germany, are you joining us?' Rupert looked at Andris in a state of shock.

'Germany! You are going with Christa?' He was barely able to voice the question.

'We are going with Irēne too... if you come as well.' Rupert looked at Irēne and said nothing but thought: *This sounds like I'm to run straight into the hands of the enemy.*

Andris looked directly at Rupert. 'If we get to Klaipeda on the coast, which is in German hands, I have some contacts there who'll be able to look after us. But we will have to be careful, the Russians will be checking the border and that means we'll have to finish our journey on foot through the forest. I know, it's not as good as getting to a neutral country like Sweden, but I can assure you life will be safer there. Now we must leave. Go and pack your bag. Irēne, I'm sure, will help. We have our things in the car. Pack as many warm clothes as you can carry.' Rupert explained he was effectively under house arrest and could not simply take off. Andris assured him that by the time his bags were packed he would have a plan to get him out of the sanatorium.

Taking Irēne's hand, Rupert made his way past the soldier in the hallway to the bedroom. He opened the wardrobe to reveal a meagre selection of clothes and a pair of leather-soled shoes, badly in need of repair. Shutting the door, he turned to Irēne. 'Surely, this is not the right thing to do!'

'Life will be tough from now on.' Irēne's voice was soft but without a hint of fear. 'But, Andris is convinced death is likely to come quicker if we stay.'

'And what about you? What do you think?'

'I am not thinking of myself, only of you.' Her reply was quiet, but firm. 'God knows what the Russians will do to you. Can we take that risk?' He sat by her and took her hand.

'The Russians have already visited - hence the soldier on

the door. It is likely I'll be transferred to a proper prison when they are ready... I would have been killed already if they were so minded.' After breathing deeply to help clear his mind, he continued. 'The Germans might accept Latvians but I'd be taken as a prisoner of war, or shot as a spy without any identification papers or uniform. In any case, I am concerned about you? What if they find out about your Jewish blood?'

'I am not thinking of myself.'

They sat on the edge of the bed for a short while and then Rupert said, 'This is like having to choose which leg I'd like to have amputated,' and, trying to lighten the mood, added, 'and I'm rather attached to both... If I stay, I'm likely to be held in detention of some kind while the Russians decide what to do with me,' and then, with little enthusiasm in his voice, added, 'maybe, when I am an official prisoner, somehow, the British Government might help.' She put her arm around him and, after a lengthy embrace, he asked, 'Do you think I'm a coward... not wanting to go to Germany.'

'You are not a coward, sometimes it is more courageous to stay and face your enemies.'

'Would you go if I wasn't there?'

'No, I would not go if it was just me.'

Making their way to the lounge, they found Uldis standing by Andris. Rupert cleared his throat and said directly to Andris, 'My dearest friend, we are not coming with you.' Andris didn't try to persuade him otherwise. He only said, 'I knew it wouldn't be easy for you to choose to run towards the nation you are at war with. I hope my worst fears for you in Russian hands don't come true. We wish you well, but it is time for us to leave now.' He helped Christa up from her seat. Rupert looked at her, with her slight frame and manicured fingernails, and wondered how she would cope with walking through dense forests.

Uldis picked up a large bag from the floor and, coming over to Rupert, said, 'I am going to take your place in that case. There is only a bleak future for me here.' Rupert wanted to say, 'No, don't leave.' But he held himself in check and wondered how long it would be before he bitterly regretted not joining them.

Rupert held Irēne tightly whilst Andris, Christa and Uldis left the building without any fuss so as not to arouse the suspicion of the soldier. Andris returned briefly, bringing Irēne's bag from the car and depositing it in the hallway. Shortly afterwards, the Peugeot was started and driven away. The substitution of Uldis for Irēne went unremarked by the soldier on guard duty who let the car depart without question. Perhaps it was a matter of tallying three people leaving against the earlier arrivals.

Irēne followed Rupert quickly up the stairs and when they got up to the bridge they saw the red car receding into the distance. When it disappeared around a bend in the road, it was as if water had been thrown on to the last ember of hope. He turned to her and said, 'What have I done?'

'Who knows,' She answered, 'but we have made the decision. Now we need to live with it without looking back or regret. What is done is done and we can only look forward.'

They then sat down on the tiled floor with backs against the wall that retained the heat of the sun's rays. He told her about his interrogation by Lieutenant Kuznetsov and she, reminding him of Brecht's play, *The Life of Galileo,* asked, 'Faced with an inquisition, did you recant your ideas?' He shook his head.

'Our conversation about Galileo seems to be from such a long time ago. Some of the reality of facing an inquisition is becoming clear to me now. It seems simple and innocent things can suddenly turn into state secrets that can't be revealed.'

'Such as?'

Not wanting to say too much about the lies he had already told the lieutenant, Rupert deflected the question and tried to lighten the tone. 'Luckily, I've no ideas to recant and, if asked to give up any secrets, I'd simply ask, what do you want to know?' The cold, clammy feeling returned, and he knew that soon he was likely to be tested beyond any measure he had experienced before. He only hoped he could be strong and careful enough to avoid implicating Irēne.

Irēne explained how she had been prevented from coming to see him. 'When I was told I was not allowed to travel without authorisation, I nearly fainted. I really believed you would take off, by yacht, to Sweden without me.'

'I would never have deserted you.'

'Is that deserted...' Rupert hugged her to him and they both smiled at their private joke.

'Did you receive the letter I sent?'

'No, nothing has come at all,' and then added, 'but, I suppose you're not allowed to write to British spies. What was in the letter?'

'Oh silly girlish things; memories and hopes for our future.'

'I would like to hear these things if denied the opportunity to read them.'

'Of course, but in summary it is this— I love you.'

A little later, Rupert considered the danger Irēne had put herself in by writing the letter. 'You did not add your name? Or address

it to me? What if the Soviets now know who you are and—'
Irēne shook her head and placed a calming hand on his arm. 'Do not worry, I did not sign it and I addressed it to the Sanatorium Manager. Nor did it show my address. I have been careful.'
Rupert breathed a sigh of relief.

Rupert's day passed much more quickly in Irēne's company. Over supper Irēne chatted with the housekeeper in Latvian and Rupert could tell they were talking about Uldis. In Irēne's company, life, it seemed, could still go on as normal.

At the end of the evening, they retired to their room. Lying comfortably, cupped together on the bed, they became aware of the sound of crickets chirping in the garden. Irēne asked, 'How do English crickets sound?'

'That's a thwack as the leather ball hits the willow of the bat.' Rupert laughed at his own joke and Irēne, turning over, prodded him in the ribs.

'That is English humour.' She kissed him and the kiss dissipated the last traces of tension. He scooped her into his arms before caressing the small of her back.

He ventured to suggest they take a bath together. Irēne looked at him, smiled, and said, 'You are full of good ideas and it would be a shame not to use such a big bath.'

Rupert went to the bathroom and turned on the huge brass taps, which he always noted with some pleasure said *hot* and *cold* in English. The taps gurgled noisily before water gushed forth. Irēne came into the bathroom wearing one of the fluffy white dressing gowns provided for guests. Whilst the bath was filling, they embraced and kissed. He could feel the tightening of his manhood and softening of his being.

When the bath was three quarters full, Rupert stopped the flow of the taps and, in the steamy mist, took off his clothes. He carefully lowered himself into the water. Irēne dipped a toe in the water but quickly retracted it, saying, 'How can you sit in that? You will be boiled.' He admitted that it did need some more cold water and ran the cold tap for a while longer. Then, she tried the temperature again, got into the bath and sat down with her back to him. As she did so, he looked at the curve of her waist together with the splendid flare of her life-affirming hips and shook his head as if he couldn't quite believe he were there.

Irēne lay back and Rupert brought his hands around to cup her breasts. The curves nicely filled his hands and he moved his fingers gently upwards to feel her nipples. After a while, he lathered up his hands on a bar of soap and began to gently caress her. Had he ever felt anything so erotic?

The bath was wide and deep. Rupert had no trouble in turning Irēne over so that he lay on top of her and, without any fuss or strain, entered her. His chest pushed up against her face and the gentle rocking set up a wave that rippled up and down the bath in harmony with the desire that coursed through his body. He caressed and was caressed in return, but, before long, his hands started to feel like prunes and he suggested that they get out of the bath. He stood up first and stepped out of the bath, then he picked up a big linen towel and wiped her dry as she stood up in the bath. After she stepped carefully out he pressed his wet body against hers and, dipping his knees, they re-coupled. He lifted her and, as she wrapped her legs around his waist, he carefully walked out of the bathroom, placed her, like a delicate cargo, onto the bed and made love with a slow thrusting motion.

Rupert woke with a jolt during the night. He had been dreaming of being swept away by the waters of a breached dam and was relieved that he hadn't wakened Irēne by shouting out in his sleep. A surge of adrenalin resulting from the dream stopped him dropping back to sleep and he listened to the faint sound of leaves rustling outside in a night-time breeze. He felt he wanted to lie like this for all eternity and, with Irēne breathing rhythmically by his side, he allowed this mood to linger, luxuriating in this rare moment of stasis. He knew that whatever happened next was likely to set off a chain of events completely out of his control. 'At least no one can take this day from me'. He cuddled up to Irēne who felt so hot it was as if a fire were raging within her.

Rupert re-awoke just as dawn was breaking. He speculated about the day ahead and considered the possibility of sneaking out of the sanatorium with Irēne and not returning. Irēne woke gently, yawned, stretched and said, '*Mana mīla* - my love.' She propped herself on her elbow and planted a kiss on his lips.

'*Mana mīla,*' He replied and then added, 'I'm wondering how we can trick the guard and disappear.'

'Oh, have you come up with a plan?' He had no time to say it was just fanciful thinking before he heard the unmistakable sound of a Soviet lorry returning to the sanatorium. His blood ran cold. *They are coming.* He seized Irēne's hand.

'If it is the changing of the guard, we are safe. If the lieutenant has returned, God knows what will happen. But just in case, you had better hide on the roof.'

Rupert dressed rapidly, kissed Irēne hard and said 'Whatever happens, stay quiet.' Then he hurried from the room, leaving her standing alone

Letters

Rupert had gone over the sequence of events leading up to his incarceration so many times it had begun to feel like he was recounting someone else's life story.

Just as he was finishing one of his very long walks in his cell, Rupert thought he heard the voice of Fricis Apšenieks, the Latvian chess champion, ask him in German, 'Is there a reality out there, or is this simply a construct of the mind?' He recalled that this was the same question asked by a lecturer in German philosophy at Cambridge. It seemed like a distant memory, but this question stayed with him as he dwelt on the loneliness of the prison cell and the madness of the outside world.

Was this outside world simply imagined? Rupert remembered an essay he had written addressing this age-old philosophical question. It had seemed to be a vitally important question at the time; one necessary to fully understand. Now, it seemed the epitome of decadent luxury, *The sort of thing*, he thought, *the privileged classes have time to undertake to stave off boredom when they don't have to face life's more mundane trials, like finding food and shelter.* Yet, he could not dismiss the question so lightly.

Rupert lay on his bed waiting for the mouse to appear. He wasn't sure when the mouse had first arrived but, encouraged by Rupert leaving some black bread by the wall each day, it would squeeze under the door and stay, longer and longer, looking around the cell. Its presence reminded him of the illustrated children's story Irēne had given him in hospital and the happy times they'd spent talking about the books they had read.

Remembering a conversation with Fricis Apšenieks, Rupert recalled some of the phrases that had intrigued him. *All living creatures are intentional. Intention enables us to operate one step ahead of our learnt behaviour and our evolutionary specified responses and, in anticipating the future, we beat the world to the punch.* On one occasion, Rupert addressed the mouse. 'What are your intentions?' To his amazement the mouse looked at him with its beady black eyes and, for one strange moment, he was sure it would answer him.

Rupert wondered, *What would my world be like if I could separate my interpretation of what appears to be there from what is actually there?*' He got up from his iron bedstead with its thin mattress and moved over to the grey wall with its chipped paint. It felt cold. He rubbed his finger along it. It felt greasy. He, very gently, hit his head against it. *Surely,* he thought, *there are physical boundaries I haven't simply imagined. After all, the mouse moves along the contours of the wall and doesn't simply disappear through it, so these physical things must exist in the mouse's world too.*

Rupert looked at the pad and pencil and knew the time had come for him to use the emergency supplies. He sat at the small desk, took the pencil, with its fat lead core, and wrote a letter to the mouse.

Dear Mouse,

I have watched you from afar and admire the way you go about your work.

Now, as I lie trapped in my cell and you move freely around, I am wondering what is the big difference between you, my big-eared friend, and me? That is after we have glossed over the largely irrelevant aspects of size and dress sense. It is clear you are going about your world with clear intentions. You are moving with purpose and direction and are even calculating some sort of likelihood of finding food here as you visit me quite often now. You make sense of the world in your mousy way and anticipation guides your actions enabling you to beat the world to the punch, or at least avoid the boot of the guard or jaws of the prison cat.

Are we not similar? Are we not continually asking the same question, 'if I do this, then that will happen, or will it?' That is always the question whether or not you can say it out loud. As we both know, the question is sometimes easy to answer, sometimes impossible to answer without further work and sometimes impossible to work out at all.

Yes, we are both active, aware, moving, choosing beings working within the limits of free choice to make the best of our world.

It is clear we share many similarities but how do we differ? Well for a start, you have more freedom than I and, from your rather fine looking coat, it seems you are doing rather well. You probably have a partner and hungry mouths to feed and you are going about satisfying these obligations with admirable speed. What am I doing? I am simply waiting.

The big difference between you and I, I hazard to guess, is that I can articulate my thoughts and you probably cannot – unless these are very mousy type thoughts. Certainly, and on this I stand firm, you are not granted a mental facility to think about your own thoughts. You are not worried you are in a prison and may never be able to see your loved ones again. You are not thinking you are a fine mouse who has yet to fully live your life. You are getting on with your life. Even with the tough life you have, and the constant threat of being eaten by the prison cat, you are moving and choosing. Oh, how I envy you.

I also write to thank you for helping me understand the nature of the world around us.

In the way I see you move around the objects that also limit my world, it is clear there is a real world out there consisting of edges and probably also acids and alkalis, light, different thermal qualities and vibrations. This, so-called, objective world, is the world you and I bump into. But what we make of that bump is, I suspect, quite different and in your case depends on whether you have long whiskers and a dexterous tail. I have been granted neither, but I am cursed with language and the ability to articulate my knowledge of the world in more complex and general terms. So I know I am in a gaol and that the world is going to hell.

You are a lucky mouse. I wish I could join you in your sanctuary of the present moment uncluttered by reflections, hopes and fear, with your plentiful supply of tasty morsels; unburdened by self-consciousness.

Yours sincerely

Rupert

With the letter to the mouse finished, Rupert looked at the amount of paper he had used, and the state of the pencil, and regretted his decision. He sat back on the bed and remembered one of his last conversations with Irēne. *What is done is done and we can only look forward.* He could not help thinking, however, that if he had accepted Andris's offer to escape before the arrival of the Russians, he would not now be going mad in a foreign land.

Dwelling on his state of mind, Rupert said aloud to himself, 'The Chinese have their water torture, but the Russians have discovered solitary confinement; such a debilitating torture.' He knew that he had to write to Irēne before he lost his ability to focus on his thoughts and desires and sat himself down at the desk.

Dearest Irēne,

It is way past Christmas and what have I got you? Only the sweetest of thoughts. Over one year ago, on your birthday, I realised I loved you and, even though we are temporarily apart, my love for you grows each day. Every day, I wonder what you are doing and think back to the time we spent in our lovely bubble.

Please let it have happened. I could not bear it, if I found out it was a dream. I seem now to doubt myself and cannot trust the words I hear myself say.

John 1.1. In the beginning was the word and word was with God and the word was God.

How many times have I heard this as a chorister? Of course it is true, but may I add something else? The word is powerful but it plays tricks. Just because there is a word for something we believe that it exists.

Have I a separate mind, a separate soul, even a separate body? It would seem I have a separate mind because I sit here at the centre of my own universe, admittedly one that has shrunken rather small of late. And, at the centre of this degraded world, I am conscious of writing these words and I'm aware of the feelings of fear and hopelessness that accompany them. I am aware of my dingy surroundings and the endless conversations I have with myself. I am aware of how one thought can trigger many other silent memories of home life in England and how visualised images of you generate the most exquisite of emotions. I am aware that the point of this pencil is becoming very blunt and there is no pencil sharpener. I am aware that, even though the outside world is becoming hazy and unreal, I am the focal point of my interactions and the centre of my experience is always in my mind.

But, despite this personal experience, is there a separation of my mind and body? No!

What is clear about the activity going on in my universe is that it is just that - activity. When I think, I am talking to myself about my predicament. When I feel the dreadful cold, it is my body that is doing the feeling. With actions, it is clear there can be no inside or outside. Thinking about you isn't in my mind anymore than talking to the prison guard is inside my throat, or walking all of seven strides across the cell is inside my legs.

Of course, in one way I am separate; I am physically alone – apart, that is, from food being deposited by a silent guard and chatting to a friendly mouse. Imprisoned and in isolation, I find my dependence on others is even more obvious.

Although I like to think of Rupert Lockart as independent and autonomous; a man constructing his own life, the reality is he is essentially nothing without his relationship to the world of things, events and ideas – and crucially of people and to one person in particular.

This me, this self, this I, this entity I call Rupert Lockart is completely dependent upon the other – the not me and in particular - you. Until I met you, I was vapour and scattered fragments carried along on a wind of opportunity. Now, this vapour has condensed into a form and the fragments have coalesced into a distinct shape because of you. I have become real through your touch and tenderness and our interactions. I am alive in a way I have never felt before. I have feelings of elation and joy as well as desire and yearning. And I feel pain, terrible gnawing pain, which magnifies with every additional day that goes by when I don't see you.

At the same time I feel very close to you. My mind is slipping into some new state; the distinction between mind, body and the world are blurring and the centre of my universe is shifting. I am still the focus of my experience, at least in waking hours, but now I am like a moon gyrating around a set of wider principles where everything is connected and interlinked. I have the feeling that body, mind and the world function in conjunction.

333

I am not a separate mind controlling a body any more than I am a separate person in control of my destiny. It is clear from my prison cell there is a physical wall separating the inside and outside but there is not a psychological one.

With every passing day, the period between sleep and wakefulness is getting longer and my dreams are more vivid. My vessel is emptying and what seemed solid is evaporating quickly as I find it harder and harder to control what thoughts I let in and what I keep out. Despite this disintegration of boundaries, I am given strength by the lived experience of you being part of me – and the hope I am a part of you. I have my arms wrapped around you, but as time passes my fingertips push back a curtain to reveal what your mother sees – a world of light and shade, good and evil. In the crumbling of my psychological walls, I am off balance and worried.

There is such cruelty here. Not physical but mental torture. I have a desk, a pad of paper and a pencil but no sharpener. I have wasted precious lead on writing to a mouse, now I have the bluntest of instruments to write what I would like to be exquisite prose. I have tried to sharpen the point against the wall but the pencil just disintegrates. Disintegration, is this almost the last word I utter? No, let it be LOVE.

Yours forever and always

Rupert

Towards Madness

Rupert ran out of memories.

During his endless pacing, he resorted to reciting the prayers and psalms that had been installed in his being when he was a chorister. He varied his pacing to match the rhythmic beat of the verses and occasionally he laughed at himself when he considered how he must resemble a monk incarcerated in his cell.

The spiritual quality this recitation induced eventually drew Rupert 's mind to God, divine intervention and personal agency.

After that, he gave up the pacing and recitation and waited for something to happen, from the moment he was given his life-saving period of exercise in the yard until the delivery of the evening meal, but it never did. He even looked back at the interrogation as a sort of highlight, a happening, at the very least, in the long litany of nothingness. He waited and waited and thought and thought but nothing happened, nothing happened. Happened... nothing. He was left alone, alone, alone. Alone.

Past, present and future merged and Rupert found that it was as if he were experiencing a perpetual now. In the confined space of his cell, which had long ceased to provide his senses with any stimulation, he felt abandoned and irredeemably alone. Even the mouse's visits had become infrequent. In this timeless vacuum, he could no longer control his thoughts. In the absence of a compelling present memory, hopes and fears alternately crowded in, jumbled and competing for dominance, or simply rotated and circled aimlessly without purpose or respite.

No longer marking off the days, he walked, ate, defecated in a continuous state of surreal meditation.

Winter slithered away down the gentlest of inclines and spring rose imperceptibly as if to embrace Rupert's descent. Gradually, his resistance ebbed to such an extent that he surrendered himself to prolonged periods of delirium, during which he was unsure about what was real or imagined. In this dreamlike condition, he could neither clearly differentiate between night and day nor between being in his room and walking in the exercise yard.

In his dim cell, when conscious and in some control of his thoughts, he doubted that he would survive his ordeal much longer. He often dreamt of Rebecca holding out her hand and beckoning him into her world. In his lucid moments, it felt that all his efforts to focus, to keep back the darkness threatening to consume him, could easily come to nothing. He was walking over the thin gauze of existence and could easily have slipped through and disappeared completely.

Like a drowning man, Rupert clutched at the flimsiest of items to keep him from slipping under. One that maintained his buoyancy more than most was thinking about how Irène would be coping with the ordeal if she were in his place. The fact that she had dealt with challenging emotional situations as a teenager and had grown strong as a result, suggested to him that she would be able to manage. This inspired him to continue to resist; she was the reason for him to survive. He began to call Irène's name softly and then added, 'I am here. I will see you again.'

In his half-wakeful state, Rupert experienced elements past and present as one confusing but interconnected narrative.

He was at Wythenshawe, he saw the early morning sun rise over the Hall and spread warmth across the large expanse of lawn edged with dahlias in full bloom. The chauffeur, Brownett, and other servants carried a large target onto the grassy sward whilst Robert Tatton and his guests prepared for archery practice. The sound of the ladies' chatter mixed with the sound of birdsong. He looked towards the statue standing on its plinth just outside the gates as it had done for centuries. He had always believed that it was a sculpture of Cromwell. Now he realised it was the Happy Prince with his faithful swallow swooping around. He called out, 'Be careful little bird, don't stay behind; you are not designed for a harsh winter. It is getting cold and it's time to follow your flock to Egypt.'

He thought of Irēne. 'How lovely you look in your yellow linen blouse and amber necklace.'

He had the most dreadful of dreams about *Hotel Dieu*. He was lying on a mortuary slab and his scream did not bring anyone running because he was dead.

A milky mist hung over the platform of an anonymous station; he was alone with Irēne. The big black beast hissed and suddenly jerked. The wheels turned and a voice shouted, 'Two o' clock sharp. Don't be late.' The last carriage passed by and receded into the distance. The rails looked like smoke trails dissipating in the light breeze. A disembodied voice shouted out *you were too late* and Rupert apologetically replied, 'Yes, Ambassador.'

Manhandled into prison, this time Irēne accompanied him. He turned to her, 'What have I done to you? You were strong and independent before you met me. Now you are being delivered here, to this stinking pit. And they are taking you into that box and asking you to strip. No don't. Get your hands off her. Don't touch her.' Bolt upright he screamed, 'Don't touch her there.'

'Irēne, what is wrong, you have your head in your hands? Sorry, my scream has so startled you that you have left your face in your hands. How beautiful is the inside of your facial mask, but I'm too terrified to look up and see your bare head stripped of its face.'

Salvation

In the middle of his wakeful dreams, the door of the cell was unlocked at an unusually early hour and warders struggled in with another bedstead. Rupert was ordered to stand to one side and, as they let the bedstead fall heavily to the floor, he felt the vibrations travel up his body. Shortly afterwards, a prisoner was unceremoniously pushed in. Rupert laughed involuntarily as the man was wearing what appeared to be a wig and a joke pair of spectacles with a large nose and moustache attached to them. Then, he wondered, *Is it right to laugh at my own dream?*

Rupert looked at the apparition. It stood stock-still. Its mouth was grimly closed, as if set forever shut, and it was impossible to tell whether its eyes saw anything as the glasses were heavily smeared. The nostrils of the large nose were flared and the long grey hair was wilted like salad left too long in the hot sun. The light coming in through the barred window created shadows across the man's face cast by deeply furrowed features. He said nothing. He just stared at Rupert.

Rupert wanted to say something but he was unsure whether it was sensible to talk to a dream or, worse still, a ghost. Eventually, the man lay down on the bed brought in by the guards and stayed in the same position for hours, uninterested even in the arrival of food, until forced to visit the washroom by the shouts of the guard. *Perhaps,* Rupert thought as the man lay and wept silent tears, *this is not a dream after all.*

The simple presence of another living, breathing human being in his cell prevented Rupert from falling completely back into his dream world. Instead, he intently studied his cellmate, as he lay inert on the bed.

The next day, Rupert ventured to say, *'Labdien,'* to the new arrival and, when that didn't provoke a response, he repeated,

'Hello' in German, Russian and English. The man lay back wearing his filthy glasses and said nothing.

Later in the day, however, he surprised Rupert by asking in German, 'Where do you come from?'

It was so unusual to hear a voice in the cell that Rupert jumped and initially wondered whether he had asked the question himself. Remembering that he now had a cellmate, he turned to him, said, 'England.'

'England!' The man repeated and then remained silent for the rest of the day.

After three days, the man introduced himself as Karlis Eglīte and Rupert reciprocated. Karlis apologised for being so distant, adding, 'But I have had quite an ordeal.'

'Do you want to talk about it?'

'No, I can't adequately describe what has happened. I don't understand why I am here. I have done nothing wrong, yet I am being punished.' He was then silent for the rest of the day. Rupert realised Karlis was deeply traumatised, so he didn't ask any questions and just gave his cellmate the space to talk if and when he wanted to. To Rupert's surprise, on the following morning Karlis asked,

'Can I trust you?' Rupert was about to say he wasn't an English spy, or placed in the cell as a stooge to hear confessions, when Karlis continued, seemingly convinced he could trust Rupert without him giving an answer. 'You are the first Englishman I have met, and I want to thank you for the help the British gave us in the battle to save Riga from the German advance in 1919.'

'Oh...' Rupert was surprised as he had expected Karlis to

talk about his arrest and imprisonment and then the year struck him as odd. '1919! I understood all fighting had ceased on the signing of the armistice on 11th November 1918.' Karlis looked pleased to be able to explain.

'There is such a belief. After all, you celebrate that day as the end of the Great War, the war to end all wars. But the armistice really is only relevant to the fighting on the Western Front.' He turned to sit on the edge of his bed. 'I will explain this to you further, but first let me properly introduce myself.'

Rupert found that a Professor of History at the University of Latvia was addressing him. Upright and alert, the Professor continued. 'Armed conflict carried on from Estonia to the Ukraine. The Baltic States especially were far too important strategically, economically and agriculturally for the Germans and Russians to give up their aims of conquest. Fighting continued here even after Latvia had declared independence in 1918 and went on until January 3rd 1920.'

Rupert appreciated that giving a history lesson must be soothing for the Professor. He listened attentively whilst the Professor talked, at some length, about how the Bolsheviks, before the end of the Great War, had renounced their sovereignty over Russia's former Baltic territories. The Professor took a deep breath, and added, 'The Germans had coveted these territories for years and, I am sure, had the intention of occupying the areas ceded to them as soon as the war on the Western Front was concluded.'

Pausing, as he might have done while giving a lecture at the university, the professor took off his thick glasses to give them a wipe on the grey sheet. Rupert half expected the nose and moustache to be removed along with the glasses but stifled his amusement.

Continuing, the professor said, 'The future of the territories, now detached from Mother Russia, was primarily determined by

Germany's dramatic military reversals in the west in 1918. After the signing of the armistice, the Western Powers would never have let Germany annex the Baltics. However,' the professor sniffed, 'that did not stop them trying. There was a great deal of confusion at this time, and the Baltic Germans saw the opportunity to make a land grab. To achieve their aim of German control, they formed the Landswehr and in April 1919, mounted a putsch against the newly formed Latvian government under Karl Ulmanis. Thankfully, the Royal Navy provided President Ulmanis and other members of the government protection whilst they were onboard the merchant vessel, Saratov, in the port of Liepaja. If not, the Germans would have crushed the fledgling state.'

Skilled in his abilities to put over detail at a pace that allowed students to take notes, the Professor again paused, this time long enough for Rupert's mind to wander. Once the professor recommenced his lesson, Rupert vaguely heard something about arms being supplied from Britain, the Cēsis agreement and the transfer of the Landswehr to the command of an Englishman. He had begun to think, rather resentfully, that he wouldn't be in Latvia or in his current predicament at all if the Royal Navy hadn't provided this protection to the fledgling Latvian government.

Rupert's speculations were cut short as the professor again paused and looked directly into Rupert's eyes. Up to this point, Rupert had felt he had been given an interesting, but somewhat detached, lecture by a knowledgeable and comical looking professor. Then the professor rose from his bed, stepped forward, formally took Rupert's hand, shook it and said, 'I really want to thank you for saving my life.'

Letting go of Rupert's hand, the professor continued, 'Some twenty years ago, I was a volunteer soldier dug in on a bank of the Daugava River waiting for an enemy shell to blow me and my comrades to smithereens.' The professor's voice was no longer that of a detached academic, he sounded emotional.

'The Russians, under the dubious leadership of Bermont, had made a pact with his twin devil, the German General, van der Golt and together they attacked Riga with heavy artillery. We were brave soldiers, but we only had old rifles. The inevitable collapse of our line was about to happen and we faced being butchered. After that, the Russians and Germans would have fought amongst themselves, like cats and dogs, to take control of the city. I had already given up hope and was awaiting my fate when the British and French warships, way out in the Bay, opened up and shelled the invading army. This allowed us to mount a counter offensive. Without those shells, God knows what would have happened to us and Latvia. On the 11th of November 1919, all the church bells of Riga rang out proclaiming that both banks of the river were back in Latvian hands. It was the sweetest sound I have ever heard.'

The professor returned to his bed and said, wearily, 'Independence was achieved at a time of weakness of the Russian and German military powers, but they have regrouped, strengthened and it is Russia's turn to claim these lands. The Baltic tide has once again turned.'

'Thank you for trusting me.' Rupert said reassuringly and found that he meant it. It touched him that this strange little man, at once so sensitive and so serious, could thank one British man for the work of an entire navy fleet.

Karlis smiled sadly and returned to his bunk. 'I don't trust anyone anymore, only now I don't care. They can do with me what they like.'

Rupert lay awake that night listening to Karlis' breathing and the creaking of the bed as he tossed and turned. A wave of relief flooded over him; he no longer felt alone. He understood that this man, who had thanked him, an unknown foreigner, for saving his life, had arrested his steep decline into madness.

The next day, breakfast arrived in the same gruff manner as usual, but when he sat down on his bed with the black bread and *kvass*, Rupert noticed the corner of a piece of paper sticking out from between his bowl and the thin metal tray. He picked up the bowl and found a page of folded writing paper. When he opened it and recognised the handwriting, it was if it were luminous parchment. He looked into the brightness and, at first, could not focus on the words of this missive sent from another world by his angel.

Rupert Dearest,

I am writing to you not knowing whether this letter will reach you but even so, I need to put my thoughts on paper and want to do it in English (please excuse my mistakes) because I feel closer to you this way.

There are perhaps two dozen words in English to describe two thousand emotions people feel but for me one prevails now – obsessive longing for your presence. I miss you – but this phrase fails to describe the depth of my loss.

I keep the ring you have given me on my finger and I imagine I turn it and the Genie arrives and asks, what is your wish my queen? I answer, I wish you to bring my beloved to me and then he unrolls the magic carpet and takes us both to Arcadia, the land where no one can separate us.

Do you believe we can create our own Arcadia? I do not mean we create a bubble, I want us to be open to the world together, there are so many things to see and learn. You have a good profession, but I can see much more in you, you are a philosopher with artist's soul.

I once asked you what you wanted to do in the future. As for me, I want to study art, to know as much as possible about great painters and maybe one day I will run my own art gallery. I have not told it to anybody, especially now everyone is distant, preoccupied with survival - even bitter.

What happens to people when they become bitter, why do we not turn to each other for help? We all walk a common path, just stumble over different stones on it, trip in different holes. You see, I become a philosopher too. Poke me in ribs and say – Irēne stop it. Let's better have a long walk and then a snooze.

I must confess to you what I do every evening, something my grandmother told me when I was little and longing for my mother's return. I put your photo on a windowsill and light a candle near to it and ask The Fairy of Light to bring you back to me. One day, you will come.

Rupert, my love, do not disappear.

I am here. I will see you again.

Yours forever

Irēne

Rupert reread the letter many times. The more he did so, the more his mind cleared of the fog that shrouded it. Finally, he folded the paper and put it under his pillow. He lay down and an irrepressible smile was the only outward indication of his inner understanding that his sanity was secured.

June 14th 1941

Karlis brought with him another gift— the date. He knew that he had be incarcerated on 11th May 1941 and with this knowledge Rupert was able to restart his calendar, savouring the certainty and reliability of time marked in numbered days and months. *Never again will I take for granted the passing of a week or the coming of a new month. To know when you are is to know a little more of who you are,* he thought. *When I have my freedom I shall buy a hundred calendars!* He realised that Irēne's name day was soon approaching and felt a heavy sadness that he was unable to get even a message of best wishes to her. He wondered, now that spring had arrived, what she'd be doing. He pictured her in the increasingly clement weather, in her linen dress with a yellow belt and carrying her flowered handbag.

By the end of May, it was clear that the prison was overflowing. Although talking at night was prohibited, Rupert listened to the constant conversations going on through knocks on the walls and taps on the pipes.

On 12th June 1941, another man, holding up his now belt-less pinstriped trousers, was thrown into Rupert's cell even though there was no bed for him. Rupert and Karlis were protective of their comfort and the man sat slumped, uncomfortably, against the wall in his suit. Eventually, after looking at the sad, intelligent face of the new arrival, Rupert relented and offered him his pillow. The man refused with a shake of the head.

The newcomer began to talk to himself in Latvian but, in his mutterings, Rupert wondered whether he had heard the odd English word. He paid careful attention and yes, he definitely heard the words *business, dollar, stocks and shares.* Rupert asked the man who he was and was surprised by the answer. The man addressed him clearly and directly, with no apparent distress. 'I am Juris Tiltins, Business Editor of *Rigascher*

Rundschau. Have you heard of the expression time is money?' Rupert responded that he had and Juris continued, but in a way that suggested he had resumed his ramblings, only this time he spoke in German. 'I should live for another forty years, what is that in minutes and seconds?' He looked as if he were making a complex calculation as he twiddled the fingers on both of his hands and then said, 'Such a lot. Is that why I am here? I possess such capital I need a guard?'

Continuing to talk in a grandiloquent manner while addressing no one in particular, the new arrival said, 'I do hope I won't let my wealth go to my head, after all, there are many people who have run out of time through no fault of their own. And such capital is easy to squander. I have let the sands of time fall too easily between my fingers. But, the balance is still in the positive - although I fear I am soon to be robbed.' He turned to Rupert. 'Can I leave you some of my capital in one-year notes? Only, I ask you to use it wisely and spend it only on those things that bring a good return.' Rupert understood these were the ramblings of a man in whose mind, perhaps through fear, something had snapped.

After a while, Karlis, clearly prompted by what Juris had said, unexpectedly started to talk. 'Time. Time... It seems to stretch forever when you are young and then it speeds up before the clock spring breaks. I have come to realise our time is a snap between two eternities of silence.'

'Is that not too bleak a view of life?' Rupert asked. Karlis turned to him in the gloom.

'I haven't detected the faintest of personal traces in the impersonal darkness on either side of my life. I have heard no organs or angels calling me from the next life any more than I heard my mother calling my name before I was born. But, what gives me comfort is the thought that I should not be worried about the silence and blackness of eternity ahead, anymore than about the eternity preceding me.' The light was then dimmed in the cell, which meant that further talking was prohibited. Rupert contemplated what Karlis had said and could see the solace in his way of thinking. As he drifted off to sleep, he imagined he heard a trumpet sound, then a Priest's lamenting voice from outside called;

The fool hath said in his heart, there is no God. They are corrupt, they have done abominable works, there is none that doeth good.

The Lord looked down from heaven upon the children of men, to see if there were any that did understand, and seek God.

Despite now being almost asleep, Rupert realised that the drip, drip of the songs and verses, which had fallen on him as a chorister, had percolated to his deepest bedrock. He shook himself awake as he felt that he had a question to answer; did he believe in God and an afterlife or not? He wanted to address it, come to a conclusion, but the answer wouldn't form.

Instead, he remembered the alabaster figure of the Virgin Mary and Archangel Michael, which stood by the door of the chapel in Pembroke College, depicting the judgement of the soul. The Archangel, now burnished in white, turned towards him with his set of scales in hand and asked, 'On which side shall you sit?' A demon then stepped from the shadow and tipped the scales to one side before the Virgin Mary redressed the balance by placing her rosary on the other scale. Rupert shuddered violently and then fell into a fitful sleep.

The next day, Juris was a little more coherent but his mutterings were not addressed to his cellmates. Quietly, but with a confident voice, he said, 'Time never passes so quick as when it is in short supply. My time is spent, but one day, and yes it may be some time off, we will base our political systems on a stronger understanding of what it is to be human. When enough people imagine another future, they will stand together, hand in hand, in a chain spanning many countries and ensure that Stalin, Hitler, Mussolini, Franco and their ilk are consigned to a brief period of the 20th century.'

Rupert brought the friendly face of Lord Simon to mind and thought, 'One day we will all have leaders like Ernest.'

On June 14th, there was an unusual commotion and Rupert was woken in the half-light of dawn by the banging of cell doors that rippled its way up his corridor. Guards shouting for people to wake, dress and stand to attention came closer. When Rupert's cell door was unlocked, guards with guns marched in. They shouted, 'Out, out,' and when all three prisoners started to move, one of the guards barred Rupert's path saying, 'Not you'.

As Juris was bundled out of the door, he said to himself, 'Time to meet my Maker. I am sure Vilis Lācis has already signed the order.'

Vilis Lācis? Rupert thought, *what has he got to do with it?* The door crashed shut with a deep reverberation that hung in the air as the footsteps receded down the corridor. Rupert was, once more, left alone.

Garoza and the Fisherman's Son

After Karlis and Juris had been removed from his cell, Rupert remained alone and unfed for the rest of the day and the following night. The next day, the old routine restarted including the fortnightly visit to the barber. On walking back to his cell, Rupert noticed that the prison still appeared to be full with the exception of his wing where all the cell doors now hung open. Rupert presumed that their occupants had been swept out along with Karlis and Juris.

It wasn't long before the cell doors nearby were once more banging shut and the nightly orchestra struck up again on the pipes as the prison was filled back up to capacity. This was confirmed when two more prisoners were pushed, unceremoniously, into his cell.

They could not have been more different in appearance. One had a round, smooth face, so bloodless it looked like the colour had been drained even from of his protuberant eyes. His mouth hung open so that Rupert could see red gums and yellow, decayed teeth. The other prisoner had a shock of thick black hair, quick darting, sharp blue eyes and the swagger of an opportunist. *He looks,* thought Rupert, *every part the petty crook.* Rupert immediately named him Garoza, after the cheating middleman in Vilis Lācis' book. Without a moment's hesitation, Garoza immediately took the spare bed and left the other man, who looked like a fish gasping for air, to lie on his thin blanket on the wooden floor. Rupert looked at the man opening and closing his mouth and thought, *So this is what has happened to the fisherman's son.*

Rupert didn't feel at all comfortable talking to these men. They seemed a notably different sort to Karlis and Juris. *Common criminals, probably used to spending time in prisons.* This was confirmed in Rupert's mind when the fisherman's son started to tap out coded messages on the pipes. Then, after two days of being cooped up together, Garoza formally introduced himself in Russian. 'My name is Nikolai Titaravo, Chief Engineer of Daugava dam project. Pleased to meet you.' Rupert's mouth fell open and for more a moment he mimicked his pale cellmate as he gulped like a halibut.

'Daugava dam! But... but what are you doing in here?'

'I was accused of wrecking after plans for new dam were set ablaze by electrical fire.' Rupert felt a pang at the banal mishap that had cost this man his freedom and thought, *When am I going to learn... nothing is what it seems in this country? At least, not any more.*

'The project has restarted?' Rupert asked.

'Yes, it's clear that electricity is needed for industry that surely will come to Riga.'

'I was also involved with the project,' said Rupert.

'So it is fate we are here together!' Nikolai laughed, 'Or is it little joke played by our captors... hm? Perhaps they are waiting to see if we are saboteurs and spies together?' He gave a short barking laugh again, 'Ha! They will wait long time.'

Nikolai and Rupert discussed the project for the rest of the day. Rupert felt his mind unclenching, as though a great knotted ball of thread was unwinding and settling back onto its spool. He had never been so happy to discuss his work.

The next day, relaxed into each other's company, they chatted about their former lives. Nikolai spoke of his uncle's experience as a gunner on the Russian Cruiser, Aurora. He finished his story with, 'He has claim to fame. He was due to leave Navy on 26th October 1917 and, day before, his fellow gunners held party on the Aurora, which was docked in Petrograd. They started drinking in afternoon and by evening it was, by all accounts, wild. My uncle, to mark his last day sent up series of blank shots from his six inch cannons on Aurora. What spectacle and what effect! Shots so scared Provisional Government holed up in Winter Palace they simply vanished. Bolsheviks opened doors and strolled in. So, my uncle started October Revolution!'

'Let's drink to that.' Rupert said and raised an imaginary glass.

Later, Rupert recalled the time he spent in Fricis' company and his words, *prediction is impossible because history turns on the smallest, and seemingly insignificant, of events.* Thinking of the raucous party aboard the Aurora, the jovial retorts of the cannons and the unintended, laughably significant events they triggered, Rupert smiled at the absurdity of it all. He was still smiling as he drifted off to sleep.

The next day, Rupert was dozing in the fetid gloom of the cell when, suddenly, the fisherman's son, who had been listening to the constant tapping of coded messages on the radiator pipes, stood up and shouted, 'Germany has invaded Russia.' His voice, unused for so long was hoarse and cracked, but his pale, limpid eyes were alight with hope. In that instance, all hell broke loose. First there was a single shout that was repeated and then built into a communal howl that went from cell to cell, floor to floor and was augmented by yelling, yodelling and shrilling sounds.

Nikolai jumped up to the window and even the fisherman's son shouted out. The next wing awoke from its torpor and likewise began to scream, shout and wail. Then, to goad their captors, what seemed like one, two, three thousand voices, all started to sing:

Deutschland, Deutschland über alles,
Über alles in der Welt,

Wenn es stets zu Schutz und Trutze
The singing rose to a crescendo,

Brüderlich zusammenhält.

Fists and stools banged on the iron doors, and Rupert joined in by picking up the end of his heavy iron bed and repeatedly dropping it in unison with many other inmates. Each massive bang and vibration filled him with elation that swelled as it was shared and echoed throughout the vast building by hundreds of men. Tin plates were kicked around the floor. The lids of waste buckets banged and the contents flung out of the small cell windows. Soon, the cacophonous, gigantic prison stank like one huge, overpowering toilet.

The siren sounded and, under its shrill ululation, Rupert heard the click, click of cell doors being unlocked. He detected the smacking sound of truncheons on ripe skulls as a roar of fury rose and swept over the prison. Eventually, the noise subsided and, after replacing the thin mattress and getting under his blanket, Rupert lay back on the iron bedstead. In a state of arousal, he imagined meeting Irēne and making love.

Later on, he thought, *How strange that there should be such an instant reaction; it was as though the prisoners had all been tuned into a radio and simultaneously learnt of Germany invading Russia.*

Despite the fact that the lights had been turned out, the tapping on the pipes continued into the night. Unexpectedly, out of the gloom, Rupert was addressed directly by the fisherman's son, whose husky whisper cracked the silence. 'Message for Englishman. Be prepared. Stay strong.'

It could only have come from Irēne and Rupert's heart leapt. *But what does it mean?* he thought, *I will be strong my love but how can I prepare for the unknown?* When sleep eventually lapped at his bedside, Rupert wondered if this was the answer to his question— *Yes. Yes, I do believe there is a God. For Irēne has found me. I have not been forsaken in my hour of need. I will be ready. I will keep vigil in my own little Gethsemane and wait for my Saviour.*

The day after the uprising, June 24th, Nikolai and the fisherman's son were ordered out of the cell without any explanation. After saying a hurried goodbye, Rupert remembered Vilis Lācis talking about a future where at least the poor struggling fishermen had a reasonable life. He was developing this train of thought when he heard the sharp crack of gunfire from outside. The hair on the back of his arms and neck stood up. *Surely not!* he thought. Never had he heard such a portent of doom.

Rupert lay on his bed recalling the slumped bodies of the men at the execution he had witnessed and tried to will himself to find some other innocent explanation for the fate of his cellmates. He jumped as a sharp bang sounded on his cell door and scrambled to sit up. *They have come for me,* he thought and an image of the bloodied, pock-marked wall of the courtyard filled his mind, blinding him.

Lieutenant Dmitri Kuznetsov entered the cell carrying a bottle of vodka. He staggered to Rupert's desk and sat down, with his customary arrogance.

Without any introduction, or hint of being drunk in his voice, the lieutenant said, 'Lying, cheating Hitler has made his most stupid decision yet; to invade Russia. Has he not read history books? Does he not know what happened to Napoleon and his army?' He paused and Rupert looked at him.

The lieutenant continued, as if talking to someone else in the room. 'Is there no one whom you can trust? Finns have reneged on Peace Treaty and are in league with Germans. With their surprise attacks they have made quick progress but Ukraine and Baltic States are long way from Moscow. Let them come is all I can say. For present time, we will take brief sojourn, tactical retreat we can call it.' His voice had taken on a petulant whine, like a spurned child.

He turned and looked intently at Rupert. 'But, what, my little spying friend, shall I do with you?' Rupert stared back. In his inebriated and emotional state, the lieutenant was less frightening.

The lieutenant's question was rhetorical. 'I could shoot you. In fact, it would make life simpler for me if I did. You have some strategic value in diplomatic circles but quite frankly you are not worth the bother of protection at this time when we have to make a temporary retreat,' He let his statement hang in the air. Rupert did not flinch. He was tired of responding to the games the lieutenant played. The lieutenant seemed disappointed and shrugged, taking another sip of vodka.

'But I am not going to shoot you. It seems you have friend; Vilis Lācis, Chairman of Council of Ministers of the Latvian Socialist Soviet Republic. You met at Kemeri. He has personally asked you are not shot.' Rupert did his best to conceal his surprise. *Lācis has spared my life? I did not think he liked me at all. Why would he go to the trouble?*

'So,' said the lieutenant, leaning forward with an unpleasant smile, 'I am leaving you to fate far worse. I am leaving you to be treated as spy by Germans. They are showing no mercy as they cut bloody path to Riga.' He tilted the bottle at Rupert. '*They* will shoot you. If you are lucky.'

The lieutenant continued, 'Maybe it will give you opportunity to learn why Russia is set to fight tyrant Hitler. Maybe it will give you opportunity to realise communism has aim whilst German imperialism is simply about grabbing land.' The lieutenant took another swig of vodka and slumped further into the chair. 'You really don't understand do you? With your soft hands and Cambridge holiday, you have not experienced what it requires, what effort and pain it takes to bring country from laughing stock where elite own everything to great nation where everyone is equal. Maybe our methods are little distasteful for your English sensibility. But ends justify means.'

With deep attention and with some difficulty, the lieutenant slowly and deliberately placed the bottle on the table before starting to speak again, although he seemed no longer to be addressing only Rupert but the room at large. 'Take my family history, multiply it millions of times and you will understand unstoppable movement – and why we will fight to last drop of Russian blood to defend our motherland...'

Pausing briefly, the lieutenant then addressed Rupert directly, his eyes sliding in and out of focus as he looked at him. 'I'm sorry for my lack of manners, how have you been since I last saw you?'

'I have met some fine people and learnt some interesting Russian words from the guards.'

'You will be able to report to the Germans we have good prisons.'

Standing up and then steadying himself by grabbing the edge of the table, he said, 'I wish you restful remaining few days in full knowledge that you, and your petite bourgeois friends at Cambridge, would have long been swept away if you had lived in Russia. But, I think you must agree, we have treated you well - in comparison to how Germans treat spies. I leave you now. Enjoy German hospitality.' He blundered from the room.

Alone, Rupert tried to distract himself from the probable death of his cellmates and the approach of the German army. He strained to recall any further morsels of his time in the sanatorium. It seemed like another age. He felt almost as if it were a story he had read, or a long and vivid dream, or else, something that had happened to somebody else entirely.

Next morning, the breakfast was delivered as normal but, later in the day, the main meal was inedible. The smell of the soup reminded him of the mud at the sanatorium and when he dipped the bread in it, Rupert watched in horror as worms wiggled to the surface. After that, no more food was delivered. No footfalls could be heard in the corridors and Rupert assumed that the Russians must have fled. He wondered if he would starve before the Germans arrived.

Exhausted, his empty stomach cramping, Rupert drifted into a half-waking dream. He found himself at the scene of the tragic stampede at the Khodynka Field. He sat astride a carousel, the painted horses bobbing as they revolved to the organ music. He turned and spoke to a fellow rider. 'Comrade Stalin, what a surprise to see you up here. I didn't think you would like such rides.'

'Oh yes', Stalin's voice was deep and his moustache twitched, 'and from top of this Ferris wheel you can see long way. Look at Khodynka Field below. See masses there waiting expectantly for their unthinking ruler. Here he comes with his entourage. Watch how disaster unfolds as easily as laying picnic blanket. Yes, it is meant to be. From here you can see Nevsky Prospect. More bloodshed. But it has to be and that is nothing I tell you, nothing to the amount of German blood that will spill across Europe. How dare they come! Hitler, look at him on that silly children's ride below. Sitting in his car saluting. Who is looking? No one. They are looking to us, to Russia. Wave now.' Rupert laughed and waved, then looked back at his fellow rider and recoiled. Stalin had become Hitler. His swastika eyes bore into Rupert's and when he opened his mouth he hissed and a forked tongue slid out. Rupert's scream brought no one running to his assistance.

From the depth of his dream, he heard heavy footsteps coming closer. *Fee, Fie, Foe Fum, I smell the blood of an Englishman. Be he 'live or be he dead, I'll grind his bones to make my bread.*

This must be his mother coming to tell him he was late for school. *Mother, your steps are so heavy and your voice so deep.* Thekey scraped in the lock. Then, he was fully awake. All time deserted the room. It was as if he were forever fixed in the photograph taken at the opera of him standing next to Irēne. Then, time rushed in again with a faint swish as the door of his cell was opened and a gruff voice shouted, 'Out.'

Prison Break

Staggering along the corridors of the prison, cell doors were open or opening in front of Rupert and dirty figures loomed and passed by. His world span around, turning and turning on the stairwell. It was if he were being dragged into a whirlpool. So many bodies cascaded down and along the ground floor and the flow bore him along. When they were flushed out through the prison block's main entrance it was as if he were a cork that had just popped up after being submerged in a torrent. He blinked. He couldn't focus properly. He breathed deeply but could not recognise the smell. It was clear and sharp and clean. It was the scent of fresh air.

Confused and disoriented, Rupert wondered whether this was a dream. Then he heard it. He heard her. A voice on the summer breeze, calling his name. 'Rupert! *Mana mīla!* Rupert!'

A wave of energy, joy and elation passed through him. He turned towards the sound and saw an angel emerging from the bright sunlight. He ran towards her. His arms reached for her. He touched clothes, skin, felt body, substance, opened his mouth to take in the swirling sweetness of her scent. She was real. She was here. He gripped onto her, held her to him, he could not bring her close enough, never could it be close enough.

Then he recoiled from her. He must not touch her. He was filth, he was a ragged animal, he was unworthy. He stumbled backwards. She caught his arms. She placed a jacket over his shoulders and took his hand. 'Come *mina mīla*', said the saving angel, 'We must run!'

Rupert willed his legs to obey.

They ran, hand in hand, joining the other prisoners spilling out of the open gates like a stream of grey moths fluttering towards a flame. Outside the prison walls, Rupert had to slow down. He started to count his steps, seven, fourteen, twenty-one, twenty-eight before he realised what he was doing. Turning into a side street, Irēne stopped by a car and Rupert saw Pēteris sitting in the driver's seat. She helped Rupert into the back of the car and climbed in after him.

'Go!' she said. Pēteris put his foot down and the car sped away.

Pēteris drove fast and the engine was noisy. Nobody spoke, but Irēne squeezed Rupert's hand. He began to recognise parts of Riga, and soon, they were in *Miera Iela* and outside Irēne's block.

Irēne hugged her father and said something to him in Latvian. Pēteris shook Rupert's hand and then wished them good luck. The car pulled away and disappeared in the distance. Then, Irēne led Rupert up the stairs to her apartment.

In prison, Rupert had tried to remember every single detail of Irēne's apartment, but it looked smaller than he had remembered it. He noticed that there was now a bed in the sitting room but didn't comment. He wanted very much to hold Irēne and talk and remember and laugh and cry. But he could not. He felt, oddly numb and he was painfully aware that he had brought into her lovely apartment the rank smells of human urine and body odour, which couldn't be masked by the glorious smell of meat cooking in the kitchen. Understanding his needs, Irēne passed him a razor, soap and towel and said that there was a change of clothes in the bathroom.

Turning on the tap, Rupert felt the luxury of hot water then looked up into the mirror and was shocked by what he saw. He wiped the surface of the mirror, thinking that it must be dusty as his face looked strangely grey, but it was clean and dust free. His face was thin and ashen, and his hair, with its golden streak no longer visible, was a mess of short matted spikes. He first shaved off an ugly, patchy beard before undressing and then, as

359

he sat in the small bath letting the water cascade and cleanse and heal, he scrupulously went over every inch of his body with soap.

After spending over an hour in the bathroom, Rupert emerged wearing the change of clothing and stood in front of Irēne. He brushed the top of his head with his hand, bringing her attention to the loss of his sun-bleached locks, before moving close to her and embracing. The human touch, the relief, the sense that his ordeal was over brought on a physical reaction; a strange sensation started in the pit of his stomach, became a short catch of his breath and then burst out as a paroxysm of huge sobs. He clung to Irēne as a drowning man would to a life belt and his tears flowed unrestrained.

Eventually, the sobs began to ebb away and the hitching of his chest shuddered and stopped. 'I am sorry,' he said. He wiped away his tears and gave Irēne a watery smile. 'You would have been proud of me, I never cried once in prison.'

'Well, I probably made up for us both.', she said, wiping away her own. They clung to each other.

'I feel so confused, disoriented.' Rupert whispered. 'One minute, I'm expecting the Germans to arrive, and then an angel plucks me away from hell. How?'

Irēne laid her head on his shoulder. 'From the moment the German invasion started, there were plans to get prisoners out. Father heard a rumour that criminals were going to be released today. You are a political prisoner and were to be kept locked up, but I managed to bribe a guard to open your cell and let you out as part of the general release. There is so much fear and confusion that the remaining prison officers are deserting their posts.'

Rupert drew back, raised Irēne's face to his own and kissed her deeply. 'Thank you.' Then he averted his gaze. 'But it is all so sudden; forgive me if I appear a little strange for a while.'

Irēne had prepared the table and brought out the food Rupert had smelt cooking when he arrived. Now the aroma of beef stew was overpowering and he wondered whether anything had ever been so mouth-watering. He sat at the table and, whilst he was being served, tried to remember his table manners but he wasn't sure in which hand to hold the knife, so excused himself, 'Just today, I'm going to eat prison style.' He took the spoon and silently, purposefully, dug in.

In the past, Rupert and Irēne would have talked and laughed but now Rupert concentrated on his food. It wasn't long before he felt completely satiated and, with his plate half full, he admitted defeat. Irēne said he would need to relearn to eat and added, 'And I am not talking about your table manners.' They both laughed and the sound permeated his head. It felt like warm, clean water was running through him cleansing parts besmirched by his long incarceration.

Rupert commented on the extra bed in the sitting room and Irēne explained that she had been lucky to keep the flat as many had been requisitioned, but they had to accept new tenants. Then, Irēne added in a serious voice, 'Unfortunately, we cannot stay here. The Germans have attacked with unprecedented ferocity. It is difficult to piece together what is happening, but it looks like they are intent on marching into Moscow before turning their attention to fully securing Latvia. However, there are reports of massive destruction across Lithuania and north into Latvia. Stories are being circulated about Jews especially, but also gypsies, being rounded up and shot as the Germans cut a bloody swathe through the country.' Irēne paused to let the urgency of the situation sink in before resuming. 'If we leave now, we may be able to get to Liepāja before the Germans arrive in Riga.'

'What will we do there?'
'Hide in my grandparents' summerhouse.'

'Oh!' Rupert wasn't overly concerned about the prospect, as anything was better than what he faced in prison.

After dinner, Rupert helped wash up and, as he stood with the tea towel in his hand, tears of joy welled up in response to carrying out this act of domestic simplicity. With dish in hand, he said, 'It seems a chance encounter saved my life. Do you remember I met the writer, Vilis Lācis at Kemeri?'

'Yes, I remember.'

'Well, apparently he had the power to stop me being shot. It's thanks to him I am here.' Irēne stopped washing.

'That is good, and I am thankful for your brief encounter.'

Irēne's voice was low and serious. 'But before you become too sentimental about your old friend, Lācis, you might like to consider that he, as Chairman of the Council of Ministers in the Latvian Soviet Socialist Republic, did not lift a finger to stop his lover, Emily Benjamins being deported and may have even signed her warrant.'

'Oh.'

'It is said he signed the warrants for the arrest and deportation of thousands of, so called, enemies of the people. It is impossible to know how many, but some say, by the volume of train wagons used in the exodus, up to fifteen thousand could have been sent to Siberia, and it all happened very quickly on 14th June.' Rupert then realised the removal of Karlis and Juris from prison on that day must have been to do with the deportations.

'I'm trying to imagine what fifteen thousand people actually looks like. The largest group of people I can visualise is the huge crowd that attended the song festival in Riga, but it falls short of that number. I can hardly believe it.'

In thinking about what had been going on outside the confines of his cell, Rupert suddenly felt selfish and self-obsessed. He had thought of Irēne every day, but never once that she could also have been classified as an enemy of the people and targeted for deportation. He realised her life could not have been easy and asked, 'How has life been for you?'

'Let's not talk about me. I got by, there was secretarial work and although it was badly paid, it didn't matter much, because there was nothing to spend money on.'

Rupert had so many things to say and ask; he didn't know where to begin. They continued with the washing up in silence whilst he tried to pull out one strand from his intertwined thoughts and feelings. Eventually, he asked, 'Andris and Christa, have you had any news? I spent a lot of time in prison wondering if they managed to get out of Latvia.'

'I have had no contact at all but neither have I seen any reports of them being captured.'

'What of Katerīna?'

'Yesterday, she left Riga for her hometown. She said, better the devil you know.'

'What about Walter Zapp?'

'I have heard no news on him.'

'Fricis Apšenieks?' Irēne took his hand.

'I am told that Fricis died in April of tuberculosis.' He immediately recalled his friend's hacking cough.

'I only spent a few days in Fricis' company, but our conversations had a big impact. I am very sorry to hear this news.' Rupert felt like he had been told of the loss of a close relative.

After a lull, Rupert asked, 'What did you manage to do in your free time?'

'At first my free time was spent writing to you until I found out letters were never delivered to political prisoners. But, I hope you received the last one. Katerīna risked a lot to get it to you.' Rupert felt he had been hit in the chest as he suddenly remembered this treasured letter had been left under his pillow in the prison cell.

'Yes, thank you. It really did save my life.'

'It seems the combined charms of a beautiful woman and the payment of a bribe were enough to fix it with your gaoler.' He remembered the letters he had written together with the ones received from Irēne and dwelt on the power of the written word to heal. Then he returned his thoughts to the prison.

'I didn't know I was a political prisoner.'

'Well you were in the wing where all the enemies of the people were held.'

Once the kitchen was tidy, Irēne informed Rupert they needed to leave soon and added, 'The Russians have blown up the railway bridge but trains are still running from the other side of the Daugava.' After the excitement of escaping from prison and with the sudden change in his regime after weeks of inactivity, Rupert felt dreadfully tired and would desperately have liked to stay and rest in the apartment. However, he realised that Irēne must know the urgency of the situation. He asked, 'Is Pēteris also leaving Riga?' She replied, 'No, we said our goodbyes properly yesterday, so now we just need to take our bags and go.'

Fetching two bags from her room, Irēne passed one to Rupert, saying, 'Here are some summer clothes from Father and, when we get to Liepāja, Grandfather will give you some more for winter.' He thanked her and, soon after, they left the apartment, locked the door and hailed a cab. Rupert was immediately struck by the bony ribs of the horse and wondered whether it had the strength to pull their combined weight.

The roads were unusually busy and people scurried along with downcast, unsmiling faces, avoiding eye contact. Rupert noted that everyone looked like they had put on their oldest clothes. He wondered whether his memory was playing tricks, as he was sure he remembered people in the city always being smart and polite and smiling at others if they caught their eye.

Driven by the novelty of being out of prison, Rupert's attention was attracted by everything; the shop signs, the seagulls whirling overhead, the grass and hostas growing profusely in the parks and even the upholstered seats in the cab. From behind, he must have looked like he had an uncontrollable tick.

As the cab inched over the pontoon bridge across the River Daugava, it was clear that a mass exodus was in progress. They crept along in a queue of laden cars and overloaded lorries, but there were similar numbers of vehicles travelling in the other direction. It was as if the whole country didn't know which way to turn.

He looked back over the large expanse of the river to the cityscape he knew so well. Apart from the chaos of tangled girders on the railway bridge, the rest of the scene was as he remembered it. The President's Palace, the fat dome of the

365

cathedral and the tiered towers of St. Peter's Church. This scene normally appeared timeless, calm, composed and redolent of history and tradition. Yet, it now radiated tension. It was as if the city was built on the skin of a giant balloon being inflated to bursting point.

Rupert knew that the Wehrmacht's needle was already heading towards it.

Escape

Torņakalns station, on the other side of the river, was crammed with people and Irēne left Rupert with the luggage whilst she joined a ragged queue to purchase tickets.

From the station, which stood on the brow of a small hill, Rupert looked back at the city. Riga was before him and, with golden clouds suspended above, it looked as proud, strong and feminine as ever. He knew the city was more than the buildings; it was the reserved but friendly people, the culture, the song and the sense of freedom. It grieved him to see that this wasn't the same city he had come to love.

The prison wasn't part of Rupert's Riga, but its powerful presence appeared to symbolise the change. It was part of a cancer eating a Goddess' body.

He looked around at the crowd milling by the ticket office. Where were the pretty parasols and polite, well-dressed people? They all stood, poorer and tatty looking, shoulders slumped as if carrying heavy loads.

Irēne returned, tickets in hand and reported, 'You would not believe the amount of pushing and shoving I had to do inside to keep in the queue.'

'I was just thinking how things have changed in Riga.' He also wondered whether she had become even stronger, more resolute.

'Yes, I will not be coming back to Riga. Not after last year and what happened to you.' Rupert wondered what ordeal she had gone through to feel so differently about her beloved city. He put his arm around her and brought her to him.

As they crossed the track for their platform, both of them were quiet. Rupert was tense, waiting for someone, he wasn't sure who, to shout, *Stoyat' na meste - Halt,* and to bar them from leaving or worse, take him back to prison.

Whilst waiting for the next train, Irēne told Rupert that it was from this station that the estimated fifteen thousand people were packed into cattle trucks and sent off to Siberia. He thought of Karlis and Juris and wondered whether they would survive in its frozen depths. He stared out along the tracks. *I do not think they even survived the journey.*

Eventually, a huge, decrepit train wheezed its way into the station. There was a great deal of jostling but they managed to clamber aboard and find a seat. Soon after, the monster, spewing black smoke, set off towards Liepāja. Rupert breathed out deeply and the furrow in Irēne's brow lessened.

Once underway, Rupert commented on the age of the train and Irēne told him that all the newest Latvian engines and rolling stock had been sent to Russia and replaced by time-expired, reserve equipment. The outskirts of Riga were soon left behind and from the window he watched as the train passed fields nestling in the gently rolling countryside. His eyes stung from the bright daylight, but he was savouring all the views and hopeful that, with each passing mile, the memories of the last months would be left further and further behind.

The train stopped at Jelgava and as it pulled off once more, Rupert rested his head against the window. The ever-changing scenes passed like the flickering images of a monochromatic film. This, combined with the repetitive click clack of the wheels, lulled him towards sleep. His eyelids closed and his head lolled forward. It wasn't long before he sat upright with a jolt, making Irēne jump, and shouting, 'Mind the slippery slope!' Fragments of tormenting dreams had returned, and he realised that it would take more than a few miles of track to shed the effects of his incarceration.

Rupert apologised to Irēne for disturbing her and drawing close, he asked, 'Can I talk to you about being in prison?'

'Of course. I want you to tell me.'

'I will skip the diet and washing regime. In prison, I had plenty of time to think over things. The reality of war and revolution hit home; it contrasted very sharply with the intellectual banter I used to take part in at Cambridge. As you once said, theory is very different to reality.'

'Yes, I remember.'

Recalling Lieutenant Kuznetsov's family story, he turned to Irēne and said, 'I have been badly treated, that I can say, but I came to understand what drives a man like Lieutenant Kuznetsov to do what he is doing. He certainly scared me on more than one occasion, but if you were able to look beyond the tough shell, deep inside you would find a little boy who had lost his father too young... Is it wrong to have some sympathy with my captor?'

'No, it is not wrong to sympathise with one's captors. No one is all good or all bad. We all do what we can to make sense of what we find before us. To show empathy and sympathy to someone who treated you so is courageous. It shows you are a good man.'

Rupert reflected on Irēne's comment and then he sat up straighter as if a weight were beginning to be lifted from his shoulders.

As the train chuffed steadily towards Liepāja, Rupert watched the landscape slip by. When he ignored the scattered farms, with their distinctive wooden roofs nestling in their protective shield of birch trees, and the occasional stork's nest, it reminded him of the gently rolling Cheshire Plains with its cows, hayricks and mighty oaks. He then thought of home and how staying in Irēne's grandparents' house would be a brief interlude before being, somehow, liberated to England.

The train pushed on towards a fiery, crepuscular sky but stopped unexpectedly at Grobiņa station. Rupert glanced out of the window, gave a cry and moved to duck out of sight. There were soldiers on the platform. His heart missed a beat. Irēne shushed him, 'Do not hide,' squeezed his hand. 'Let me do the talking.' The train jerked to a halt and, as the soldiers clambered on board, Irēne whispered, 'Latvian.' The soldiers simply ordered everyone off. The passengers milled, bewildered, about the platform beside the train, which was now producing a sound like the breathing of a wounded animal.

One of their fellow travellers addressed a question to the soldier who seemed to be in charge. He replied gruffly and waved his rifle in the direction the train had just come from. Then, the passengers raised their arms in what looked like disgust or frustration and in ones and twos trudged off down the line in the opposite direction towards Liepāja.

Irēne took Rupert's hand and led him away from the station towards the town before saying, 'The soldiers have been told to send the train back to Riga. They don't know why, and it is up to us to finish the journey as best we can.' He was relieved the soldiers had not been ordered to do anything more, not even to check passports, and asked, 'Where are we?'

'We are about ten kilometres from Liepāja, but Grandfather's summerhouse is out beyond the town, so we have a long walk in front of us.'

'We had better get going in that case.' Rupert was flagging, the long weariness of his incarceration still aching in his bones, but he wanted to sound positive.

Their shadows were already long as they headed through the small town centre and they wondered where they would sleep. After walking through a park, with what appeared to be the remains of an old castle at its centre, they came to a row of houses, one of which had a sign painted on its façade saying *Viesnīca*. Rupert surprised himself by knowing that this meant hotel and pointed out the building. They decided to see whether they could stay for the night.

Rupert pulled a chain hanging by the entrance door and immediately a loud bell began to ring and continued to ring for a long time without anybody coming to the door. They were about to set off when an upstairs window opened and a great mop of grey hair spilled out. The grey mop called down for them to wait, and eventually an elderly lady, wearing a long traditional Latvian dress covered in embroidered ethnic motifs, opened the door.

Irēne explained in Latvian that they needed a bed for the night. The lady, smiling in a kindly way, replied and Irēne translated. 'The lady says the hotel has been shut for more than a year.' Rupert had picked up his bag and was ready to go when the lady spoke again. Irēne nodded her head, said, '*Paldies*,' and explained to Rupert that the hotel was shut under the orders of the Russians, then added, 'If we wait for a while in the lounge, she will prepare a bedroom for us.' He turned to the lady.

'*Paldies*.' His simple thank you was heartfelt.

The lounge, at the back of the building, was warm and its windows looked out onto a garden full of apple trees. In the twilight, Rupert could see a number of beehives. He smiled and said quietly, 'Zoumm, zoumm'. They both laughed. He sat back in a comfortable armchair and couldn't quite believe that, in the morning, he had been festering on his prison bed in a hallucinated world inhabited by terrifying figures. 'What a striking difference,' he thought and was surprised to find out he had spoken out loud.

'Yes it must be.' Irēne replied.

The old lady came to show them to their room and on the wide wooden staircase she started a conversation with Irēne that continued whilst standing outside the door of their room. Rupert fidgeted, itching to fall into bed and welcome sleep. Finally, Irēne and the lady finished their conversation and embraced. Irēne thanked the lady once more as she left them in a room lit by the vestiges of a glorious sunset.

As soon as Rupert lay on the bed he was overcome with exhaustion. By the time Irēne had taken a nightdress out of her bag he was fast asleep, still fully clothed, on top of the bed. He awoke briefly in the night and struggled at first to understand where he was and how he came to be sleeping on what felt like a cloud. He slipped off his shirt and trousers, turned down the top of the sheet and blanket and gently got into the bed. He tried not to disturb Irēne, who lay on the very edge of the bed, as he gently pulled her close and snuggled against the contours of her body.

Rupert awoke and knew it was early by the faintness of the light. He gently touched Irēne's cheek and thought, *How lovely, pure and delicate. Creation, love, hope encapsulated in this wondrous, delicate person. How beautiful. How beautiful!* His thoughts seemed to wake Irēne. She stretched, yawned and gently blinked her eyes open and turned to him. 'You were tired last night.'

'But not this morning.' He pulled himself up and lent over to kiss her and she gave a little sigh of pleasure. He felt the now familiar sensation of simultaneous melting and tension and moved his hand over her body. Had he dared to think this would ever be possible again? Now, with all his senses straining, he cuddled up to her and she said, 'Welcome home,' which made him smile all the more.

There was no rush, no clamour, only the swish of clean linen and the sharpening intake of his breath.

They lay still, resonating to the deep frequency of passion, like the fading reverberations of church bells. As he raised his head, he saw her eyes fill with tears and, as they swelled and rolled down her cheek, he wiped them away with his little finger. 'It was so lovely.' She whispered, 'It was so lovely, don't move.' He said nothing, only softly kissed her, and he took her gentle sobs to be a sort of bliss.

Rupert inwardly smiled as he understood that the same body that drove him to a frenzy could also becalm him like a sailing boat on an unruffled sea. Passion and peace existed together in one body. He lay inert, knowing that his healing had begun.

Once Rupert had rolled away, Irēne propped herself on her elbow to study his head and torso. 'You have many different kinds of hair,' she said to him, 'on your head you have a mousey coat, your chest is nearly all black with the exception of one or two grey hairs but the hair on your arms is still blond.' He was surprised he had any grey hair and, triggered by her description, wondered how his friend, the mouse, was getting on without him. Then, he realised that, in making his sudden and unexpected escape, he had forgotten to pick up the letter he had written to Irēne.

Rupert did not want to dwell on his time in prison and, instead, recalling Irēne's lengthy conversation with the lady the previous evening, asked her what they had been talking about. She replied, 'We talked of loss. Not just physical loss or the disappearance of loved ones but the loss of trust. When you cannot trust anyone for fear of being denounced, this is probably the greatest loss of all.'

Rupert was struck by what she had recounted and wondered how long it would take for the people of Latvia to regain a sense of mutual trust.

On Mushrooms and the Nature of Time

Rupert and Irēne waved goodbye to the lady who had provided the much-needed accommodation and set off towards Pāvilosta. They were told that it was a long but straightforward walk, as they just needed to keep to the main road. However, it had turned cooler, a fine mist hung in the air and threatening dark clouds suggested this wouldn't be a comfortable journey.

It wasn't long before the thin mist turned into fine but persistent rain of the sort that soon soaks through to the skin. Rupert turned up the collar of his summer jacket and gritted his teeth. The road led them into the Latvian countryside and the forest, enclosing them on either side, seemed to bend towards them as if the trees were also plodding through the rain.

Rupert struggled with walking and carrying his bag. He was weak after his imprisonment and his right leg, still not fully recovered from the accident, soon started to ache. Quite often, he had to stop and rest and, because of the persistent rain, there wasn't a great deal of talking as they trudged on in the gloom of the overhanging trees.

Walking along for some time, Rupert was surprised that no one had passed them on the road. He was just about to comment about this when he heard the sound of a horse's hooves coming up behind them. He then turned to see a man driving a cart appearing out of the middle distance. As the horse and cart drew close to them Irēne waved to the carter, who then pulled back on his reins and stopped the horse. She spoke to the man in Latvian and then turned to Rupert and told him that they could get up onto the back of the cart nearly full with chopped logs. There was just enough free space for them to stow their bags and perch on the back of the cart. As the carter shook his reins and encouraged the horse back into motion, Rupert was relieved but distressed that he had been unable to walk very far without discomfort. The damp and cold of the prison had not aided his recovery and despite the pacing that had kept him limber, a pervading stiffness had entered the joint of his knee. Now, in the inclement weather, it had begun to ache again and he could feel it seizing up as he settled back on the cart, his arm around Irēne.

The cart jolted and bounced them along the road for about two hours. Encapsulated in the thickening mist and grunting in pain every time the cart went over a pothole, Rupert was uncommunicative. Finally, to his great relief, the cart stopped. The driver indicated this was where he turned off the road and, after helping Irēne clamber off the back of the cart, Rupert said testily, 'I'd rather walk slowly than have every bone shaken to pieces.' Once they had waved goodbye to the carter, he apologised for being in a bad mood, and added, 'It looks like I can't be pleased today.... I am very aware I'm not being very chatty, Thank you for not pushing me to talk.' She took his hand.

'You are doing well. It is impossible for you to be in the best shape after what you have gone through. Now, let us take it easy; we are out of the city, there is no rush. We have plenty of time in the future for you to tell me what your experiences were, but don't dwell on them now. We can find somewhere to rest tonight and finish the journey tomorrow.'

'Sounds like a good plan.' He tried to sound positive.

They walked on and, thankfully, the isolating rain stopped soon afterwards. Shortly afterwards, they arrived at a clearing in the forest and near to the road was a large, flat rock, which Irēne suggested they sit on for a while to rest. Poking up through the grass nearby was a cluster of large, white, flat-capped mushrooms and Irēne lost no time in picking them. Offering one to Rupert, she bit into another without hesitation while he looked on with some alarm. He was reminded of how one of the boys in Wythenshawe had picked and eaten mushrooms from the woods and then had hideous dreams and was violently sick for days afterwards. Irēne noticed his surprise and said, 'Don't worry, this is a national sport and we know what we are doing. In a few weeks, when they are more plentiful, everyone will be out and about looking for mushrooms.'

Rupert bit into the cap of the mushroom and savoured its nutty flavour. After finishing her mushroom, Irēne turned to him and said, 'Rainy weather brings out these beautiful mushrooms in profusion under the firs and birches in our forests. There is a special smell in the shady recesses – it is a satisfying mixture of damp moss, rich earth, rotting leaves and fungi. But the search is never easy. You have to poke and peer for quite a while at the cushion-like, forest floor before you find something really nice, such as a *baravika*.'

Recounting the story of his friend's experience of picking and eating wild mushrooms, Rupert admitted to being wary of eating them. Irēne commented that he didn't know what he was missing and then added, 'You rest here and I will go and search for more mushrooms like these that we can eat without cooking. But I must admit to preferring them fried in butter and thickened with sour cream, then mushrooms are the very best delicacy.'

Carrying a headscarf, Irēne set out on a mushroom picking expedition. No more than fifteen minutes later, she emerged from the edge of the forest, her woollen coat covered by tiny, countless drops of moisture creating a kind of misty halo all around her. She came over to Rupert from under the dripping trees, her scarf tied into a sizeable parcel, her face beaming with obvious pride and success. On reaching Rupert, she let her scarf sag as if carrying a heavy weight and then opened it to reveal an astonishing heap of freshly foraged fungi. She lay them down in front of him and bowed slightly as if bringing an offering. 'I have collected too many for us to eat now. But you never know how these might come in useful; mushrooms are Latvia's passion and may buy us some help en route.'

Starting on their way again and, fortified by the mushrooms and soothed by the sun that now broke through the cloud, Rupert felt revitalised and managed to walk with renewed vigour. As the afternoon wore on, however, and the evening shadows lengthened, they both realised that they needed to find somewhere to shelter. As the sun sank towards the horizon, they saw a barn sitting at a little distance from the road. They crossed the field as swiftly and silently as possible. The barn was empty except for a few bales of hay that would provide comfortable seating, and they sank down onto them with relief. It wasn't long before Rupert nodded off in the warmth of the shielded evening air.

Rupert suddenly jolted upright thinking that the guards had banged on his cell door, and then he heard a shout. He wasn't sure where he was and was still trying to clear his head when he heard Irēne plead, 'Nešaujiet.' Rupert's heart raced as he understood this meant, 'don't shoot', and then he saw a man by the barn door pointing a large, old-fashioned shotgun in their direction. Irēne stood up and said something, and to Rupert's relief, the man pulled back his gun and dropped the butt so that it was no longer pointing at them. There was a further brief but friendly exchange between Irēne and the man. She then turned towards Rupert and said, 'The farmer has asked whether we would like to rest for a while in his house.' He was amazed by the man's sudden transformation and unexpected generosity.

The farmhouse was close to the barn, but well hidden by the surrounding trees, and they were soon inside the small dwelling. The front door led straight into a rustic living room with wooden walls, bare floorboards and a large table made out of roughly hewn logs. A threadbare sofa, tucked against one wall, was the only obvious comfort in the house except for the fire that burnt in the stove even though it was the height of summer. The rest of the room was taken up with a loom with a half finished woollen blanket stretched across it.

The farmer's wife, who had a healthy-looking complexion and big, round rosy cheeks, came out of the kitchen and welcomed the farmer as if he was bringing back old friends for supper. She listened to what the farmer had to say and then, after returning to the kitchen, she came back into the living room with cake. Irēne was carrying her headscarf full of mushrooms and she handed it to the farmer's wife who opened it out on the table and then clapped her hands as if Irēne had just laid priceless jewels before her.

Sitting on the sofa in the heat of the room, Rupert soon fell back into a doze. He only awoke when the farmer's wife brought a steaming pot of mushrooms, cooked in a creamy sauce, into the room. Rupert tasted the dish and let out an involuntary sigh of pleasure. The rich, earthy flavour of the mushrooms had softened to a malty sweetness and a mossy tang unlike anything he had ever experienced. 'It is the food of the gods.' he said, so sincerely that the farmer's wife, looking to Irēne for translation, clapped her hands and laughed, blushing with delight. Irēne, the farmer and his wife chatted away as if they were long lost friends whilst Rupert sat back and listened to the soft crackling of the fire, watching its gentle light flicker over the warm wooden walls.

There was no spare room in the small house in which Rupert and Irēne could sleep, but the farmer provided a small churn of milk and a blanket before escorting them back to the barn. The bales of straw were easily reconfigured to provide a comfortable mattress, but first they sat down together and chatted through the day's events and their good fortune.

With the sky outside darkening, so that they could hardly see each other in the gloom, Rupert started to talk about his experiences in prison. 'In the long months of solitary confinement, familiar things became strange; borders and barriers ceased to exist.'

'It is strange that in prison barriers ceased to exist.'

'Well, unfortunately physical barriers remained but the distinction between mind, body and the world became very blurred. Nothing is as separate as we like to think. Everything is in constant interaction and that includes the past, present and future.' He paused, recalled his time in the sanatorium and then added, 'I once had a conversation with Fricis who said that time is circular. In prison, I began to understand what he meant. Time changed and so did my sense of connection to the wider world.'

Putting her head on Rupert's shoulder, Irēne gave a little 'Hhmm' noise and he continued, 'Time ceased to exist, at least not in the linear way I was used to. Clock time rules our life from the blowing of the factory whistle to the organised silence marking the armistice at 11am on the 11th day of the 11th month – by the way, I was sorry to miss your birthday!'

'You can make it up to me next year... But please tell me about time.'

'Clock time is completely fictional. The division of time into twenty-four hours and its constituent minutes and seconds is a human invention. It is a kind of a linear measurement and although it is useful, if you don't want to be late to the factory for instance, it also misleads us into thinking the arrow of time is a one-way direction of travel.'

'Are you suggesting you went back in time?'

Rupert realised he had started a conversation in which he might lose himself and Irēne faster than if he had ventured into the forest without a compass. Nevertheless, he persevered and answered her question. 'No, not exactly. Of course, what has been said can't be unsaid; we can only go forward and elaborate on what we have said or done. Yet, clock time misleads us. Time isn't running anywhere and it's certainly not aimed at a specific point in the future.'

'I have never had a watch, is it worth having one if it is wrong?' Rupert again smiled.

'Now, I'd be crazy if I was saying everyone needs to get rid of watches because they are telling us lies. But, in one way they are. In clock time there's no present moment. In the continual movement of the clock hand, we are either waiting for the present moment or it has just passed.'

In the gloom of the barn, Irēne made a grab as if catching a mosquito and clenched her fist. Bringing it towards Rupert she opened her palm.

'Oh, I thought I had caught the moment.'

'You have.' He replied with almost glee in his voice. 'The present moment is all we ever experience. In fact, in the living present, time isn't moving anywhere. It surrounds us all. It wraps around us. Time is spherical.'

Shuffling herself to sit upright and looking directly at Rupert, Irēne asked, 'Are you sure you have not been eating the wrong sort of mushrooms.' She poked him in the ribs and added, 'No, I joke with you, please go on.'

'Did the farmer's wife put some dream-inducing mushrooms in the pot?' He chuckled. 'Well, in my mushroom-induced fantasy, I realise that, in the living present, the past and future are intertwined.' He paused and realised that what he was saying was difficult to follow. Then he pressed on, 'The past is not as fixed as I once believed. My loss of memory made it clear to me that the past is not stored as a series of postcards that remain unaltered. We remember what we last remembered and in the process of remembering we edit and change our memories.'

'I understood from my own experience that memories change over time, but I still don't understand what you mean when you say time is spherical.'

Remaining silent for a while, Rupert tried to muster his thoughts and then said, 'I mean... nothing is fixed. In the present moment we are continually retelling stories and in the retelling, the past and future change. What is more, the stories we tell ourselves determine the quality of the present moment.' Rupert realised he had talked quickly, probably too quickly for anyone to follow, and then said, 'I'm sorry, I am in danger of losing myself and you too, but I hope you understand.'

'I certainly understand nothing is fixed.'

They sat in the gloom listening to the slow crick, crack and creak of the contracting rafters in the cool night air. Eventually, Rupert used Irēne's comment to restart the flow of his thoughts. 'What I am trying to say is that there is good news. Nothing is fixed, there are no inevitabilities... there's no hand of fate directing us. We are beings in time but time is not running anywhere and it's not aimed at a specific point in the future. We are not commodities, resources or unthinking pawns in someone's game. We are free to choose even if there is no certain future out there.'

'I wish there was a certain future out there for us.'

'Oh me too. But what if that certain future, shaped by Stalin and Hitler, looks like hell?' It was a rhetorical question and he carried on. 'Whether we like it or not, the future is not already determined, so life isn't just about waiting for time to unfold.' Rupert paused and then to finish off he added, 'Let's imagine a very different life for us together.'

'I do want to. I really do.'

Again recalling the conversation he had with Fricis, Rupert thought, 'Our future is imagined but unfortunately, it probably won't turn out as we imagine it to be.' He refrained from voicing this and turning to the shadow that was Irēne's face, he asked, 'Does that sound like a lecture?'

'Yes, but a very interesting one!'

'I'm sorry. I didn't mean to sound like that. But before I finish... with the blurring of the distinctions between mind, body and the world, I came to realise how your mother must feel.'

'Really!'

'Yes, when the fine screen between reality and our dreamworld is removed life can be a very scary place. If you hadn't arrived when you did, I hate to think where I would have ventured... What I have come to understand, is that your mother is perhaps just a sensitive soul who cannot tune out the terrible state of the world from her own life. When this is all over, there must be some help we can find for her. I am determined.'

'Thank you.' That was Irēne's only comment but she took hold of his hand.

They both lay back on the straw waiting for sleep to overcome them, but it was elusive. Eventually, Irēne said, 'I am not so sure. You talk as if we make our own future. I am more a believer in destiny than you. What if you had gone to a fortune teller before leaving England, do you think she would have predicted such a strange turn in your life?'

'It would have been interesting. She probably would have said, *you will travel to distant lands and meet a beautiful, tall, dark stranger.*'

'Fate!' She laughed. 'If you were able to go back in time,

what would you have changed?' Rupert propped himself up; such a question needed proper consideration.

'If I could go back, would I have been more sceptical of Chamberlain's *peace for our time*, and not set sail? Or having come, would I have decided to make my own way back to Riga rather than being Stanley's passenger? No, I wouldn't meddle because that would mean that I wouldn't be here, right now with you.' He lent over and planted a kiss on her lips.

5th July, 1941.
At the Crossroads

After a few hours sleep, Rupert woke early to see shafts of light radiating through the rafters of the barn illuminating a shower of dust motes in the air. Irēne also stirred and, soon afterwards, they were both up and ready to go. When they went to the farmhouse to say goodbye to the farmer and his wife, they found that the farmer had already left to tend his cattle. However, the farmer's wife was in the kitchen, and she gave them a wrapped piece of freshly prepared curd cheese and a small churn of milk to sustain them on their journey.

Retracing their steps to the main road, they turned in the direction of the Baltic coast. The mist and rain of the previous day had given way to a clear cloudless sky and, once in his stride and having shaken off the grogginess caused by too short a sleep, Rupert felt like he was a man on a walking holiday rather than a refugee. At one point, he even broke into a rendition of *Onward Christian Soldiers,* but as he started the last verse, Irēne hushed him to stop. They turned and, in the distance, they heard a mechanical rumbling approaching. As of one mind, they ran for the cover of the silver birch trees that lined the edge of the pine forest.

By the time they reached the safety of the trees, the rumbling was appreciatively louder, and they could make out multiple engine noises. It soon became clear that it comprised a sizeable formation, perhaps a battalion, of soldiers, identifiably German because of their tell tale helmets, being transported in a convoy of army trucks. They dropped flat to the ground and waited for the noise to fade away into the distance before, half biting his lip, Rupert said, 'I think the walking holiday is over.'

'It will be if we are captured by Germans. I think I recognise where we are, but ahead there is a great deal of open ground.'

'So we could be easily seen! Any suggestions for what we should do?'

'I think if we turn left ahead,' Irēne waved her hand vaguely in a westerly direction, 'and then skirt the edge of the forest we will eventually come close to the coast. From there we can follow the coastline towards the north until we reach my grandparents' village.'

Later, after reaching the northern boundary of the forest, Rupert and Irēne walked over fields, through copses and thicker woods heading towards the coast. They made slow progress as the ground was soft, and they took a meandering course to make best use of the available ground cover. The sun rose high in the sky, and the crickets hummed, unseen in the tussocky grass. Rupert's mood had sobered, and he no longer felt the need to sing. As the sun reached its zenith, Irēne suggested that they stop in the welcome shade offered by a clump of birch trees and eat some cheese and milk. The rest and refreshment enlivened them both. They chatted about reaching Irēne's grandparents and wondered what they would say when the two of them showed up at their door.

In a much-improved mood, they set off again and, after a relatively short walk, they found a sandy road that headed in their general direction. Telephone wires traced its edge and Rupert commented on the stork nests comprising huge baskets of twigs and sticks that perched precariously on top of scattered posts. Irēne compared their own journey to that of the storks and said, 'Let them give us some encouragement. They fly from Africa each year to return home to the same nest.' He walked on with a longer stride.

They carried on along the road for what seemed to be an age and, as the sun arced through the sky, both became lost in their own worlds. Rupert recalled the German troops passing them and, brushing his spiky, roughly cropped hair, he hoped that he'd never have to compare a German prison with a Russian one. It was only when the road came to a crossroads that their thoughts returned to the situation they faced.

Putting his dust-covered bag down, Rupert said, 'Another crossroads. Turn left and we have afternoon tea with Uncle Joe. Turn right and we're entertained at Adolf's pleasure. Maybe straight on would be best but is that just a barren area crisscrossed with tank tracks?' He looked at Irēne and, slightly shaking his head, asked, 'Was there ever a harder decision to make?'

'It is certainly a metaphor for life.'

'If only I'd read more books about Native American trackers, I'd be able to make wise decisions. Now, I would trade my Cambridge degree for their uncommon skill of being able to put my ear to the ground and say, German tank, two days.'

On both sides of the road were freshly made haystacks. Their loose construction gave them a limp appearance mirroring how Rupert felt, and he suggested they sit by one whilst they worked out what to do next. Once they sat down, they realised how tired they were. Rupert said, 'Let's rest for the night.' Without waiting for an answer, he got up and tipped the haystack over. 'Here's our bed and a night under the stars, how romantic.'

The hay was still soft and provided a surprisingly warm and cosy bed, but it didn't protect them from the mosquitoes that buzzed about in the gathering gloom. Rupert slapped his arm to prevent a bite and, in a dramatic voice, said, 'Fee, fi, fo, fum, I smell the blood of an Englishman.'

'Isn't that what your mother used to say to you as she chased you up the stairs to bed?'

'You have a good memory.' He remembered a dream he had in prison, with the monstrous voice that boomed the same words and he shivered.

Finishing off the cheese and milk, which had warmed in the sun and turned slightly bitter, they rested, hand in hand, happy not to talk for a while. The sun dipped and, as the sky dimmed, a crescent moon rose casting only the faintest of shadows. Rupert looked closely at Irēne and noted, once again, the shape of a crescent moon in her left eye. He remembered exactly when he had first seen this imperfection; *Or rather, perfection,* he thought. Now, huddled beneath a haystack and hunted by German soldiers, that moment seemed as if it were a memory from a different lifetime.

Looking up at the few stars that could be seen in the still light sky, Irēne asked, 'When you look into the vast cosmos, is it not asking you what is this life all about?'

'Yes indeed... I think there were times before prison when I felt that everything revolved around me. Now, looking at the night sky I feel infinitesimally small, the merest speck of dust in the vastness of history.'

'You haven't lost your poetic quality in prison.'

'Hmm... I didn't see the stars in prison, but I nearly went mad there trying to make sense of my life. I tried to see how the watermark of my own life was stamped. I have come to realise that many, many forces beyond my control have shaped me... In fact, I seem to be a minor player in the play of my own life.'

'I can have a word with Brecht; maybe he could write the screenplay?'

Rupert smiled and said, 'The play would be very simple. Scene One; young boy enjoys idyllic home life. Scene Two; boy grows up and, as a man, comes to work in a foreign land. Scene Three;

man falls in love with beautiful native girl. Scene Four; man imprisoned on the orders of the chieftain. Scene Five; man escapes with sweetheart. Scene Six; couple chased by chieftain. Scene Seven; not sure how it ends.... but really, I don't think it is the stuff that Brecht would be interested in.'

'On one level, the play is a simple love story; two young people meet, are separated and are then reunited,' Irēne sat back on her heels whilst playing with a long piece of straw, 'but is it not also about more than this? Surely it is about fate and destiny and who is in control of our lives?'

'Yes,' He replied with an ironic tone, 'the play could be spun into some philosophical tale. *At the Crossroads of Life*, maybe that's what it should be called or perhaps something more enigmatic, like *Distant Light.*'

'Yes, that is a nice title for the play.'

Irēne settled down and rested her head on Rupert's lap and he said, 'Here we are sitting at a crossroads. The choice to go on, or left or right is down to us. I don't feel our past is compelling us to take one or other of the paths, neither is fate guiding us. Yet, are we not being fooled?'

'Fooled!'

'Whilst we tell ourselves we're actors starring in our own play, the director seems to change the story and scenery at whim.' Rupert remembered the brief time he had spent with the Latvian Chess Champion and said, 'I remember Fricis saying *we are free to choose but doomed to be out of control.*' Remembering that he was now dead, and struggling with rising emotions, he added, 'Now I know exactly what he was talking about.'

In the twilight, Rupert noticed the surrounding haystacks looked, eerily, like silhouetted people gathering around, but he didn't say anything. Instead, as the temperature had dropped, he covered them both with straw. After a long pause to look at a twinkling star, he continued, 'The stories we tell ourselves about being in control are amusing. If you ask a man to explain how come the coin toss of life fell nicely for him, he will undoubtedly tell you it's a result of his well-thought-through considerations of how to reach a clear goal. Unless, that is, he finds himself lost in a foreign land, one step ahead of a German jackboot. Then, he'll blame forces beyond his control.'

Irēne turned, poked Rupert gently in the ribs and said, 'I am more a believer in fate than you.' She said. 'There is a force out there greater than us and our actions are guided by the cosmos. So, we might be sitting by the crossroads weighing up the options, but we are being drawn to take the right hand fork.'

'So, that's our direction tomorrow?'

'Yes.'

'Fate... more Lady Luck,' thought Rupert but kept this to himself. He recalled what Fricis had said about randomness and smiled, as he understood that randomness seemed to characterise his life. 'Is there any other conclusion?' He thought, 'After all, I was a trigger click away from being shot because of a tenuous connection with Orlonsky, being employed by Metro Vicks and owning an innocent camera. Certainly, if I hadn't bumped into Vilis Lācis at the sanatorium I'd be dead now. Randomness, chance, luck, call it what you will.'

Settling back on the straw, Rupert reviewed his time in Latvia and all the things he had gained and lost. He didn't dwell on the hardships of prison life but instead focused on the time he had spent in hospital, recovering from his serious accident. Then, he asked, 'Do you remember the book of Latvian Fairytales you gave me?'

'Yes, of course.'

'You were going to translate some of the stories. We had so much to talk about that we never got around to it.'

'Well we have time now, would you like me to tell you one?'

'That would be lovely.'

Irēne turned, placed her head on Rupert's chest, looked up at him and began. 'Once upon a time, there lived a man who had a clever son. However, the man lost his life in a terrible accident and thereafter his mother never allowed her young son to go alone into the woods. The boy grew up loved and sheltered from the outside world.'

'This isn't the famous lad from Wythenshawe, by any chance?'

'Sshhh, not all stories are about you.' Irēne raised her hand to pinch Rupert gently on the cheek before continuing. 'One day the young man came to his mother and said,' Irēne's voice dropped an octave, '*Mother, I had a dream. I saw a beautiful princess in a distant land over the sea, but she was very ill and doctors could not help. I saw her lying in bed and her beautiful eyes were full of tears, and I could read in them that she wanted me to save her. Mother, I want to go and save her.*' She then resumed her normal tone. 'The mother understood she could not stop her son and off he went.' Rupert recollected the last time he had seen his mother. She was standing at the gate of her cottage clearly holding back tears that would be shed when he was gone. He did not share the image and Irēne continued.

'The young man's road was long and difficult and he became very tired. He came to a small house and knocked on the door to ask for water, something to eat and a rest. A small, old man who, curiously, was playing chess by himself opened the door. When the weary traveller expressed his wish, the old man said,' Irēne's voice croaked, '*I will give you what you want, but first you must pick all the apples off the tree. You see that I am small and old and cannot do it.* The young man was very tired, and the tree was heavy with ripe apples, but he could not refuse the old man and did what he asked. The old man let him rest, gave him water and bread and, when he was ready to go, said, *I know that you are going to find the beautiful sick princess, and I know how to cure her. Here is one red apple from my tree, brush it over the princess's lips, and she will be well again.*'

Rupert brushed the back of his hand over Irēne's lips and she kissed it softly before resuming her story. 'At last the young man reached the land where the beautiful princess lived. The land was green and beautiful but cold. A cruel king ruled it, and all the people were suspicious and unfriendly, but he was shown the road to the castle and allowed to see the princess. The princess looked very ill, she was pale and thin, but when the young man brushed the red apple over her lips, the miracle happened, the princess became like a flower in full blossom, beautiful and strong. The young man and the princess looked into each other's eyes and did not see anything else. Only the young man was a little shy, and the princess had to give him the first kiss.' Rupert looked down at Irēne; her face glowed, luminous in the gloaming. He remembered their first kiss, and how Irēne had initiated it.

Irēne continued, 'The young man wanted to take the princess back to his own land, and they went to ask the king's permission. But the cold and cruel king looked at the foreigner with his dreamy eyes and gentle soul and decided that he was not the son-in-law he wanted. Therefore, he said,' Irēne's voice took on a commanding tone, '*I will shoot an arrow, and it will fly far. If you find it and bring it back to me, the princess is yours,* but he knew he had set an impossible task.'

Irēne swished away a mosquito before continuing, 'Despite the impossibility of the task, the young man kept on searching and searching until one day, he fell down exhausted, unable to move. The young princess, who had been told about the foreigner's plight by the old man, saved him. After she raised a leather pouch to his lips and let him drink the water of life, the young man sprang up and he took the princess in his arms. Back at the cruel king's castle, they mounted the king's best stallion and rode off whilst the king and his servants were in deep surprise. By the time the king and his troops started to ride after them, the young man and the princess had already reached the sea where a sailboat was waiting to take them to the land of their destiny. As night fell, they sailed off to towards the distant light of freedom.' Irēne rounded off with a triumphant sounding, 'That is it.'

Rupert had always enjoyed the way Irēne fluently recounted stories, and as, he lay thinking of what he had just heard, he noted the curious resonance with his own experience; the love that had kindled between them and how they had been separated and reunited. 'Who wrote this fairytale?' Rupert asked.

'I just made it up.'

'How wonderful.' He paused and remained quiet for a while looking towards the purple tinge of the horizon. Then he ran his fingers through his princess's hair before saying, 'In our fairytale we have already tried to escape by sea in the yacht to Sweden, so how we get back to our land of destiny is still to be written.'

They lay cupped together on the makeshift hay bed, but the buzzing and biting of the mosquitoes prevented them having a restful night. Rupert could not believe it was less than two years since the strands of fate, or sheer coincidence, had entwined their lives. His last conscious thought before finally drifting into a fitful sleep was, *Entwined we are, but what does the future hold? Will there be a happy ending to our fairytale?* He was assailed by doubt.

Towards the Distant Light

The romantic star-filled night was followed by a prosaic, dew soaked dawn. Rupert and Irēne awoke and, despite feeling groggy from lack of sleep, they were able to laugh at their untidy state with bits of straw clinging all over their hair and clothing. After they had helped each other to pick the pieces off their clothes, they started walking towards Pāvilosta.

The straw had made a good bed, but they now itched because of its remaining fragments and their numerous insect bites. As they walked through the grass and then onto the right hand fork of the road, they concentrated on the dew that had collected on their shoes. It wasn't until they looked up that they saw they were surprisingly near the coast.

The road formed a vantage point with the Baltic Sea stretching out ahead of them, grey and cold looking. A lingering mist smudged its interface with the morning sky. Irēne pointed to the right and said, 'We are close to the village, I am sure it is only a few kilometres further on.' The idea of getting to the summerhouse and having a hot drink spurred them on, and they reached the outskirts of Pāvilosta in what seemed like no time at all.

Irēne recognised where she was and knew how to get to her grandparents' house. They walked rapidly through the deserted village, managing to scare the crows, which were not expecting such an early morning disturbance, so that they lifted off languidly into the air, screeching as they did so. The summerhouse was on the other side of Pāvilosta. By the time they reached it, Rupert understood why they had bought a house there as the village, comprising traditional wooden houses, was scenically situated around a small harbour populated with painted boats, their masts standing tall and ghostly in the still air.

Nearing the summerhouse, Irēne pointed to a window where a figure watched their approach and she cried out, 'Grandma.' Rupert was surprised that Irēne's grandmother was up at such an early hour and wondered whether the crows had disturbed her, or if she could not sleep. Irēne ran the last hundred metres to the red-painted house and hugged her grandmother who met her on the porch. Rupert saw an older version of Irēne. Her hair was grey and uncombed, but she had the same high cheek bones and smile as Irēne and was, unquestionably, still a beautiful woman. Irēne's grandmother talked in an animated way, but Rupert could see she had been crying, as her eyes were red and slightly puffy. After Irēne introduced him, Rupert rather formally went to shake her hand, but she took hold of his hand in both of hers and, drawing him closer, gave him a hug.

Ushered inside the summerhouse, Irēne and her grandmother began to talk with each other in Latvian. Although he didn't catch every word, Rupert understood that Irēne's grandmother was upset and worried. Concerned for her he was, but he desperately needed a cup of tea and was gratified when it was offered once Irēne had calmed her grandmother down. Irēne explained that her grandmother was very afraid for her husband, as he should have returned home last night but had failed to do so. Rupert now understood why she was up so early.

The house was a single storey wooden building with rooms leading off a central corridor. Irēne showed Rupert their bedroom dominated by a large iron bedstead covered by a colourful, handmade, patchwork eiderdown. Rupert asked whether she would mind if he had a wash and went to bed. Irēne replied, 'Of course not and, after I have reassured Grandma, I will join you.' A large wash jug and bowl stood on a cabinet at the edge of the room. Rupert poured some water from the jug into the bowl, washed his hands and face, lay on the bed and was asleep within minutes. When he awoke much later in the morning Irēne was next to him, and he put his arm around her. In doing so, he disturbed her and she turned towards him. He then heard a man's voice and, immediately, Irēne jumped up and ran out of the bedroom shouting, 'Grandpa.'

When Rupert joined the others in the kitchen, Irēne's grandfather broke off from the animated conversation and welcomed Rupert in German, introducing himself as Jacobs. As Rupert shook his hand, he noted his beard was still without grey hairs although his head was balding. Jacobs started apologising for his late arrival, but Irēne broke in and said, 'Grandfather has had a terrible night. The arrival of the Germans has given some of the locals an excuse to ransack his shops.'

Rupert was shocked, and was about to say how sorry he was to hear this, when Jacobs turned to him and said, 'Yes, we have had our own *Kristallnacht.*' Rupert didn't understand him but didn't comment. Jacobs continued. 'Of course, since the Russians came my shops have been State property, but it is painful nevertheless and I think this is just the start. God knows what racial hatred the Germans will whip up when they really settle in.'

Hugging his wife, Marta, Jacobs spoke further in Latvian to her and Irēne, then, apologising that his wife did not speak either German or English, he suggested that they go through to the sitting room. Tea was brought in by Irēne's grandparents and, whilst Irēne poured, her grandfather said, 'I understand you have suffered at the hands of the Russians and want to stay here for a while. We would love to have you for as long as you both want, but I don't think you will be safe... even here. The Germans are spreading out quickly from the towns to check on possible resistance in the villages and they are repeating what they did in Poland. As soon as the war started, thousands of Polish, so called, enemies of the state were targeted for execution. These included Freemasons, Catholics, Communists but by far the majority were Jews like myself.'

Rupert shook his head and Jacobs continued. 'Yes, I am afraid you need to believe it. Hitler has given the call to arms to exterminate the Jews.' He didn't try to impersonate Hitler but quoted him in a stern and uncaring voice. 'I will start fundamentally from the expectation that they will vanish. They must go. We must annihilate the Jews wherever we meet them. The war will not be ended merely by the defeat of the enemy's armed forces.'

Irēne asked her grandfather whether he had heard any news from Riga and he replied, 'Crowds have welcomed the Germans... Germans are already organising death squads under Victors Arājs. I have brought the paper back with me today, I didn't want to show it to your grandmother, but I think you need to know the danger you are in.' He took out the Latvian paper, *Tēvija* and translated one paragraph of an advert. 'All patriotic Latvians, *Pērkoņkrusts* members, Students, Officers, Militiamen, and Citizens, who are ready to actively take part in the cleansing of our country of undesirable elements should enrol themselves at the office of the Security Group at 19 *Valdemara Iela*.'

Thinking about the advert, Rupert said, 'I can't imagine any Latvians signing up to this.'

'Your naivety is oddly refreshing,' Jacobs replied in a kindly tone, 'but we have heard that, yesterday, Arājs and his henchmen trapped about twenty Jews in the Riga Synagogue on *Gogoļa Iela*. There, they were burnt alive while hand grenades were thrown through the windows.' Rupert felt physically sick, as he had passed the synagogue many times when he lived in Riga and couldn't imagine such an atrocity occurring there. Irēne took her grandmother's hand and addressed Jacobs.

'Such wickedness! Do not tell Grandma, she is already frightened enough.' Irēne urged.

'Latvians joined the KGB, now others are signing up for the Gestapo. It is the biggest crime for a nation when brother turns against brother. You can forgive the enemy, but never your brother'. Jacobs shook his head.

The four sat around the table and drank their tea in silence. Then, Jacobs said to Rupert, 'You have just arrived, but if I were a young man, I would take my wife and make an escape by boat to Sweden.'

'Is that really possible? Can you get to Sweden from here? I've never sailed before.' His voice ebbed at the end of the sentence.

'If the wind is from the east, which it is at the moment, all you need to do is launch the boat, paddle quietly out of the harbour then put the sail out and you will be carried to Gotland. There may not be much wind at night, but the morning normally brings a steady breeze. On a clear day, you can even see the island; it is not too far. The only danger is that a German patrol may spot you, but they have yet to secure the coast.' Rupert didn't want to contradict Jacobs but thought, 'That is odd, there was no wind this morning.'

The need to escape and return to England had become almost irresistible, but Rupert had never considered that achievement of this would be so recklessly placed in the lap of the gods.

Jacobs must have realised he had presented Rupert with a great deal to think about and lightened the mood. 'After lunch, we will go down to the harbour, but now, why don't you two rest?' Irēne took Rupert out onto a veranda attached to the house. It was encased by stained glass windows and had doors opening onto a flower-strewn garden. Sitting together, they admired the tranquillity of the setting, the wild flowers growing in profusion and the striking birch trees at the back of the long garden. Irēne pointed to the yellow painted, intricately carved privy partially hidden by a clump of rhododendron bushes.

'Does that remind you of home?' She asked and in laughing, some of the tension of making yet another leap into the dark was eased.

Referring to their conversation with Jacobs, Rupert said, 'By the way, I've never heard of *Kristallnacht*.'

'I can hardly believe that. I thought everyone must have heard of it. Where were you on 10th November 1938?'

'That must have been the day I set sail for Latvia and thinking about it, after I arrived I was not listening to news, because I was so busy starting work on the project.' Irēne nodded and told him what she knew about this night when Jewish homes, hospitals, schools, synagogues and businesses were ransacked across Germany and Austria. Rupert shook his head, partly in disbelief that he had never heard of this dreadful night. Irēne continued. 'I mentioned that I lived on Fassenstrasse in Berlin. On *Kristallnacht* the synagogue there was totally ransacked. We had left Berlin long before then, but I saw a picture of it and it was as if a whirlwind had gone through the building. It is in a lovely peaceful area of Berlin with apparently friendly neighbours.'

'It must be hard to understand how it could ever have happened.'

After a lunch of boiled tongue, potted shrimps and a wide selection of pickles, Rupert and Irēne were escorted down to the harbour by Jacobs, who pointed out one particular boat gently bobbing by the side of a small jetty. He said, 'Launch this boat at two o' clock in the morning. It is not completely dark then, but it will be the best time not to be seen. Don't even whisper as any noise will carry far on the still air. We won't tell Martinš, the owner, you are going to take the boat, but I will make sure he can afford to buy another.' Rupert recalled the fairytale of the night before and thought, *So this is how the prince and princess really do make their way to the land of their destiny.* He realised Jacobs wouldn't understand and kept this to himself.

Jacobs explained how to raise and set the sail and use the rudder. Rupert nodded and was aware he was pretending to understand more than he did, as he had done when Walter demonstrated the Minox camera. After a brief discussion to clarify the plan, they made their way back through the village to the summerhouse where afternoon tea and biscuits awaited them. This homely setting and activity turned Rupert's thoughts towards seeing his mother and how they might have tea and biscuits in the parlour, given that his return home with Irēne would warrant such an unusual excursion into the best room.

Wondering how Irēne felt at the prospect of leaving her grandparents and both of her parents, Rupert asked, 'With luck and a following wind, I'm on my way home, but what about you? How do you feel about leaving your family?'

She hesitated before replying, 'As you know, Mother is completely in her own world; in truth I lost her shortly after we left Capri. As for Father, I think, if he keeps his head down in the countryside, he will survive and one day, God willing, we will be reunited. I am most worried about my grandparents, they are too old and settled to leave but are in real danger. I just hope that my grandfather's influence and money will keep them safe.'

That afternoon, Irēne talked with her grandparents and helped prepare the evening meal. Rupert felt relaxed listening to, what seemed to him, the normal chatter of daily life and the tinkle of crockery. He didn't want to contemplate the potential ordeal ahead and, instead, let the atmosphere wash over him. Dinner was served and, over a feast of rabbit pie and roasted vegetables, they swapped stories of everyday life and pretended all was fine.

Just as Rupert was about to offer help with the washing up, they heard a crunching of feet on the gravel path outside. This ordinary sound created the same reaction as a gun being fired. They all froze. Rupert shot a glance at Irēne then Marta, who looked like she was going to cry out hysterically. Jacobs took hold of Marta, then whispered to Rupert and Irēne, 'Slip out of the back and go and hide in the woods; we will stay here. It is unusual for anyone to call at this time, but it is probably nothing.'

As silently as they could, Rupert and Irēne left the house through the veranda door and, keeping to the long shadows of the bushes in the late evening sun, headed to the wood.. They remained hidden there, crouched behind a grassy bank for a while, listening out for a call from the house indicating that all was clear. Instead of a call, they heard the sound of trucks. Rupert recognised the note of the engines from the previous day but did not voice his concerns. Irēne, though, didn't need any prompt and said, 'My God, Germans!'

Talking in whispers about what they should do, they soon realised there was nothing they could do; only hope and pray that they were mistaken. Once dusk had settled over the countryside, and after the trucks had moved off, they ventured back to the house. It was empty. Irēne brought her hand to her mouth to stifle sobs.

Sitting in the gloom, at first unthinking through shock, Rupert put his arm around Irēne, and he could feel waves of emotion flowing through her. Then, he began to think about what he could do and asked, 'Let's go to the neighbours and see if we can muster some support.' He knew it was a futile task, but he was surprised by Irēne's vehement response. 'You cannot trust the neighbours. The butcher in the village hates Grandpa, and it was probably he who brought in the Germans.'

In the wolf light of late evening, Rupert spoke, 'I don't think we have any choice.' It was clear Irēne knew what he meant as they both got up simultaneously to pack a bag of warm clothes for the journey ahead.

Sitting back on the settee on the veranda, Rupert recalled his sudden release from prison, and how happy he had been only a few hours earlier. He could not believe happiness was so fleeting. He was also daunted by the fact they now faced an ordeal that he was completely ill-equipped for.

Thinking about the real possibility of capsizing, sinking, being blown off course or shot by the Germans, Rupert began to feel an urge to pray. He recalled the unanswered prayers he had said before his father's death and the subsequent anger he had felt towards God. He remembered his rage at the window of the prison. Yet, at the same time, he understood he had been angry with someone or something, so he could not fully discount God, even a God who rarely intervened in the affairs of humanity.

Rupert recalled what Karlis had said in prison, *life is a snap of the fingers between two eternities of silence... But what gives me comfort is the thought that I am no longer bothered about the silence and blackness of eternity ahead anymore than the eternity that preceded me.* Now, faced with the possibility of an eternal void, he could not find the solace this idea seemed to promise.

Rupert smiled as one final memory surfaced and shone, a light on dark water. Turning to Irēne, he repeated the question he had asked. 'Against all the forces of darkness that seem to be around, can love eventually triumph?' She nodded and responded just as she had done before.

'I am an optimist, and a romantic, so my answer is yes.'

Tentatively, to himself, Rupert said;

For thine is the kingdom,
The power, and the glory,
For ever and ever.

Irēne squeezed Rupert's hand and he wondered whether he had said the prayer out loud. Then, he thought she must have been reading his thoughts.

Rupert didn't want to worry Irēne but, sitting in the silence and gloom, he couldn't contain his thoughts about death. 'Of course, the chorister should welcome the opportunity of eternal life; think of all that organ music and singing. Only, if it was to end today, I will have lost you and the opportunity to grow old with you. Now, that is something I cannot think about.' Irēne put her head on his chest and remained like that until the gentle chime of the clock told them they had been tipped into their day of destiny.

Although the light faded, the darkness did not become absolute. There was a hush in the atmosphere and the overpowering scent of the mock orange in the garden.

In the stillness of the night, they left the summerhouse and made their way to the harbour where the boats were silhouetted by the silvery sliver of a rising crescent moon. The sea looked luminous, as if it were lit from within, providing no cover or shadows in which to hide. In the far, far distance lay Gotland. This was unseen, but the weak afterglow of the sun, dipped below the horizon, marked its direction.

On reaching Martinš boat, Rupert turned to look at Irēne. Despite the gloom, he saw the crescent moon shape in her eye revealed by the reflection of the true moon and wondered, *Was this destiny already written into her soul?*

Off to their right, the slight rise and fall of the water in the small harbour broke the moonlight on the surface. They heard the creaking of small boats straining at ropes and the soft clunk of wood on wood as the vessels nudged each other gently in the gloom.

At fifteen minutes past two o'clock on the morning of 6th July 1941, Rupert and Irēne untied the fisherman's boat and stepped into it as noiselessly as they possibly could. Even with the gentlest of movements though, the resulting creak of a floorboard and lap of the disturbed water sounded as out of place as a gunshot and they, flinched, willing the ignorance of the enemy.

After pushing the craft away from the jetty, Rupert, who was sitting on the thwart, looked at Irēne and saw no fear but he was sure the beating in his own chest must be audible from afar. Glancing behind, the moon's faint, bloodless light marking the harbour entrance, he gathered the oars and began to row towards the distant light of freedom.

Postscript

The tide referred to in the title is the human one that has swept back and forth over the Baltic States. As the book describes, in the twentieth century, Russia laid claim to the territories until after the First World War when there was a brief period of independence. Then, there were successive waves of Russian and German occupation.

After the Second World War, the Baltic States of Latvia, Lithuania and Estonia were incorporated within the Soviet Union.

On 23rd August 1989 approximately two million people joined their hands to form a six hundred kilometre human chain through the Baltic countries, thereby demonstrating their unity in their efforts to achieve freedom.

Full independence of the Republic of Latvia was asserted on the 21st of August 1991, during the coup d'état attempt upon the government of Mikhail Gorbachev in Moscow. Latvia's independence was fully recognised by the Soviet Union on 6th September 1991.

Historical Context

1938

12th March 1938. Germany annexes Austria (Anschluss).

30th September 1938. The British Prime Minister's aeroplane lands at Heston Aerodrome where Neville Chamberlain speaks to the crowd declaring that the agreement signed with Hitler was symbolic of the desire of the two peoples never to go to war with one another again.

1st October 1938. Germany begins the annexation of the Sudetanland then part of Czechoslovakia.

9th and 10th November 1938. Kristallnacht. Over one thousand synagogues are burnt and over seven thousand Jewish businesses are either destroyed or damaged in Germany and Austria.

1939

15th March 1939. Germany invades Czechoslovakia, creates the protectorate of Bohemia and Moravia, turns Slovakia into a fascist state under Josef Tiso and occupies the Lithuanian port of Klaipeda (Memel in German).

7th April 1939. Italy invades and annexes Albania.

23rd August 1939. Signing of the Molotov-Ribbentrop Pact between the Soviet and German Governments. This ostensibly sets out a mutual agreement of non-aggression, but includes secret provisions dealing with 'spheres of interest' that facilitates division and annexation of other states in eastern Europe.

1st September 1939. Germany invades Poland.

2nd September 1939. British liner Athenia is sunk by a German submarine.

3rd September 1939. Britain, France, Australia, New Zealand and South Africa declare war on Germany.

17th September 1939. Soviet Union invades eastern Poland.

27th September 1939. Warsaw surrenders.

5th October 1939. Soviets negotiate with representatives from Finland about ceding territory.

30th November 1939. Soviet invasion of Finland commences.

14th December 1939. Soviet Union is expelled from the League of Nations.

1940

1st February 1940. Stalin appoints Senyon Konstantinovich Timoshenko to be in charge of the Soviet forces on the Finnish front.

12th March 1940. Finland surrenders to the Soviet Union.

21st March 1940. Finland ratifies the Moscow Peace Treaty with the Soviet Union ceding Karelia and leasing the Hanko Peninsular to the Soviet Union as a naval base for thirty years.

10th May 1940. Chamberlain resigns and is replaced by Churchill.

13th June 1940. German army enters Paris.

17th June 1940. Soviet troops enter Riga.

5th August 1940. Latvia is 'accepted' into the Soviet Union.

1941

14th June 1941. The Soviet Union begins deportation of 60,000 Estonians, 34,000 Latvians and 38,000 Lithuanians to Siberia.

22nd June 1941. Germany, Finland, Romania and Hungary launch a surprise invasion of the Soviet Union (Operation Barbarossa). The German army crosses the Soviet frontier early in the morning on a broad front from the Baltic Sea to Hungary.

24th June 1941. The Soviet Union massacres prisoners in Poland, Bessarabia and the Baltic States.

26th June 1941. Finland and Hungary declare war on the Soviet Union.

End June 1941. Soviet troops retreat from Riga.

1st July 1941. The German army enters Riga.

Historical Figures

The main characters in this book are fictional. However, their story is set within a historical context and many of the people referred to and described in the book are real. Short biographic summaries of these individuals are provided below and are listed in order of appearance.

Arthur Neville Chamberlain, **PC, FRS** (18th March 1869 – 9th November 1940) was a British Conservative politician who served as Prime Minister of the United Kingdom from May 1937 to May 1940.

Joseph Vissarionovich Stalin (18th December 1878 – 5th March 1953) was a Georgian-born Soviet revolutionary and political leader, governing the Soviet Union as its dictator from the mid-1920s until his death in 1953. He served as General Secretary of the Central Committee of the Communist Party of the Soviet Union from 1922 to 1952 and as Premier of the Soviet Union from 1941 to 1953.

Ulrich Friedrich Wilhelm Joachim von Ribbentrop (30th April 1893 – 16th October 1946), more commonly known as Joachim von Ribbentrop, was Foreign Minister of Nazi Germany from 1938 until 1945.

Vladimir Ilyich Ulyanov, better known by the alias **Lenin** (22nd April 1870 – 21st January 1924) was a Russian communist revolutionary, politician and political theorist. He served as head of government of the Russian Republic from 1917 to 1918, of the Russian Soviet Federative Socialist Republic from 1918 to 1924 and of the Soviet Union from 1922 to 1924.

Vyacheslav Mikhailovich Molotov (9th March 1890 – 8th November 1986) was a Soviet politician and diplomat, an Old Bolshevik, and a leading figure in the Soviet government from the 1920s when he rose to power as a protégé of Joseph Stalin.

George Armistead (27th October, 1847 – 17th November, 1912) was an engineer and entrepreneur and was the fourth Mayor of Riga.

Eugen Berthold Friedrich 'Bertolt' Brecht (10th February 1898 – 14th August 1956) was a German poet, playwright, and theatre director.

Walter Zapp (4th September 1905 – 17th July 2003) was a Baltic German inventor. His greatest creation was the Minox subminiature camera.

Sir Charles Orde, **KCMG** (25th October 1884 – 7th June 1980) was a British Diplomat. He served as Envoy Extraordinary and Minister-Plenipotentiary in Riga between 1938 and 1940.

Asja Lācis (19th October 1891 – 21st November 1979) was a Latvian actress and theatre director.

Thomas Egerton Tatton (31st May 1846 – 2nd December 1924) was Head of Household and owner of the Wythenshawe Estate.

Robert Henry Grenville Tatton (2nd March 1883 – 1st March 1962) was the High Sheriff of Chester from 1936 until 1937. He was the last member of his family to own Wythenshawe Hall and its estate, the ancestral home of the Tattons for six hundred years, and the last male member of his line.

Ernest Emil Darwin Simon, 1st Baron Simon of Wythenshawe (9th October 1879 – 3rd October 1960) was a British industrialist, politician and public servant. He was the Lord Mayor of Manchester in 1921–1922 and was a member of parliament for two terms between 1923 and 1931 before being elevated to the peerage and serving as the Chairman of the BBC Board of Governors.

Kurt Gerron (11th May 1897 – 28th October 1944) was a German Jewish actor and film director.

Gothards Vilhelms Nikolajs Munters (25th July 1898 – 11th January 1967) was a Latvian diplomat and served as Latvia's Foreign Minister between 1936 and 1940.

Sir Robert Hamilton Bruce Lockhart, KCMG (2nd September 1887 – 27th February 1970) was variously a British diplomat journalist, author, secret agent and footballer.

Fanya Yefimovna Kaplan real name Feiga Haimovna Roytblat (10th February 1890 – 3rd September 1918) was a Ukrainian Jewish revolutionary who tried to assassinate Vladimir Lenin.

Fricis (Fritzis, Franz) Apšenieks (7th April 1894 – 25 April 1941) was a Latvian chess master.

Kārlis Augusts Vilhelms Ulmanis (4th September 1877 – 20th September 1942) was one of the most prominent Latvian politicians of 20th century, serving as the first Prime Minister of the independent state. He was exiled from the country and died in prison at Krasnovodsk in the Soviet Union (now Türkmenbaşy, Turkmenistan).

Peggie Benton was a civil servant and worked in the British Legation in Riga from 1938 until 1940. She is the author of Baltic Countdown, A Nation Vanishes.

Vilis Lācis (12th May 1904 – 6th February 1966) was a Latvian writer and communist politician. After Latvia was incorporated in the USSR in August 1940, he became Chairman of the Council of Ministers of the Latvian Socialist Soviet Republic and served in this position from 1940 until 1959.

Prince Georgy Yevgenyevich Lvov (2nd November 1861 –

7/8th March 1925) was a Russian statesman and the first post-imperial prime minister of Russia, from 15th March to 21st July 1917.

Alexander Fyodorovich Kerensky (4th May 1881 – 11th June 1970) was a Russian lawyer and key political figure in the Russian Revolution of 1917. After the February Revolution of 1917 he joined the newly formed Russian Provisional Government, first as Minister of Justice, then as Minister of War, and after July 1917 as the government's second Minister-Chairman. On 7th November 1917, his government was overthrown by the Lenin-led Bolsheviks in the October Revolution.

Viktors Arājs (13th January 1910 – 13th January 1988) was a Latvian collaborator and Nazi SS officer, who took part in the Holocaust during the German occupation of Latvia and Belarus (then called White Russia or White Ruthenia) as the leader of the Arajs Kommando.

Other Relevant Publications

Article 58
By Russell John Connor

Sent from Latvia to Siberia at the age of only fifteen, this is the story of a young man's endurance, survival and love. It is set against a cruel political system that identified millions as 'enemies of the people'.

It ends on the day before Stalin's state funeral; a day which proved that from his coffin the twentieth century's most brutal dictator had not lost his capacity to deal out death at random to his subjects.

A Life in a Day
By Hilkka Polvinen Mednis

Through the lens of a single day, we are offered a glimpse of the whole life of Hilkka Mednis.

One of five daughters of Pauli and Anne Polvinen, Hilkka enjoyed a happy early childhood until her mother died in childbirth. Then, at the age of thirteen, on the invasion of Finland by the Red Army, she, together with her father and three of her sisters were deported to Siberia.

On the day she finds out her son, an up and coming ballet dancer, has defected, Hilkka describes her experiences including the interrogation, and, in so doing, we are dipped into the tough, mundane and, sometimes, sublime nature of Soviet life.

Whilst the book is set in the past it deals with very current issues of mental health and post-natal depression. It is about determination, grit, bravery and resilience, the Finnish term for which is 'sisu'.